What the
River
Wants

What the *River* Wants

Arthur Byrd

iUniverse®

WHAT THE RIVER WANTS

iUniverse books may be ordered through booksellers or by contacting:

iUniverse
1663 Liberty Drive
Bloomington, IN 47403
www.iuniverse.com
1-800-Authors (1-800-288-4677)

*Because of the dynamic nature of the Internet, any web addresses or
links contained in this book may have changed since publication and
may no longer be valid. The views expressed in this work are solely those
of the author and do not necessarily reflect the views of the publisher,
and the publisher hereby disclaims any responsibility for them.*

*Any people depicted in stock imagery provided by Thinkstock are models,
and such images are being used for illustrative purposes only.
Certain stock imagery © Thinkstock.*

ISBN: 978-1-5320-0823-8 (sc)
ISBN: 978-1-5320-0825-2 (hc)
ISBN: 978-1-5320-0824-5 (e)

Library of Congress Control Number: 2016919086

Print information available on the last page.

iUniverse rev. date: 12/13/2016

For Vickie

So we beat on, boats against the current; borne back ceaselessly into the past.

—*The Great Gatsby*

Acknowledgements

I'd like to thank Rob Johnson for his early insight and encouragement as well as my wife, Sally, Lee McMichael, Bobbie Pritchard, Janet Gee, and Bernie Pfahnl for their kind support as I began this adventure.

Many thanks as well to James Lubas for the author photo of me in my New Jersey garden, a place I love dearly.

But most of all let me express my gratitude to my mother who served as inspiration for this piece of fiction and to my father who was the first person ever to tell me I should become a writer; I miss them every day.

Chapter 1

South Mississippi, 2010

I.

The idea didn't seem as good now that Lee was on the bus heading down to see his grandfather Tom. The zeal he'd felt originally faded as Picayune got closer and the Greyhound pumped out a diesel fog that drifted noxiously into the last row of seats. All his excitement about seeing his grandpa for the first time in three years suddenly evaporated leaving instead a hesitation not only to deal with the past but also to uncover things perhaps better left buried.

The drone of the engine and nauseating fuel smell left Lee dazed, but he was happy to be away from his sisters for a couple of days. The eleventh grader had gotten off to a rough start this school year. When he went to register for the special half-semester elective class on the stock market, it had been filled, so instead he had to take the session on genealogy that the boys in school referred to as a "chick class." Now he only wanted to be done with the burden. First, however, he had to interview his estranged grandfather and gather as much family information as he could.

Tom Bradburn was definitely an odd character. For over three years now, he'd simply withdrawn to the Catchahoula River in Pearl River County, Mississippi, a secluded area near the Louisiana state line about fifty miles from New Orleans. Lee always had been close to his grandpa, having grown up hunting in the woods around Picayune from the Honey

1

Island Swamp to the Wolf River, but since Tom had withdrawn from the family, no one really knew how he was making out these days. Feeling hopeful, Lee intended to investigate.

Part of the teenager's angst grew from the surprise nature of this trip; his grandfather wasn't keen on unannounced visitors. Tom had no phone or mail, so the only reliable contact anyone had was through his oldest friend, Mike Hamlin, who drove out occasionally to deliver a little flour and sugar to his old buddy. Tom pretty much lived off the land the rest of the time by hunting and fishing, raising a fruit orchard, and growing a sizable garden. But Lee had this thorny idea Mike had been almost too eager to help set up the river visit, so new concern about his grandpa began to simmer.

Tom and his grandson had always shared a special relationship. Glenna, Lee's mom, had three kids, the oldest and youngest being girls, so Lee as the only boy was the one who had spent much of his time on the river with his grandpa. From day one, these two had known a bond that didn't require much talk—just a fireside on a chilly night or trotline to check, hoping to catch a little supper. Lee's childhood had been one filled with girl talk in the house most days, and fishing and hunting with his grandpa on weekends helped balance his world. Harold, Lee's father, drove a big semitruck and lived on the road most of the time, so in the early years, Lee spent countless hours stomping around the woods with his idol, Tom.

As the bus bounced into the station, Lee saw the Roy's Burger Stop sign where his mom took him for a cold root beer nearly every time they visited her hometown. Hattiesburg being only fifty-five miles north of Picayune, weekend trips to see her parents tended to be common when Lee was a boy. Today, all alone back in the town where he'd spent many a summer at his grandmother's house, Lee Mitchell recognized the familiar burger sign but didn't feel welcome yet. And the faded old reminder seemed remote, a place he couldn't quite remember.

Standing in the parking lot, Lee spotted Mike shuffling toward him, his old flannel shirt with barely any color left, a thin head of white hair freshly combed, and that familiar beaming smile.

"Good Lord, Lee, look how big you are. My heavens, you must be six feet tall already."

"Hello, Mr. Hamlin. Yeah, I'm pretty much six one these days—and still growing, I think." Mike grabbed Lee's hand and gave him a bear hug, nearly squeezing out all the air in the boy's chest. The happy glint in Mike's eye told Lee everything he needed to know about the silent gratitude for this visit, and in that moment Lee felt welcome again in Picayune.

"So tell me," Mike said, "what are you now, 'bout fifteen?"

"Yes, sir. Comin' up on sixteen—that is, if grandpa don't cook me up for supper."

Mike chuckled. "Oh, don't worry. The old codger is tough as shoe leather, but he ain't too mean. He'll try to scare you a bit, but most of the piss and vinegar is out of his system these days, and he's pretty darn mellow. Heck, he's seventy-five, so he ain't got too much to bother about—or shouldn't have, anyways." Mike faltered ever so slightly, but the old man quickly gathered his thoughts. "Hey, you hungry, son? We could stop by Roy's for a root beer float if you want."

"Naw, I'm good," Lee said. "Had a couple ham sandwiches on the bus. I'd rather get on out to the creek."

So, the Ford pickup began its journey one more time to the river as Lee explained that the teacher's workshop had given him the Friday off. Watching the woods get thicker and the afternoon sun slip lower, his thoughts drifted back to days when his grandpa had sometimes felt like his best friend, maybe his only friend, and Lee wondered if his visit might help them both.

"You better hold on there," Mike said. "These roads are in some bad shape after that storm last month. Lemme put 'er in four-wheel drive. This dang creek road is about shot, I tell you." And so they slowly skidded and spun their way deeper and deeper into the Catchahoula swamp, back to the cabin Tom had built overlooking his primary world, the river.

The old man grinned as he spoke. "It's a good thing you're coming to see Tom like this. I know boys like you got better things to do, but a feller like your grandpa ain't one to ask for help, so it's good you took

3

the initiative. Yeah, you wait for Tom Bradburn to invite you down, and you'll need to keep time with a calendar."

"I know, Mr. Hamlin, but I got this project for school I'm doing, a genealogy thing, so I thought grandpa would be a good place to learn some things about the family. Since Granny Oui died, he kinda disappeared. My mom's worried too, but she won't come out here with no electricity; she's more a hotel kind of camper."

"Yeah, I reckon so." Mike seemed to concentrate carefully. "Tom took your grandma's passing hard. Used to be he'd come to the cabin to hunt or run lines, but when Ouida died, he just quit going home, kinda like an old live oak stuck on the creek bank." The old man pointed out the bobcat that crossed the muddy road and how the pine trees up on the ridge looked brownish green in the fall light. Jostling around the mud holes and craters, Lee began to wonder if he could get out of here if he needed to find help.

"Mr. Hamlin? If anything happens while I'm here, what should I do? Where should I go?"

"Well, there ain't much you can do except walk it out; I doubt that worthless ole truck of your granddad's will crank. This road is about five miles to the cutoff, and once you're out there, you'll see a car or something. But don't worry; nothing is gonna happen. I'll come out tomorrow to check on you and then again on Sunday to pick you up and take you back to the bus. You'll be fine." The words helped, but Lee wasn't consoled. All the oaks along the road seemed draped in the heavy gray of spanish moss, and the dense underbrush spread darkness early over these woods. The slightest inkling of worry formed about dropping in on someone who had dropped out for a reason, but Lee trusted his grandpa would be happy to help with the genealogy investigation.

"Don't you worry. Your grandpa is about the best woodsman in these parts; ain't nothing in nature he can't take care of." With that assurance, Lee fell silent, wondering why his grandpa had retreated to such a desolate place, what he hadn't been able to handle that left him so stranded from people.

Moments later, Mike broke the silence. "Okay, I see smoke coming out the chimney up there; your granpappy must be home." Lee's anxiety rose another notch. Then, as the truck turned by the woodpile, the cabin came into view. Quite to Lee's satisfaction, the scene wasn't at all what he remembered.

When he was last here nearly five years ago, the place was a dismal little hole in the woods with not much to it but a small porch and trees pushed up close to the house like mushrooms next to an old log. Now the trees up close had been cut, and light came down broadly all around. To the left, a nice fenced-in garden soaked up the sunshine, sporting greens and tomatoes, onions and cabbages, all kinds of life. There were even flowers growing in the yard and some rudimentary chairs made out of vines and tree limbs situated around logs cut in half lengthwise that obviously were benches. A long, heavy wire hung between two oak trees, and from it dangled round hoops of beaver skins stretched to dry. A half dozen of them twisted in the breeze. "The ole place looks pretty good, don't it?" Mike spoke with pride.

"Yeah, it does. I'm a little surprised it looks so homey." Lee couldn't wait to get out of the truck.

His grandpa's time here became quickly evident as Lee did a slow rotation, taking in this secluded world. The tree with the hook used for skinning catfish, the little hammock under the maple trees, and even the old chest freezer serving now as a container for raising worms destined to be used as fish bait. On a make-do little table, Lee spotted the coffee grounds and raw vegetables for fattening the squirming creatures, and an old memory popped into his head of his grandpa pulling huge night crawlers from a pile of rotting leaves left by a river flood. Over the years, Lee had learned much about self-reliance from Tom, and standing before the cabin, seeing fingerprints of his grandpa's existence all over the property, that old bond found connection to the present moment.

A beaten path to the river showed regular use, and down in the shady lower area Lee heard water sloshing against the old skiff he remembered so well. With the easy breeze cooling his face and without thinking, Lee found himself walking toward the dark brown creek flowing endlessly down the banks headed to the gulf, and he knew that this was a special place. His mind filled with summer days lazing in the current or checking limb lines for a fresh catfish dinner. This crook in the river with its tiny cabin linked Lee not only to the past so recently missing but to the joy of simply being alive, so often misplaced beneath the stress of adolescence.

"Is that two robbers I see up there trying to steal all my expensive stuff?" The happy sound came from down the path even before Lee could see his grandfather.

"Yeah. But where's the silverware?" Lee said with a smile.

Tom popped out from the dark overhang, his gray hair poking out from around his red cap and his big walking stick pushing back a small bush growing out of place in the meandering path.

"Well I'll be dang gone. Look what the bobcats drug up—a couple of useless city slickers." Then with a grin, Tom hugged his grandson, the hug lingering a little longer than Lee expected. Turning to his old friend, Tom slapped Mike on the back with a heavy, strong hand, gripping the top of his neck with a friendly squeeze.

"I got a pot on the stove inside. You boys want a cup? Made it myself just this morning." So the afternoon settled into some stout caffeine, several good laughs, and pan-fried catfish with river greens picked only an hour earlier. As Mike drove away trying to catch the last of the afternoon light, Lee watched with apprehension though he knew his visit had been a good idea. A slight memory of his mom's hopeful face at the bus station lent pale encouragement.

II.

Lots of work had been done inside the cabin. A little loft Tom had built above the small living area became his bedroom while the rudimentary couch served as cozy bed for Lee. A wood-burning stove anchored the far wall, and the small kitchen had its own little eating table, so everything appeared orderly and efficient.

Soon, chatter filled the room about school, the family, his research project, and things of general concern, but little was said about the life in the woods the old man held to so adamantly. As Lee stretched out on his make-do bed by the wood-burning stove, he looked at the ceiling now golden red in the flickering light. He remembered when he was a boy.

Times when he visited the old house his grandpa and grandma lived in at the edge of town, big pecan trees outside, homemade chocolate fudge all packed with nuts, so many wonderful thoughts. Those years of squirrel hunting, camping, running lines on the river, all those summers swimming in the tinted water, translucent as it glided over the white river sandbars. Hundreds of sensations, sounds and tastes, sights and memories of childhood gone by, glimpses of his grandmother now taken by cancer. The flood of images left Lee feeling almost old as he thought of all he'd lost over these past few years.

"You still awake?" Lee whispered.

"Yeah."

"Do you miss Granny Oui sometimes? I think about her all the time, and it's like she's standing next to me, helping me remember things and showing me her face so I won't forget." His voice trailed as he suddenly became self-conscious.

"Yeah, I miss her too, a lot. We were married forty-eight years, so it's kinda like waking up one day and one of your hands is gone. You can see it ain't there, but you still can't figure it."

"Yeah, that's it," Lee said. "Same for me too, like something is there but not. Grandpa, do you believe in heaven? Can Granny Oui really be there waiting for us?"

"Son, I got no idea 'bout that; other folks will have to figure that one. I don't really think that way myself. I'd rather focus on things I can touch than worry about places I can't go. But I'm pretty sure Ouida is here in this cabin right now, watching over me and you."

"Grandpa, I know you're tired now, but tomorrow will you help understand some stuff about the family, things you can remember? I got a bunch of information from Mom and people, but I don't know much 'bout your mom, and I'd like to hear more. She died when I was so young, I can't remember things now."

"Yeah, I'll help you. Your great-grandma was an amazing woman, a force of the earth like few others. She's a difficult story, though. Saralynn didn't like people getting too close; she made finding the truth like prospecting for gold, a lot of work and tiny reward along the way. We'll talk in the morning." And with warm memories refreshed, both drifted to sleep.

III.

The smell of coffee and meat frying filled the cabin. A couple of blinks, then Lee caught a glimpse of his grandfather shuffling a cast-iron skillet on the potbelly stove.

"Hey there, sleepyhead. You hungry?" Tom asked.

"That sure smells good. Fillet mignon, I expect?" Still stretched on the couch, Lee enjoyed the day's slow beginning.

Tom chuckled. "Oh yeah, its fillet all right, fed on nothing but fresh leaves and nuts, right out of my little pecan grove."

The idea seemed unfamiliar to Lee as his typical breakfast was a root beer and a bag of salted peanuts, but he remembered this breakfast from his grandmother's kitchen and the many times she'd made biscuits and eggs along with a big slice of sizzled ham and a couple of fried squirrels cooked up fresh. Most people winced at the thought of eating squirrel meat, but to Lee, it was a reminder of the old days when his grandpa lived in town socializing with people, when Lee grew up around the loving relationship of his grandparents.

"Tell me, son, how's your mom and dad doing? And those pretty sisters?"

"Oh, everyone's good. Mom keeps us all straight, but Victoria is the queen, of course, Lucy her princess in training."

Tom laughed. "Oldest girls always end up running the show as I recall."

Lee wanted to mention his dad too, though he had a hard time thinking of what to say. "And Dad, uh, well, I saw him last week. Still doing those long-haul runs, so he's pretty busy. Okay though."

Pouring a cup of dense black coffee made from a mixture of coffee grounds and tree bark tea his grandfather had gathered, Lee slid comfortably into the chair next to the small kitchen table. The cabin stood another world from his daily life, and there in his head danced all the times he had awakened at his grandmother's house to her cleaning and cooking turkeys, ducks, rabbits, dove, quail, and an endless list of creatures his grandpa hauled home. It all felt strange to think of everyday existence now so sanitized with plastic-wrapped everything and how different his life now appeared from his grandmother's warm little house with chickens out back and a mulberry tree where he built a clubhouse.

Feeling at home, Lee nudged his grandpa into conversation. "Can you tell me a little about your life as a kid? Mom told me how your family got here from Scotland and all, but I don't feel like I know much beyond you and Granny Oui. What was your family like?"

"It wasn't much," Tom said flatly. "Had an older brother that turned out kinda worthless; lost all Mom's money in some scam he got tricked into. My sister was about as useless—only thought about her important social status. She lives in Atlanta now, but I don't know where."

Not much to talk about with the uncle and aunt, Lee stuck to the subject that had begun to intrigue him. "How 'bout your mom and dad? I heard they were both interesting characters." Glenna had already hinted there might be some stories her dad could share about the old days.

"Yeah, I suppose so. I've been trying to think of how to tell you some of this history. Lots of it I don't remember; parts of it were never clear to me. You see, my mom was born just outside of Slidell in the first decade of the twentieth century. Her family was poor, and her dad, John O'Brian, had come over from the UK and finally drifted down the East Coast to Slidell where he fished and trapped to feed the family. My mom was born Saralynn O'Brian, one of seven kids and pretty much in the middle of the lot with both older and younger brothers and sisters. She had a closest sister, Katie, who was only fifteen months her senior but wild as a March hare. That girl was always in trouble, as mom told it, and always counting on her younger sister to cover for her."

By the time breakfast ended, Lee knew about all the brothers and sisters and what they'd done with their lives. Though he gathered details for his report, Lee had a sense that important pieces of information for some reason were being omitted. Deciding to narrow the investigation, Lee focused on Saralynn.

"Grandpa, do you know how your mom met your father?"

"Well, yeah, I do. Harlan's parents owned a café in Picayune. I think it was called the Corner. While in high school, your great-grandma worked there as a waitress on weekends and sometimes during school if one of the regulars needed a day off or was sick. School wasn't too strict in those days, so skipping wasn't a big deal, but my mom had reasons not to cut class, though she always needed the money."

"What was that? Was she like a brainiac?" Lee asked.

"No, that wasn't it. Though Mom was a good student, at the time she actually was one of the best women's basketball guards in the state. The family had moved into Picayune when she was young; her dad took a job as a carpenter remodeling places. Worked for some shyster and was gone a lot. I don't know much about all that, but my grandmother Zelma wanted out of Slidell. Not quite sure what happened down there, but they put Slidell behind them and moved to Leetown, just outside of Picayune.

"Anyway, Mom played on the Picayune basketball team. In those days, it was six on six for girls, with three guards at one end and three forwards at the other, and only the forwards could score. Each group could only play up to the half-court line. Saralynn was only about five foot six, but she was quick and made a ferocious guard, or so her reputation went. She told me once her friends called her Hornet. Anyway, when she was in eighth grade, she played for the varsity, and for five years in a row Picayune went to the state finals; the last three years running, they won the state championship. Saralynn lettered five years straight."

"Wow, she must've been really good," Lee said with a sense of pride.

"Yeah, she was. That's how she got the job at the café, because everyone knew her, and also how poor her family was. They always wore homemade clothes to school but were clean and proper. My grandmother Zelma made sure of that. She had no truck with dirty kids or disrespect, and all her children went to school, did their best, and helped the family by working, hunting, or fishing."

"So, how 'bout Great-grandpa Harlan? Where'd he come in?" Lee asked.

"Harlan's parents owned the Corner. He was eight years older than mom, so he'd been off in college for a few years when he returned to Mississippi to open a little hardware store. Over time, he got to know Mom in the café, as that's where he ate a lot of his meals, being a bachelor and all ..."

10

The back and forth between Tom and Lee went on for almost two hours before they needed a break outside; Tom suggested they go check some limb lines he'd set the afternoon before and which were now long overdue for a rebait. The morning had been interesting, and Lee had a whole new library of stories about the family to think over.

They cruised up the river, enjoying the nice fall day. Checking the lines, they unhooked the two, small catfish and then headed back to the cabin.

"We lost some good fish 'cause we checked the lines so late. In the morning, let's get out early." Tom acted a little displeased, and Lee understood that checking lines wasn't entertainment; it was livelihood.

"Sure thing, Pop. Daylight tomorrow it is. You want me to take these volunteers up to the cabin and clean them?" Lee asked, proudly remembering his grandpa always called the fish they caught "volunteers."

"No, just throw 'em in the holding pen there."

On the river's edge, a dammed area with rocks created a reservoir about six feet square but which allowed a trickle of current to flow through.

"Awesome idea, Grandpa," Lee said. "Can they live here?"

"Yeah, a while. Gotta watch the flooding water so they don't escape, but I pitch 'em in there and then fish out the size I need to eat every day. If Mike drops by, I sometimes need a few extras. He eats like a horse. Oh yeah, you gotta watch out for snakes too. Moccasins visit me regularly." Tom's grin reminded Lee this was not a supermarket.

After situating the gear and having a drink of well water, the two walked down the sandbar a ways to enjoy the creek tumbling over logs. Such a peaceful mumbling often made unusual sounds—almost like words, Lee thought, voices from the river. Soon they took a seat on a fallen sycamore sprawled out on the sand, and Tom rejoined his storytelling.

"Son, I haven't been fully honest with you about your great-grandma or even Harlan, so I want to set a couple of things straight." Lee looked up quietly, not wanting to disturb the somber tone but pleased with himself for already realizing that, as raconteur, Tom had been editing.

11

"My mom was a force, no doubt about that," Tom said. "Tenacious, fierce, almost ruthless, one of those small people you know you don't want to cross. Athletic, tough minded, she focused on whatever task she had at hand by setting goals and tracking progress. Made us kids do the same, whether it was washing clothes or doing homework. And she loved to create stuff. I saw her write dozens of poems about life and draw pictures all the time even though she wasn't much of a writer or a painter. She believed in focused, intentional effort whether painting birdhouses, growing plants, or rearranging furniture. My dad used to joke that when he came home, he would never lay down in the dark 'cause the bed would probably be in a different place from where he last saw it. She loved to rearrange furniture and would do it all by herself, hauling big bureaus around and pushing armoires to the other side of the room."

Tom took a deep breath and looked down the river at the fall colors showing their design, a heavy look on his face. Lee was sure something big was pulling at his thoughts.

"Mom was a peculiar combination of unbelievably positive and at the same time secretive, even devious. Like she wasn't always telling you everything she could."

"Okay," Lee interrupted, "so I got that she was a relentless person when she was locked onto something, but tell me more about that strange side of her. What was she really like?"

"About the most loyal, intense human being I've ever met, especially about her family. And believe me, everyone knew it, and few crossed her. Problem was she absolutely believed she always in the right—I mean *always*. I remember thinking once if she was an animal, it would be a snapping turtle." Lee smiled, hoping for some action stories, but Tom stayed with his serious train of thought.

"Funny though, what she usually wanted was exactly the opposite of what she needed. Take my dad for instance. Harlan was a good-looking, well-off local boy who everybody liked; had a college education, a family with some means, and a personality that could have made him a politician if he'd had any ambition. The problem was he didn't. All he wanted was to play cards, drink, and chase women, and though he straightened up enough to marry my mom, his old ways won out, and he didn't make much of a husband. So there was Saralynn raising three kids with no help, and she made it all harder by pretending everything was perfect. It was weird, but she knew how to be optimistic with her kids and didn't let imperfect reality get in the way.

"It took me years to understand why Mom worked so hard to maintain the illusion that her marriage was healthy and that Dad was a good husband. To us kids, it was pretty obvious all he wanted to do was drink and come home late, but to the outside world, Mom maintained a steady image of him 'travelling on business.' Yeah, business all right— personal business." Tom paused almost as if he'd lost his train of thought, then began again.

"She grew up hard and had been laughed at her whole life for wearing sewed-up flour sacks and secondhand clothes, so when she got married, she thought all that embarrassment was behind her. So, with my dad, she got what she wanted but not so much what she needed."

"Really, your dad was that bad?" Lee said. "I never knew that; I always thought he'd been interested in work more than anything else." Lee knew he was learning some good stuff now.

"Well, it wasn't that he was bad, just spoiled. He'd been raised a rich kid with everything handed to him, so he didn't respect how hard life was, especially for someone poor. Dad was kind of worthless really, but likeable. And the more aloof he became, the more pressure it put on Mom to keep up appearances. Over time, that stress changed her in ways that made her seem odd to folks."

Boom!

"Did you hear that?" Lee said, jumping to his feet. "Sounded like a gun."

"No, it wasn't a gun. Just a car up the river; got water in the tailpipe and backfired. Probably Mike, but once in a while the game warden or such types drop by." Tom's face contorted, though his words didn't sound overly concerned. "I don't like surprises."

The last comments struck Lee as curious, but he knew they had plenty of time to talk and wanted to keep his grandpa in as good a mood as possible, so he let the words pass.

Walking back to the cabin, Lee began thinking about how Saralynn was coming to life through stories, and he wanted more. Could it be that his grandpa was a lot like Saralynn and might be finessing the truth a bit, maybe even hiding some kind of secret? The clear morning air awakened a creative urge, and suddenly Lee wanted to know as much about his family history as possible. Collecting stories never sounded like schoolwork before, but the mission now became to uncover hidden information, maybe even help his grandpa get what he needed.

IV.

"Hey there, boys. Figured you might be tired of eating tree bark and river grass, so I brought you some doughnuts and hot chocolate." Mike had a big grin on his ruddy face, but Tom, suddenly frowning, ignored the comment.

"Well, I'll let you boys poison yourselves on that stuff without me," said Tom. "I gotta run to the smokehouse and throw another log on the fire." With animated steps, he headed to the edge of the clearing where he'd built a little shed to cover an old freezer converted into a wood smoker. In that little locker, quite a few deer roasts and turkeys and heaven knows what had soaked up oak and hickory, or pecan and apple wood, which helped preserve the meat Tom ate. Lee took the opportunity to quiz Mike a little about the past.

"Mr. Hamlin, Grandpa has been telling me all about his mom, and it's real interesting. I was wondering, did you know her?"

"Well, sure I did. But for starters, since you're grown now, call me Mike, okay? Now, let me see. Heck, I pretty much grew up hanging around your grandpa and got to know the whole family pretty good. They were nice people for the most part. Harlan was a little rowdy, but he was gone a lot anyway."

"Yeah, that's what grandpa was telling me, about how Harlan liked to drink and gamble."

"Shoot, he was a legend 'round here. That guy could shoot pool with the best of them. In Old Man Granger's barbershop, there was a poker game going on in the back room pretty much twenty-four hours a day, and Harlan not only played a good chunk of that time, but he was the dealer most of it. He could handle some cards—now let me tell you. Unfortunately, when he was drinking, his handling got a little less careful."

"So everybody knew it? I thought the family kept his carousing a secret?" Lee said.

"Saralynn did keep things quiet, but everybody knew anyway. She pretended nobody saw how he acted, and folks let her think what she wanted. Truth is most people thought Tom's mom was a little nutty—you know, not crazy but just a little extreme, I guess you could say. She had one reality, and everybody else had another."

"What do ya' mean?" Lee asked.

"Like for instance, she had 'bout the worst temper you ever saw, and if you ever got a look at it, you didn't want to see it twice. Once when Tom and me was in sixth grade, before I got held back that year, we were changing classes and talking in the hallway when Mrs. Cressler told us to keep it quiet, but we kept talking anyway. She whopped us both on the seat with her paddle. No big deal. The 'lady was seventy years old, but she culled us out of the crowd and made an example of us.

"Well lemme tell you something. When Saralynn heard what happened, the next day she went straight to the school and waited till the last bell rang and Mrs. Cressler came out to go home. Saralynn walked straight up to her, poked her finger in the old woman's face, and a blue streak of curse words and warnings came out like vomit from a sick baby. Man, that woman had a tongue as sharp as a razor and a temper to go with it. I remember all us kids standing there listening, terrified to say a word; we'd never seen a teacher get in trouble before. Poor Tom; he pretty near died of embarrassment that day."

"Wow, so what happened afterward?"

"Everything cooled off okay, but Saralynn was banned from walking on school property. That was too bad too 'cause she was always the room mother that organized all the good parties, brought cupcakes and decorations for Easter and stuff. Tom's mom was the center of most everything fun we got to do in school, and when they banned her, we never had another decent birthday party or Christmas celebration again. Too bad really."

After stirring the bed of hot coals and putting on a nice piece of green hickory for smoke, Tom strolled back to the cabin where Mike and Lee were deep in conversation.

"Okay, you guys look like you're having too much fun over here with these sugar bombs, so let's knock off the party and get serious. You boys want to go horseback riding? There's a makeshift barn 'bout a mile and a half down the road toward town; you might have seen the trail to it on the way in. The fellow there lets me ride any time I want 'cause the horses need the exercise; he's got four animals. No saddles, of course, but horses anyway."

"Gee, that sounds like fun," Mike said, "but I got to get back to town and shove some bamboo shoots under my fingernails, so I'll beg off for now." With a chuckle, Mike stood slowly, his body a little weary of the log he'd used as a chair. Lee was up in a flash, ready to go. Mike looked so much older than his grandpa, and Lee realized how much more fit Tom seemed due to his austere lifestyle. But Lee also noticed how much more somber his grandpa was than his best friend; clearly, socializing was more effort for Tom.

As the old red truck pulled away, Lee turned to Tom. "You think your old truck will crank, Grandpa?

"What for? I got a shortcut over there. Only a mile or so." And with a grin, Tom walked to the road.

More and more, Lee began to absorb a new sense of his grandfather, a young man's perspective replacing the boyhood images he'd collected years earlier tagging along riverbanks. Clearly his grandfather was still strong physically, his sparse life forcing him to stay active and use his strength as well as cleverness, and Lee understood Tom enjoyed that challenge. But his granddad struggled at the easy work of talking to people, tending to stiffen up every time someone came around, even if it was only Mike. Lee wondered what could have triggered his granddad's withdrawal. Had it been Ouida's death like everyone thought? Or was it something unknown that Tom kept to himself, like Saralynn would have?

The horse stable visible in the distance got closer as Lee snuck quick glimpses trying to spot something new about this man he loved so much and yet was only beginning to understand. Tom simply strolled along letting his ears pick up every sound of squirrels barking in the sloughs along the river, doves cooing in distant fields, and the wind tinkling the maple leaves turning orange now in the weakening autumn sunlight. Studying each little twitch, Lee wondered how it felt to be someone knowing the twilight of life approached.

Lee finally ventured a question. "Mike said your mom acted a little strange sometimes. Was she a little crazy maybe?"

Tom answered as if already in midthought. "I don't know; it seemed like Mom was always one of those people too big for her own life, like she was large enough to reach around other people and take them in, shelter them when they needed it, as if nothing could hurt her. Lord knows how much grief she took covering for my aunt Katie. That girl was always sneaking out at night, drinking moonshine and smoking cigarettes. She was trouble, but Mom would lie for her, tell Zelma and John whatever they needed to hear to get the heat off Katie. Then Mom would take the fallout for herself, like it didn't faze her, like her shoulders were bigger than anybody else's. Somebody called her a martyr one time, and I guess that was it. She wanted to show people how strong she was, and she could back it up too." Tom paused, seemingly distracted by a passing thought, and then began again.

"Aunt Katie told me once some girls cornered her about some boy she flirted with in high school. She said Mom came out of the school and beat the crap out of all four of them, dang near breaking the biggest girl's arm behind her back. They had called her "flour sack" and names, and that set her off. Mom was not a big person but was bad news when she got mad, as those girls found out."

"Man, that's cool," Lee said. "Saralynn the bouncer girl. But it's kinda weird, ain't it? Always bailing out her sister? I mean most brothers and sisters try to get each other in trouble, not take the wrap for one another. It's odd."

"Yeah, maybe, but Saralynn knew how much Katie needed her, like she didn't trust Katie to survive unless she got that help. Of course, Katie was the most conniving person I ever met, and I know she took advantage of Mom all those years, but it made Mom feel important to be needed, gave her confidence that she was up to life. It was also an intimacy, something secretive she could share with Katie. Mom always liked her secrets, and she didn't do too well with making friends."

As if searching for someone who might be listening from behind the trees, Tom began to look around with a nervous twitch across his face that appeared uncomfortable. Then he spoke. "I never told anyone this before, and I want you to keep this part just between us, but a few years ago, I found out something I didn't know about Mom, something she'd always kept to herself. It slipped out in the hospital when she was delirious under the cancer medicine and talking out of her head. I snooped around afterward though and found out what she'd said was true." Tom took a deep breath, the years unwinding as his face took on a distant stare.

"My grandmother and granddad raised their family as well as they could, but they were poor, real poor. John did his best, but he wasn't a great provider and unfortunately tended to drink a little more than he should. I always knew that part, but I didn't know that sometimes he got mean and hit Zelma, and even the kids. It seems things got worse and worse till he came home drunk one night and shoved my grandmother. She hit the corner of the bed, knocking her out cold. Everybody got all upset and panicky evidently, but Mom went straight to the kitchen and got a butcher knife. As Granddad bent over Zelma trying to revive her with a wet washcloth, Saralynn snuck up behind him and put the knife right up to one of his kidneys, telling him if he ever touched her mom again, she'd kill him in his sleep. I'm pretty darn sure he believed her too.

"My uncle Roy was Mom's oldest brother and real close—stayed with her till she died. He told me those details, though I had to pull it out of him. All Mom had said in the hospital was, 'I'll kill you if you touch her. I'll kill you in your sleep.' It took me a while to piece it all together, but I finally did."

"So, did he stop hitting her?" Lee asked.

"He did for a while. Then a few months later, here it went again. Now everyone was all worried about what Saralynn would do, but she surprised everybody—I mean *everybody*. Mom knew her dad was watching her and didn't trust her, so being the devious type she was—shrewd-like I mean—she did something I still can't believe."

"What? What was it? Tell me," Lee said.

"Well, Mrs. Shultz lived right next door to my grandparents for thirty years and was best friends with Zelma, always baking together and canning things. Mom used to go over there all the time just to get out of the noise and hear the two ladies talk about the old days and the Bible. Anyway, Mom discovered that Mrs. Shultz kept money in a coffee can under a floorboard in the bedroom. A couple days after John hit Zelma again, when she knew Mrs. Shultz was at the grocery store, Mom slipped through a side window and took the money, took it all, two hundred and twelve dollars."

"Why'd she do that?" Lee was truly puzzled.

"She did it so she could buy an escape for her mother, which she did, and lickety-split before anybody knew what happened, Zelma had money in her purse and was in New Orleans where her sister lived. Mom didn't tell anyone where her mom went and had evidently told Zelma the money had come from saving her tips at the restaurant. But the point is she got her mom outta there while she stayed to face the consequences."

"So did John beat Saralynn up?"

"No, not exactly. He didn't have to. As soon as Zelma left town, Mom went straight to Sheriff Walker and confessed she'd stolen the money, even before Mrs. Shultz knew it was missing. The law put Mom in jail straight away. Roy told me it was such a big mess 'cause it came to light John had been beating his wife and how Saralynn stopped it, so finally the judge told Mom to pay back Mrs. Shultz the money and that she'd be on probation for five years. He also told John that if he touched any of his kids or wife again for any reason, that he'd go to jail for assault."

"Wow, that's amazing," Lee said. "She really was quite a woman, wasn't she?"

"Yes, she was. Unfortunately, the whole thing sunk Saralynn's chance to play semipro basketball after high school 'cause now she had an arrest record, but that was the price she paid. After a few months, Zelma came back home, and John quit drinking, so things settled down, but Mom sure left her mark on the family, and after that, people both admired and feared her as they weren't quite sure what she was capable of doing anymore. Some people thought she was crazy, and some said she was the strongest woman they'd ever seen. All I know is that nobody messed with my mom. Having her around was like wearing protective armor, and her brothers and sister knew it too."

Tom and Lee now retreated into their separate silence, Lee wondering if he had any of that heroic strength in him. Learning more about his great-grandmother had brought forward new ideas never considered before. If there was a crisis of some sort, how would he react instinctively? The morning's chat filled Lee with new impressions about his own life and increasingly about his grandfather's.

After Tom put the bridles on the horses, with a little hop and leg swing, both mounted their steeds, though precariously at first. Tom rode every couple of weeks and quickly eased off at a comfortable pace, but Lee was less experienced and oscillated between trying to hold on too tightly with his legs, which told the horse to go faster, and pulling back on the reins, which told the horse to slow down, a confusing sequence for both man and beast. Soon, however, Lee found a comfortable balance by emulating Tom's upright posture, and the two followed a well-worn path parallel with the river.

Studying Tom from behind, the fierce independence that had made him strong all his life seemed obvious, that clarity about what he demanded. Saralynn had that singularity of purpose, that confidence that she could master any obstacle, and Lee felt a thrill at being related. With idealized simplicity, Lee saw his grandfather as the strongest man alive, the one most certain of his choices in life. Instinctively, the boy craved that same fortitude for himself, as lately adolescence offered more confusion than clarity. An important idea had begun to germinate, and understanding how Tom and Saralynn lived such lives of control inspired Lee to seek his own choices about the future and not be ruled by the decisions of others. A vicarious energy flowed from Tom to Lee as the boy absorbed the heroic image he'd begun building in his mind, and as if the miasma of his adolescent years began to clear, Lee glimpsed the man he wanted to become.

After a half hour, Lee spoke up. "Hey, Pop, can we take a little rest? Sally June's backbone is killing my butt."

At first Tom didn't react and continued plodding along in silence. Then, as if the delayed request had finally shown up in his brain, grinning, he turned to Lee. "Yeah, sure, son. Let's take a little break." A nice patch of blackberries lined the trail where they dismounted, and Tom produced an empty tin from his knapsack. There it was again, his grandpa's mastery of the moment, always in charge and prepared.

Someone had cut a stack of firewood there, so they pulled up a couple of logs to sit on, and Lee began his investigation.

"You know, we were talking about Granny Oui last night. I know you miss her—heck, we all do—but what I'm saying is after so many years with just one person, how do you put something new into your head to fill up that emptiness? I mean, moving on must be tough." Lee had felt confident about his question until he began speaking. Then in midsentence the idea tried to drift away.

Tom looked straight ahead at the blackberry bushes as if he hadn't heard, and Lee was convinced his grandpa simply wouldn't answer. As Lee scrambled for another question, Tom released a little gasp, like a leak of emotion from behind his stoic exterior. The old man peered off into the woods with a listless stare leaving Lee with the impression some sudden weakness had robbed his grandpa's strength. Then Tom found his voice.

"There's a few things I think about every day. Oui is the one I think about every minute. It's not easy to say how it all works, but it's just like how one of your hands knows the other is there and what it will do. Your brain doesn't need to get involved to know some things. That's the way Oui was for me, like the part of me I didn't have to think about. There ain't no moving on to something else. Oui was the one thing in my life whose absence can't be filled."

After a moment of quiet, Lee wanted to break the emotional grip. "Sometimes I wish you'd leave these ole woods and come back to us, Grandpa. You know, we all miss you that same way too. And Mom, well she ain't been the same since you left; it's like some part of her slipped away, and she can't find it anymore."

Tom jumped to his feet, face flushed red. For an instant, Lee felt afraid of the sudden power unleashed so quickly by a few simple words, and before him he witnessed another vestige of his great-grandmother.

"We ain't gonna talk about that—nope," said Tom. "I'm out here 'cause I want to be, and nobody can change that. It's my choice, you hear me? I ain't taking orders from nobody anymore." And with that surprisingly volatile response, Tom slid back up on old Bucky, who had waited in the shade for Tom to tell him what to do, and the day's pleasant ride was over.

Sorting out things with his grandpa was proving to be more delicate than Lee had envisioned. This withdrawn, hard spirit he'd come to visit had taken time to insulate from the world, and introducing outside opinion was the last thought that interested Tom. But a sense of mission had begun to germinate around the important idea that both Tom and Glenna may need a little help with life.

V.

The tension remained heavy all the way to the horse barn and then on the walk home, but neither spoke. Expressing his mother's sense of loss hadn't garnered the reaction Lee had planned, though surely he hadn't meant to be invasive or judgmental. But the eruption had been too volatile not to arouse concern.

Back at the cabin, the somber mood combined with a tacit dread almost tangible. "I'll be back in a minute," Tom said. "Why don't you wash those sweet potatoes there and put them on the stove?" With that, Tom stepped outside for some air.

Soon, dinner steamed on the table, a sumptuous hunk of smoked pig with delicious apple and pecan-smoked flavor all permeating the meat after hours of slow cooking. Loading his plate, Tom heaped the sliced persimmons ripe with the autumn chill, dripping in juicy liquid stored from a long summer's growth.

The fresh air and big meal relaxed the men, but Lee decided to pull back his probing and talk more about less painful matters. Light conversation helped finish the meal.

"That crazy Sally June," Lee said, "is one wacky old horse. Did you see when she tried to knock me off? Yeah, she kinda bucked as she hopped over that pine log just to see if she could lose me. Didn't fall off, but I probably should have."

"Yeah, she gets feisty sometimes; wants you to know she ain't too old yet."

Not sure if there was a hidden message, Lee didn't say anything. His response worked, and all through the rest of supper they chatted about how sweet the fruit was and how good the applesauce tasted with the smoked pig.

After dinner, the sweet blackberries savored and dishes all cleared, Tom stoked the fire with a fresh oak log then sat back in his favorite chair, an old homemade armchair made of scrap wood now laden with quilts giving it a soft inviting appeal. The dancing red light revealed crevices on his face now stone-like in the glow. Gray hair still full but wild, he looked to Lee like a wise man from some unknown people, an earth knower trapped in the pull of civilization. An idea came to Lee that his grandpa appeared stranded, snagged almost by the briars of his old life that kept him from moving on. Tom stared deeply into the fire.

"I'm sorry I was so rough today," Tom said. "Didn't mean to be. It's hard for me to think about the past. Too many places there to pull me backward."

Lee said nothing, allowing his granddad the slow moment he needed, just as the hard oak wood resists a flame and then slowly yields to the heat.

"I'm an old man now," Tom slowly began. "Don't really know how much time I have left; sometimes don't know how much time I even want. When I'm down on the river or digging in the garden, I sometimes stop and feel the wind and let the sun fall all over me, and I don't have to do a thing except feel my root to this ground. That's the moment I need now in life, that quiet acceptance as the river talks and the wind holds me gently. Not sure I need a lot of talking and people."

Drifting into silence, Tom watched the oak log catch its flame, brightening the cozy cabin with a golden light. Lee had an unspoken idea of spirits without bodies, shadows examining his emotions. The sensation passed. Tom's words about the wind holding him and the river speaking became a slowly fading echo, and an inkling of his grandpa as a poet scratched at Lee's silence. He thought of Saralynn and her writing and painting, and a lifting joy slowly filled the quiet. As the fire crackled, Lee wondered if religion and art had been conceived originally so people could imagine life without pain.

The glow of the cabin filled Lee with a surge of hope, and then, grounded again, he spoke. "Does my being here hurt you?"

Tom's blue-gray eyes looked at his grandson with the loving glint of a parent proud to see a child take a first step.

"No, son, it doesn't hurt me. It helps. Helps me remember times when I was strong, when I cared about people. It's all getting harder now, Lee—harder to remember those good things." And with that, Tom slowly rose and headed for bed. As he passed the couch, he laid a rugged hand on his grandson's shoulder, squeezing his neck in that familiar way, the way that felt like a full-body hug, a handprint as substantial as a footprint, Lee thought, a connection of men outside the frailty of words.

VI.

Early Sunday morning, the creaking footsteps on the porch awakened Lee. Not moving, he only blinked at the daylight coming through the window and wondered what Tom had been doing outside so early. "Probably checking a trap," he thought out aloud as he pulled the warm blanket up close to his shoulders, wondering what the day might bring.

Seeing his grandfather's independence and unwillingness to compromise had stoked Lee's teenage urge for independence. Tom's defiance of social expectations rendered the old man heroic in Lee's mind, a man who knew exactly what he wanted. How liberating it must be not to need other people or listen to orders and rules, not to worry about stupid things like reports and tests. In his mind, a life of freedom seemed the only solution to the ennui he felt so often, the frustration with the rigidity that life imposed. Lee wanted Tom to know he was a hero for not conforming to pressure from others.

After a half hour of far-flung imagination and fully awake, Lee was ready for the world, ready to stay with his grandfather or join the army, maybe go around the world as a merchant marine. Soon the door opened, and Tom moved quietly back into the much warmer inside but said nothing. Lee knew Tom was not an easy man, so he held his enthusiasm, waiting for the right moment when coffee percolated, and bacon sizzled, and men could be men.

"That smells good. Is that from that pig you smoked up?"

"Naw, it's from the Farmer's Cart in town. Mike brought it out; he was afraid you wouldn't like that stinky old swamp pig." The words didn't exactly harmonize with Lee's idealistic notions of living life alone in the wild, but he took the news in stride, still filled with his newfound invincibility.

"Where'd you go this morning, Pop? Check a trap or something?"

"Naw, just sitting and thinking. That ole fog this morning sure was pretty, had that kind of steel-looking color. With the creek whispering and that soft little breeze, it was mighty pleasant."

"Personally, I liked this nice warm quilt myself; it was pleasantly warm." They both had a laugh.

"I don't know if I've helped you much with your report," said Tom. "Seems we talked about a lot of personal things but not too much about lineage, I'm afraid. Really, I don't even know much more than what your mom probably already told you. Hope that's okay."

"Yeah, it's fine. I got what I needed. To be honest, I really just wanted to see you and make sure you were doing okay. We talk about you all the time." Lee sensed this might be a good time to expose how much respect he had for the fierce autonomy he so admired in his grandfather, so he slowly rose to his feet, gathering his thoughts.

"Grandpa, I want you to know I admire how strong you are and how free you live your life. Lots of older people tend to lose some of that and start to count on families more, too much a lot of the time, but not you. You did the opposite; you don't need anybody."

"Yeah, well I wouldn't go too far down that road if I was you," Tom said. "I'm kind of an old crank, and sometimes I'm my own worst enemy.

Living out here all alone gets kinda boring, and my mind tends to think about the wrong things."

"Well, I reckon, but at least nobody is telling you what to do all the time. Man, I get tired of other people giving me orders and deadlines and chores. I feel like a slave half the time."

"You know," Tom said, "one of the things I've figured out by being half stupid my whole life is that the stuff I hated wasn't all bad, and the stuff I loved and thought I needed wasn't all good." Tom went quiet.

Conversation soon turned to activity with Lee putting out plates as Tom scrambled eggs fresh from his chicken coop. Then as they were finishing breakfast, a horn blew down the road. A few minutes later, Mike barged into the cabin with a Barq's root beer in hand and a bag of salted peanuts, Moon Pies, Honey Buns, all various "poisons" as Tom called them. Lee was ecstatic. The abstemious life was fine in theory, but peanuts in a root beer for breakfast approached nirvana in his teenage world.

"Didn't know if you were half-starved yet, so I thought I'd bring you some vitamins," Mike said with a devilish grin. "You can always take them on the bus with you as sustenance." All three laughed as long-lost pals happy to be together again. Lee noticed the respect Mike had for his lifelong friend, the man he'd known as a boy and now as headstrong spirit living alone on the river, and he wondered what Mike might know about his grandpa's withdrawal.

Since the first rays of daylight, it appeared something had begun thawing inside Tom, like a shallow creek frozen in winter releasing to a warming sun. Tom's face was brighter with color in his cheeks, and Lee considered that a little company had been a good thing to give his grandpa.

Tom even moved with alacrity as he grabbed his old cap. "Hey there, boys, what do you say we go check the trotline and do a little target practice down at the river? Heck, Lee ain't even shot a gun since he's been here. Then maybe crank up my ole Chevy to get Lee on that bus. Maybe even stop by Roy's first. I got a hankerin' for some onion rings."

The pronouncement shook the little cabin like an emotional earthquake but one that must not be noticed. Lee glanced at Mike, who gave the boy a quick wink. Then both went about their business, not wanting to draw attention to Tom's rare openness. Lee furtively studied his grandpa's stare and what almost looked like a tear as he stood at the cabin window.

VII.

After getting into the little skiff, Lee expected to head upriver, but instead Tom pointed the now overloaded twelve-foot boat down the shallow current.

Mike too was a little confused. "Where you going, Tom? Did you move that trotline you had up at Mussel Hole bend?"

"Nope. This is something different I put in a couple of days ago but ain't had a chance to check yet. It's in a place I call the Devil's Throat. You and I were there years ago, but it's different now."

Lee looked at Mike, showing mild concern, but it was a nice, warm day, so a little boat ride didn't seem too bad. Surely the Devil's Throat was only some joke name.

Mike offered a reminder. "Don't forget, we gotta get this boy to the bus station this afternoon."

"Okay, okay, it ain't far. I hadn't been to it in years, but the big flood two springs ago changed everything; really filled in that old pond and made it a pretty nice-sized lake. Found it when I was turkey hunting this spring and finally decided to set a line there. That little piece of swamp is now full of water and looks interesting. Spooky though."

Again Lee and Mike caught one another's eye. The sangfroid tone with which Tom delivered his monotone response sent a shiver through Lee as visions of dark stygian haunts began to conjure in his imagination.

"Great, just what we need, a little trip to hell before we head to town." Mike's quip lightened the mood, but Tom didn't flinch.

After a few quick minutes, Tom eased the boat to the right side of the river where a small cut carved into the woods next to a slender sandbar. This spot was so desolate no one except Tom had probably walked in there for years, but now he stepped onto the sand and started unscrewing the outboard motor from the back of the boat.

"What are ya' doing, Grandpa?"

"We'll leave the motor here. Too heavy, and we don't need it where we're going; too close in there. Come on. Grab a side of the skiff and let's drag it over this bar. I got a trail going there."

Mike growled at having to pull the boat over land, but Tom paid no attention.

The little aluminum boat was pretty light, so the effort really looked harder than it was, but once over the rise behind the sandbar, Lee saw what they were in for. An ink-black dead river lake staged out in front of them, barely visible for all the tree growth reaching out over the water. The lake was about thirty yards wide at their end with huge willows growing along the edge, reaching toward the center where a little path of water stretched out largely unobstructed by the reaching tree arms from either bank. Waiting ahead was a watery trail just wide enough for the skiff.

"Let's put the boat in here and sneak down this little open area to where I put out my line. I'm thinking there's a lunker in here somewhere."

Soon they were knifing through the opaque black water. Dense willow limbs dangled in the stillness, and behind them large oaks and cypress trees, all dripping with gray spanish moss, stood motionless as if stoically observing the unwelcome humans trudge through the density.

The muffled sound in the thickets left a turbid heaviness almost impenetrable in the overabundant growth, an eerie silence punctuated only by the buzz of mosquitoes. No birds moved, and no river gurgled this far inland, only lush growth smothered in a blanket of insects.

Tom sat up in back with the paddle, and Lee noticed for the first time the ivory handled .38-caliber pistol tucked into Tom's belt. Clipped into a rack on the side of the boat, the old Winchester pump .22 rifle hung as well. Lee felt comforted by the two guns but wasn't quite sure why.

Tom was in command. "Watch your head here, girls. Hold the limbs up a little, and I'll paddle us through. Lee, keep a good look out for us, okay?"

Lee grimaced, a little unsure what his grandfather wanted, but given the cryptic instruction, he assumed there must be a handkerchief or plastic bottle marking where the trotline was tied off, so he looked for what he wasn't quite sure of, doing his best to spot it anyway. The only sound to guide him was the gentle dip of the paddle into the still water. Twice, low limbs jabbed the boat, but the thickness opened up just ahead, and it encouraged Lee. The afternoon light dimmed in the heavy growth where the lily pads donned their late-season brown as waxy green surfaces sensed the seasonal light and cool night air of this unwelcoming world.

"Man," Lee said, "how'd you find this place? It gives me the creeps. No way I'd come in here by myself." Then, as Lee began to expatiate on the spooky grays and blacks of everything, a loud thump hit the center of the boat, just to the side of where he sat between Mike at the front and Tom at the stern. Tom was looking backward as his hat had gotten snatched off by a limb, so he reached behind the boat to retrieve it just as Lee saw the unknown object fall two feet from where he sat.

At first it looked like a tree limb—fat, four inches or so in diameter, and a little over two feet long—but then not only did it move, it turned toward Lee, opening its huge mouth, bright white inside with two gigantic fangs on top.

From the front of the boat, Mike yelled. "Snake, snake, Tom!"

Lee barely knew what had happened, but as his grandpa turned forward, his legs moved, and the snake struck at his boots twice, very quickly, hitting the soles fortunately. Lee, without thinking, instantly grabbed the abandoned paddle and hit the snake with the thin, sharp side—a swift, direct blow that pinned the stunned animal's head in a crevice between the floor and bench seat. Again with pure reflex, Lee quickly stuck the second paddle under the stunned snake and with a sudden heave lifted it, vigorously launching the heavy mass over the side of the boat without complaint.

Mike yelled, "Crap, Tom, you trying to get us killed? That dang cottonmouth almost crawled up your dungarees. Holy crap. You know how mean them things are. He could a hit us all."

Tom sat dazed but quickly caught himself as he turned to Lee.

"Quick thinking, son. Sorry, I didn't see him in that tree. I was futzing with my cap back there."

"It's okay, Grandpa. None of us saw him; he was the same color as the tree, and I thought it was a limb that fell in the boat. Man, that scared the kageebees out of me." Lee slumped back, head against the boat side, throwing open his arms and laughing. Mike finally cracked a smile as he caught Tom's eye, but Tom never smiled or laughed, never released the tension in his jaw.

"Jesus, let's get outta here," Mike groused as Lee looked at his grandfather with the loving respect he'd always had.

"No, way," Lee said. "We gotta check that trotline. Heck, that's like hiking to the summit of a mountain and stopping before you reach the top because your feet hurt."

Tom's voice got stronger. "The line is right here Mike. Won't take a minute. But this time instead of napping up there in the front, could you keep your eyes open for varmints? Geeze, you take these old guys out with you, and all they want to do is siesta with the snakes."

As Tom began to paddle toward the tie-off, a cacophony of birds began screeching. The commotion in the boat had no doubt awakened everything in this dank hole, and though Lee didn't say anything, he had the creeping suspicion that an alligator might be on the prowl after all this racket, and that's what could be frightening the birds. Suddenly, Lee became very uncomfortable with being this far off the river, this far back in the still waters where the shade ruled and the closeness of things suffocated.

After pulling in two three-pound catfish, Tom cut the trotline and rolled it up on the piece of large bamboo he used to carry the line. He flashed Lee a quick grin, then handed the boy the gleaming pistol. "Okay, boss, you're the new sheriff in town. Let's keep the bad guys on the other side of the paint and the old guy up front awake, if you can."

VIII.

The Chevy truck cranked with sluggish complaint and the ill will of a hangover, but after a few minutes of coaxing and a battery jump from Mike's Ford, Lee and Tom began the jostling ride to town. Mike followed in his truck. The first few minutes passed with both men listening carefully to see if the pickup might falter, but after the first half mile, all seemed well. Lee noticed his grandfather's face twitching as if speaking to himself in silence. Tom finally brought words to the surface.

"Son, I appreciate you coming down here. I know I ain't the most pleasant company, but it means something to me."

"Are you kidding?" Lee said. "I would have paid money for this trip. That snake striking your boots is the most exciting thing I ever saw up close." Lee knew he sounded adolescent, so he pulled himself back, though he still wanted to keep the mood upbeat.

Tom picked up Lee's thread. "Yeah, Mike was so shook up I thought he was going to jump out of the boat." Lee sat back allowing the balm of a happy thought to work a moment on his grandpa. But as they bounced along the rutty road, Lee began considering how significant this trip to town was for Tom, and he couldn't wait to get home and tell his mom all about it.

The weekend had helped Lee gain perspective on his own life too. Now a new idea began to ferment as he considered the strong, reliant person his grandpa had always been. That dependable character was a strain of Saralynn, and it also flowed through his own youthful veins. With that thought, a smile broke out, so he decided to press his grandpa a little further.

"I still want to know more about Saralynn. Okay, Pop? I'm starting to see things in me—and even you—that are part of her. I want to know that better." Lee felt tentative but glad.

"Well, okay," Tom said. "I'll have to give that some thought." And Tom went quiet for a good five minutes, letting the gouges in the road shake the truck enough that a little truth might fall out. Finally, he spoke.

"Since we got a few minutes here, let me tell a little story my mom told me from when she was in high school. Oui and I were about to leave Picayune and move to Yazoo City for my new job. Both Mom and Mike were pretty upset. Anyway, seems that way back Mom was the favorite student of the chemistry teacher who always let her run errands to the office and such. At the end of the school year, she asked Mom to work on inventorying everything in the chemistry lab, all kinds of beakers and tubes, different elements and the like.

31

"Well, Mom became intrigued by a tiny little ball of mercury she found in some abandoned bottle in the back storeroom, so she took a little dab of it for herself, then snuck it out of the school in a tiny little bottle. Said she loved to put that stuff in a bowl and break it up, watch that little ball roll around, divide into other silver balls, then join right back up again like nothing ever happened. She had a serious look the day I was to leave town, and I knew she had something profound on her mind. Mom always did have a philosophical way about her. I'll never forget that little story of the quicksilver and what she said afterward.

"'It's good you're leaving Picayune, Tom. But you'll be back. We're all just shiny little pieces rolling around, bouncing off one another like we're separate. But we aren't. We're all one family. And one day we'll all be together forever.'

"Took me a while to absorb Mom's words. But now I see, for her, heaven and earth were the same thing. She was right too; I did come home to Picayune. I guess we all look to get back to that bright shiny source we start as but can't quite comprehend until after we bounce off one another for a lifetime."

Tom finished with what Lee was certain to be a tear in his eye, but each managed to look a different direction. Not sure what to say, quietly letting the image of the silver ball dividing and rejoining sink in a little, Lee focused instead on the great effort it took his grandpa to tell that story. And the remainder of the drive passed peacefully.

After onion rings and a double cheeseburger, they finally got to the bus station where Mike crushed Lee's hand again amid a shower of appreciation. With both arms, Tom hugged his grandson in a way Lee had never felt before. Images of silver balls still caroming in his mind, the boy finally said, "I'll be back, Pop. I'll be back."

Soon the bus turned north as Lee studied the miles of pine trees lining Highway 59, realizing again how few people actually lived in Mississippi, how easy it is to be alone. And he imagined the cabin, the garden, and the skiff, all separate images now of a world that rarely included outsiders; but connections remained.

Trees and cars zipping past the huge bus window brought a surge of excitement, and Lee thought again of his craving for adventure.

Yet even as the future tugged, he found himself reaching back to his grandpa and to that link so valuable to the family. Curiously, his mind drifted to the trotline as he wondered if it had been baited—or had the worm bed been turned and the coffee grounds added? Images pulled Lee back to the cabin, closer to his grandfather's world, and for a dreamy second he imagined that the two realities of the riverbank world and his Hattiesburg home were really only one reality after all.

Leaving Lumberton, headed to Purvis, Lee opened Mike's bag of junk food, a sudden craving for a Moon Pie now in control. There he discovered something new, a light pink envelope. Lee pulled it out. On the front, handwritten in blue ink, was only one word, "Tom." He carefully pulled out the note, also in pink but containing as well a small piece of folded white paper. First the pink note:

> Dear Tom,
>
> I wanted to write you before my surgery tomorrow, as at my age you never quite know. This whole sickness has been hard for us all. I know that, but you and Oui have simply been angels for me. I wouldn't have made it this long without you. So do me one more favor, son; promise me that no matter what happens tomorrow that you will take care of yourself. You are a good man, a man with heart, and I could never have asked for a better son. You have given me strength and love, and now I want you to give yourself those same things. You deserve it.
> I love you.
>
> > > Mom

Lee stared at the note, stunned as if he'd peered through a window into a secret dimension. Here were his great-grandmother's own words calling forward a moment only days before she died. And Lee saw the power, the optimist, the stickler for efficient execution of her wishes. Here he witnessed that strength and unequivocal love flowing through the family vein, and the cascade of truth left his youthful soul rumbling.

A tear welled, and Lee joined his grandfather's great sadness, his loss at Saralynn's profound imprint now fading with time. There the cabin seemed so much farther away than moments ago, and time rose as a great wall too lofty to climb.

The bag fell from his lap, and the white paper slipped to the floor. As Lee bent to pick it up, his head brushed against the pink note, where he caught a faint smell of something he couldn't quite recognize, a scent almost of baby powder. Had it been something on Saralynn's hands when she wrote the note? Or was it a favorite perfume Tom would recognize? Was it a footprint of the past accidentally fossilized as a written note? Intuitively Lee sensed how such vestiges of life connect people with unspoken language, a brush of souls outside the filter of mind.

With trepidation, he flipped open the small white page: "Lee, tell Glenna I'll bring a smoked turkey for Thanksgiving. Tom."

Chapter 2

I.

At the bus station, Glenna waited alone for Lee. Her two girls were at a church function, and Harold had left earlier in the day and wouldn't return for a week. As she sat in the car listening to the radio, she glanced in the mirror. The image of the forty-something-year-old housewife with the beginnings of gray hair almost shocked her as she had been feeling so vibrant waiting for Lee to come home from Picayune. She appeared overly tired. Without warning, a tear formed as she choked back the urge to cry. "What's wrong with me?" she said aloud, wondering why lately she felt so disjointed and emotional.

A touch of lipstick and quick hair comb helped her mood, but lurking in her thoughts was the growing discontent of her life, and particularly her marriage. She knew this pressure must vent itself soon, but as she caught a glimpse of Lee coming out of the station, the day brightened.

"Yoohoo. Need a ride there, good-looking?" Lee hadn't seen his mom.

"Depends. What do you charge?"

Glenna popped out of the car to give her son a huge hug. A hint of desperation lingered, but sensing Lee's strength gave her the needed strength she'd missed all day.

"Where's everybody?" Lee asked as he got into the car.

"Oh, the girls are at church. Some kind of woman speaker and a dinner afterward; they are talking about missionary work. And your dad, well, you know. He left today to take a load out to Seattle. Won't be back for nearly a week." Glenna felt her energy fade as the sentence spilled out, but she didn't want to think about this cycle of absenteeism anymore.

"I see." Lee looked out the window and then turned to Glenna. "It's like he doesn't want to be around us anymore." Glenna's face went pale. Lightheaded, she scrambled to invent an excuse even as Lee moved quickly to avoid the breech he'd opened.

"So I got great news. Grandpa is coming to Thanksgiving. Said he'd bring a smoked turkey too." If Glenna had won the lottery, she could not have brightened more quickly, and instantly she was hugging Lee and kissing the top of his head like he was three years old.

"I've got to hear all the details about your visit; let's go to the Coney Island Deli and have ourselves a nice fat sandwich. We need to celebrate Dad coming home to the family. Oh my goodness, I need to start cooking as soon as I get home." Glenna, fully refreshed, began planning the holiday meal.

"I think you have time. It's still over a month away." Lee got a good laugh seeing his mom so excited. Then he turned to Glenna with a cautious look. "Do you think Dad will be home for Thanksgiving? Last year he said he had a club sandwich in El Paso."

"Hope so, son; sure hope so."

Soon they enjoyed milkshakes and steak sandwiches along with trip details and laughs, Glenna's staunch equilibrium having magically returned with having her boy home again.

II.

The afternoon spent getting Lee to the bus station proved to be the most fun Tom had treated himself to in months, and before the day was out, he had won fourteen dollars shooting pool with some old buddies. He and Mike teamed up as partners, and they held the table for over an hour. Tom even had a couple of beers, an extremely rare event.

But the next day back at the cabin with a little daylight still hanging on the treetops, Tom visited the smokehouse to tidy up. Then, around back, he admired the creation he'd worked on for weeks. He loved his time in this private spot because no one ever visited there but him, and he treated these moments as sanctuary where he loved to paint. The shed's back wall had an eve built out, so it stayed dry where Tom kept a few saws and tools. But primarily the area sported a large mural he'd painted on most every day for weeks. His idea for the picture was a landscape view of his cabin world. There he worked using different dyes and stains conjured from plants along the river. A high-level view of all things around the cabin was his ultimate goal, including the smokehouse, garden, fruit orchard, and the dozens of other places Tom illustrated in his secret retreat.

The homemade paints faded more quickly than store-bought oils, but Tom didn't mind. He enjoyed making his own brushes from feathers, corncobs, and animal fur, knowing they were far from perfect, but there on that wall was a summary of the three years he'd withdrawn to this spot, all laid out as an integrated world.

He loved the color variety concocted from the flowers and roots, bloods and mud from up and down the river, and though he saw them fading with time, the violets and greens still made him feel alive.

Almost every time he did a little painting, his mind drifted back to his childhood and the pieces of wood bark and old boards his mom used to paint, the birdhouses she decorated with her own colorings to give as Easter presents. These memories of Saralynn were important, a link to a distant world Tom could never quite find the words to describe; only the stains of wild cherries and blackberries mixed with honeysuckle could speak that truth. So he painted in the present but lived the past.

Standing back to take in the breadth of the picture, he saw where he wanted to place Mike's red pickup with Lee and his old friend standing next to it, exactly like they had done earlier in the week. The image swelled, and though he didn't know how to share his secret, he was sure the act of painting mysteriously linked Mike and Lee to his world and to the fullness he struggled to express.

With day turning to evening, Tom sat on his porch recalling his time with Lee, the tentacles of new memory settling gently. The soft quietness of his cabin without the heavy strain of words relaxed him even more knowing days must now turn to putting the garden in order and storing as many onions, potatoes, and green tomatoes as he could and to working his river lines for fish hungrily anticipating winter. Not having to think too deeply about the effort of his familiar life brought a sense of well-being that Tom enjoyed as he watched the sun fall below the graying tree line.

After a big meal of smoked duck and tomatoes, his overtired body yearned for bed as fresh memories echoed. He'd made tiny dots with pure egg yolk to look like the golden ripe pears now hanging on the trees, but in trying to remember his earlier walk to pick fruit, both the orchard and mural became one fuzzy blend, a distorted smear suspended from the rules of time. Tom walked on in his mind, lost in the sensations of color and chirping birds.

Going to town had left emotions sloshing out of normal equilibrium, and even now, days later, all that talk about the past and death weighed too heavily as he tried drifting off to sleep. He preferred to avoid thoughts with such sticky attachment, but the outside world had intruded, leaving him vulnerable to a storm of guilt he couldn't quite comprehend, as now he'd been forced to realize the impact of his absence on Glenna and Lee. A wobbling sensation of self nestled into his quietness, intruding on privacy yet again as Tom realized that he wasn't truly alone.

The next night, a heavy frost covered the garden, making the broccoli happy but treating the tomatoes roughly. Tom's little cellar under the cabin brimmed with pears, persimmons, apples, and hard green tomatoes, and he knew he must save as much food as he could from the cold.

Each evening now, he sat alone on the porch watching change come to the woods. Here acceptance fell to each living thing opening itself effortlessly. The winding flow of the river welcomed the seasonal rotation yet demanded nothing, and Tom knew his own spirit must acquiesce to the upheaval he perceived ahead. Summer's riot now a faded glimmer, the chill of a new season spoke with familiarity. So Tom waited.

Restless hours followed. But deep into the early morning he awoke before daylight to find himself sweaty and exhausted, standing in the open doorway from the porch. Fitful memories churning, fragments from his entire life strewn in unrelated sequences, moments with his dad playing baseball, the night he spent in the woods lost when he was ten, and the Christmas his sister had to be taken to the hospital with an appendicitis. Countless images of his family washed over Tom, spreading fertile sediment from receding years.

A particular dream occurred for three nights, but Tom didn't remember the first night's episode until the same dream recurred the next evening, a strange sensation of déjà vu. Bewildered, he saw himself standing on a curbside with Oui and another woman he didn't know. All three looked around, up and down the street, when the other woman said, "Where is that Donald? How long does it take to bring the car round?" Hearing that one sentence, Tom then saw himself alone, both girls gone suddenly without explanation. Next, a car drove by slowly. At first he couldn't see who was inside until it was right in front of him, his friend Don driving with the two girls inside and two other men he didn't recognize. Then the car sped off as everyone laughed. It was the third night Tom realized that in the dream he stood in front of the Spaniard Inn restaurant. It wasn't in Yazoo City like it was supposed to be but in Picayune instead, down by the pool hall. The details seemed surreal, out of place, disconnected. But each night the movie replayed.

Most every morning now, Tom found his way outside to the rocker to watch the sun rise.

The first piercings of morning amethyst and pink inevitably brought joy, as did the frogs and birds chirping in the distance, chatting the morning news of coming winter. And the old broken chinaberry tree stared at Tom. It had been hit by lightning years earlier but stood still against the backdrop of the oaks and willows stretching down the riverbank. In the blue fog, the deformed old tree took the shape of a looming giant, a dark presence draped in spanish moss reaching down as if a dutiful matron tasked to lift the cabin from darkness. And each morning, Tom studied the daily mystery that helped dispel the ugly shape of thought he did not want to know.

The last months of Saralynn's life became a familiar theme drumming constantly. How she settled into the knowledge that her life was almost over, how she accepted her end without regret, that unforgivable abandonment of a defiant spirit, as Tom judged.

Each day the river murmuring over downed trees sounded like words, mysterious spirits speaking to Tom about the past, times as a boy working in his garden when his mom sat on the porch reading Whitman poems aloud, off in the distance from his garden but audible. Those echoes returned now, as did the image of his mother, destitute after lending her life savings to her older son, Louis, who squandered the money, never to be repaid. A floating river of sounds and images passed each day through a less and less attentive mind as Tom lost himself in the emotions of the past, barely able to find the present.

An image stuck of a little old woman headed to church, rather than the fiery warrior of her youth. Where had that vigor gone? Where was the hornet shooting hoops with him in the driveway, teaching lessons about how to guard people, how to watch their belt buckle because it cannot fake out a defender the way arms and heads can, how the center of someone is the only part that matters, as the extremities can be false? Tom considered how words are extremities, how people use them to cheat, how even when people try to be honest, they don't know what to say, and he pondered whether it is even possible to live without lying.

Lee had only been six when Saralynn died, and the thought made Tom feel old, as he knew he must balance truth and myth for the boy. And with each breaking day, there again her shrunken face and those last words: "The Lord has been good to me."

The daily ritual of studying the chinaberry's reach toward Tom with that soft light of the river behind reminded him how nature had become his home now, his school and work, the place he spent the conduct of his life, and the idea felt right, uncomplicated, a place he didn't have to tell lies. Saralynn had understood people and how to move them, guard against them, trick them yet be among their ways even when at odds with them; she knew the heart and the hope life needed, how to share the rhythm often so troublesome for people yet necessary like a heartbeat in the soul. And the rising chill of each morning filled Tom with fresh sadness that he did not have the skills of his mother, that for him loneliness had become too close a confidante.

Fluttering down into the moving current, the fall foliage mesmerized Tom while the yawning sun painted the riverbank, and he knew this was his only home. His family, these trees and paths, these shacks that greeted him each day had become the familiarity of his existence, and he knew they were alive in their own way.

But thoughts of home reminded him too of his unshared secret and the demons of the past. Those surly words of Sheriff Barker: "The state of Mississippi now owns this land, and you have ninety days to vacate. Defy this order and you're going to jail where you belong."

That sneer hauled up the old grudge, and that smirk of power so cruel that Tom wasn't quite sure if he had dreamed the moment or was it real. Then his feeble protest: "But I have written permission to live here, from the owner." The pusillanimous tone made him nauseous.

"I won't go." Tom spoke aloud to himself, his mind unable to pull forward any such image. So he decided not to reveal this embarrassment to anyone, his failure as Tom saw it, and a usurping starvation of soul began its deep-rooted growth.

Long walks as distraction filled the days, or dabbling at his mural where Mike's red truck now rested happily in the side yard with Lee next to it. With each session, the picture grew richer with a thicket of birch trees or the broken windmill down the road. But increasingly Tom drifted from his contentment to visit times past and people lost to him.

One morning standing before the mural, the wide perspective tripped a thought. The river could be faded into the distance, revealing several bends along the way where houses and things from his past might be sketched in ...

Honk, honk, honk. A loud car horn sounded from up the road, piercing the intensity of memory. Reflexively Tom knew Mike was coming. Usually intrusions bothered him, but the familiar truck sound reminded him of the past, so Tom decided to cook up a fresh batch of Muscatine tea he'd been experimenting with; he wanted his old friend to have something to complain about when he arrived.

The truck settled into the yard, and Mike yelled out the window: "Hey, anybody home?"

Through the cabin door, a gruff voice, "Not if you blow that dang noisemaker again. I'm old, not deaf," Tom groused, revealing a slight smile.

41

"Just making sure. You're pretty decrepit these days, and I wasn't sure you could hear this sweet, purring new vehicle of mine." With that, they shook hands, and Tom shoved Mike with a little push toward the porch, trying not to let the word "decrepit" penetrate that vulnerable center so exposed these days.

"Come on in here, you old pain in my butt. I made you some tea I think you'll hate."

"Oh, great, I can hardly wait. What is it, pecan shells and onion skin?" Mike said, looking almost serious, but then he had a new thought.

"Hey listen, I heard from your daughter; she wanted me to tell you she can't wait to see you at Thanksgiving. Wants me to come along too since my sister is gonna be in Memphis with her husband's clan. Heck, I figured I'd give you a ride up to Hattiesburg in style since your Chevy has already had its cranking for this year. I told her I'd bring some of that oyster stuffing my wife used to cook."

"Well good," Tom said distractedly. "Did she say anything about Lee—you know, 'bout his genealogy report?" Tom watched his own reaction as if it were another person, saw how happy and anxious he was to find out about Lee, and for a moment he could almost remember what it was like to live among people all the time.

"Naw, she didn't say nothing about the report but did say Lee had a good time coming out here and thanked me for getting him to and from. I told her it was always a pain to have to deal with you, but I didn't mind helping out the boy."

"Uh huh. Drink your tea, you old coot." For the next couple of minutes, both blew on the hot, sweet-smelling tea, Tom taking the moment to think about his mural and that idea of making the river much longer in the background.

Mike spoke with a pleased smile. "You know, this tea ain't half bad; sure better than that wild mint stuff you made up. My mouth was bitter for two days after I drank that stuff; more like castor oil than tea I'd say."

"Yeah, but I bet you weren't constipated, were you?" Tom croaked as he realized the pain he put Mike through every time he came out. For a second, Tom flashed back to what it was like to have his mother take on his troubles when he was young, how she did what was necessary and never needed to be thanked, never wanted words as payment. That familiarity seemed so close now to how he saw his old friend in light of the new changes lifting family memories from the silent past. The sheriff's demand stabbed him with sudden turbulence, so Tom went silent in his thoughts.

After a couple of minutes, a restlessness awoke. "You want to go with me to check my lines?" Mike was on his feet before the words cooled. So they both sidled down to the river. Tom liked to go upriver a few bends and then cut the motor, just let the current do the work as he paddled from tree to tree checking limb lines and the trotline set out over the deeper water. Coming downstream so quietly, he often saw squirrels, or ducks, or even a deer or pig coming down for a cool drink or swim to the other side. Sometimes Tom would take a shot at something for dinner, but it seemed lately he only pondered the moment of ambush more than engaging, preferring to float undetected instead.

Today he didn't even carry the gun, as he felt a little more taciturn than normal, wanting only to enjoy the sound of the water and the well-grooved presence of his only real friend. Soon they were drifting toward home. Mike was in heaven sitting up in front of the boat, scanning the riverbank like Tom's faithful old hunting dog, Shep, who'd died a year ago. Tom couldn't bring himself to break in a new dog. So on down the river floated these two friends who'd grown up on this creek and knew pretty much every deep hole and eddy.

"I got something kinda weird I want to talk to you 'bout." Tom brought the words out slowly. "Don't worry, I ain't sick or nothing. It ain't like that, but I been having this weird dream lately and can't figure it."

'Hmm. Okay. So what are you dreaming of? Moving to a busy place like the moon?"

"No. Just listen. Anyway, I see myself and Oui with another woman waiting on a curb for Donald Newland to come pick us up in the car. We're in front of this restaurant I used to go to in Yazoo City, but the dang place is in Picayune in my dream. When I turn around, the two girls are gone, vanished. Then Don comes by, and there the girls are in the car with two other guys. They go speeding off without me, everyone laughing their heads off." With that, Tom stopped speaking, sitting perfectly still as if he'd performed a great labor leaving him devoid of strength.

"That's it? That's what was bugging you? Heck, that don't mean nothing. That Donald fellow, he's the one that got you fired back in Yazoo City, ain't he? Good Lord, Tom, that was thirty years ago. It ain't nothing but that awful tea you make that's squeezing off the blood to your brain. That's probably all it is."

Tom smiled and shook his head agreeing, but he knew it was odd to have the same dream three nights in a row, especially about something that didn't make sense. Those days at Overland Container, Don had been so treacherous and threw away a longtime friendship as hunting and fishing pals, all for a stupid job. For the millionth time, Tom pondered what had possessed Don to do something so wicked.

"Yeah, guess you're right, don't mean nothing." Both men looked away to the far bank, not really wanting to talk anymore. Tom felt slightly embarrassed at having brought up the past like that and now wanted to put new images into the present to overwrite this long-held angst he could never seem to resolve. Mike simply studied the shoreline for movement.

After a few more limb checks and rebaits, the two men had four nice volunteers, so they headed back to the cabin for a quick lunch of hushpuppies and fried fillets. The early afternoon settled into familiar discussion of how the weather had gotten cold so early and why perhaps there would be an early spring down the road. Just the slightest hint of tension hung in the air, and then Mike confessed he'd brought some real coffee from town that he had stuffed in his pocket like an illegal substance.

As the old friends enjoyed a taste of town together, Tom's mind drifted to the gray color he wanted to add to the chinaberry tree on the mural. He'd found a dark silver lichen on a rotting tree that had a brightness to it, the perfect touch to lighten up the tree bark, Tom thought.

"Hey there. Listen, before I go, is there anything on your mind?" Mike said. "Seems you're a little distracted these days—you know, with all this sudden talk about the past. Has anything happened to get you going over all this old stuff again?"

Tom considered whether to tell Mike his new problem, but in his mind he saw the sheriff's laughing derision again, and he didn't quite know what to do yet, so Tom decided to study the matter a little more, to make sure he was certain of things.

"Naw, everything's okay, just a little off my game 'cause of the weakening fall light. Always makes me a little unsteady."

III.

In Glenna's home, the family tried to have a meal together usually three nights a week; at least she and the kids did. No other friends around, no television or music, only Lee and his two sisters, and occasionally his dad if it happened to be a leap year, Glenna sometimes joked. These evening meals helped with day-to-day planning and weekly schedules, which were hectic, but the conversation often swerved into serious territory.

Lee's older sister, Victoria, had been testy lately, so Glenna paid close attention to the talk around the table. As a senior in high school, her older daughter felt the pressure of college approaching, and continuous boyfriend conflict kept her more edgy than anyone wanted.

"I can't believe Grandpa lives in that hut down there. There must be snakes and alligators all over the place. It's just uncivilized." Victoria was in a mood. Lee was not in the mood.

"Don't you think that's kind of stupid?" Lee said. "You got it all wrong. He's fine. And the cabin is awesome. You should see the porch Grandpa built and furniture made out of vines and trees. And what a garden; it's huge." The details Lee thought impressive only left a sour look on Vic's face.

Then, Lucy, Glenna's younger daughter, chimed in. "I'd love to see that and go fishing with Grandpa. Did you get to shoot any guns?" Lucy, being a bit of a tomboy, loved getting dirty, so things like fishing and hunting excited her, though she'd only been fishing a few times with Lee.

Glenna jumped in at the first minor pause. "I have some news for you guys. Daddy and Mike Hamlin will be having Thanksgiving dinner with us. I asked Mike to come along to make sure Dad gets here okay. You know how hard he is to get off the river these days. Your grandpa is bringing a smoked turkey, and Mike makes about the best oyster stuffing I ever tasted. It should be really fun."

Victoria snarled as Glenna had mentioned the visit earlier, but she kept her sarcasm silent. Lucy, who hadn't heard the news, clapped with joy.

"So," said Glenna, "tell the girls about your visit with Dad, especially that Devil's Throat part."

But before Lee could answer, Lucy said, "So what did you guys do out there? Kill things? What did you kill?"

"Na, that's not it. Grandpa ain't out there for killing; he's out there to show the world he don't need anybody. He's living all by himself, catching and shooting his own food, making his own clothes, growing his own vegetables and fruit trees; he's living life the good way, out of the racket." Trying not to let her face show any emotion, Glenna felt a wave of uselessness pass through her.

Victoria, a year and a half older than Lee, tended to be prim and proper, with great attention to her long, dark hair, clothes, and eye makeup. She couldn't resist a sour comment. "Sounds boring to me. How does he take a hot shower? Yuck, can you imagine cold-water bathing in the winter? Crazy if you ask me."

Lee erupted. "Well, I didn't ask you, so you can keep that for yourself. You don't even know what you're talking about anyway. Grandpa has built a complete world for himself where everything relates to everything else, and he's happy. He's got his boat on the river, he rides horses down at a neighbor's barn, he listens to nature better than anybody I know, and most of all he don't give a flip what anybody thinks—not you, nobody."

Glenna saw the discussion heading toward a personal argument, so she stepped in to calm things. "So tell us what you found out from Dad about our family lineage. I'm sure he had some good Saralynn stories." Glenna wanted to keep the discussion civil and productive.

"Lots of stuff. How she had this wicked temper and wouldn't take any guff off anybody, how she was a great basketball player and could have gone pro, how she one time got all over one of grandpa's teachers, warning her never to touch her kid again. Granny Saralynn must have been a real firecracker; I sure wish I could remember her better."

"Well, let me tell you, my grandmother was more than a firecracker; she was a full-blown bomb. That woman had more energy and tenacity than anyone I've ever known. Every time I saw her, she was in high gear. Never sat down, walked miles a day drinking coffee and smoking cigarettes, and could talk a blue streak. She was exhausting to be around sometimes."

"Mom," Lee said quietly, "did Saralynn change toward the end? You know, slow down any? It was funny, but Grandpa let it slip once that she seemed to run out of gas at the end and got real passive. Did you see that?"

"She was like everyone else in life, living like we're never going to die, and then one day we realize we are. It's that moment we all have to prepare for, and I think that's what she did. The fight was over; she'd raised her kids and lived her days, and she was ready to go to heaven." A shrill thought shot through Glenna's head as suddenly she realized Saralynn's whole life had been dedicated to her kids, and creeping disquiet crawled even deeper inside that ever-widening cavern Glenna had trouble hiding these days.

Victoria chimed in, "Mom, you don't really believe that baloney about heaven, do you? Nietzsche said that religion is just a tool for keeping poor people down, letting them think they are superior to rich people so they won't feel as much hatred for not having any money. It's a tool for oppressing the masses."

A bit miffed, Glenna glared at Vic. "I don't know where you come up with this stuff, but that's crazy. Your grandmother's religion is what kept her strong her whole life; it let her feel that no hardship on earth could hold her back from salvation. I believe the same thing too, and I don't want to hear you talking about that God hater anymore."

Lucy chimed in. "Oh that's just Brad's words. He knows everything." Victoria threw a hateful stare at her little sister while Glenna took careful note that perhaps a clue may have been revealed as to why Vic had become so difficult lately.

Lee continued, "You know, Grandpa said at the end all she wanted to talk about was how good the Lord had been to her. It all seems so different from everything else I heard about her."

"Your great-grandmother battled cancer for three years, two surgeries, and multiple chemo treatments; she saw the end coming from a long way off. Saralynn wasn't one to do something spontaneously. She was a planner, and you can be sure she thought it through, and rather than feel bitterness and spite toward anyone or toward her disease, she accepted it as the Lord's calling for her."

"But did Uncle Louis really steal money from her?" Lee asked.

"What? No. He didn't steal anything. He borrowed the money and planned to pay it back, but he got swindled by a so-called friend in Little Rock who lost it all. What really happened was he was so embarrassed he didn't want to see anyone in the family and didn't come back home until three years after we buried Saralynn. That whole thing broke him. He always felt like a failure. I've only seen him one time since all that happened. I don't even know if he's still alive."

"Sounds like he didn't much take after his mom like grandpa did," Lee said. "He must have been the runt of the litter."

"Lee, don't talk that way. You have no right to judge Louis or anyone else. His life is his own, and his decisions are not for you to see as right or wrong. He was a sensitive man, one too trusting in people, and when he realized his friend had tricked him and that he'd let his own mother down badly, it broke him, just broke him down. It's a sad thing really."

Lucy jumped up with a screech. "It's Lee's night to clear the dishes." And before too many words of excusing from the table passed, both Lucy and Victoria were off to their bedrooms. Lee sat quietly glancing at his mom. In his eyes, Glenna saw that sweet boyish love she knew filled his heart. Then, as if she could read his thoughts, she detected a tinge of doubt, that mild ache to grasp the certainty of life. Her son broke the spell.

"Will you think some about Saralynn and tell me what you can remember? Not tonight, I understand, but over the holidays. I need to hear more about her life. I want to see how much of her is in me."

IV.

The day Tom was to head up to his daughter's house for Thanksgiving had been a shadow of dread and anticipation, until finally the beep of the old Ford up the road sent a cold streak up his spine. The idea of being the center of attention left Tom nervous, and all he really wanted was to slip in Glenna's back door, have dinner, then drift home again. But he knew that wouldn't happen.

All week he'd gotten ready to smoke the turkey and ham while imagining a dinner table with people badgering him about the last three years. He considered claiming to be sick and sending the meat along with Mike but knew that would only raise concern, so instead Tom tried to conjure answers to indefinable questions not yet posed. Surely Lee would be at his side to help push away some of the noise so words would have time to form.

As the old red truck pulled into the yard, Tom saw his friend sporting a nicely pressed, pumpkin-colored shirt, and he couldn't help but smile as Mike hadn't bought a new shirt in probably ten years. But there he was, handsome as a game show host.

Tom offered his usual warm greeting. "You're early. Can't you tell time?"

Undaunted, Mike was prepared. "Yeah, I can tell time all right; it's time you got your worn-out hide off this porch and back to see them grandkids of yours. I done had three calls from Glenna making sure you wouldn't duck out. I told her I'd tie you to the bumper and pull you outta here like a stump if I had to."

"Well, I ain't ducking out. Course, I ain't got no high-falutin' shirt on neither, but that's okay because I always like hanging around with rich folks. Makes me feel important." Both men slapped each other on the back at the same time, and Mike got a look at the huge turkey and ham Tom had smoked.

"Good Lord, Tom, where'd you get that bird? That thing is a monster."

"Yeah, ain't it? I trapped him in a live trap 'bout three months ago; been feeding him field corn ever since to fatten him up."

"All right, let's get out of here; we got a ride ahead of us. You got everything? Don't forget your manners. I know they been missing for a few years."

Tom took the jest with sober recognition and only looked at the ground. Then both men climbed into the truck for the long bounce out. Each sat quietly, studying the rutted path and the bare tree limbs along the way, neither saying anything but simply enjoying the simple voice they'd shared between them in silence for decades. Soon they hit the interchange road and the interstate heading north, windows cracked and the wind howling through the truck.

Thanksgiving being less stressful than Christmas, Tom was almost cheerful knowing he didn't have to go through lots of present opening and fake happiness. Though a trace uneasy, he trusted his daughter and grandson to help things go right, and some of the good responses he'd thought over all week skipped through his mind, though he had a hard time keeping them sorted. Finally, he focused on "It's good to see you." Tom felt a little dense as the words failed him but knew he had love in his heart and faith in his family. He also knew Mike was much more sociable and would stick close to make sure things went okay, the way he always had.

Mike broke the silence. "You remember that time we hitchhiked back from Florida and that couple from Colorado dropped us off on this highway? It was right over by the *Purvis, ten miles* sign. Man, that was a fun trip. Seems like a million years ago."

"That was a million years ago, but it was Wiggins on Highway 49, not this one, you old fool. Heck, I can't even remember what we were doing down there."

"Well, don't matter much, I reckon. Just thinking about how long we been friends and some of the good times we had, that's all."

"Yeah, these old roads are a history book for what we've done over the years. A lot of it I wish I could forget," said Tom jokingly.

"Funny you should say that, 'cause there's something I want to tell you that I been trying to figure how to say," Mike said. "I decided to wait till now 'cause I got you trapped here in the truck, and I know you can't go nowhere."

"What are you talking about? What have you done now?"

Mike's strong resolve weakened. "Well, it ain't nothing I've done recently but something from a long time ago I was sworn to secrecy over. It's been enough time that it should be okay to tell you," Mike said.

Tom leaned against the passenger door not knowing yet how serious this confession might be.

"You remember the other day when we were on the river and you mentioned that crazy dream you kept having, the one with that Newland fellow?"

"Yeah." A hint of impatience showed in Tom's voice.

"Well, I got something I need to tell you about that guy. Now I know you ain't gonna like it, so I'm asking you kindly to sit there and relax." Mike's pleading sounded almost desperate.

At hearing Newland's name, Tom flashed instantly, sitting straight up, his hand instinctively grabbing Mike by the arm. Mike calmly stared at the grip and then looked up to meet his friend's eyes as if to say, "Now that's not what I call relaxed." Tom let go of the sleeve, then slouched, feigning boredom.

"Listen, you got to get this straight without flying off the handle. It's something Oui asked me to do thirty years ago and swore me to silence on my mother's life. You hear me? I need you to think about this from Oui's point of view not from that righteous anger you quick draw on people."

"Awright. Good Lord, get on with it, old man." Tom clearly had lost patience.

"After you got let go from Container, you called to tell me you were moving back to Picayune, remember? Well, I was so excited I couldn't stand it. I mean you and Ouida coming home unexpected like that ... Anyway, you said Oui was coming down early to find you guys a place to live and you'd be along in a couple of weeks with the furniture."

"I'm getting old over here waiting on you to get to the point," Tom said. "I remember all that, so spit out what you got to say."

Mike was prepared. "I told you to sit and relax. I'm only making sure you understand the background. At any rate, I picked Oui up at the bus station, and for a few days we looked at houses. Three days before you were to arrive with the furniture, Oui told me something that really worried me bad."

"Mike, damn it." As soon as the words blurted out, Tom knew he had overreacted, so once again he slid down into the seat.

"Oui told me she felt like somebody needed to know what had happened in Yazoo City—you know, why you lost your job and such. She said Donald had connived and done some things but that you got the blame. But listen, it wasn't for the reason you thought." Tom sat up attentively but didn't speak. "Oui and other folks made sure you believed that Don was ambitious and wanted your job and that he manipulated everything to make you look bad, but that was only half-true." Mike paused to collect the next words carefully.

"Oui told me that right before you got fired, you went on a management retreat to Natchez with a bunch of the managers at Container. Do you remember? It lasted like three days, and you all had to go?"

"Yeah, I remember. So what? All we did was sit in meetings and have fried catfish at night; wasn't nothing to it, I swear."

"No, no you old fool, it wasn't you. It's what happened while you were gone. Oui said Don came over the night you left, and he was drunk. Had a bottle of champagne with him too. He knocked on the door and just barged in as soon as she cracked the screen. She was terrified 'cause Don started talking about how he loved her and wanted to marry her. She said he even grabbed her and tried to kiss her and got rough with her."

"What the hell! I'm gonna kill that son of a bitchin' Judas. I'm gonna kill his ass." Tom turned crimson. "Stop this God-damned truck right now. Let me out."

Mike only accelerated. "Are you crazy? I ain't stopping. We're ten miles from Hattiesburg, and I ain't going to Glenna's and telling her I let you walk your way there. Now just shut up; I ain't finished." A hand grenade sat next to Mike and he had to make sure the pin didn't get pulled.

Tom could no longer think in words, only in wild images of driving to Yazoo City and bouncing Don's face off a baseball bat. Violence raged with a language of revenge, and Tom had plenty to say.

Mike became a little afraid Tom might try to jump out the truck door. "Now listen here, Oui made me swear not to tell you or she'd never speak to me again. She said Don had acted so weird that she wanted someone else to know the real story just in case something unexpected happened. She told me he came over sober the next night and tried the same thing all over again but that she slapped his face and threatened to call the police. Evidently that ended it, but he swore to Oui that he'd ruin you no matter how long it took and that it would be her fault. Well it took him a couple of months after that to get you canned, but, my friend, that's why you got fired."

"I should have killed that traitor. I may yet. But I don't understand something; why are you telling me this now?" Tom said.

Mike was not ready for the question. "Well, I don't know. I honored what Oui asked me to do, and now that she's gone ..." Nonplussed, Mike finally remembered the last time they checked lines on the river. "You remember telling me about that recurring dream about that Spanish restaurant? After that, I knew something deep was bothering you, maybe stuff I don't even know, but I had a piece of the truth, and I felt guilty keeping it from you. All these years, I knew if I told you that you'd go crazy and probably end up in jail, and none of that sounded even half-right, so I shut up and did what Oui asked."

Tom stared out the truck window with tears running down his cheek, emotions long ago suppressed now suddenly released into the fury of unfulfilled revenge. And the burden Oui had carried all those years and never yielded deepened his heartache.

"If it makes any difference," Mike said, "the day before you came back to Picayune, I found Newland's number you'd given to me in case of emergency. Anyway, I called him. He of course denied everything, said Oui was lying, said you were fired because you were incompetent, and so on."

Tom looked at Mike now with subdued frustration, the initial surge of anger passing, but his flushed face hinted of the residue of long-held pain. Motionless, he waited to hear what else Mike had to say, what other old news hadn't yet found the liberating moment of words.

"Well," Mike said, "I told that lying scum he was a two-faced coward and lower than snail shit and that if he so much as ever spoke a word to Oui again that he wouldn't have to worry about you coming up there and whipping his sorry ass because I'd do it myself, and there sure as hell wouldn't be need for a second dose of that medicine."

For a moment, Tom's heart lightened, and he cracked a painful smile. Finally, he spoke. "Dang, you're kind of a violent old codger, ain't you?"

The next twenty minutes passed in sluggish silence with Tom considering how to find Donald Newman. Seems Tom still had some things to catch up on with his old friend, and maybe a little chat might set things right for the future.

Chapter 3

I.

Glenna tapped lightly at Lee's bedroom door. "Hon, are you awake?"

"Yeah, sure. What's up?"

"Can you let me in? I've got something for you?" Glenna said.

Checking his watch, Lee thought ten o'clock to be awfully early for a Thanksgiving Day, but he was intrigued with the idea of a gift.

Carrying a cardboard box, his mom stepped into the room. "I'm sorry to get you rolling so early, but Grandpa will be here around two, and I need some help in the kitchen. I also wanted to give you these." She handed an old carton over to Lee. "When Dad moved to the cabin, he didn't have much room out there, so he asked me to keep some stuff for him, mostly old letters from his mother when he was in college and some books and things. I really don't know what's there but figured you'd want to take a look."

"Really? Letters from Saralynn to Grandpa? Thanks." Fully awake now, Lee couldn't wait to rummage the new treasures, but as usual, his mom had already orchestrated how the morning would develop.

"Look, half hour, okay? Then come down 'cause I want you to set up the furniture on the porch; I think we'll eat out there since it's a nice day. I already put the tablecloth and everything out for you. When you're done, I'll get the girls to set the table." With that, Glenna disappeared with barely a sound. Lee looked down into the old vanilla wafer box, two feet by three, filled with letters and mementos.

First he noticed the pink and blue envelopes that his great-grandmother had used as stationary over the years, several different styles and shades of color all disheveled but with her scribbled handwriting on them all. He couldn't help thinking how this box held more vestiges of his family's past than almost anything he'd found on his own, and he wondered why his mom hadn't shown it to him when he was writing his report. Had she forgotten? Or was this collection a bit too personal for a school report? He thought of the letter his grandpa had slipped into the junk food bag, the shading of the envelope's color, the faint hint of fragrance, the very personal message from the eve of Saralynn's death. What might be hidden in this box? What had escaped discovery all these years?

He figured the first thing to do was sort them into rough piles, so away he went on the mission. Dates on the letters were smudged and difficult to read, so he instead decided to sort by envelope color and style. Some had little borders of flowers the same pink or blue color as the envelope, and some were merely plain, so he decided they must all have common roots in time if they represented the same pattern.

Soon, four piles of blue and five piles of pink envelopes sat on the bed along with an old manila envelope and some badly faded photos. There were a couple of pins with "Picayune High School" on them and one maroon letter P that must have been Saralynn's high school basketball letter. It had four white bars on the low parallel line of the P, indicating five years of varsity lettering. Lee thought this must be the greatest treasure of all, the thing that must have been so important to Saralynn. He settled back against his bedpost to contemplate his trove, feeling as if his great-grandmother had entered the room through some mysterious door of time.

The pictures seemed fragile, a yellowish shade of brown, but there Saralynn stood with Harlan, Tom, Louis, and her youngest daughter, little Clara. It must have been a Sunday because they were all dressed up, standing among the pine trees in the sunshine, getting their pictures taken. Harlan had such a full head of hair, and Tom looked so muscular and athletic, but it was Saralynn who stole the picture. Her sharp features and wry smile spoke of silent power, restrained in the moment but ready for the call at an instant's notice. She stared defiantly at the camera with a little grin, not one of "look at me" but rather one of "better watch out for me."

A new world lay before him with a couple of old watches, a small gold ring, and several books, though he hardly paid any attention to them given his interest in the letters. The one book that caught his eye was a volume of American poetry that was pretty ragged, and when Lee opened it, the spine fell limp to a section of Walt Whitman poems. Lee almost stopped breathing as he remembered his grandpa talking about how when he was a boy working in his garden, Saralynn used to sit on the porch reading Whitman aloud, and Lee imagined he heard that distant voice just as his grandpa had but then realized it was Glenna calling from downstairs. Lee flew down the stairs, bubbling with excitement.

"That box of stuff is awesome, Mom. Did you ever go through it before? It's full of treasures."

Glenna smiled. "No, I didn't. It seemed personal to Dad, and I didn't really feel comfortable. I know he wouldn't have minded; heck, he gave the stuff to me to keep for him, but it never seemed right."

He wasn't quite sure he understood his mom's logic, but Lee didn't care; he felt no uneasiness at investigating. On his hands, he smelled the dust from the box and the faint scent given off by the letters as they slowly decomposed in the dry attic, and he imagined Saralynn's fingerprints all over those envelopes, her DNA literally helping to fill the box with her presence.

Outside setting up the big table, Lee saw his basketball resting in the corner next to the wicker couch, and he wondered how many times Saralynn must have grabbed a similar ball and found some other kid to shoot hoops with or guard like the demon she must have been. At that instant, he decided to hang the old picture of his grandpa and Saralynn on the mirror where each morning he could remember them as he combed his hair. Almost like a little shrine of sorts, he wanted Tom and Saralynn always to live in his room among his things so he could find some of the strength they found together as mother and son. The thought felt comfortable, like he'd discovered a hidden talisman he would always carry in secret.

II.

Harold had called with the bad news that he was stuck in Memphis with a truck breakdown, but the family was ready for their other guests anyway. When the doorbell rang, Lee sprang into motion. Anxiously turning the lock, he prayed the day would go smoothly.

Sunlight from outside showered the white tile of the foyer, almost blinding Lee with its contrast, but even with some squinting he saw two gentlemen all dressed up in their best clean clothes and smelling like Old Spice. Mike looked handsome in his starched and pressed pumpkin attire, and even his grandpa's old flannel shirt was neatly ironed, though Lee couldn't figure out how that had occurred. Both men smiled when they saw the tall, lanky slouch standing in the open door.

"Hope everything is fine," Tom blurted out as if he'd been practicing the line all day and just couldn't wait to deliver it. Mike only smiled as he and Lee caught each other's eye in appreciation of Tom's awkward gesture.

"Yes, sir, everything is fine. And we've been waiting for you two young fellows." Lee walked straight to his grandpa and reached around him with both arms.

Mike was beaming. "Well hey there, Lee, you're looking mighty sharp yourself in that nice green shirt. I saw one like that in town last week; a manikin was wearing it. Sure liked it too." A bright red engulfed Mike's face, and Lee understood the poor fellow had suddenly become self-conscious about his Picayune fashion commentary, so Lee moved on quickly.

"Well, I tell you, I look like a tractor jockey compared to you in that sweet potato shirt of yours; that thing is snazzy. We better lock up all the single women in the neighborhood today." All three had a good laugh and passed into the den with slaps on the backs and small talk about how long it had been since they'd seen Glenna's house. Lee felt as proud as a new parent seeing his grandpa voluntarily walking into their home and hearing his voice trickle through the rooms again. He couldn't help thinking of all the years his grandpa and Granny Oui had visited, bringing little gifts to help warm up the place—the nice birdhouse out back, the homemade mailbox, even the little table in the foyer. The house echoed moments from days when the family shared time together every holiday and oftentimes in between. Today, those times warmed Lee, and he knew he would make sure everyone had the best time possible.

"I think I hear a couple of special men in my house," came the happy words from the kitchen as Glenna popped into the hallway, wiping her hands of the meringue from the lemon icebox pie she'd just made, her dad's absolute favorite dessert. Tom took a long look at Glenna but only smiled; Lee wondered if his grandpa noticed the extra fifteen pounds she gained or the hard lines forming on her face, at least partially because of Harold's continuous neglect of the house.

Tom finally spoke. "Wonderful to see you and the kids. The house looks great." Lee felt a sharp pain to the heart, but Glenna beamed.

"Looks like you're making some good stuff there too," Tom said. "I know lemon icebox when I smell it."

"Oh, Dad, you know I wouldn't forget. I made a pumpkin for Lee, a pecan for Mike, and a lemon icebox for me." Lee saw his mom give a little elbow to Tom to make sure he caught the joke.

Clearly his grandpa's social acumen hadn't had much exercise lately, but he finally spoke up. "Oh, you mean me, right?" Everyone laughed, and then Glenna hugged her dad. The day had gotten off on a very pleasant note—no awkward moments, no feelings of resentment about the past three years, no stupid questions to veer the conversation in the wrong direction. Glenna had coached the kids on making their grandfather feel right at home, and both Lee and Mike were at full salute to the needs of the day as they focused on making this meal the best family get-together in years, certainly the best since Oui died.

Ever the social director, Glenna guided the crowd. "Come on, everybody; let's go sit on the porch. I've got lemonade and some cheese and apples we can munch on while the potatoes are cooking. Everybody, go on out and have a seat."

As soon as everyone was on the porch, Lucy immediately wanted to show Tom her new playhouse, so she led him to the corner of the yard where Victoria was on the cell phone with Brad. Only Mike and Lee now sat under the ceiling fan, enjoying their cool drinks and a moment of peace.

Mike tried to be friendly. "So how'd that report turn out, Lee? Did you get it turned in okay?"

"Yeah, Mr. Hamlin, I did. Made a B- on it, so it wasn't great but better than a C." Lee stared at the floor as if shy to tell Mike the truth, a little embarrassed he'd gotten so many people to help him and yet hadn't made a better grade. "I should have done better."

"Heck, when I was in school, a B- would have been cause to celebrate. Reckon I wasn't the best student in them days. Too much hunting and fishing, you know."

"Yeah, I understand. It's a little different these days, and people seem a lot more serious about school, like it's the only way to go. Heck, when you and Grandpa or Saralynn went to school, nobody really cared, did they?"

"Sure they did, son. Heck, Tom was a real good student and won prizes for stuff all the time. Saralynn was all business 'bout his schooling, and when he got lazy, she parked his butt at home till he started doing better; he knew there was no sloughing off with her around."

Lee leaned in to talk to Mike more seriously. "Before Grandpa comes back, is he doin' okay? Everything fine after I left?"

"Yeah, it's all good. Tom seems a little agitated these days, but coming back up here had him anxious, so it's only natural. He'll be fine," Mike said.

"Okay. I was a little worried when I saw him at the door; he looked kind of distracted, you know, like he wasn't sure where he was." Lee tried to be serious but not overly dramatic.

"Yeah, that's my fault. I told Tom some old news, bad stuff from way back, and I got him all riled on the drive up here. My fault really." Mike himself looked a bit distracted now.

"What'd you tell him?" Lee asked.

"Oh, it ain't nothing, nothing at all. Just some two-faced feller he knew in Yazoo City a long time ago. Forget I mentioned it, okay? It kinda slipped out."

Lee wasn't quite sure what had happened, but he was sure Mike was trying to conceal something. At that moment, Victoria ended her noisy cell call and came back to the porch, so Lee had to hold his curiosity for a while. All day, it seemed vestiges of the past refused to rest quietly, and the more Lee tried to think normally, the more unexpected events kept pulling him into strange new areas.

III.

Soon the porch took on the lively appearance of a festival with platters of raw oysters, cheeses, fruit, and dips with a variety of chips and fresh-cut vegetables. The spread was so massive everyone was sure there wouldn't be any need later for turkey and dressing.

Tom mingled comfortably as he watched his grandkids interact and his daughter scurry to make the festivity perfect. Relieved not to be the center of public investigation, he appreciated how Lee, Glenna, and Mike hovered around every comment to make sure no one forced an uncomfortable question. The more he got to sit back and observe, the better he enjoyed himself, and the afternoon unfolded with oddly warm weather and a greatly improved sense of belonging. Today, Tom could barely remember why he'd wanted to be so alone for so long, and he allowed the rhythm of conversation to guide him slowly through winding bends of the reunion, the day's twists and surprises presenting sounds almost as soothing as the chattering river that typically kept him company.

Victoria caught Mike's attention with her flamboyant style. "My how you've grown these past couple of years. So, what grade are you in these days? Must be 'bout eleventh, I reckon?"

"That's close; actually, I'm a senior." To the casual observer, Victoria seemed ultimately confident, but Tom saw her drop her gaze as she answered, and he thought that curious.

"And she's got a boyfriend," Lucy blurted out with more volume than she intended, leaving her blushing.

Lucy's moment of exuberance humored Mike, so he turned to Vic to probe a little deeper. "So what's the lucky feller's name?"

"Aaaahh, well, his name is Brad. He's in my grade, plays trumpet in the marching band."

Lucy, having regained volume control, rejoined the chat and again ratcheted up the intensity. "He thinks he owns her." Vic glared at her sister, clearly invoking powers of telekinesis to silence her, but Lucy was immune and instead enjoyed her moment of victory before deciding she wanted more of that delicious blue cheese.

Twitching at Lucy's comment, Lee turned to Vic. "What does that 'owns her' even mean? Does he make you wash his car or something?" Lee noticed no one else thought the comment funny. Lucy only stared at her plate, searching for something suddenly lost there, but Vic finally responded.

"No, nothing like that; he's just possessive, that's all. Because he really likes me," Vic said.

Tom sat quietly observing the exchange, remembering his own difficult teenage years. Even after all these decades, he still felt clueless about how to converse easily with women, how not to irritate them unnecessarily and yet not appear weak. Tom could wrestle an alligator better than hold comfortable chitchat with a member of the opposite sex, so he gladly accepted silence, happy not to be on stage. But finally, the tension between the girls prompted him to change the subject entirely. With a warm grin, he turned to Lee.

"So, tell me 'bout your genealogy report. A B- is a good grade, huh?"

Lee wasn't quite ready for the direct question and fumbled. "Well, uh, uh, yeah, I guess it was okay. Mrs. Gibson said I didn't 'investigate broadly enough and focused too much on stories.' That old bitty don't like me."

"Let's not talk that way, okay?" Glenna said. "You need to show your teachers more respect than to call them silly names." Her perfunctory response had the tone of a regularly issued complaint, and Tom admired his daughter's handling of her kids, thinking Glenna definitely showed a streak of Saralynn without even realizing it.

Lee continued, "I don't care much about the grade anyhow; I just wanted to get that class over with. I'm taking a stock market class starting after Christmas." Tom stared at his grandson, knowing Lee enjoyed the first class but didn't want to admit it in public.

A clever feeling came over Mike. "Oh yeah, good; maybe you can make us all some money since I can't seem to win the lottery."

But Lee's façade gave way. "I did learn some things from that report though. The stuff you guys told me about Saralynn was really interesting, and now I think I see a lot of her in our family—you know, traits she gave us all." His comment rolled out slowly, carrying a gravitas that took everyone by surprise.

Glowing with pride, Glenna returned to duty. "So tell us what Saralynn traits you see in us." The conversation marker issued, as Glenna often did at the dinner table, she relaxed, but Tom seemed a bit lost from the speed of the discussion. Clearly words at the Mitchell table were more facile than the ones he shared with Mike on their biweekly trip to check the trotline, but he enjoyed his grandkids' alacrity and tried to listen as fast as he could.

Obviously, Lee had thought about his great-grandmother lately, so he responded easily. "Well, I think I got a good bit of Saralynn in me. I've been playing basketball down at the park lately, and I think I'm pretty good. One of the guys there plays on the varsity B team, and he wants me to try out next week; said I got a good move to the basket. Heck, I never even thought about basketball much before my report."

"That's great, son," Tom said. "Just like Mom." He thought back with pride to the old days when he'd played high school football.

Rolling now, the speed of Lee's talking accelerated slightly. "I've also got some of her temper and maybe even some of that free spirit she had. I've even been thinking about becoming a forest ranger." But his words trailed off at the end, and his face brightened to a tomato juice color. Tom smiled to himself, though he also noticed Glenna's immediate frown. Mike jumped in to fill the void.

"That's a fine idea. With all Tom knows about the woods, he could really help you learn some things about rangerin'. Of course, he ain't the best one in the world to stop with a limit, if you know what I mean." Everyone howled at that comment, as it was common knowledge that Tom took from the woods and river what he wanted, what he needed, and rarely paid much attention to the rules. Tom did not defend himself but knew he did not abuse his relationship with nature and instead considered himself a conservationist, only taking what he needed. All the little animals he'd helped mend, the homes he tried to engineer for them, the many trees and plants he'd cultivated as food for animals blinked in Tom's mind, a comfortable reminder of his respect for nature, even if he did harvest abundance when available without being beholden to arbitrary government rules. Tom caught Lee's eye, and he knew the boy understood.

Then Lee continued, "See, that's exactly what I'm talking about. Grandpa has his own way of living just like Saralynn did. He lives where he wants, hunts and fishes when he wants, and doesn't ask permission from anybody to be free. That's the kind of thing I want to do one day."

Clearly Tom had to speak up as once again he saw how Lee misunderstood the lifestyle he enjoyed down on the river, the withdrawal from life he'd chosen.

"Whoa there, son. That ain't exactly correct. I do live the way I want down at the cabin, and I enjoy my peace and quiet, but running off and living like a muskrat ain't always that much fun. You know, being on the Catchahoula the past three years has taught me a lot about being alone, 'bout missing my family too. I been sorting out things, but I also feel like I let too much pass me by. You know there's current flowing up here just like down on the river, life I mean. Before you go jumping off into that freedom stuff, you might want to think about what you already got right here."

Glenna's face stalled in dismay as Tom scanned the room. Delivering intimate speeches about family wasn't exactly his forte, but he saw how his daughter loved the sentiment and how he had helped her keep Lee thinking the right way. Tom's intense ponderings over the past weeks had driven these clear thoughts to the surface of his awareness, and now those same images had found their way not only into words but into public sharing. He felt a little embarrassed at being so soft as he saw things, but he knew this would be a Thanksgiving to remember as his grandkids continued their long march to adulthood.

Choking with emotion, Glenna's voice cracked. "Here, here, Dad; that was beautiful. Let's have a toast—so, everybody, raise your glasses. I want to thank everyone for being here today, for remembering that love is more potent than anger, and that life finds its way into the future through our children, and we must cherish that responsibility. Thank you all."

Her little speech impressed Tom—how Glenna could think of all that without any planning—and he remembered so many little sermons Saralynn had delivered to everyone she met. And so the day had finally arrived when the family was back together. The legacy of Saralynn thrust a whole new spirit of individuality as well as unity upon the changing scene, and Tom was proud of his mother's spirit. But as he sat quietly remembering, the barb of Sheriff Barker jabbed again at his peace.

IV.

Dinner soon followed with too many choices for any single person to try, but everyone put forward serious effort. The turkey and dressing with a side of ham were a big hit naturally, and the girls decided they loved oyster dressing, but Lee's favorite was the candied yams and string beans with little slivers of almond and onion. Sitting on the back porch until well past dark, one favorite taste gave way to another until finally an overflow of pies made their way to the table and the family finished their feast with a whimper of overstuffed regret.

Hours had passed with each member of the family taking turns leading the dinner conversation and opining in public, but boundaries had been faithfully regarded with minimal damage to personal feelings, so everyone felt satisfied with their contribution. Lee basked in the aura of his libertarian ideas, proud he'd gotten to underscore his admiration not only for his grandfather but for the downstream family ripples that Saralynn had set in motion.

Soon the disquieting snore of overfed old men rattled in the living room, and the kitchen sparkled clean again. The cleanup crew now drifted to their various haunts in search of deserved silence, with the day closing more successfully than anyone could have expected.

As Lee softly shut the door to his room, he remembered the box on the bed and thrilled at the sight. Soon into his warm-ups and favorite

T-shirt, he pulled the weighty cardboard down to the floor, beginning the exploration.

The piles he had sorted earlier gave a good start. Soon he identified items with no postage stamp that had been obviously hand delivered. Others had been ripped across the postage mark so the date remained illegible. With each envelope style representing a point in history, once sorted Lee hoped to be able to estimate roughly which generation of stationary preceded the next, and that strategy excited him.

The rough sort didn't take long, with a couple of stacks being smaller than the others, and Lee calculated those missing letters must have gone to other people, but a rough count yielded over a hundred letters.

He discovered quickly that most of the letters were short one-or two-page editions, handwritten with consistent features in a scrawl not unlike his own untidy handwriting. Almost all letters addressed a calendar event, birthday, Father's Day, Valentine's, and so on through the Hallmark parade that Saralynn obviously tracked assiduously. Lee couldn't help smiling at how orderly the progression was, how meticulous she had been about making sure she acknowledged each event arbitrarily established as important by marketing forces but which in reality meant little other than profitability for card and candy makers. *Could it really be that Saralynn kept up with Arbor Day?* Lee joked in his mind.

Lee thought of the stories his grandpa had told him about Saralynn's regimented planning, and he saw in this collection her adherence to structure not only along calendar lines but within each epistle as well. Nearly all had some kind of quotation from the Bible or motivational apothegm, copied in her own hand or cut out of a magazine or church bulletin, then included as a special little prize in every letter. Frequently her own words or those of the quotation she included were underlined to make sure each special message received full import.

Soon Lee understood the rote nature of the letters, the mechanical structure, the laser-like focus of the mini-sermon Saralynn offered each time, but he also saw the newspaper function his great-grandmother served for the family. In each letter, there was an update about aunts and uncles, local basketball or football successes, even accomplishments by nephews and nieces surely to go unnoticed by the average family member, but here was Saralynn documenting everything in orderly, periodical form, her own little blog well before the Internet existed.

Many of the names in the notes seemed unfamiliar—family members long since drifted away or dead, neighbors no longer around as houses and people crumbled under the roll of passing time. There was great Aunt Clarise who committed suicide, and Mrs. Shultz's son who was arrested for bootlegging, and the doctorate in chemistry Saralynn's second cousin Terry received. Lee was thrilled to know better the private lives of people he'd never heard of before and to observe times when families cared about small details. This casual chronicling meant something now decades later, carried a currency of those days that could be savored the way a tray of warm biscuits in the oven lends itself briefly to the inviting hearth of a kitchen memory.

After about a third of the letters had been scanned, Lee got a little tired, deciding to continue later. Then he noticed again the old paperback books also in the box. Thoreau's *Walden*, Melville's *Moby Dick*, *Leaves of Grass* by Walt Whitman, a King James New Testament, along with the volume of American poetry he'd seen earlier.

All the pages crinkled when touched, and each had a dark yellowish color of old age and too much heat, but he knew they carried a history with them, as they had not been discarded long ago and for some unknown reason lived in this box alongside Saralynn's personal diary of the family for three decades.

Then he noticed something important. On the inside flap of each book, Saralynn had signed her name below an inscription, "For my son with love." Flipping slowly through *Moby Dick*, Lee found a white envelope, something that had been separated from the other letters but also different in color—pure linen white. It seemed innocuous enough, as the envelope was the small note size similar to the others, but this one had gone through the mail system and had a postmark of July 3, 1979, addressed to Thomas Bradburn from Saralynn Bradburn. Lee figured one last letter for the evening couldn't hurt; it was probably just a Fourth of July vintage.

Dear Tom,

Hope you, Oui, and my granddaughter are doing well. I'm still up here in Jackson with Aunt Katie. She's very sick, but we're all praying for her and you too.

Ouida called me a couple of days ago to tell me about your trouble at the factory. She was a little vague, but I managed to get out of her the story of that backstabber Donald Newland and how he lied about you. Hard to imagine those people at the plant could be that stupid and believe him, but the Lord makes all kinds of folks so he can test us before he takes us home.

Anyway, I managed to track down Newland at work. Don't be mad; I know how you get sometimes, but I couldn't stand for what he did. After the third call, he told me he wouldn't get a restraining order against me if I promised not to contact him ever again. So, let's let sleeping dogs lie, okay? I think he got my point.

I love you, son. Jesus one day will set things right for us all.

Mom

Lee rolled over on the floor, facing the ceiling, holding the letter like it was a thousand-dollar bill. How priceless this little leftover tidbit of the past was for him, how it again showed the simple Saralynn attitude and style, completely decisive. This little vignette awakened again the romanticized image of his great-grandmother, and Lee stretched his mind to hear her voice excoriating Don Newland on the phone. How he would have loved to hear that call, to see her anger rise again to protect her child, even if he was forty years old at the time.

The box of treasure lay solemnly in front of Lee, and he vowed that tomorrow he would read every single letter to soak up all the Saralynn he could find among the underlined phrases and statements of fact. At that moment, Lee connected to a past he'd never understood before, and his life began accelerating in directions he had only begun to grasp. But a queer thought appeared that this one separated note seemed so much more personal than the other more perfunctory ones, almost as if the whole situation had been prearranged for effect. Were there other treasures hidden away somewhere, even more profound snapshots of the deeper Saralynn? Lee simply knew there were and that he would find them.

As he flipped off the light and snuggled down into the covers, the word *backstabber* reverberated in his brain. Saralynn had used that word in her note to Tom. Was it remotely possible that this Newland guy was the same *two-faced feller* that Mike had referenced earlier?

V.

The next morning, Lee had plans to shoot hoops at seven thirty with a few of the guys in the neighborhood. If they could play early, the day didn't have to be as schedule challenged, as everyone seemed to have holiday company. He rose at a quarter to seven slowly, still sluggish from the heavy sleep and the previous day's activity, but soon slipped down the small back staircase that led to the kitchen, a bowl of Fruit Loops his mission.

At the bottom of the back stairs, a quick little left turn led to the kitchen. Making the last step, Lee heard voices, so he stopped short as Glenna spoke again to her dad.

"I can't tell you how much the kids love having you here; it's all they've talked about for two weeks now, and you saw them yesterday—they couldn't get enough of family talk."

"Yeah, I know," Tom said. "Means a lot to me too. But you know, I miss Harold too. Sure wish he was around. Funny, but you don't talk about him much. Is everything all right?"

"Of course, sure, everything's fine. He works too much, that's all." Lee inched closer to the door, as he wanted to hear everything. "Truth is we aren't that close anymore; I guess we don't see each other enough." Glenna's voice faded to barely audible.

A little insecure with the subject, Tom spoke softly. "I understand. It's hard these days, especially with your husband gone so much. But, darling, these kids are going to grow up and leave one day. When that happens, Harold may look a lot more interesting."

Lee smiled, as he too had been concerned about his dad being gone so much but didn't know how to say so.

"Hadn't really thought of it that way, Dad. Guess I should." And Glenna found a reason to look in the refrigerator.

"By the way, I forgot to mention it, but a strange thing happened a year or so ago you might want to know about. It was right before Thanksgiving, and the doorbell rang. I answered, and there was an older gentleman there. Said he'd been a friend of yours a long time ago but couldn't get hold of you in Picayune. Somebody had given him our address here, so he just dropped in unannounced."

"Yeah, who was it?"

"He said his name was, uh, uh, I can't remember, but I wrote it in my address book here right in front so I wouldn't lose it. Yeah, here it is. Donald Newland. That's it. Lives in Yazoo City, and I got his phone number and mailing address if you want it."

The next few seconds went silent, but Lee's imagination flew into action. He knew this Newland fellow was someone important and that his grandpa was hiding something that had a family history. This was the guy who threatened to have Saralynn arrested if she kept harassing him. Lee yearned to see Tom's face but remained hidden as he detected the cool composure in Tom's voice.

"Hmm, is that so? What else did this feller say?"

"Well, not much really. He was kinda quiet and polite, took his hat off but wouldn't come inside, as he didn't want to bother me. I liked him. He seemed sincere and friendly. Just told me to tell you he dropped in. So, here you go. Maybe give him a call."

Snuggling closer to the doorframe and sneaking a quick glance, Lee didn't notice anything out of the ordinary on his grandpa's face, and the seconds seemed like ages as he stood trying not to make any noise. Finally, Tom responded.

"Do you remember that fellow from when you were a kid? You must've been six or seven, I reckon."

"Not really. He was only a baldheaded older guy to me. I'm sure he looked different thirty-five years ago. Who was he?"

"Oh, nobody, nobody at all—just a guy I worked with at the plant years ago. Hardly even knew him, to tell you the truth; didn't really know him at all." Lee knew his grandpa was lying. Something very

70

strange was happening, and Glenna had no idea, but Lee intended to find out more.

"Well, maybe they're having some kind of reunion or something and want you to come," Glenna said. "Could be a good thing he stopped by."

Tom maintained his sangfroid coolness. "I don't think so, but let me have that information there. I'll check with him to see if there's anything between us we still need to talk about. You never know; a little chat might be in order." The mysterious flavor was unmistakable, and Lee spotted the false disinterest. Having spent some private time with Tom lately, he was familiar with what sounded genuine, and this response definitely sounded fake.

"And, sweetheart, let's keep this between us, okay? Mike had some issues with this fellow a long time ago, and I don't want to bring up any ill feelings. No reason to get Mike all riled; he's pretty decrepit, you know." The kindly words had a mischievous undertone, but now Newland was linked with both Mike and Saralynn. A secretive game was being played, but Lee wasn't sure why, though Saralynn's misdirection gene had clearly shown up in his grandpa's actions. In an odd way, Lee was almost proud to see his grandpa's maneuvering.

Back upstairs quickly, Lee kept his discoveries secret. The whole story of Don Newland's visit didn't sound right; some piece of information was missing. He laced up his tennis shoes, deciding to forego breakfast, but planned to copy the Newland contact information from his mom's address book as soon as he could be alone in the kitchen.

Within seconds, he was out the front door and off to play ball. The fresh air felt crisp, helping clear his head. Something peculiar was emerging, old relations and long-hidden secrets leeching into the present in ways no one quite understood yet, even Tom. Maybe this was one of those family traits where someone got what they wanted but not what they needed. Instinctively, Lee recognized that his grandpa needed his help but didn't know how to ask.

Soon, two hours of sweat and a few elbows to the ribs cured Lee's imaginative curiosity, but the physical release left him clearheaded, even though the previous day's food had added an extra pound or two. As he rounded the corner to home, Lee saw his grandpa and Vic sitting on the front porch having a one-on-one conversation, so not wanting to interrupt, he slipped down the side of the house to the backyard. Sipping a cup of coffee at the edge of the veranda, Mike studied some cuttings rooting along the edge of the deck. Here was a chance to talk privately.

"Well hey there, sport. Where you been? You look all sweaty," Mike said.

"You better believe it. Two hours of basketball. Kinda muggy this morning."

"Sure is. Them clouds to the north might bring us some sprits here in a while."

Lee had an idea. "Hey, you want to see the car Dad and me are working on? It's out in the garage."

"Sure, what is it?" Mike asked.

"A yellow 1968 Chevelle Super Sport, 396 horsepower, Hurst shifter, chrome mags with baby moons, Holly four barrel, the works! Dad and me are fixin' her up, and he said I can drive it on my birthday."

"Yeah, let's have a look."

So off to the back of the yard the two men strolled, talking about headers and carburetors. Lee chattered like a mockingbird while Mike nodded, not wanting to disrupt the boy's flowing trance.

Soon the black stripes on the hood shone in the sunlight. Inside, the interior had been totally removed and was being reworked, but most of the bodywork had been finished.

Mike beamed. "She's a beauty. Reminds me of a '68 Impala I had once. I made a racer out of her. Them girls liked her too." The boy looked up to catch Mike's eye, but the old man scooted to the other side of the car so as not to explain the comment.

After the thrill of showing off his baby, Lee eased around to his original intent, hoping Mike would be caught off guard.

"I forgot to mention it when I was in Picayune and want to ask you about something." Lee knew he was about to fib a little, but he'd just seen his grandfather do the same thing, so he gave himself permission since it was about family matters.

A happy calm engulfed Mike. "Sure. What's that, son?"

"You know, doing all this genealogy stuff, I heard mention of this guy Grandpa used to know, but I can't quite figure out his story. Grandpa don't reveal too much, so I thought I'd ask you. The fellow's name is a Donald Newland."

Mike stopped cold, no expression, not even a sign of breath that Lee could detect. Seconds passed with no response, only an implacable stare at shiny chrome rims.

The jovial mood disappeared. "You'd best leave that one alone," said Mike. "Your grandpa don't have much use for that man, and I think you'll find more shell than bean if you ain't careful. That temper Tom carries around ain't one you want him to pull out if you can avoid it. Ancient history, so let it go."

"Yeah, I know; that's why I'm asking you. His name has popped up a few times in the family, making everyone always seem jittery. But I don't know why. You know I wouldn't do nothing to hurt Grandpa."

Shaking his head, Mike headed out of the garage. "I'm not gonna get into this with you. You best leave it alone. Don Newland was a traitor, and you ought not to be foolin' round with that."

With that, Mike hustled out of the garage and back to the house while Lee closed the doors. Whatever had happened in the past sure had everyone antsy these days, but Lee was certain it was all a lot of noise about a little thing, the kind of thing small-town affairs are full of and that old men who hate to talk much just try to hide from the light of discussion. As he locked up, he wondered if the letters might offer any more clues; it seemed Saralynn was the only one willing to speak up about things or to take action other than to hide secrets, and Lee still wanted to know the facts.

Chapter 4

I.

The Thanksgiving reunion ended successfully with pleasantries all round and changes newly set in motion that could alter the future. As a spring flood finds its way from the confines of the riverbank, too-long silent emotions now rushed to invade places unaccustomed to their pressure, especially for Tom, as Don Newland had once again entered his life.

The trip home to Picayune began normally, with big hugs in the driveway and a sincere kiss from Glenna as her dad squirmed from the group's attention. But Tom managed the perfunctory minimum then retreated to Mike's truck for the trip home.

Occasional glimpses found Tom staring out the window and motionless as a statue, not a twitch, a syllable, a comfortable repositioning on the seat, just Buddha-like stillness peering blankly into the ordinary afternoon. Mike figured Tom must still be upset about the Newland news, but now wasn't the time to revive that discussion, though Tom's rage did seem to have oddly subsided. Something had changed, and Mike was sure his old friend was sorting the world anew after all the family reconnection.

Trying to distract Tom's stare into nothingness failed to register a response, but Mike continued to point out the old Pontiac like Oui used to drive and the pickup truck with the six-point buck laid out on the bed as hunters looked at it with self-importance. Even the sight of Aunt Bettie's Famous Hamburger Steaks café outside Poplaville hadn't produced a reaction, though they'd eaten there dozens of times over the decades. Nothing seemed to touch Tom in the place he'd withdrawn to—no new sights or sounds, no triggered memories, only a numbed tiredness.

Always the optimist, Mike kept trying to engage. "Hey listen, I could drop into the north exit if you wanted to run by the grocery store and pick up some supplies. I see where they got chocolate on sale for Christmas if you wanted to splurge."

Only indifference. Tom seemed not even to hear the words, or if he did, he chose not to show it, or perhaps couldn't. His frozen stare never moved in the hour drive, his complete absence from the moment unchanged in any perceptible way. But Mike didn't give up.

"Hey, how 'bout some onion rings? I got a hankerin' myself. Why don't we hit Roy's?"

At least this time Tom turned his gaze straightforward but not toward Mike. "No. Take me to the cutoff. I'll walk."

"No need to do that; I'll run you out to the cabin. It'll only take a minute."

"No, I'll walk."

Twenty minutes later, Tom crawled out of the truck barely looking back at Mike but finally uttering a muffled, "Thanks." And that was it. Down the rutted road he started his walk that would take two hours.

Blowing the truck horn, Mike yelled out the window, "Hey, you forgot your clothes and food." Never once did Tom look back with a smile or wave, nothing but total preoccupation with walking back into the world Mike couldn't help thinking Tom should not have left these past two days.

Not having prepared himself for the moment alone, Mike now had his own remorse; surely he had made a serious mistake by telling Tom about Don's advances on Oui. His plan to vent his own festering guilt and to address Tom's recurring dream scratched at Mike, and he felt stupid as if he'd fumbled the whole deal. How could he have made such an error of judgment? As the old red truck putted back to town, he wondered if he'd ever be able to put the flood back within the banks of the past. This venture back into the normal world might have been too much for

Tom. Seeing his family had been strain enough, but now that test had been made much more difficult by the burden of corrupted knowledge. Tom hadn't needed to know about Newland, but now the worry could not be ignored. And yet Mike simply couldn't get out of his mind the idea that something was missing; there had to be another element agitating his old friend from the withdrawn shadows Tom kept so guarded.

As the old red truck bounced past Roy's, then the Farmer's Cart, Mike knew his oldest friendship had reached a divide in the river with a dangerous flooding of uncertainty pulling at Tom. Ahead Mike sensed impending danger, and though he didn't quite know how to anticipate actions that might need to occur, he remained certain that he and Tom together could handle most any challenge. With that, he decided to focus instead on the positive step of the holiday weekend and to keep close touch with Tom until life on the riverbank settled back into its normal bounded flow.

II.

The Sunday before returning to school, Lee spent the morning playing basketball at the park. In the beginning, he hadn't actually liked the game and was only trying to discover a little of what Saralynn might have experienced as a teenager. Now things had changed, and he played every opportunity he got. The game had begun to matter.

When practice ended, Shelby, the tenth grader who had always lived down the street, slapped him on the back. "You're getting the hang of this game. Like I told you, Coach Barnes wants you to try out for B-team varsity. You should."

Not feeling like chatting, Lee started walking away. "Maybe." Lee loved the idea but didn't feel comfortable sharing that information with this kid who wasn't really his friend.

Shelby tried again. "Listen, my mom made a big pitcher of lemonade and about the best pecan fudge you ever tasted. She told me to invite you over after practice for a little sustenance, she called it." Lee felt crowded.

"Better not. We got company." And Lee had the strangest feeling, almost as if he wanted to go hang out and simply be with another teenager, but some barrier controlled his answers. The two boys parted, and Lee felt a little guilty at being so cold. But he was sure Shelby didn't really mind.

"Too bad," Shelby said. "You're missing out on some good stuff, and I got two new computer games that are awesome. One of them is even teaching me to play chess like a Russian master." At Shelby's final comment, Lee smiled, though he never turned back to the boy, instead merely raising his right hand with a little side-to-side wave as he walked away.

The rest of the day was spent sifting and organizing the remainder of the letters. He'd forgotten to ask his grandfather about the paperback books and hoped the family might reconvene for Christmas, but no plans had been firmed up. His grandpa had returned to his world, the place where the willowy sounds of the river tangled with erratic bird calls or windy chants down the open water, those places and noises that felt comfortable, like his grandpa's family of sorts. The idea of Tom checking the lines or building a fire or maybe setting some new traps felt thrilling as his grandpa's retreat into the world of solitude left idyllic traces Lee too imagined following someday. Now, with each Saralynn letter, the family tradition of fierce independence imprinted the canvas of Lee's romanticizing imagination.

The letters didn't produce any profound insights, but there were a couple of other references to Don Newland, though vague. One letter made mention of some rough patch Tom and Oui had gone through early in their relationship, but Lee couldn't understand what had happened, and evidently everything had worked out okay because after that Tom finally went to Mississippi State. Saralynn continued documentation of every holiday, editorialized her observations of human behavior or important events, usually someone dying or being born, but overall the letters seemed ordinary. An idea began to form for Lee that something was missing.

What he knew of Saralynn's innate vigor struck Lee as contrast to the superficiality in her written notes, and he wondered if that journalistic style was a technique to maintain control by revealing minimal tidbits about herself. Was Saralynn's emotional depth blocked off by a life of too much maturity at too early an age? This idea fascinated Lee, and he hoped one day he could ask his grandpa that question. It would be interesting to see his emotionally constricted grandfather respond to such a sensitive personal question, and the reaction might unveil some hidden family truth.

If emotional distance was one of those passed-along family traits, could Lee use this same technique of psychological separation? The idea intrigued the boy. Then he thought of how his mother seemed to have walled off his father, how they treated each other like strangers, sharing only mostly perfunctory details of weather or daily business. Confusion crept in, as he couldn't quite decide if he was inventing some opinion of Saralynn's personality or if he had truly spotted a family trait passed along by habit.

Having no girlfriend and not even a best friend since elementary school, Lee wondered why he resisted people getting close to him. Working on the car with his dad and the nightly dinner conversations with his mom and sisters represented the closest imitation of friendship he'd had for years now, and the idea was perplexing. Perhaps that was why going to the river had been so meaningful; reconnecting with his grandpa touched that lost friendship nerve Lee had forgotten. All the debates with his sisters, the arguments, were an exercise rather than genuine family closeness. Only his mom had ever developed deep trust with Lee, and that idea gave foundation to his new consideration of what friendship means to a person.

Look how close Mike was with his grandfather, Lee considered, their friendship exactly opposite of who his grandpa truly was. And what about how his grandpa missed Oui after she died? Maybe Tom wasn't so unavailable after all. The more Lee tried to penetrate this idea of family intimacy, the more circular things became, with no clear answers. Perhaps time simply had to take an unforced path. Perhaps one day he would find his own love and maybe even have a lifelong friend. Thinking about his grandpa's life had offered a modicum of hope—until Lee considered that maybe Tom, like Saralynn, would always be a loner.

Images from his own life swirled with the stories his grandpa shared. In that shifting flux, friendship and family relations seemed too opaque to grasp, and Lee wondered how he was supposed to know which human connections were real, until he had the thought that word labels didn't matter and the only thing that counted was closeness that could be trusted. Family sometimes didn't feel that meaningful. Heck, Lee had cousins he didn't even know. The whole idea of genealogy seemed irrelevant, and what Lee really wanted to understand wasn't lines of marriage and birth but clusters of life-filled moments, instances people share and then pass along to other generations, the kind of knowledge his grandpa and Mike could pass back and forth all day long without effort.

Saralynn's life stretched out as a giant mosaic being pieced together. So were the times he sat on the porch with his grandpa, nights listening to his sisters bicker, and moments watching his mom herd her kids like pups. Each of these instances rose up in a landscape fragmented in time but gradually synthesizing even if not yet fully grasped.

Tromping around with his grandfather, walking the river, skulking through the woods with guns, and a thousand other images passed through. Those Catchahoula times when he was a kid now felt strangely superficial, emotionally immature, the same kind of interpretation he got from this new batch of Saralynn's letters. Except that one special note that got separated. And he envisioned himself a child lost between the present and the swirling past whose existence he hadn't known. And the pull of memory moved him forward. As a child, then, his closeness with Tom had not been superficial; it had been the deepness of life without words soaking into his child-rich soul, nutrition for the complexity of person he would soon become. Something transformational was occurring. Lee knew it; the flat plane of his life now warped and molded to forces he had begun to perceive, and slowly an emergent person was forming, the man he wanted to be.

For the first time ever, Lee began to perceive his grandfather's limitations and not just his strengths, to see where his grandpa struggled with life, not just where he excelled. The impression felt like the internal conversation he had when he thought of his own life, secret but real. The bonds of his family, the connective tissue of blood and behavior, began unraveling into an objectivity difficult to accept. Lee became intuitively aware of the subtle mingling of separate lives, where the negative in one connects with the positive in another, where his grandfather possessed great closeness and insurmountable distance all in the same personality, all in some closed world of self.

Intuitively, Lee recognized this shuffling of lives was energy, the actual way people became friends or learned to be family, lives swirling like constellations rising and falling, separating and joining across the deep space of time and the close space of human life.

The letters lay disheveled on the floor, that messy collection of separates reaching with invisible tentacles in search of another piece of life to grasp, those letters now that fell as inert pages ripped from a living life that knew and loved. Family was about the interplay of people, and so was friendship, each a place a person could grasp. No artifact could capture that.

For a moment, the muddiness of life had cleared into a search for what his mind could hear but which words could not yet touch. He could learn to understand without labels this emerging identity as a person. Then, as if with the tick of a clock, the artful insight closed, passing now as daydreams ephemeral as flecks of dust across his eye before the staring sunlight.

III.

It took Tom over two hours to make the walk home. The road was muddy from the previous night's rain, and his step strained under the labor of a heavy mood. Slowly by the old bridge, the horse barn quiet now with the animals inside, and the ancient graveyard lying unattended off in the shadows, he dragged himself willfully. Some of those graves went back to the 1700s, and rumor had it that several slaves were buried there as well, but most of the headstones were so beaten by weather that barely a letter could be made out, let alone a date or name, identity of the past completely lost to time. Less reflection seemed to be Tom's prescription, a hiatus from examining life, and with only images of the waiting cabin filling his mind, he walked in a trance of deliberate concentration.

An hour before sunset, he finally saw the opening where home stood and then took the shortcut where his garden plot lay shut down for the season, though boasting still a few cabbages, turnip greens, and a stand of broccoli. The fenced area offered warmth as he saw the rails and chicken wire steady at their task and could even recognize the two days of growth on the greens. The afternoon had turned colder, but thoughts of home steadied Tom. Sighing unconsciously as he stepped into the yard, the heavy countenance he'd carried all day lifted slightly but not so much as to smile. Instantly his senses turned to the sounds and sights of home, scanning to see if anything had changed, but all looked normal from the side yard, until he reached the porch.

When he came around the front of the cabin, something was strewn on the floor, toilet paper or perhaps napkins. He halted to listen for a sound—nothing—then stepped onto the deck, seeing the door half-open. Inside the cabin was only darkness as he had closed the shades before he left. Hunting mode instinctively took over. Soundlessly to the door he crept, opening it with the walking stick he kept leaned against the post supporting the porch roof, ready in case anything moved. All was quiet.

Inside, the place was a wreck—furniture knocked over, kitchen ransacked with food containers everywhere. At first he thought Sheriff Barker had invaded to harass him, but after a closer look, whatever had gotten inside had been looking for food, as the kitchen was the most devastated place of all.

"Dang gone door, must have blown open. I got to get a new latch," Tom muttered to himself. Then he saw paw prints on the counter, tracks through the flour he had stowed in a coffee can.

"Coons. I'll be trapping your ass tomorrow."

And so Tom's reentry went less smoothly than anticipated, being greeted by a huge mess, almost no usable food, and thickening loneliness as company in the dying light. The happy solitude of a month ago drifting further into the backwater of distress, he knew the battery on the truck was likely dead, and because he'd been so gruff with Mike, he might not have a visitor for days or weeks. But to Tom, the abject realization seemed almost appropriate, like he deserved the bad luck he'd created.

Again the nameless graves down the road hovered in his thoughts, and a dim awareness peered through the opaque moment that his idyllic world was unraveling. Outside forces demanded change, and the synchronization he'd known with nature at the cabin now became so distorted that even simple creatures easily unbalanced his wobbling life. An odd sense of not belonging rose, this river world now something less than home where Tom was the intruder, and yet he hadn't belonged at Glenna's either. The initial warmth of his return to the family began to float down the river of memory with Tom recalling only the annoying clutter of too many people. A miasma of futility settled over the sanctuary he'd been so anxious to reclaim, but suddenly no place felt like home, and Tom simply didn't know what to do or where to go. His one clear wish was to be with Oui.

Bitterly frustrated, he walked outside to see floured paw prints on top of his little porch table and the seat of his favorite chair ripped, and Tom wanted to give up. He didn't care about the cabin or food, about his newly revived family or Mike, or anything. The garden simply looked like work that needed to be done, and the hides on the line reminded him of the tedious, nasty work ahead to finish the stretching process and tanning. A world once full of his touch, the things he most loved looked like drudgery, and darkness swelled like he'd never known, not even after Oui or his mother had died. In the fading light, Tom stood utterly alone, a silhouette standing on his porch against the rising flood of night.

Demons would haunt the sleep ahead, and as Tom studied the last image of the old matron in the yard, leafless in her own despair, he slumped against his world, wanting suddenly to break everything in the cabin—the furniture, the stove, the window, everything. The thought actually gave him energy and purpose, but he knew that too would only end in regret, that circular disappointment bred from trying. Exhausted, he fell into bed, thoughts aching as his stomach growled its plaintive reminder he'd forgotten his leftovers in Mike's truck.

Night passed as a glacier retreating. Once, Tom heard a voice calling from down at the boat but couldn't find the strength to get up and investigate. Drizzle at daylight woke him to mild but unexpected encouragement. The cabin now looked as if it could be handled with some organization, so he began sorting damage from confusion. Most of the food was lost and a few cushions ripped, but they could be repaired. But first catfish for breakfast and some steamed broccoli from the garden sounded just fine.

By noon, the gray sky brightened, and the cabin was reasonably reassembled. Tom had a nice meal of fish and vegetables which lifted his gloomy mood, but increasingly he sensed being trapped. The cleanup helped with distraction, but with menial tasks completed, the vista of his life opened again onto the world he'd claimed. Always so easy, the project of self-construction now perplexed Tom, but he knew instinctively that action was his only course.

Down to the river and then out into the boat carrying his twenty-gauge, he needed to get away from the mess at home and go upstream away from the lingering damage done to his confidence. Lee would be so disappointed if he could hear this self-doubt or the weakness about how to handle the sheriff. Demons flew in the sky, but Tom was glad to be alone out of the glare of sharing, here where self-doubt consoled itself with its close friend loneliness.

Nothing moved on the river—no birds, squirrels, deer, pigs, nothing, only the lazy current slightly encouraged by the morning rain. All the trees held gray as limbs dominated the skyline and trunks automatically took Tom's gaze to the ground, to the dead leaves and limbs decaying after their usefulness, and he wondered, had his life's run come to an end? Had he, like his mother, come to where the trouble of living outweighed the joy?

By midafternoon he tied off the boat then walked straight up the hill to the smokehouse. There, he took an old hubcap used to hold screws and nails and filled it to the brim with charred wood from the smokehouse firebox. Each piece, midnight black, almost bright in its darkness, shone as dangerous beauty to Tom as he sorted the largest pieces. Around back of the smokehouse, he looked at his colorful mural—the bright, sunny grass, the cute little cabin and garden, even Mike's old red truck with Lee standing in the sunlight, all those laden fruit trees and his little boat eager for a job, all waiting cheerfully.

Then Tom selected the largest chunk of charcoal. Holding it to the afternoon light, he thought it looked like some object from another solar system, some alien thing sent to teach him the secrets of a fading life, and so he rubbed hard the blackened chunk against the wall where soon several inches of detail around the entire perimeter disappeared into a night of self-destruction. Tom as creator began destroying his own world. The frenzied assault on the cheerful picture left instead a ransacked image as if devastated by a madman or crazed child. Soon, he stood staring blankly, the glaucoma of a dispiriting soul continuing to shrink the edges of his collapsing will.

Deciding whether to climb through the damage into that shrunken universe, Tom remained emotionless, no pain of loss, no regret from the strident assault on his artistic secret, and yet he could not bring himself to completely destroy his creation, only to maim it. Left were Lee and Mike with his old truck, even the little boat tethered to the cypress, and part of his garden. But gone now was so much of the enveloping nature Tom loved, the pear trees and willows, the giant oaks and luscious orange maples, the mulberry trees flowering and ripe, all blackened now.

With the same suddenness of decision, Tom went inside to rest, his secret creation now half-alive, and he agreed with the symmetry of the moment. The tranquility of loss felt safe, as if it were the place he could hide from the searching eye of his thoughts, and Tom was sure he heard his dear mother calling him from down by the river, but too exhausted to abandon the cabin, he slept deeply instead.

IV.

As basketball practice ended and all the boys headed to the locker room, Coach Barnes pulled Lee aside. "Good practice today, son. Wanted you to know I like your hustle for the ball, that third and fourth try for each rebound. You got something special, Lee. Keep working hard and something good is gonna happen." Lee felt ten feet tall.

Leaving the gym later, he thought how he actually loved the tiredness in his legs after practice and the feeling of physical sacrifice during the game. Each day he learned more as his skill improved and his natural instincts matured. Even more confident around his teammates, his chatter during practice became more crisp and functional, though afterward he struggled to relate to the other boys. But easiness had begun to develop, and Lee almost felt comfortable reaching out to his peers.

Soon he found himself talking about how girls too hated the tedium of school and other topics Lee would never have broached only weeks earlier. The other boys considered Lee serious, but he played skillfully, so tension slowly subsided, and Lee's amiable nature began to emerge.

Occasionally he accepted a ride home from Randy or Louis, two seniors on the team, but lately he preferred instead to jog while carrying his books in a small backpack. The extra physical effort helped build endurance, all part of Lee's long-term plan.

Shelby had made the team as well. Riding with Randy one Tuesday after practice, the two boys stopped to chat with Lee. "Hey, dude, awesome half-court shot you made today," Randy said.

"Just lucky," Lee responded, still awkward at chitchat.

"You want a ride?" Randy asked.

With a slight smile, Lee turned to the driver's-side window. "Not today. Need to jog. Don't want to get fat and lazy like you seniors." And the quip lightened the stiffness that frequently overtook Lee. But the tenuous thread had begun connecting, and he discovered that joking was easier than being serious.

The weather remained chilly but not too cold, so a slow run sounded good. Passing through the high school parking lot then onto the street, Lee saw a red flash of his sister Victoria's jacket. Over near the outside edge of the student lot, it disappeared as quickly as he'd seen the familiar color, so he paused to take a look. Her head popped up between two of the cars again but this time with her boyfriend, Brad, holding her by the neck, his right hand pushing her back against the driver's-side window of an old Chevy pickup. Lee flew to his sister.

Approaching deliberately, Lee didn't say a word, only stared at Brad—no sound, only intention. Slowly to within eighteen inches of Brad, Lee watched the boy twitch as his personal space collapsed. Victoria broke loose and scampered away. Face-to-face, the two boys glared. Brad was a year older than Lee and about the same height, but Lee looked fit, leaner, and athletic as he shoved his face six inches from Brad's nose.

"Now here's the thing, Braddie, this here is my sister." Lee moved his chest to almost touch Brad's. "I'm only gonna tell you this once. Touch her again where she feels uncomfortable, and you'll be playing that horn of yours butt style. Understand?"

Three or four other kids now drifted over to the scene as everyone could see something was happening, though there were no loud voices, no yells or belligerent behavior, only calm, serious redefinition of the situation. Brad stepped to the side and gently held Lee back with a diffident hand to the chest.

"This ain't none of your business, Lee; it's between Victoria and me, so you can just clear out of here. Besides, she slapped me first."

With those words, Lee backhanded Brad, his right hand moving so fast Brad didn't see it at all. Then, again Lee stepped close to the boy who now breathed heavily.

"I guess slappin' buttheads just runs in our family," Lee quipped sardonically. "Braddie, we're not ever going to have this conversation again."

A whimper from Victoria broke the moment. Lee wasn't sure if she was angry or terrified, but he did know the crisis was over. A strange combination of pride and dread swelled, as he knew his mother would be upset at his public behavior, and probably Victoria would be furious, but he knew he'd done the right thing. Oddly, he wondered what Saralynn might have said to him or for that matter to Brad, and then he knew he hadn't gone too far.

V.

The day after returning to Picayune, Mike began to worry about Tom and his long walk home. More truthfully, he worried about how the Don Newland news was sitting with his old friend. Seemed a visit was necessary. Tom had given Mike money some time ago so that when he came out he could bring a few things like flour, sugar, and cornmeal,

WHAT THE RIVER WANTS

WHAT THE RIVER WANTS

but no matter what Mike brought, Tom always complained that he didn't need it. Getting a little milk from the dairy three miles away seemed to be all Tom really wanted, as his chickens and garden served him well enough. Anything he didn't have he simply learned not to need. Today, however, Mike decided on a different approach.

Stopping by the Wal-Mart at the edge of town, Mike bought a new truck battery. While at it, he also picked up a tune-up kit with spark plugs and wires, a can of Fix-A-Flat because he was sure at least one tire on Tom's old truck would be low, and new air and oil filters, along with six quarts of oil. He figured this might not be all Tom needed, but it was a good start and would give the old grump something to work on the next few days. Mike kept playing back their time at Glenna's, studying how things were changing for Tom. Perhaps these days Tom simply needed more contact with people.

Jostling down the rutted road reminded Mike how confused Tom acted lately, missing that certainty of things that was his typical nature. Could there be something in Tom's head he had forgotten to share with everyone else? Who knew? The reconnection to the family appeared to have been a good thing, but he also recognized that the holiday had cost Tom emotional energy. Had he made an egregious mistake telling his friend about the Newland fiasco? A cold shudder sobered Mike, and he calculated whether he should share his one remaining secret about Oui. Or was it too dangerous? A stomach lump of guilt formed. This ancient secret Mike had held since he and Tom were teenagers, but the timestamp had run out on this buried memory, and it needed to be exposed.

Almost breaking a tire rod, at last Mike turned into the cabin yard. Things instantly looked different. No smoke came from the chimney, cushions and fabric lay strewn all over the front porch, and the woodpile on the porch had been used up, with only a couple of sticks remaining even though no fires burned. Mike began to worry.

"Hey, you old goat? You home?" Then he blew the truck horn a couple of times, not knowing what else to do. The cabin door lay slightly ajar, so slowly pushing open into the darkness, he saw utter chaos, everything still disheveled from the raccoon rampage. Tom had cleaned the place but had not returned order to items now scattered everywhere.

"Oh my God. What the …" Tom was normally meticulous; this disaster could not be a good sign. Mike needed to find his friend. To the bed, nothing. Back outside to the smokehouse and then the river, all round the edge of the property where the fruit trees stood bare limbed, nothing.

At a loss for what to do, he grabbed the shotgun from his truck. Three shots and then he waited for a response. Nothing. Then after about fifteen seconds, Tom's old twenty-gauge fired off upriver, and he knew Tom was headed back. Realizing he had a few moments to look around, back inside Mike went to see what food was there. Not much, just some dirty dishes and cooked potatoes. Outside to the smokehouse where the fire had pretty much gone out, but some kind of meat hung in the smoker. There on the step he saw the hubcap with the black, messy charcoal remains, and he couldn't imagine what Tom used that for. Finally, in the distance, the putt-putt of the Johnson engine came down the river, so over to the bank he strolled.

Soon the little skiff came around the bend with Tom sitting deliberate as a preacher on Sunday. He didn't acknowledge Mike at all until he pulled up to the cypress tree to tie off. He finally looked up but didn't say a word.

"I was beginning to think you might have fallen in the river and drowned." Mike tried to make a joke.

"You couldn't see the boat was gone?" No humor in Tom's voice, only a cold, sharp response laden with irritation, certainly not a welcome.

"Yeah, I saw."

"What are you doing here snooping around? Glenna send you?"

"Well, I'm not snooping around for starters, and, no, Glenna didn't send me. I ain't talked to her since you did. Why you so grumpy anyway?"

"Since you wasn't snooping around, you probably didn't notice that the coons got inside the cabin while I was away wasting my time in Hattiesburg. They tore everything up, ate all my food, made a mess."

"Now that you mention it, I did notice it was a bit disorderly up there. I figured you'd had some wild river women over for a party." Mike's deadpan delivery so caught his old friend off guard that Tom actually smiled.

"You old coot. You're the Romeo around here. I ain't the one that goes to that dance club. That would be you, my friend."

With that, Mike helped pull Tom ashore and gave him a strong arm to grab as he stepped from the unsteady little boat. "I brought you some coffee and stuff; thought you might be running low. Should have brought a coon dog, it looks like." And they both laughed a measured release as they headed up the hill. Tom brought along the four catfish he'd caught and the one squirrel he'd shot.

"Good, I need a hot cup," Tom said. "You ready for some lunch? Next time, it'll be coon, I promise you." And so for the millionth time, the two old pals cleaned up the fish and squirrel and cranked up the stove for a hot cup of coffee and some nourishment from the Catchahoula, nutrients and friendship more important now than ever as the outside world continued to close in on Tom's sanctuary.

"I brought your ice chest and clothes back from Glenna's. She'd packed you a pie and some yams, you know. Guess a little family ain't all bad, huh?"

VI.

Lee's door slid open as his sister peeked around to see if he'd heard her slight knock. Still a little shy after the episode with Brad, Vic didn't know quite what to say but wanted to see Lee before the family sat down to dinner.

"You awake?" she asked.

"Yeah, come on in," Lee said.

"Hey look, I wanted to say thanks for what you did with Brad. I was kinda mad at first, but you were right. I broke up with him after you left."

"Good. He's a punk. You can do better."

"Yeah, I know." Lee saw how timid his sister became as she crossed her arms and seemed to shrink two inches in height.

The earlier pep talk from Coach Barnes left Lee in a positive mood even after the spat with Brad, but he knew that Vic was having the opposite kind of day. Though normally the typical brother and sister with predictable rivalries, Lee began to see his relationship with Vic could be more personal. He decided to use some of that Saralynn optimism his grandpa always talked about.

"Look," Lee said, "I know you had a rough day, but sometimes when things go bad it means they will go better next time." His skill at coaching needed a little work, so he went for a more personal angle. "You know, you're about the smartest person I know, and you have a good way with words," Lee said. "You don't need to put up with crap from a loser like Brad." The comment jolted his sister, not accustomed to such sensitivity from her brother. She smiled, looking at the floor.

"You know, being a senior, you have a lot of things to take care of this year," Lee continued. "Maybe just focus on schoolwork and make some good grades so you can get out of this crappy little burg one day. Go to college and find a real guy who appreciates you." This time Vic almost started crying. Lee wasn't quite sure what to do but instinctively kept moving ahead. "You don't need this small-town trash, so don't settle for it."

A look of desperation enveloped his sister's face. "I know. But I get scared, like I'll get left behind or something."

Standing to give Vic a sincere hug, Lee felt the moment become less intense, having a renewed sense of the friendship he'd always shared with Vic, one he'd never really thought about too carefully. "Heck, we all think we're different and maybe don't quite have what others do, but that's not true most of the time." Lee looked around, having an idea. "Try to get what you need, not what you want."

A curious brightness returned to Vic's cheek. "What does that mean?"

"It's something Grandpa told me, how Saralynn always pushed hard for what she wanted, but when she got it, it usually was the wrong thing for her. I think we all might be that way." Lee sat back against his headboard.

Then he had another thought. "See all these letters? It's a whole pile of things Granny Saralynn wrote. Old stuff from forty years ago. I've been studying them trying to figure out who she was—you know, all that strength and cleverness she had. And temper too."

"Really, like what?"

"Well, look at this one. No date on it, but it looks like it's from when Grandpa and Granny Oui were dating. Check this out ..."

Dear Tom,

So sorry to hear you and Oui are having some trouble; I know you'll work it out. She is a good woman, son, with options, you know—good options, and you're just one of them. That other fellow has just as much right to call on her as you do until she makes a choice, so rather than pester her about who he is, you need to show her what you're made of. Jealousy is for people that don't have a true north in their soul. Show Oui who you are, then let her choose. That's a marriage that can stand.

Mom

"See what I mean? Granny Saralynn had a way of helping other people. Maybe she didn't make the best choices for herself, but she was good at seeing stuff for her family. These letters show who she really was, and you get to see that temper of hers. Whew, nasty."

Encouraged, Vic spoke optimistically. "Do you think we got some of that strength in us? I don't feel too strong right now. Maybe her DNA got diluted before us."

"Naw. It's there, but you got to use it. Like doing this basketball stuff has really affected me—gives me focus and a way of using my body instead of crawling around inside my head all the time."

Vic inched closer. "Weird but I see that in you," she said. "You're happier lately. I wasn't sure why. And what you did today with Brad, I didn't recognize you."

From downstairs, Glenna's voice echoed up the stairs. "Okay, guys, come on down. Supper is ready." Victoria stood up and for perhaps the first time in her life hugged Lee's neck as if truly grateful. He blushed, suddenly at a loss for words.

"Thanks. You're a good brother. But don't worry, I won't tell anyone." She smiled and then slipped out the door. A strange expansion pulled at Lee, and oddly it felt like friendship.

Ready to go downstairs, he caught a glimpse of the family photograph and wondered where his grandpa was at that very instant as the cabin glimmered in his thoughts. The homey, warm glow faded now to mundane concern as dinner appeared with chattering girls excited over some pep rally, but Lee had wandered distantly from his normal life tonight. And the cabin and warm fire reached out to him again, a happy thought of men secure with their freedom, their bond as family. A new door of self was opening, and the sounds of his sisters with images of the cabin flickering in his mind pulled at Lee from the center of the new memories he was ready to create.

A voice broke the spell. "I made banana pudding." Lee saw his mom's face floating behind those soft words, comforting as a child's blanket. That silent awareness Glenna carried with her, that massive character people too often forgot to note, for a moment lit brightly. And at that very tick of time, Lee remembered his mom too was a part of the legacy of Saralynn. In Glenna lived the same potential for guiding her little flock with that gracious smile of protection and that strong arm of character. Then, instinctively he realized his grandpa too needed help finding his way home, even if he didn't know it.

VII.

Lucy became rambunctious at the table leaving Glenna to reset the rules of order. "Listen to me, do not make fun of your teacher that way. Mr. Ford can't help it if he has a little stutter. You don't know; he may have gotten it in the war or had some kind of disease as a child." Probity reestablished, Glenna wanted to move on to the matter she was anxious to discuss.

"Let's change the subject, shall we? I had an interesting phone call this afternoon." Both Victoria and Lee cast peripheral glances at one another. "Yes, it seems that Brad's father gave me a call."

Without pause, Lee effused a defense well before any accusation of blame. "Now listen, Mom, it wasn't my fault. He was being a jerk ..." But Glenna simply put her forefinger to her lips, indicating silence.

"As I was saying, Mr. Parker called me, screeching about assault and intimidation and various egregious behaviors, so I let him rant on before I could ask a few questions myself. Lee, it seems you slapped his son after he accidentally shoved your sister against the car." The table moved as Lee sprang to his feet. Again, Glenna held up her forefinger.

Anxiously, Vic spoke up. "Mom, Lee didn't do anything wrong. Brad was getting rough with me because he thought I'd been flirting with Tim Songa; that's what happened. Lee just told him to keep his hands off me."

Glenna turned to her son. "Is that what happened?"

"Well, sorta'. I kinda slapped him and then maybe threatened him a little if he ever touched Vic again. I didn't hurt him or nothing, but some of his friends did think it was pretty funny."

"Okay, well that's that. Lee, I want you to stay away from Brad—and you, Victoria—"

But before Glenna could issue a directive, Vic interrupted. "I broke up with him."

Smiling at the easy resolution, Glenna continued. "Fine, if that's your decision. If you two are not suited to one another, then a little distance is probably best."

Both Lee and Vic looked at each other quizzically, and then Vic addressed her mom. "You seem awfully calm about this whole thing, Mom. What did you say to Mr. Parker?"

In a moment of subdued joy, Glenna responded, "Well, not that my personal conversations are any of your business, but I did have a word with Mr. Parker. He kept yelling, so I told him that his son was a churlish brute that deserved to be smacked for using physical force on an innocent girl. I think I might have added that if he ever so much as touched Victoria again that I would personally break his knees with a baseball bat. Then I wished Mr. Parker a good afternoon."

Everyone at the table howled. Lee slapped the table so hard that his water glass tipped over. An odd moment hung over the family just then, a comfort with themselves as a group, as defenders of each other's right to live a peaceful life, and though Saralynn was not around to enjoy this spirit of family loyalty, she no doubt would have found the moment rewarding.

VIII.

All afternoon, Mike and Tom worked on the Chevy trying to get it back into reliable condition. They removed, repaired, or cleaned until their knuckles looked like they'd been in a fight, and after about three hours, the truck cranked with a new sense of pep. But Mike had a bit of unwelcomed news.

"You need a new distributor cap. This one has a crack in it. While we're at it, let's put on a rebuilt starter too; this one sounds pretty worn."

The advice irritated Tom. "Dang, I ain't trying to race at Talladega; I just need to get to the store once in a while."

Ready for the complaint, Mike threw a zinger. "And to Glenna's house. It would be nice if you'd drag your worthless butt up there and see them grandkids sometimes. They're gonna be grown and gone before you know it. Then you'll be complaining they moved away too far."

"Yeah, yeah, whatever," Tom groused. "Just figure out what we need. Shoot, I'll need to sell half this mighty plantation to pay for this little tune-up." Mike smiled, but Tom realized his slip, and the thought of not only money troubles but of eviction returned. His social security checks and small pension weren't a lot and barely met expenses. After leaving Container, Tom really never had another job that paid taxes, so he worked for cash, painting houses, trapping, and general carpentry back in those days before moving to the river.

Again he thought how silly his comment about the plantation was since he didn't even own the place, and now the gnawing growl of the sheriff's eviction had a new grip on Tom's confidence.

The repair continued with few words passing between the two men. Having a little company had been pleasant, though Tom would never admit it, and since the trip to Glenna's, his mind had been disturbed from its normal rhythm, leaving him strangely detached from the natural world, normally so calming. The old news that Don accosted Oui had dislodged his emotions, and now the idea of treachery had taken on a whole new drama with Newland looming as sexual predator. Old memories no longer felt familiar in this new phase of disorientation.

Distracted, Tom wondered why Don had reappeared after such a volatile end to their friendship. Those days remained poignant, but increasingly Tom knew the truth had not yet been fully revealed.

The recurring dream flitted at the edge of Tom's mind, and the deep analysis he'd performed of every word and glance lined up for review. Perhaps he had missed something; there must have been a clue.

Decades smoldered as Tom sorted reality from suspicion. Then, as if a voice from the clouds speaking, he heard Mike.

"Hey, you're daydreaming there while I'm doing all the work. I'm gonna renegotiate my contract if you keep this up." So the men retreated to the porch for a fresh pot of coffee while they planned the next day. The afternoon waned with Mike wanting to get down the road before dark, but he had time for a little rest and some store-bought caffeine while resting on the make-do furniture, chipper but tired.

"Dang, this is good coffee. It ain't much pay for half a day's work, but I guess it'll have to do," Mike said.

His daydream paused, Tom was ready. "I'd say it's just about what you're worth. After all, I still can't drive the old bucket of bolts. At least it cranked before, sometimes." Tom then nestled into his steaming relaxation.

"Before I leave, I want to ask you something," Mike said.

"No, I won't marry you, you ole coot," Tom replied.

"Well good, I'm glad we got that out of the way 'cause I do have something serious to say."

Being a little worn out himself, Tom was amenable. "Awright, shoot. My life is pretty much already screwed to the hills and back, so lemme have it."

The opening animated Mike. "You see, that's kinda what I'm talking about. You seem a little different to me now that we returned from Glenna's, and I want to make sure I'm not missing anything. I been a little concerned I caused you this downswing when I told you about Don making moves on Oui. And I regret that. I never meant to dredge up hardship."

The sincerity touched Tom. "Yeah, I know. Look, it's awright; I'm fine, just a little out of sorts. That trip north reminded me of the things

I've lost—Oui, my mom, even the closeness to Glenna and the kids. I sit here in these ole woods all alone, trying to live in the past, maybe find some peace with nobody around to bother me, and for a long time that worked. But it ain't working anymore. I used to not say a word for days, not even think about anybody except my family, and the river song was all I needed to hear. Now things have changed."

Mike kept pushing. "Why don't you think about moving back to town? I got an extra bedroom, and you can stay there for free, just help a little with the food and utilities."

A little chuckle from Tom eased his mind. "Naw, I don't think so. I ain't ready to be a roommate just yet, but thanks for the thought. Right now, I got to sort out some things, and I need peace and quiet to get that done."

"Hmm," said Mike, and then Tom changed direction.

"Maybe this summer I could get Lee out here on the creek with me. Show him some stuff about trapping and living on the river—you know, rangerin' kind of things." This time Mike chuckled.

"Oh yeah, that's what every sixteen-year-old wants, to spend the summer alone on the river with his grandpa, skinning coons and raising worms. You might want to talk that over with him before you get too carried away with that notion."

Though he'd successfully eluded Mike's probe, Tom sunk into his chair, thinking how he couldn't seem to catch the pace of things anymore, how no matter what he thought or planned, it always turned out to be a little bit off. Aging for Tom left him increasingly forlorn in his thoughts even as he continued to choose more isolation, a cycle firmly grooved after Oui's death and one without much impetus for change, until now. Tom knew he had to confess the real root of his distress, the threats from Sheriff Barker, but he couldn't bring himself to that humiliation yet. And so he decided to save that chat for later and quickly changed the subject.

"So, old man," Tom said, "did Glenna tell you that Don Newland came to see her last year?"

"What? No. Why would he do such a crazy thing. Lookin' to get shot, I reckon."

"Who knows. Said he just showed up before Thanksgiving last year and knocked on the door. Wanted to talk to me but was real calm-like, Glenna said. Left his address and phone number too." Tom played his response as deadpan as possible, studying Mike for a reaction.

"Hmm, seems odd that feller would pop up after all this time," Mike said, more confused than insightful. "Maybe he's feeling guilty."

The idea of remorse from Newland enticed Tom. "Yeah, maybe he's got something else to say. Who knows. Can't imagine it's anything for my good though."

"You're probably right. Some more poison, I suspect." Mike didn't seem particularly intrigued by the unexpected visit. That nonchalance piqued Tom to a more aggressive approach.

"I want to go see Don," said Tom. The direct approach left both men a little stunned.

Moving to his feet suddenly, Mike spoke more earnestly. "You sure about that? That guy ain't done no good for you; he might be planning to drop another crap bomb if you ain't careful."

But Tom's determination had begun to build. "Maybe, but my life is a mess anyway, so I'm not sure I'd even notice the smell." Tom looked directly at Mike. "Will you go with me?"

Mike sat back down. "I ain't anxious to do that for sure, but if you insist, I will. One condition though."

"What's that?" Tom said with a victorious little smile.

Again Mike stood. "You can't kill him. I'm too old to go to jail." And though Mike chuckled and Tom smiled, they both knew a real truth had unfolded in front of them.

Feeling a little cocky with the offered support, Tom said, "Well, if I do, I'll make sure you ain't with me at the time."

So the day ended with Mike inching the Ford back to town while Tom continued the cleanup, but both men knew a new epoch was opening. For Tom, perhaps the chance to settle this long held confusion had finally arrived. A confrontation might even be the final chapter in a saga that could let him finish out his last few years with a little peace. The idea sounded so good that in the same swoop of thought, Tom made up his mind he wanted to go to Glenna's for Christmas, then on to Yazoo City the next day.

Chapter 5

I.

The news that Tom and Mike would arrive on Christmas Eve sent the family into yet another whirlwind of preparation. This time Glenna wanted to cook a Christmas goose, and Tom would bring a smoked deer roast, so everyone was excited about the unusual menu.

Tom called his daughter from the thirty-year-old pay phone at Roy's after his third unscheduled trip to the car parts store, and then he and Mike took a break for a well-deserved hamburger and chocolate shake. After four days of car mechanic torture, they were tired of grease and aching knuckles, but finally the Chevy came back to life. Tom grew increasingly excited about the trip to Hattiesburg and then on north to Yazoo City, and having his truck in such new condition was a significant emotional lift.

"They can't wait to see us again," Tom said, "so I guess we just have to live long enough to get there on Christmas Eve."

"That's good," Mike said. "Did she mention Lee's car at all? He might be done with it." Mike couldn't wait to inspect the Chevelle for progress.

Talk about the car irritated Tom. "Don't know, didn't ask. Harold will be home though. Ain't seen him in years."

Mike had another thought in mind. "Hey, listen, you going to call Donald before we go up there? I mean, give him a head's up since it's Christmas?"

A cold stare. "Nope. He dropped in on Glenna, so that's the protocol. Besides, I want to catch him off guard. That guy's up to something."

Mike had already drifted to a new thought. "Hey, meant to tell you I got you something. My neighbor a coupla' weeks ago cut down that big oak tree in his backyard after lightning struck it. He had a nice tree swing in it that ain't no use to him no more. Two good ropes and a seat made out of white ash, hard as steel. Thought you could hang it from that chinaberry by the path. Maybe if your grandkids come down this summer, it would be fun for the girls."

Incredulous, Tom stared at his old friend's sudden sensitivity. "Okay, thanks. Can't say the idea would have occurred to me but sure. You can help me hang it up there since you're being so extra considerate these days."

Grinning, Mike was ready for the comment. "Way ahead of you. Already got a plan."

So the banter continued as Tom felt more cheerful than in weeks. "Nice to see you're on the ball for a change," Tom said. And with that, the meal of burgers and shakes carried forth in silence with Tom already planning what his first words to Don Newland might be. He was torn between "Hello, jackass" and "Why the hell are you bothering my daughter?" but wanted to stew on the felicity of his expression so as to catch the perfect blend of fresh outrage and fermented bitterness.

Savoring his future revenge, Tom noticed a police car drive by slowly as if looking for someone. One of the deputies that had come to the cabin with Sheriff Barker glared at Tom, but no words passed, and Tom shook his head slightly, as if to say, "Later, my friend."

The hard stare at the police car caught Mike's attention. "You looking for a ride somewhere?" Mike asked.

"Oh, no, thought I recognized somebody, that's all." Mike seemed confused, but Tom pointed out how good the onion rings were, and the nearly exposed secret slipped back into the unobserved moment.

II.

Victoria had drifted into a quiet withdrawal since breaking up with Brad. He still chatted with her at school and called occasionally, but she had a decisiveness that now left him with foggy importance. She relived

ARTHUR BYRD

that last day they were together, and though still harboring animosity about how Lee had treated Brad, she knew the right thing happened.

The normal routine in place, Glenna was organizing for dinner as she gave direction to Vic. "Darling, can you help me set the table? Lucy isn't feeling well, and I want her to rest for now. I made some homemade soup, and I'll take her a bowl later."

"Sure. I'm done with my homework anyway. We having salad?"

"Yeah, some sliced pears with grated cheese. I've already got them set up on plates."

A little cheer came to Vic. "Oh good, my favorite. Yum."

Glenna saw the opportunity for a personal moment, so she eased into a chat. "I never got to ask you what really happened with you and Brad; it all ended so sudden like, and you've been a little down ever since. Is everything okay?"

Vic felt relief, as she needed to talk to her mom. "Everything is fine. It's only that things stopped so quickly, and I wasn't quite ready in my mind." Her words faded at the end.

Glenna maintained an unemotional stance. "I know you need your privacy, darling, and you don't have to explain anything to me, but if there is something I can help with, I'm always here."

"Yeah, I know. I keep replaying the whole thing in my head and trying to see what I did wrong," Vic said.

"Well, honey, maybe you didn't do anything wrong. Maybe it simply happened, and it's for the best. Or maybe Brad was the one that did something wrong. You know you're too hard on yourself, and you put too much pressure on trying to be a perfectionist. Heck, I ought to know; I always did the same thing."

Vic's mood brightened. "You're so right. I do that to myself all the time. It's like I don't think I'll be good enough, so sometimes it's easier not to try than fail."

Her mother did not like those words. "That's the wrong way to see things. You know I've always encouraged you to do your best, but I also wanted you to try new things. You know, like when you tried out for the chess team. You did a lot better than you thought you would, and that third-place trophy on the mantel is proof."

100

"I know," Vic said slowly. "But I get tired of not being really good at anything—As and Bs, not straight As, cute but not beautiful, that sort of stuff."

"Victoria, I have to tell you that is the silliest thing I've ever heard you say. Do you know how many girls would love to have your looks and your brains? You have the full package, sweetheart, and you don't have to be a combination of Marilyn Monroe and Bobby Fischer to feel good about yourself. You're not missing anything you need."

A slight tear formed in Vic's eye. "You always make things so simple, like anyone could figure it out, but when I think about things, they always seem so hard, like I'm not smart enough."

Now Glenna began to wrestle her motherly emotions. "Goodness, darling, you are a lot smarter than me, and prettier too. You're more educated now than I was at your age, and I had to work hard at school. Years ago, I finally got tired of beating myself up and figured that if I was ever going to be happy, I'd better start noticing the good things in my life and stop concentrating on the bad things or on stuff I didn't have. You know who helped me see that? Your grandpa, that's who."

Vic's mouth gaped open. "Really? Grandpa? He hardly ever says anything; I can't imagine he would explain something like that to you."

"Well, he did. You know, you didn't get all the outdoor time with him that Lee did, or even I did growing up. That's too bad. My dad is quite a profound person, but he doesn't express that too easily, at least not in talk. But you should see what he can write; it is so beautiful. Years ago he wrote me a letter about the woman I could be, and it was one of the most amazing things I ever read. Unfortunately, it got thrown out accidentally years ago, and it broke my heart. Anyway, when he comes up for Christmas, why don't you spend a few minutes alone with Dad. Shoot, ask him a couple of hard questions and make him squirm a little; that's kind of fun in itself." And the two women squealed with laughter at the thought of big, tough Tom having a hard time answering life questions from a complex teenager.

Glenna took a fresh view of her daughter, the sensitive, doubtful side she kept so quietly guarded behind a sharp tongue and a capable persona. She remembered her own adolescence and the pain of rejection because she was overweight, the trauma of self-discovery that still lingered unresolved in the shadowy parts of her life. Vic needed guidance, but unveiling her own vulnerabilities left Glenna afraid.

In a rare moment of deep self-investigation, Glenna questioned her own ability to cope with her ever-widening estrangement from Harold. And there too was the old nemesis roaming her thoughts, the pervasive sense of failure with her life. What if Harold decided to walk out? As she looked at her daughter's timid steps forward into womanhood, Glenna knew she had no time for weakness; Vic needed a mother's strength.

With what looked like fragile trepidation, Vic, with hands to her lips as if praying, took a step toward her mom. "Brad wanted me to have sex, but I said no. That's why we argued in the parking lot."

Rich, hot blood swarmed into Glenna's shocked demeanor. She paused to allow equilibrium and then instinctively held out her arms to her daughter, and Vic's soft whimper soaked into Glenna as medicine for the spirit. Brushing her daughter's bangs aside, Glenna studied the girl's pale face and hungry eyes, and she knew there was undiscovered strength they each shared and yet hadn't found a way to touch fully. A gentle kiss on the forehead, a mother's anointment for the long journey ahead, and the wordless moment began its long linger as memory.

III.

The days before Christmas filled as Tom labored to put his world back together. Taking almost everything out of the kitchen and the sitting area, he cleaned the entire cabin, meticulously getting rid of all the dusty flour particles everywhere in the cabin. Soon, he sewed the ripped cushions, threw out the cracked dishes, and replaced anything damaged. His world reordered, an improved mood followed. But soon, concerns slipped beneath the contentment. What would the holiday journey produce? Should he go see Sheriff Barker and plead for an extension? So without realizing, Tom soon busied himself with distractions, not noticing that these concerns were not being addressed. Soon enough, he would find a way; he always had.

Having his truck running again gave Tom a new sense of hope. He could go to town when he liked or pick up supplies without having to wait for Mike's sporadic visits. Tom even went to the pool hall for a game of snooker and a fresh rack of lies from his old buddies. Over those red and colored billiard balls, Tom discovered who had fallen on hard times, who ended up in the Cornucopia retirement home, and who simply hung around without much to do or say but spent a lot of time working at it. The proximity of people didn't annoy Tom so badly with that powerful urge to disappear so often gripping him these past years.

Mike continued his visits, and projects together with Tom took their normal slow pace. They replaced the steps to the deck at Mike's house in town. Then they extended the porch off the tool shed to accommodate the new radial arm saw and gas-powered generator Mike inherited from an uncle in Gulfport. And the two men hung the swing from the big chinaberry limb.

All the effort leveling the two ropes seemed too much trouble, but Tom humored Mike, and soon the new touch of hominess brightened the yard so overfilled with functionality. A summary judgment captured the mood. "Geez, looks like regular people live here now," Mike said. The ripened message passed as Tom could only think of what Oui might say if she could see the new addition.

Each visit, Mike pumped the ropes hard to swing high. Tom observed, wondering if his friend could see over the tree line out to the next world. The regular event always made Tom chuckle to see the old man swishing away as if ten years old, and he admired how Mike could still find the happiness in ordinary moments.

Never tempted to swing, Tom didn't want to look foolish. For him, the ticking of daily time became trudging, a weighty journey of thought mired in the passing ordinariness of life. He had largely forgotten how to function without that containerizing boundary where responses to everyday moments struggle with habitual patterns of analysis and classification. For him, home wasn't so much a place but a state of awareness where comfort settles around menial events rather than things fun. Seeing Mike kick his feet and pump those ropes brought back lost youth and the simple joy Tom had known as a boy. So he relaxed and taught himself to disallow the immediate reaction of foolishness. More and more, Tom learned to suspend, and then gradually, unpredicted happiness leaked back into the present, and without realizing, he didn't feel so alone or aware of his world shrinking.

One crisp morning on his way up from the boat, Tom noticed sunlight bouncing off the white board so luminously that he actually put down the cords and sinkers he carried and took a seat in the swing. His weight pulled against the solitary limb above, but the swing was strong. Looking up into the old tree, he recognized the familiar ill-formed branches as the shadowy figure he could see from the porch each day at dawn, but today the old crone looked so different, so much more inviting, alive in the sunlight, flexing her strength against the challenge of the swing. And Tom felt eager to play.

With feet lifted and a couple of pumps, the slight breeze intoxicated the old man. Ropes against the weight, arms pulling, the lightness of youth lifted him higher as the earth disappeared. Untied from the world, leaning toward the sky so blue and deep, then the pause of going backward, Tom was happy to have forgotten the utility of daylight and instead enjoyed a moment of escape. He suddenly understood why children need swings as he flew himself into the newness of life, and for half an hour, Tom heaved in the breeze, a child at recess.

For an instant, time froze, and Tom pushed Oui in the churchyard swing. Then, slowly her laughing in the sunlight disappeared as he stopped pulling the ropes, her laughter hiding in the trees. Where had those years gone, those images lost until now? But her presence lingered in the mild euphoria, her hand still touching his soul. And even as the white ash swing glided slowly, Tom's reaching thoughts sailed again into the thrill of memory's daylight.

Moments later, stepping onto the porch, he noticed the swing still moving gently, and settling into his chair, an unknown idea floated into his head. An innocent spore at first, so tiny as to remain largely undiscovered by the hovering rule of consciousness, but the idea urged itself to fruition and then hid deeply beneath words and reason. In an instant, Tom no longer dreaded facing Newland or even the sheriff. A new will had begun inoculating him against fear, and though he did not yet fully comprehend his new power, he knew he would use it.

IV.

Two days before the trip to Glenna's house, Mike trudged to the cabin with bad news.

"But why can't you go? Glenna is looking for both you and me for Christmas; she'll be disappointed," Tom said.

"Look, I understand, but I can't go. My sister had to cancel her trip to Memphis because of her bursitis; can't make the bus ride. I'm not leaving her alone for Christmas."

"Well, how 'bout if she goes to Glenna's with us?" Tom pleaded.

"Don't be crazy. She's in pain, can't travel. Besides, if we go off to see that worthless Don Newland, what's she going to do? Sit around Glenna's all by herself? Maybe you and me can make another trip later in the spring."

"Nope, that ain't gonna work," Tom insisted. "I'm going if I have to do it alone. Hell, you'd think I'd know by now I gotta do everything myself." And Tom stormed off the porch down to the river.

Familiar with his friend's overreaction, Mike remained calm. Long ago he'd learned that there are times for talking reason to Tom and other times when words become incendiary elements best kept away from the fuse of Tom's anger. So instead Mike strolled down to the swing and waited quietly.

Twenty minutes later, up the path came the perfect image of a chastised schoolboy with a head full of humiliation.

"I'm sorry; you're right," Tom said. "I'll head on up to Glenna's and see everybody. Then we'll see about Don later."

"That's good," Mike said. "It'll be fine just seeing them grandkids. That's what you should keep focused on." The moment passed, but a devilish grin on Tom's face hinted that he had a different plan.

Though wanting to avoid discussing the potential trip to Newland's house, Mike spoke before his brain had fully engaged. "Listen, if you do decide to go see Don, you ought to work through how you want the conversation to go. You know how you fly off the handle sometimes." Mike sensed he'd insulted Tom, so he maneuvered quickly. "You know, since I won't be there to pour cold water on you if you go catching on fire."

Tom was already irritated. "Look, you old goat, I don't need you there like some kind of nagging wife. I can take care of myself. Hell, I ain't no kid, you know."

Though he'd won the spar, Mike wanted to make sure Tom understood fully. "You see, that's exactly what I'm talking about right there, shooting off your mouth without your brain being loaded. Damn, Tom, you can't be doing stuff like that with strangers. It scares them, they think you're crazy, and I ain't sure they're wrong."

Both men went silent as they digested the exchange, but after a minute, Tom stood looking as if a whole new thought had captivated him.

"Awright, I'm fine. But listen, I got one more thing that's been bothering me."

"What's that?" Mike asked with piqued interest.

"Well, you see ..." But in midthought, Tom paused to look out the window at the smokehouse, then abruptly walked outside without a word.

The midsentence departure left Mike wondering what had happened, and he had an unsettling sense that something big had occurred. Now he needed to find out what Tom had on his mind.

After a few minutes, Tom wandered back into the kitchen, chipper as a chipmunk at a bird feeder.

"Okay there, fellow, now that we got that business out of the way, what do ya say we go pull us a big boy off the trotline before you head back to town? I got a new spot, and it's been working good for me." The moody countenance from earlier completely gone, Tom now acted like he'd had two pots of coffee.

Though important details might have been fumbled, Mike didn't want to sour Tom's pleasant mood with probing questions, especially since the news that he wouldn't be going up to Hattiesburg had gone so well, so he decided to let things drift. There hadn't been a big argument, so what could be wrong with taking a nice fish home for dinner? How could that be a bad thing?

The afternoon passed with fried fish and a couple of nice fillets for the freezer. Opening the truck door, Mike took a pack of gum out of his pocket then noticed his old friend standing dreamlike in the sunlight, happy to be in his world where he could control things the way he liked. Here was a lucky man, a free person living his fantasy life of escape and enjoying perfect synchronization with the natural world. Mike appreciated what his oldest friend truly was at that instant, a river dreamer, and he studied his crotchety ally while a flickering thought skipped through his head that a person could do worse than be a river dreamer. Yep, a lot worse.

And with those silent words, Mike readied himself for the ride. But before he left, he wanted to give Tom one more chance.

"'Fore I leave, I wanted ask you something. You said earlier there was another thing you wanted to talk about. Then you took off to the smokehouse without telling me." Tom looked perplexed.

"I don't remember. Didn't I tell you already?" Tom said. "I think I did. Anyway, it don't matter." And without another word, Tom disappeared into the cabin. Sure his friend would remember later, Mike let the matter pass as he noted a plan to revisit the lapse another day.

V.

Harold beamed, as proud of the Chevelle as he was of his kids, maybe more so, as he behaved more naturally with machinery than he did with people, or so Lee always thought.

"You like this color?" Harold asked. "I tell you, I think it came out great. That pale yellow with these black pinstripes looks fine to me, much better than that canary color. And these mags with the baby moons, bud, this is a muscle car."

"I know, Dad. Can't wait to drive it." Lee had drifted into heaven.

"Soon, soon. I want to wait till this cold weather is past and the streets ain't slippery. Then we'll take her for a spin. I got to leave on the twenty-sixth for a run up to Portland, but maybe when I get back, the weather won't be so gloomy." Harold never had a talent for intimate conversation, so he slipped in the bad news about leaving the day after Christmas while Lee was distracted.

"Aw, really? You gotta leave that quick? But you just got here."

"Hey, gotta make a buck, right? How do you think we paid for this baby? She ain't been cheap to fix up, you know." Lee listened to his father and once again recognized that money and things had priority. People were important but more like a spare tire than chrome wheels.

Clearly disheartened, Lee tried to be upbeat. "I know. But I was hoping we could go hunting with Grandpa, go out to the old Eli place and stomp up a deer maybe."

"Naw, can't do it; got to be gone," Harold said, relieved. "Maybe you and Tom can go; he'll be antsy to get out of the house."

Lee tried not to show his feelings. "Yeah, I'll get Grandpa to go with me."

Problem solved, Harold tried to make small talk. "Your mom told me you got into it with Vic's boyfriend. Said you slapped him for getting rough with her."

"It was nothing, a few words, no big deal." Lee did not want to have this talk.

Looking almost proud, Harold continued. "If I was you, I'd stay out of Victoria's business. I'm pretty sure she don't appreciate you interfering with her love life. Most women prefer a man who keeps his mouth shut; they like it that way."

"Yeah, thanks. Good stuff, Dad." Lee almost revealed his sarcasm, but Harold had moved on to adjusting a seat lever as Lee wandered out of the garage.

In the kitchen, Glenna had a warm smile; she'd been watching from the kitchen window.

"I see you got to spend time with your dad. What did you men talk about?" Glenna donned her most cheerful persona.

"Nothin' much. He gave me some advice on how to stay out of Vic's business. Said I should keep my mouth shut 'cause that's what women want. He's a good motivator, you know." And before Glenna could respond, Lee left the kitchen.

A tear welled as she looked out the window again, Harold under the car, looking up at the engine, intent on finding that thing that was so interesting, apparently not even aware his son had left the garage.

Chapter 6

I.

On the morning of Christmas Eve, Tom awakened early as usual and arranged all his things for the visit. Since Mike wasn't making the trip, a strange freedom to plan the day the way he wanted had settled over Tom as he decided to leave an hour early, wanting to drop by a place he hadn't seen in several years.

A quick lunch at Roy's, and the taste of root beer still lingered as he remembered all the years of stopping to cool off with a frosty root beer draft. Days of Oui and Glenna, even boyhood years drifted through as the hamburger stand stood testament to the passing of his small-town life, and the stream of time these images captured filled Tom with nostalgia.

This overcast day instead of shooting out to Interstate 59 for the hour drive to Hattiesburg, Tom decided instead to take the old Highway 11, the one he'd used much of his life before the new roadway bypassed the small towns of Poplaville, Lumberton, and Purvis. Filled with sentimental holiday emotions, a slight detour to see some of the old sights seemed appropriate.

But before leaving Picayune, Tom took a right at the Methodist church and wandered back into a neighborhood he used to spend a lot of time in when he was younger but now rarely had reason to visit. Onto Currant Street he veered, and like the beginning of a movie, his life opened up to the past when he was in high school and dating Oui.

Slowly he approached the big white Victorian house with the wraparound porch and the bowed-out bedroom where Oui had been raised. Giant azaleas still grew three times the height of a man, and their lush greenery of small leaves stood dormant against the old house in the winter chill.

The huge live oak growing outside Oui's old bedroom hovered majestically in the side yard with its horizontal arms pointing directly at any onlookers. Nearly six feet in diameter, this giant had already been full grown when the house was built in 1906, and that permanence soaked as medicine into Tom's soul. On the other side of the structure near the back door, two other giants spread deep shadows on the back of the house, and mossy green squeezed from cracks in the cement patio now severely uprooted.

Tom wasn't sure if Oui's sister had moved out to Cornucopia, as he'd lost track of his wife's family and felt a little estranged even looking at the yard again. Around the side, he saw the three pecan trees where he and Oui had picked a million nuts off the ground to make chocolate fudge. And there the lovely fig tree that produced the largest, most delicious purple fruit that Oui canned as fig preserves and gave away at Christmas.

All around the cool air under the trees nestled up to the house, providing an aura of the past. Yet the place seemed distant even as he thought he heard Oui's voice round the corner and imagined sitting on the soft grass chewing sprouts rich with sweetness while the smell of fried chicken wafted from the kitchen. Was that Oui's mother singing "The Old Rugged Cross"? Those innocent years had their own angst as he remembered in tenth grade Oui's dad dying of a stroke, his bedroom inside just above where Tom stood in the yard.

Foggy scenes interleaved everywhere, voices and laughter forever hanging in the quiet of Tom's stalled life now awakened in the shady chill. This place was a home for Tom, somewhere he'd known love yet now which stood in exile, and the numbness from another lost sanctuary passed through his spirit.

A mockingbird sang her complex song from a barren dogwood near the front door, out of step herself with the season as a car horn sounded up the street near Mike's old homestead. Tom had forgotten too that simple house where he'd sat on the porch a thousand times with Mike's mom sipping iced tea. Looking down this street became a visit to the museum of his youth, and without ever moving, Tom visited friends from this home neighborhood where he never lived.

Soon a misty drizzle prodded a quicker step around the house back to the truck. All those people in his life, girlfriend and wife, her mother and father, the countless aunts and uncles he'd shared Sunday homemade ice cream with, where were those lives he could almost hear? And Tom had difficulty remembering who he was, or why he stood lost in this saturating cold.

As the truck turned over responsively, the heater brought gratitude as it pushed out its reminder that Tom wasn't alone. And a last glance at the azaleas paused for the season triggered the germinating thought begun days ago at the swing. Stretching its tentacles of memory, the idea ingested fresh energy from the winter abandonment, and it began to grow. Still not exposed to words, the inkling had begun to live, gnawing now at his fading spirit and feeding on the ambrosia of despair.

Soon back on the highway, each road sign took him back to his college freshman year, the forsaken scholarship to Mississippi State, the yearning for Oui waiting back in Picayune.

Tom had never imagined then that Oui would one day leave him, yet here all alone he drove his faithful Chevy through the canyons of their shared past, and the solitude of oneness wandered the walls of time.

The turn to Smithfield Lake where all those picnics sorted the lives of two teenagers peering at adulthood, and a vast cavern of memory opened before the dauntless truck. There too the day Oui broke up with him, giving back his high school class ring. His clueless recoil into dismay. But Oui said it best they not rush. Life could have ended for him that day as he misplaced the unwavering image of their future together. What a child he had been, a boy acting like a man hoping to be loved in a way he couldn't even describe. He'd yielded his power to Oui, given her control of his happiness because he thought that was the way to win her, to capture her love. But now neither those days nor the present made sense, and Tom muddled along as a latent pathogen of doubt stirred in his soul.

The noise of the rain beat against the metal roof, and Tom appreciated the solace of distraction, fixating now on the squeaky wiper blades panting to keep pace with the downpour, until magically Glenna's house appeared. Pulling into the driveway, Tom realized he hadn't even noticed the past twenty minutes of driving. Then an unexpected thought—without Mike around, maybe he should ask Glenna's advice about visiting Newland. But Tom could barely remember if he was still angry or not, so he wasn't quite sure what to ask.

II.

With the ringing doorbell, Lee sprang to the sound even before his dad or Lucy could begin to move. Then, a silhouette appeared in the sunlight on the porch, Tom offered the bouquet of yellow flowers he'd brought from Picayune.

"For me, Grandpa? You shouldn't have," Lee joked as he hugged Tom's neck with a strong grasp to show him a sincere welcome.

"No, dummy; they're for your dad." And they both laughed as Tom stepped inside, feeling triumphant with his smooth entrance and clever remark.

Soon Tom was enjoying *Miracle on 34th Street* with the girls and Harold, waiting for Glenna's return from the store.

"I see we have company!" Glenna said. "Oh, Dad, it's so good to see you here. How was the trip? That drizzle earlier was so messy, but up north in Tupelo they're having sleet." After a long hug and a kiss on the cheek, Glenna brought Tom a nice mug of hot chocolate.

"Here, try this; I got some great new coco as a Christmas gift, and it makes the best hot chocolate. Yum. Listen, relax a while and let me unpack my groceries. Then come on in the kitchen and let's catch up a bit. No rush."

Moments later Tom followed scrambling to find pleasantries and trying to appear normal. "So, how is everything? Looks like the family is doing pretty well, and it's good to see Harold."

Glenna hoped to chat more about Harold, but for now she merely set the scene.

"Yeah, we're all fine. Harold doesn't get to spend much time with us these days, but we understand." She looked as if she was getting emotional, then Glenna quickly changed the subject. "And that Lucy, she's a handful, I'll tell you. That girl is going to be a tornado when she's a teenager; hope I have the energy left to deal with her."

Tom saw his daughter's edginess. "You know," he said, "I can see a good dose of my mom in Lucy. She's got that 'I'm always right' look about her—even overshadows Victoria sometimes, doesn't she?"

Glenna picked up the idea. "Actually, that's what I wanted to chat with you about, to see if I could get you to help me a little. Vic has been really down lately since she and her boyfriend broke up. He calls her, but she won't have anything to do with him. Brad even had a little run-in with Lee, so everything got complicated."

Tom shook his head. "I see. So what do you want me to do? I don't know much about women these days; I'm a little out of practice."

"Yeah, I understand," Glenna said. "But what I mean is that Lee came back from his visit with you so charged up and confident that he's been like a different person ever since. You've always had lots of time with him, being a boy of course, but I was hoping you could find a few minutes just for Victoria, to encourage her a little. She's so smart, but she doesn't believe in herself and depends too much on what other people think."

Instantly Tom understood. "I see. Well sure, I'd love to chat with her a bit. What say I ask her to go to the store with me to get something, and we can talk while we're gone."

"That would be great. In fact, this gallon of milk I bought has a leak in it, so you could take that back and get us another. Perfect excuse. Vic can show you the new grocery store over by the high school."

"Sounds like a plan," Tom said with commitment. "By the way, everything okay with Lee? I thought we might go for a walk in the woods sometime. He said his dad has to leave the day after tomorrow, and it seems to bother the boy a little."

"Lee's at that age when he'd like to be treated more like a man than a boy," Glenna said, "but Harold still thinks of him as being six years old; sometimes he doesn't realize how the kids have grown."

A swath of pain spread across Glenna's face, so Tom tried to steer the conversation back to a less sensitive zone. "I have to keep reminding myself too of how they've grown up. Maybe I can catch up with both of them while I'm here."

So, after making an excuse about the damaged milk jug, Glenna sent Tom and Vic on a mission. He drove so she could enjoy being out of the house that for days had been nothing but preparation.

Still warm and cozy, the truck felt comfortable, so after a few minutes Tom eased into his chat. "So, how's things going with you at school? I hear you're a smart one with the books."

Vic's eyes immediately looked away before she responded. "Not really, I do okay. Lots of girls are smarter."

With the opening so apparent, Tom moved cautiously. "I doubt that. Even if they were, I bet they're not half as pretty." Victoria gave a half grin then looked blankly out the window. As the high school appeared on the right, he had an idea.

"This is your school isn't it, hon? Let's pull over and let me take a look. Seems like it's bigger than I remember."

"Yeah, it probably is. They added a music and arts building and made a separate parking lot for the faculty. Some kids got caught messing with a teacher's car, and nobody can go near their stuff now."

With a chuckle, Tom took the big step. "So Glenna tells me Lee and your boyfriend had a little scuffle; what was that all about?"

Victoria turned to look at the school. "Nothing really. Brad grabbed me, and Lee saw it. Lost his temper and kinda threatened Brad." Her attitude seemed curiously unemotional to Tom.

"Sounds like a good thing," Tom said. "Why'd the little punk, I'm mean young fellow, grab you?" His deliberate smile relaxed the girl even more.

A prepared story was ready for sharing. "Nothing. We had a little disagreement, no big deal. I could have handled things myself." The weak tone spoke more than her words.

"I'm sure that's true; you're a strong girl. You remind me of my mom. And, buddy, let me tell you nobody ever laid a hand on her." My aunt Katie told me once how some girls were giving her a hard time, and

Saralynn, who was only fifteen at the time, came out of the school and saw what was happening. She singled out the biggest girl, and before anyone knew it, Mom had her on the ground. Dang near broke the girl's shoulder."

Vic turned toward Tom. "You know, Grandpa, Mom gave Lee this whole box of letters from Granny Saralynn, lots of old stuff, and Lee has read every one of them ten times. He's been showing them to me too. I saw where she said a bunch of times, 'You can do and be anything thing you want, but you have to believe in yourself first.'"

Her comment caught Tom off guard. "Haven't heard that line in a long time. Mom used it all the time in her letters, usually when I was a little down and confused. She had a way of being optimistic."

"Was it real for her? I mean did she really believe that everything is possible stuff?" An earnest plea bled through his granddaughter's words, and it touched Tom's heart.

"Mom meant it. She saw the possibility of every situation and focused on it knowing she could make anything happen. To be honest, a lot of the time she was off base and what she wanted was wacky, but no matter, once she locked onto something, that's what was going to happen."

An unexpected laugh popped out as Tom remembered his mom. "Years ago, she got banned from school for yelling at a teacher. Of course, it was because I got in a little trouble being stupid, but she came home and told all of us she was going to run for the school board. Three days later, she had her bowling league, her garden club, the ladies' reading club, and practically every disgruntled parent in the county out putting up signs for her and writing editorial letters to the *Picayune Tribune*. It was a blitz, and she drove it like she was running for governor."

"Did she win?" Victoria was genuinely excited.

"Hell yeah, I mean, of course. Mom didn't know what failure was. She got the fellow that banned her blackballed from every social function in town even before his mistress came forward and ratted him out. Ugly, but Mom never looked back. Sat on the board for ten years; that's why we got a girls' track team in Picayune—because she demanded that if the boys had one, then so should the girls. When she retired from the board, they gave her a key to the city, and her picture still hangs in the administration building in the Great Citizens of Picayune section."

Vic was ecstatic. "That's awesome. Mom always told me Saralynn went through life like a lawnmower, leaving everything nice and neat but always exactly the way she wanted it."

"Definitely. And she liked being that mower." A rapport had begun to build, and Tom was sure he could help his granddaughter.

"Did you know Lee is getting pretty darn good at basketball?" Vic asked seriously. "He's one of the best players on the B team, and this is only his first year."

"Glenna told me. I'm not surprised, as Saralynn was an unbelievable athlete. You know, girlie, we all got those genes somewhere in us." These words surprised even Tom.

"Not me, I can't dribble. But I can run fast. I've been thinking of going out for the track team, but I don't know; most kids start in ninth grade and get better every year."

Tom put his arm around his granddaughter's shoulder. "That may be true, but it doesn't mean you can't do it anyway. Is that what you want to do? If it is, then do it. Focus on the doing part."

For a good half hour, they talked about things Vic was good at doing, like math and chess, and with a little nudge from Tom, she declared making the track team to be the new goal.

Now ready to get on to the store, Vic opened the truck door, then leaned her head in. "Brad tried to make me have sex with him. When I wouldn't, he started saying mean things about me and other boys at school. That's why we broke up." The confession had little emotion to it, so Tom knew the girl was adjusting.

He shut off the engine he'd just cranked. "See. Told you were strong, and there's the proof. If you want to be something in life, you got to be decisive. Maybe right now all you should focus on is running. You can worry about boys later when your feet get tired." And with that, they eased on to the store for fresh milk.

Neither Tom nor Victoria had much else to say, and Tom drifted back to those years with female talk around him about people and feelings, and he knew those times with Oui, and Glenna, and his mom had done his soul good. He felt proud he'd been able to talk to Vic and even a little amazed that it seemed so easy, but she had stiff challenges ahead as a woman in this slanted old world, and he worried that she needed that strong hand from someone to help her. Maybe it was time to have a little chat with Harold as well.

The quiet ride gave one more moment for Victoria to ask a question. "Why did Mom give all those letters to Lee? Did you ask her to?"

"No, I didn't. Forgot I even gave them to Glenna after Mom died. Not even sure which ones Lee has, as I never went to the trouble to organize them too well. I reckon Glenna was trying to help Lee's genealogy project, but it sounds like they might have helped you both. That would make my mom happy. She'd be real proud to know someone still cares to read through those things because she spent a lot of time scribbling thoughts and little poetry tidbits to all kinds of people."

"Grandpa," Vic said softly. "I think maybe I got a little of the poet from Saralynn in me too. I won our English class competition for memorizing poems, and the teacher said my performance of Wordsworth's 'Lines Written in Early Spring' was the best in all four classes."

"Really now, that's great. Mom used to read me all kinds of things when I was young—Tennyson, Whitman, Blake, Cummings. Heck, it was always something about nature and the cycles of life. She wrote some poetry too, but she really loved to read out loud; used to drive my dad crazy reciting things at the dinner table. As a boy, when I'd work in my little garden, she'd sit on the steps and read Walt Whitman to me out loud. Funny how I never thought that was strange at all, but as I look back now, people must have thought Mom was pretty weird, especially my dad. She never quite cared what people thought of her; only did what she wanted. I loved that about Mom.

"Vic, honey, you better believe if my mom was here right now, she'd grab you and hug you so hard your eyeballs would pop. She'd tell you to park all that wrong-headed thinking about what you can't do and get yourself busy making your life important. Heck, Mom wouldn't tolerate laziness or stupidity, and, darling, you ain't either. You're a slice of Saralynn as sure as I'm a grumpy old fool." Both got a good laugh but also a shot of hope for the soul.

After he parked the truck, Tom gave Victoria one of those rare hugs he didn't often feel comfortable sharing with people, but he too needed this day.

"Oh yeah, one more thing," Tom said. "You tell that Brad fella that he don't want me to come visit him if he bothers you again."

III.

The remainder of the Christmas Eve festivities went smoothly as the family told stories about each other and the old days. Eating being the most popular activity, Glenna had baked pumpkin, pecan, and apple pies, plus all kinds of dips and things to munch. All afternoon, the family sat around the kitchen table enjoying the tastes of food and familiarity with barely a ripple of disagreement.

Having dreaded so much company, Tom relaxed, surprised how quickly time sped. Though the two girls got into one big spat about who helped out most around the house, and Harold got a little drunk on beer and began mouthing off about how much money Glenna spent on frivolous things like Christmas ornaments and a nativity scene spread out on the hall table, everyone knew not to look too closely at faults this day.

All through the afternoon, Tom studied how each family member carved out a little personal world and lived comfortably within its parameters, often negotiating with each other about boundaries. Clearly the two girls had their own argot about women's matters, nail polish, moisturizers, shampoos, and the like being the most basic but also the more sophisticated perspective of how women were breaking through the traditional boundaries of society. Victoria was sure Mississippi would one day have a woman governor, and Lucy insisted she would earn all the money in her family and have her husband stay home and cook for her.

The ideas that swept around the table generated a torrent of passion with everyone offering a unique point of view. For Tom, seeing the family so vigorous patched the emotional hole left by his guilt of having abandoned them for three years. Though he joined in the fray a time or two, the pace sped too quickly, and he preferred listening and watching the faces of the girls.

Lee too participated, but he talked about basketball and hunting, as those were the two things he most loved at the moment. He enjoyed the social contact of sport, its physical demands, and the competition, but when talking about the woods, his love of nature merged with the deep recesses of his individual spirit.

"No you got it all wrong," he reprimanded Lucy. "Fishing on the river isn't about survival of the fittest; it's about letting the earth talk, whisper secrets of who we are and what the world really means." Tom thought Lee poetic as thoughts of his mother reading Whitman flowed through his head.

His granddaughters' conversation took a different businesslike path. Vic lectured Lucy on stereotypes, but Lucy had her own ideas.

"It's more than traditional roles, Vic. Women have carried the burden of family and will continue to, but men have those responsibilities too. We can't accept that one person earns and another person nests."

With inspired response, Vic raised her voice. "Right. It isn't the responsibility of men to support women; it's the responsibility of both to support the home. Men can't skate on this obligation anymore, thinking all they have to do is bring home a paycheck." Victoria's authority sat everyone back in their chairs, and Tom smiled, thinking this was the same doubting young girl he'd talk to earlier. Harold slumped into the chair.

"Yeah, I know." Lee wasn't finished. "But even in a team, everybody has to have a specific role. If everyone does everything, then that sets up confusion. There is a productivity problem with looking at everyone exactly the same."

"Look, you two, this isn't a sociology class, so let's just chill a little, okay?" Glenna had heard enough about abstract social concepts.

The veiled reference Victoria implied about her parents intrigued Tom, and Lee's uninspired defense of traditional roles sounded forced. This family was hiding secrets behind this atmosphere of openness and sharing, and the idea poked Tom's guilt about his own secrets.

Everyone obscured and shared, and the paradox felt normal as Tom silently drifted away to an image of his mom watching the quicksilver divide then rejoin. His life on the river needed more connection. He needed to restore his attitude of pursuit so drained lately by concern of eviction. And again he thought how nature these past years had become his family. How when he'd first moved to the cabin, the absence of human contact and his immersion into life alone had recharged him the way he now saw Lee invigorated by his success in sports. But Tom knew his energy was not recharging as it had in earlier years and considered that perhaps absorbing the exuberance of his grandchildren might help. So, he sat collecting their thoughts and energy while pondering a whole new project.

But a sinking truth wrapped its grip around Tom as he realized he no longer had a permanent home. On the river, his world had reduced to a forest cabin with a river flowing past. So the emergence of darkness reached through the long shadows of the day to touch Tom alone in this crowd of family, and as he studied his daughter and her husband ignoring each other, he wondered what inadvertent lessons he'd taught Glenna with his withdrawal.

IV.

The noise became so loud that Glenna asked everyone to clear out for an hour while she finished the goose. People went all directions, but when Tom saw Harold slip out the back door, he followed, making small talk about long haul driving and basketball. Sensing that Harold was ready to head to the garage to fiddle with the Chevelle, Tom decided to probe deeper.

"You know, when Lee came down to the river, he talked a lot about how he missed you 'cause you were always gone. Vic told me the same thing. Of course, you realize these kids are gonna be grown 'fore you know it." Not meaning to be as direct as the words sounded, Tom still placed a dead-eye stare on Harold, hoping to elicit a response. Then he pressed further. "Seems Glenna is pretty lonesome too. She's got a sadness to her."

Anger sparked. "Well, maybe if her dad hadn't abandoned her, Glenna wouldn't be so sad," Harold said. Instantly Tom moved toward Harold with his fist balled, only to be interrupted as the back door opened.

"Oh good, Harold, please help with this goose. It's too heavy for me," Glenna said.

The two men glared but said nothing. Realizing yet another social blunder, Tom wanted to withdraw, so flushed with emotion he walked around to the front porch.

In the kitchen, Harold moved the goose onto the carving platter but hesitated before going back outside. His words strained under a tight, angry tone.

"Your father gave me a hard time about not being around for you and the kids. Did you say something to him about me?" Instinctively Glenna looked at the door to the den to see if anyone was listening.

"Of course not. I never would. Dad makes his own conclusions, but he's not far wrong. You treat this place like a hotel." She paused, feeling the flame of emotion. "You don't love us, do you?" she said. Almost to tears and terrified Harold might lose his temper, she moved quickly to the sink, anticipating the worst. Harold did something astonishing.

Stepping within two feet of Glenna, he whispered, "I'm not around much because I thought you didn't want me here." She tried to react, but he placed his index finger to her lips. "Glenn, ever since Victoria was born, you've treated me like a second-class citizen. And with each child, it got worse. We ate what they wanted, went where they wanted; I never had a voice. All your affection was for them, and I figured you stopped loving me."

Unable to speak, Glenna's eyes filled with tears.

"You remember a few years ago when we went rafting down the river in Tennessee?" Harold said. "Well, I do. We walked up to the boat, and you, Lee, and Vic jumped in along with two other strangers. Luce wasn't there. I asked you where I was supposed to sit. You looked me dead in the eye and did that hitchhiker thumb thing like, 'Back there in another boat.' You know, Glenna, at that very moment, I knew I didn't matter."

Lucy barged into the kitchen, breaking the tension, but the truth had been freed, leaving Glenna and Harold looking at each other but unable to remember their lives together. Then he kissed her forehead and stepped through the back door, turning at the last moment to offer a quick wink.

V.

As Vic entered the kitchen, Glenna immediately assigned duties. "Please, girls, clear away these appetizers and set the table for dinner." Then turning to Lee: "You get the pleasure of clearing the table after dinner, so how about entertaining Dad a while. I know he wants to talk to you."

"Whatever you need, Mom." Leaving the kitchen, Lee paused waving Glenna into the hallway for a quiet word. "Mom, did you ever think of any Saralynn stories for me? Maybe some stuff I could ask grandpa about?" Realizing she'd forgotten her son's request, Glenna recovered quickly.

"Why, yes, I did; sorry, I've been so busy. I remember Aunt Katie told me about their neighborhood clubhouse when they were kids. Just pine straw and limbs. But every spring Saralynn would call a meeting for the annual raid on old man Parker's apricot plum trees. The kids waited until the fruit turned slightly yellow, so timing was important. Saralynn planned each invasion with military precision, assigning duties to each kid and organizing platoons to create diversion for Mr. Parker's dog, divert the local constable, everything. It was a real military exercise." Glenna paused to wipe her hands on her apron, so Lee piped up.

"So Granny Saralynn was kind of like the general in charge? Was she the oldest kid?"

"Not at all. There were some younger and many older, but Aunt Katie said everyone knew Saralynn was the planner and leader. It was always that way in her life; people looked to her instinctively for guidance."

Lee loved it. "Awesome. Think about it, a girl as general even in the early 1900s."

Glenna felt distracted. "Definitely. But we'll have to talk later; this goose has a date with my fillet knife, so you go talk to Grandpa." Lee instantly wondered did he have some of that same Saralynn bravado? Walking back to the den and hearing Glenna issue a new set of directives to the girls, he even had a flash of himself in a military uniform leading a charge into some future battle.

"Hey, Grandpa, come on up to my room; I want to show you something."

A little bored, Tom was happy for diversion. "What's that? You got a girlfriend stuffed under the bed?" Peculiar thought, Lee surmised, but Tom moved quickly up the stairs, leaving his red-faced grandson reminded of how talking to girls intimidated him and wondering what it would be like even to have a girlfriend.

"Have a seat—real comfy chair," Lee said.

"Yeah," Tom said. "I could take a nap here."

Thrilled to have Tom in his room, Lee became a chatterbox. "Oh, I have snoozed here plenty of times, especially when we had to read *Romeo and Juliet*; man, that stuff was awful. I don't even think it was in English." Catching himself, Lee realized he needed to focus. "Anyway I wanted to ask you something about Saralynn."

"Sure, son. Shoot."

"Don't know if Mom told you, but she gave me this whole box here of letters and stuff."

Immediately Tom picked up the old photos. "Would you look at that? I was pretty darn young then, and look how beautiful Mom was. See that sharp, tight look on her face? She always had that, like she was on alert at every moment, never relaxed completely, like some kind of wary animal."

The comment fascinated Lee. "Hmm, I see that. You know, I've read every one of these a bunch of times. Hard to make sense of the order 'cause most of them are about birthdays and stuff, but there are some interesting things."

"Like what?" Tom's face seemed to search back to this collection, trying to remember exactly what was there.

"This one, for instance, looks like it was written when you had left some job up in Yazoo City. Granny Saralynn talks about a Donald Newland and how she called him and chewed his rear end for treating you wrong. Do you remember any of that?" Being a trifle deceptive provided Lee with a jolt of excitement.

Tom turned red, and his voice tightened to a higher pitch. "What? Let me see that. This letter was in the box Glenna gave you?" Lee thought the comment odd.

"Yeah. But it was stuck in that book of poetry there."

Clearly Tom had become anxious, and to Lee he seemed suddenly confused. "Let me see."

Handing the book of American poetry to his grandpa, Lee said nothing.

The ragged, old book fell open to a familiar verse which Tom stared at in silence.

"Do you remember this letter?" Hoping for a fresh anecdote, Lee felt his pride swell at his masterful management of the Newland investigation.

But without any indication as to why, Tom became stern and his voice unemotional.

"Yes, I remember it. My best friend got me fired, so he could take my job. I was stupid for trusting him; my fault for being so gullible."

The pusillanimous tone in Tom's voice in conjunction with the secret knowledge of Newland's treachery irritated Lee in an unexpectedly volatile manner. "What? You're kidding, right? This is some kind of lesson you're trying to teach me about turning the other cheek and crap like that, right?" Lee leapt to his feet, a sudden rebuke instantly born, and though he paused to collect himself while having the clearheaded thought that he was overreacting, his surging emotions burst out of control.

"That's just bullshit, Grandpa. There's no way you were wrong because this jerk lied and got you fired. That guy's a traitor, and you should have beat his ass." Lee observed his eruption as if from across the room, admiring its vitriol and yet confused by the disrespect he couldn't seem to harness. In his mind, two people existed side by side, one railing against his grandpa's unfamiliar weakness and the other frothing to defend Tom against an unavenged enemy.

"Now calm down," Tom said. "You don't know the facts. Besides, beating him up wouldn't have changed anything, only gotten me arrested." Tom dropped his eyes to the floor as if he didn't believe his own words, again infuriating his grandson.

"Okay, what else don't I know? Tell me why you take the blame and a backstabber gets a pass. I want to hear it." Lee, again seeing himself as if from across the room watched Tom sink into the reading chair.

"Sit down, cool off." Tom tried to rally. "I'll tell you but not now. You're too worked up. Later. When we go hunting. That'll give me some time to think this through. I need to study it more." And for the first time in his life, Lee thought his grandfather looked small, and the image flowed from a fresh wellspring of guilt.

"Okay, guys. Come on down; this goose is cooked."

Chapter 7

I.

Christmas Eve dinner drifted past inside the hermetic enclosure of Tom's mind as he stared blankly. Echoes caromed with words and faces popping in and out, but he had little desire to engage. Barely glancing up throughout the whole meal, he simply became another person from the one who knocked at the door earlier in the day.

Once Lucy asked him a question about the drive up, but Tom didn't hear it, and later Glenna remarked on the nice red shirt he wore but again no response, not even a glance. Tom withdrew deeper into that place so inviting to him now, that repose out of the light where people couldn't see his fading will and where words lost their threat. He was on the river again as a boy, lying on his back in his boat, feeling the sunshine bathe his face and the exhaustion in his arms from rowing against the current. There too the smell of honeysuckle and the trill of river water lilted through the air. The dinner sounds now transformed to the gurgle of the creek tumbling along, of birds squawking and the scramble of squirrels racing through the leaves to hide. Here in his sanctuary, no one could enter, and Tom could not, or would not, leave.

Glenna became increasingly concerned. "Dad, are you okay?" Tom looked up at Glenna as if through boyish eyes, hoping it was his mother come to make the sickness leave.

"Here, have a sip of water." She said. "Everyone at the table stared at Tom's strangeness, and the heavy air suffocated his light breathing. Out of the corner of his eyes, everything had an angelic halo, blurring the family into a fixed, gawking frame that Tom struggled to understand.

"Only a bad headache." He said. "The drive up strained my eyes." Those words coming from an unfamiliar source took all his energy. As he attempted to stand, he noticed Lee's stare, thinking it odd, but he couldn't recall why.

Soon in the big easy chair with a plate of dessert, he listened carefully for that big gobbler he'd seen near his garden that morning. The funny stories and conversation at the table passed by as muted clouds of sound while Tom concentrated hard on tracking that wily turkey.

Then a breaking plate in the kitchen snapped his attention, and the disagreement with Lee resurfaced. Why had the boy gotten so angry? The insistent tug of confusion pulling against his will, Tom floundered to avoid becoming lost. Scrambled awareness spinning on a bicycle sprocket with no chain, sounds and images circled in blurred thought. Then something gripped, and the spiraling sensation gave way to a hum, steady, almost as if Tom could touch the levelness of the sound. He wanted to stand, to escape the swirling pull of thought, but instead slumped again, now seized by a moment of rest.

The meal ended almost in a whisper as everyone crept quietly to distant places in the house and Lee helped his mother clear the kitchen. Glenna didn't quite know what to say. "Did anything happen between you and Dad? He seemed disturbed when he came downstairs, like he was upset but didn't know why."

"We talked about some Newland fellow from Yazoo City," Lee said. "Seems Grandpa thinks he did the guy wrong."

II.

Morning arrived as the ceiling hinted a pearly white, and the Christmas tree left a sunset hue over the room. Quickly to his feet scanning the room, all was in order, so Tom sat again in the easy chair where he'd slept, the bizarre ending to the previous day now echoing as only a dream.

The burden of embarrassment returned when he remembered Lee's disappointment. But Tom understood the boy now. Lee had been right. And suddenly sick of dissatisfaction, he wanted to make things clear in his head.

A shadow from the architectural column between the den and dining room reminded Tom of the gloomy old chinaberry, then the stoic cabin with no Christmas tree, no stockings, or people to visit, and the lost feeling of gratitude returned as he remembered he wasn't alone. But how Tom missed his river sanctuary with its shrunken mural, and he decided to add back the pear trees as Lee had so enjoyed their sweet flavor.

Into the kitchen, and soon the smell of strong coffee cheered the room though the coffeemaker sounded alien. Everywhere gadgets, microwave, blender, toaster, so many tools for comfort that he didn't have at the cabin—or want—but along with the modern mechanicals, other prompts brought cheer. Here was Lucy's jacket, Victoria's backpack; there schoolbooks and a gym bag, strewn images of family life, of people living together normally rather than as holiday exception. Tom viewed himself an anachronism dropped into this modern world, lost in its rapid purr. The tools of thought he possessed seemed inadequate to his challenges, yet people still expected competence, that assured quality his life had always demonstrated. But today a rising tide of spirit so missing lately arose to pull him toward the resolution he both dreaded and needed.

Soon, scurrying sounds upstairs, and then Glenna slipped into the kitchen, her blue robe pulled up tight against the chill before the furnace revived.

"This sure is good coffee, Dad. I forgot how strong you like it, but it tastes dee-lish."

"Yeah, don't need many cups, but I do like 'em to count." Tom was grateful not to be questioned immediately.

As they sat at the breakfast bar, both holding their cups as if warming hands against a hearth fire, Tom peered at Glenna, who seemed intent not to catch his eyes directly.

"Look," he began slowly, "I'm sorry about last night; overtired I guess. I'm not used to being up past seven, you know. Night comes early on the Catchahoula."

"No worries. You missed some good food, but there's plenty left, and I'm going to make a blueberry cobbler today to go with some homemade ice cream."

Squirming, trying to figure how to talk to Glenna, Tom calculated that saying absolutely nothing would probably be the best way to proceed. But he knew dealing with women wasn't like living alone or talking to that thick-skinned friend he could ignore at will. Soon, he gathered the courage to scramble a few words.

"Listen, I had a little spat with Lee about some stuff Mom wrote a long time ago. I didn't handle it too well. My fault."

Certain that avoiding last night's disagreement was a good idea, Glenna decided that for now everyone had talked enough. "It's okay, Dad. Lee said it was about that Newland fella. I don't need to know any more about it, so you just rest up and maybe we'll talk later."

Though Tom saw his chance to avoid the moment, he also knew his behavior had called some serious questions into the open, and he wanted Glenna to have a better sense of what was happening. "Listen, Glenn, one of the letters explained how Saralynn attacked this Newland guy on the phone for getting me fired. You know how Mom was."

"Oh, I see. What happened with this fellow?" Glenna was mildly curious.

Tom paused as he collected the details from those years, but all the images jumbled out of sequence. "Oh nothing; we all went our separate ways."

The words poured out emotionless, empty of judgment or passion, like cold motor oil from an engine that had sat overnight. Glenna had no real sense of what her dad described, so she moved the conversation along. "Well, he probably wanted to apologize last year, so looks like things might have ended okay after all." Then she poured another cup of coffee.

Without realizing it, Tom missed his chance to exit the discussion. "Yeah, you're right, but you know, at Thanksgiving, Mike told me that Don had made a pass at Oui, and when she blew him off, he got mad and threatened revenge. Now I guess I know how he honored his threat. Wish I'd known that thirty years ago; that guy would be dead."

Immediately Glenna sensed danger. "How come I never heard anything about any of this? Good Lord, this sounds like a big deal. And Mom never said anything to you either?"

"No," said Tom. "Oui kept it to herself. Can't believe it really." Staring at his coffee, only the echoes of birdsongs from outside moved about the room.

"You were a little thing then," Tom said, "even liked Don in those days. Called him Uncle Don. Do you remember how sudden like we moved?"

She tried recalling those long-ago years. "Not really. Seems like Mom left first. Then we all came down to Picayune, but I really don't remember. I kinda recollect Mom being sad in those days but maybe not."

Turning squarely to his daughter, Tom spoke seriously. "Mike was supposed to come with me this trip so we could go see Don. I need to know what he wanted. Clear the air, if possible." Tom's face filled now with wrinkled lines suddenly over-red in the weak kitchen light.

"Maybe everyone should just let this whole thing pass," Glenna said. "It's not worth getting all worked up over."

"Yea, but I been trying to blame myself for a long time, and Don too. I'd like to know what really happened." Then he wandered over into oblivion remembering the anger he'd carried all these years and the nagging wonder as to where all that fury had disappeared to, especially after the eruption in Mike's truck at Thanksgiving. And yet lately, he'd lost that vengeful motivation. He even recognized Lee's insolence as the reaction he himself used to possess, the outrage of youth so unwilling to compromise, so offended by weakness. So Tom began to think about how to find the truth he needed.

III.

Slipping quietly out the back door to go shoot hoops, Lee was long gone before Tom knocked on the bedroom door. Not quite sure if Lee was only ignoring him, Tom tiptoed downstairs, regretting they wouldn't get to talk before the big Christmas day meal. Glenna was already cooking up a roast and every side dish imaginable, and Tom wanted to make the gathering a success for her after the fiasco the previous evening.

Everyone helped in the kitchen, cooking, setting places, vacuuming and though most of the talk sounded more like military orders, the family was in good humor. No one dared mention Tom's absence the evening before or the disagreement he'd had with Lee, not that they even understood, but clearly Lee's silence at dinner and Tom's withdrawal meant something had happened. Glenna had warned everyone to be on best behavior.

Unexpectedly, the doorbell rang.

Hands soaking wet at the sink, Glenna looked at Tom. "Would you get that for me? I invited a friend to eat with us; that's probably her."

A subtle choke followed the word "her" slipping innocently from his daughter's lips, but surely that was nothing to fret over, so Tom opened the front door. On the steps in the bright sunlight stood a woman of perhaps sixty, dressed in a bright blue, tight-fitting dress with a cut neckline and a row of pearls perfectly placed. Her red hair lit up like fire in the light, and a piercing blue eye shadow lent a showgirl effect to her glamorous entrance.

"Hello there, handsome. I'm Wanda Spencer; you must be Tom, or is it Mike?"

Almost forgetting he had to talk as well, Tom lurched to respond. "Tom. I'm Tom, Glenna's dad." Then he began to relax. "Come on in." He felt surprisingly comfortable with Wanda as she had a disarming effect on people with her bright smile and garrulous way. This woman was the kind of person that could carry a conversation all by herself, and that would be fine with Tom on this day when he felt a bit tentative.

Bravely, he moved forward. "Why you're a pretty thing. Glenna didn't tell me we had a movie star coming." Tom almost gasped after the words left his mouth, and he realized how flirty he must have sounded. Not imagining where that impulse came from, he focused on trying to remain calm.

A large Macy's bag at her side, Wanda allowed Tom to relieve her of the obvious weight.

"Thank you, love. You're such a dear—and cute too." With that, Wanda swished down the hallway to the kitchen, and two seconds later another explosion erupted as she made her grand entrance.

Beaming, Glenna's mouth hung half-open. "Look at you! I love that dress, and your hair is stunning. You're such a sprite, I tell you." Glenna dried her hands and hugged her friend as the girls stared in amazement; they didn't know Wanda at all.

Introductions made, everyone knew that Glenna and Wanda had met at a church charity function a few weeks ago. Wanda's husband of thirty years had died eighteen months before, and she had more or less locked herself away for quite a while but now wanted to circulate and meet some new friends. When Glenna discovered Wanda's daughter would be spending Christmas with her fiancé up in Canada, she of course invited her to the Mitchell festivities.

Slowly Tom made his way from the hallway into the kitchen. Peeking into the bag, he spotted two large bottles of wine, one red and one white, and a bottle of sherry along with a few small wrapped gifts.

"Oh, there he is; this handsome gentleman helped me with my things. I think he deserves a drink." Tom turned Santa Claus red at being called handsome in public, and he didn't quite know what to do, as no one in the family really drank alcohol, except Harold, who was strictly a beer man. Glenna jumped in quickly.

"Yes, he does." Glenna winked at her dad. "We don't normally partake, but since this is Christ's birthday, a little celebrating seems in order. Tom couldn't utter a sound. Wanda grabbed the sherry bottle with gusto.

"Listen, Mr. Good Looking, you do the honors." As Wanda placed the bottle in Tom's hands, he noted that her fingers touched his hand ever so gently. A two-karat diamond on one finger and diamond-studded Rolex also served to crisp up his mental fog, and suddenly Tom was alert. Wanda offered a quick wink and without realizing it, Tom had opened the sherry bottle. Glenna beamed while the girls sat slack-jawed not knowing what to think. Wanda had taken control of the party.

"Okay, Mitchells and Bradburns, or whatever you all are, I've brought you all a little something from Mrs. Santa Clause. Since I'm barging into your family gathering, I wanted to make the day a little more special."

The back door opened, and Lee stuck his head in, then stopped with a squeak of his shoe as he saw the stranger. "Well, hello there, scrumptious," said Wanda, and Tom grinned with impish pleasure at the way Lee glowed red. The boy's hands absently ran through his wet hair and sweat-soaked T-shirt as he looked from Glenna to Tom and back to Wanda.

Their guest took a step toward Lee as if she might eat him, but Glenna sprang to his rescue.

"Oh, Lee, this is my friend Wanda Spencer; she will be joining us for Christmas. Is Harold coming up from the garage now?"

"That's great. Yeah, hello, Mrs. Spencer. A pleasure to meet you. And, ah, yes, I saw Dad locking the garage." Lee fidgeted uncomfortably, instantly consumed with Wanda's divine perfume filling the room.

Undeterred, Wanda continued her torment of the poor boy. "Honey, I've seen many a ..." Then she caught herself, realizing this was a teenager. "So, ah, good timing there, Lee, is it? I'm passing out Christmas goodies, and you're on the list."

Glenna again directed traffic. "Okay, Dad, I'll take one of those sherries over here for the cook." The family looked at Glenna as if she'd ordered a toothpaste sandwich.

Glenna's huge smile filled the room like a balloon drop as Tom swept into action knowing she hadn't had a sip of alcohol in probably ten years. Clearly this day would be one to remember at the Mitchell residence.

IV.

The next few hours proved delightful. Even Harold had a good time once he came in and had a couple of beers. The girls loved the Chanel No. 5 perfume Wanda gave them, and Lee's solid brass compass looked quite handsome attached to his belt. For Tom and Harold, she had given silk handkerchiefs with their initials embroidered, surely things they would never buy for themselves and probably would never take out of their sock drawers, but everyone thanked Wanda and smiled, recognizing that she'd not only gone to the expense but to the trouble to choose these

ARTHUR BYRD

things herself. Glenna felt a little left out as everyone looked at their presents, praising Wanda for her kindness. Soon the jabber died.

With faux surprise, Wanda looked at Glenna and began her act. "Oh my, I forgot to give you your present, didn't I? Forgive me, dear. I'm getting so absentminded in my middle youth."

"Oh, Wanda," Glenna said, "that isn't necessary; you know your friendship is more than enough for me." Tom thought Glenna's graciousness didn't have that genuine ring she was so noted to possess, but she made the good effort.

"Don't be silly, Glenna. I wouldn't even be here if it weren't for you. I got you something special, so here, Merry Christmas." Wanda handed Glenna a package about the size of a small toaster but thin, with a red bow and green wrapping paper and the most gorgeous golden lace stitching around every corner of the box. Glenna looked almost fearful as the wrapping was so expensive, then suddenly a pall of inadequacy fell upon her. Taking the gift, her hands trembled.

"Go ahead, open it. I thought it would be something you would love, a cheese grater." Wanda took another sip of sherry.

Glenna opened the box. The object inside appeared electronic, about the size of a hardcover book with a glass screen. She looked at Wanda with embarrassment. "I love it, but what is it? Is it really a cheese grater?"

Wanda howled. "I knew you wouldn't know what it was; you live such a sheltered life, dear, you really do. It's one of those electronic book readers. This thing can download a book in one minute from some cloud somewhere, and you can get almost every book in the world right now. I have one, and I adore it."

Never so taken aback in her life, Glenna knew this must be expensive and was something she never in a million years would have given herself, so she simply stared in silence. Harold, who had given her flannel pajamas for Christmas, helped out. "Geez, Glenn. You can read in bed now without having the light on."

Tom watched his daughter's happiness, the devotion she'd always shown her family rewarded by an outsider. And he enjoyed a social moment that didn't require overplanning. It was impossible not to think of Oui's smile, her kind heart, and that faithful mother who must be in heaven weeping tears of joy for her beloved daughter.

Sipping his sherry, Tom realized that perhaps being around people wasn't quite the bother he'd calculated, but the thought was framed in a troubling disquiet, a hint of things he did not want to remember. So instead he floated on the family's happy aura, realizing he was lucky to be exactly where he was this fine day. And he hoped Glenna would like the hummingbird he'd carved for her and painted with his special river paints.

V.

Soon the kitchen smelled of food, and the warm oven gave the house a homey, comfortable snuggle. A couple of glasses of sherry, and the adults drifted, but Wanda entertained with her stories of Paris in the spring and how her daughter was completely spoiled. With wine and attention available, Wanda didn't care about judgment, merely laughing her way to the place where she could do no wrong.

The huge afternoon meal unfolded with the kids describing their Santa Claus presents to Wanda while Tom ate, quietly enjoying the family conversation. Lee remained aloof, gradually lending a smile his grandfather's way. Soon, Lee moved to calm Wanda's antics.

"So, Mrs. Spencer, Mom tells me that you have a daughter; she's visiting up north this Christmas?"

With a sharp cut of the eye, Wanda followed Lee's lead. "Why, yes, that's right. Jocelyne couldn't wait to get away from me this year." Wanda seemed woozy, the sentiment clearly too personal to be rolled out in public like a dim sum tray, but self-control wasn't her focus at the moment.

The blunt response softened Lee. "Was your husband close to your daughter?" His attempt to bring a more somber tone fell short, however, and Wanda simply slammed the lob back hard.

"Oh no, they hated each other. Jocelyne is a little bee-ach, you know, and doesn't appreciate anyone. Ernie was a good man, husband, and father. I miss him on holidays like this."

A sadness floated about Wanda, and Tom thought of his own loss and adjustment. Studying her vibrant style, he wondered if Wanda ever slowed enough to examine her life. Did she relive the past the way he did or merely glance back then blunder ahead?

Slowly he joined the conversation, speaking softly to Wanda. "I know how hard it is to lose someone close for so many years; it's been five years for me since my Oui passed. How are you doing with finding your own life?"

Glenna's radar went off immediately. "Now, Dad, I don't know that we have to put Wanda on the spot like that; I'm sure she's doing fine. Would anyone like some of this good hummus I made? And these apples are so crisp." No one sprang at the chance.

Almost sobered, Wanda spoke earnestly. "It's okay, Glenna. Tom didn't mean anything. He's trying to be sensitive, that's all. I appreciate a man not always pushing and explaining but willing to listen to a woman's perspective. Ernie was a great listener. He had this gentle way about him that never ruffled people, except maybe Jocelyne, but she has this contumacious way about her that ruffles everyone." Tom looked around the table as the big word spilled so effortlessly into the conversation, realizing this was an interesting, educated woman hiding her pain with antics.

Glenna spoke gently. "Do you miss him, Wanda?"

The fierce redhead sighed and sat back in her chair, wiping her lips very properly before speaking. Her eyes flitted with great energy, but now Tom thought she seemed to be assessing things with deeper reach for the truth. "Yes, Glenna, I miss Ernie each day. I have his pictures all over the house and the things he gave me, but I realized something a few months ago. I have a duty to Ernie to live my life, to continue soaking up the fun of being alive just like he and I did. That's what he would want me to do, not sit around in some dolorous mood thinking of all I've lost. It's lonesome sometimes, but I'm living life for the both of us now."

Her words touched Tom; he saw the love in her fingers gently stroking her wedding band. Tom recognized a familiarity with her strength even as his own recent weakness spun about his head, how he'd begun to give ground to life. Wanda's words sank into his thoughts pushing up the idea that perhaps the time had come to find his own new path, and he wondered if this was a new friendship.

Without knowing where the words came from, Tom spoke before he realized. "Wanda, you're quite a woman, and your husband had himself a very special wife. I want to propose a toast to the love you had and the love you still carry." Tom raised his glass, as did everyone at the table. As he finished, a flood of thoughts filled Tom's head, brilliant things, quips to make Wanda smile, but the words failed, and the simple lifting of the glasses completed the moment.

Sensing the mood needed to be lightened, Wanda rejoined her familiar persona. "Now, Tom, are you flirting with me again? I must say, I wonder if your friend Mike is as naughty as you are. I wish he could have been here too; nothing I love more than a harem of good-looking men. Lordy mercy, what a day." Wanda, with practiced social acumen, returned the party to the proper balance as Glenna toasted the air yet again.

For the first time in months, Tom's melancholy disappeared. He was young, energetic, and happy to be with people genuinely glad to see him. Hope began to flow as tinkling glasses and tantalizing food sang siren songs of happiness, allowing the rare luxury of once again feeling young at heart. And the clock of life ran backwards for an afternoon.

Chapter 8

I.

After dessert and coffee, no one at the table could even consider another morsel of food. Stuffed beyond normal limits but also satisfied that the day had filled an unspoken need simply to be normal, the now quieted group enjoyed the peaceful calm of a completed feast. Wanda had been an unexpected catalyst, her antics releasing quietly held tensions in need of venting. Almost as if a grand emotional exercise joined them in commonality, the congregation of family and friends understood the nurture each had received.

As everyone rose to clear dishes, Glenna insisted Victoria show Wanda around the house while she and Lee cleared the table, so off the girls went upstairs. Tom stepped over to Glenna and hugged her neck, showing his deep appreciation for all her hard work but also acknowledgment for her role as connector of the family. More clearly now, he recognized that Glenna functioned as head of the family, and though he held the titular role, Glenna was the living soul of this family clan.

"Hon," Tom said to Glenna, "you go sit down and rest yourself. Lee and I will knock out these dishes. We're a pretty good team." With a quick glance Lee's way, Tom wanted to call a final truce to the misunderstanding of the prior evening.

Of course, Glenna resisted. "Don't be silly. I don't mind."

"Now listen," said Tom. "You can't keep this boy all to yourself forever. After all, I don't get to see him as much as you do." So Glenna retired to the den to watch a Betty Davis movie just starting. Harold even made them some popcorn and poured another glass of that red wine Glenna said was so good, and they sat together on the couch.

Closing the kitchen door to keep the noise level down for Glenna, Tom and Lee dove into the mountain of dishes littered across the kitchen, the workload affording both men convenient cover for hiding.

Each busied himself with soapy water and dishwasher management, allowing the distinct chill in the air to dissipate into preoccupation. Soon a cant about where this bowl went or that pitcher energized the dialogue, but Tom knew the chatter meant nothing. They were jousting in warm up intended only to delay communication. After everything was put away, Tom made the first deliberate move. Wiping the countertop one last time, he spoke casually.

"We still going hunting tomorrow? Thought you wanted to go to the old Eli Lott place and walk around a little."

"Oh yeah," Lee said, "well, I got basketball practice first thing, but we could go after that. Maybe just target practice, if you want. Dad's leaving early, so it'll just be us."

Lee's basketball practice afforded Tom the chance to skip the hunting trip, but he knew the discomfort needed to be cleared. "Sounds good. I forgot my hunting boots anyway. You still got that Winchester pump .22 that I gave you? I'd love to shoot that old thing again."

Having had a little time to think, Lee realized his own teenage frustrations had gotten tangled up with what he saw as an inherently unjust thing Don Newland had done, and his overreaction had been out of balance. At the thought of the rifle though, Lee decided simply to keep his focus on supporting his grandpa and not worrying so much about trying to make decisions for him; and for an adult moment, Lee understood the challenges of guiding family without being overbearing.

"Are you kidding? I shoot that gun all the time." Lee said, remembering when Tom had given it to him on his thirteenth birthday. It had been Harlan's rifle, and the gift a rite of passage to the next generation. Now it would serve as peacemaker.

Already Tom's strategy was working, and Lee spoke quietly. "Look, I'm sorry I was so smart-mouthed yesterday. Got all riled up when I thought about that Newland fellow and how he treated you. Don't be mad at me, but you should fight for what's right."

The clarity of Lee's thinking struck Tom as a vestige of his own past when life played out in simple choices of right and wrong, times before thought became too entangling for action, and with a quick squeeze of Lee's neck, Tom remembered his temper flaring in Mike's truck, that same temper unexpectedly dormant now but not to be underestimated.

"Tomorrow when we go shooting," Tom said, "I've got something I need you to help me sort out. But you gotta promise to stay calm, okay?" Without realizing, Tom had obligated Lee to some kind of partnership in the resolution of Don's old affront, but he wasn't quite sure why he'd done that. The thought had slipped out. Instantly Tom began to worry what he would say to Lee, but then he had the clever image that he was treating Lee's volatility exactly the same way Mike had treated him back at Thanksgiving, and for the first time that day, Tom remembered his old friend and wished he was there to help make sense out of all the commotion.

"Okay, Grandpa, you're on. But you gotta be honest, okay? I mean no finessing things, no matter how sticky." Tom knew he'd probably lost this negotiation and began to feel weary again from the strain of playing truth and hide with reality, that artful balance Saralynn had mastered with many a well-conceived canard but which Tom had difficulty handling these days. So they left the kitchen, Tom considering he needed a story to tell tomorrow so perhaps Lee wouldn't notice his ambivalence, Lee wanting only to see his grandpa take action.

II.

In every direction, Victoria found parts of the house she wanted Wanda to see—the nice wallpaper Glenna had hung in the hallway, family photographs, even old drawings her mom had done as a child. They studied pictures of the girls as infants, of Lee winning a baseball trophy for best outfielder, and of Tom and Oui holding Glenna as a baby. Wanda stared with a fascination most strangers don't usually show when looking at family moments that have no sentimental value to them as outsiders. Instead she seemed to crave those images, to need their nourishment as she stood estranged that day from her own family. And Vic sensed a starvation in Wanda as she peered into each photograph.

Eventually the girls drifted into Victoria's room; by then Lucy had become bored with the twenty minutes of examining photos in the hallway, so she disappeared. As Victoria opened the bedroom door, a beautiful world of femininity unfolded.

With a slight gasp, Wanda stepped inside. "Oh, it is lovely. I adore this beautiful baby blue with all the white lace curtains. And look at this doll collection; there must be fifty of them."

Proud of her personal little world, Vic was in heaven. "Mom and Dad give me a new doll every year on my birthday. It's my favorite part of growing up." Vic noticed Wanda's almost sad expression, so she remained quiet and let her new friend take in the moment.

"I grew up in Biloxi in a big house that looked almost like this one," Wanda said. "Hurricane Camille destroyed it. But I still remember my pink bedroom with the windows overlooking the courtyard with all those giant wisteria vines and a little goldfish pond." In midthought Wanda went silent, leaving a hole in the moment, and Vic knew this lady had lost much in her life.

On a small table sat a child's tea set. Wanda picked up the little cream pitcher. "I gave Jocelyne a set like this on her seventh birthday. A week later, she took a hammer to it because she couldn't have a new bicycle like the new one Samantha down the street had." Vic could almost feel Wanda's sharp regret of motherhood, the pain it had caused. Then with a gentle smile, Wanda turned, and a waft of hope entered the room.

"Are these your trophies?" Wanda asked while pausing at the door.

"Yes. Chess trophies. I've won a few, and all these ribbons too. I like puzzles, math, that kind of stuff."

"I see," Wanda said. "And a tennis racket; do you play?"

"Not much; we don't have any courts close by, so it's hard to practice." Vic halted, then started again. "But look at my track shoes here. Aren't these cleats cool?"

"Why, yes, that is interesting; they are only on the front half of the shoe?"

"Yeah, 'cause when you run, you're leaning forward; it's not like walking. I'm trying out for the track team in a couple of months, so Mom wants me to run around outside and break them in on nice days."

"Your mom is really something, isn't she, Vic? I just love Glenna." Wanda sighed.

"Mom is the best. It's like she can read your mind or something, like she knows what I'm thinking even before I do. Mom can fix about any problem."

A huge smile crept over Wanda's face. "Oh, darling, you're so lucky, you know that? You must be so happy. And I bet the boys love that beautiful hair of yours too."

Vic turned red. "Well, uh, yeah, I guess, I don't know really. I'm not too good with boys; they confuse me."

"Yes, well," Wanda said. "Welcome to the club. They make all women crazy, don't you know? The only thing you need to remember about boys is that their brain is in their pants, and if you keep them unsure, then you're always in control. Boys are easy; it's girls that are complicated." And they laughed, giving each other a big hug, one that showed Victoria she had a new friend, someone who understood the world and how women fit into it.

"Thank you so much for the tour; you're such a delightful girl. You keep those track shoes on. Make those boys chase you, and you'll have all the trophies you want." And yet again Wanda gave Victoria a sincere hug that Vic thought carried with it just the slightest twinge of a mother's desperation.

III.

After what seemed an endless morning, Tom escaped the chatter of women and finally picked up Lee from basketball practice. With barely a greeting, the two found themselves in the Chevy heading out for some target practice. Lee had been gone all morning while Tom piddled in the house fixing a broken hinge, shaving off the bottom of a sticking door, and looking at all the trees and bushes in the yard, noticing how tidy Glenna kept things and, of course, engaging in small talk with Glenna and her next-door neighbor, Sue, who talked incessantly about absolutely nothing.

The previous day's excitement now returned to pedestrian family life, and Tom enjoyed its simplicity. Still, he missed the river, its sonorous sound never stopping to rest, passage the reason for its physical being. Even the birds didn't sound as chipper here in town, almost as if they too felt trapped by the clamor of too many people.

Back in his truck, Tom welcomed the mesmerizing whine of the tires studying the highway. The passing trees, occasional farmhouse, the abandoned gas station along the way all harkened back to many years before when he used to come to this place with Mike. Eli Lott had been a great-uncle of Mike's who left the old farmstead to the family, never to be sold until the last living Hamlin could make the decision alone. An abandoned anomaly along the Leaf River, this five-hundred-acre wood sprawled with ancient pine and hardwood forest, a twenty-five-acre lake nestled in the middle after the river changed course eons ago, and the old crumbling farmstead with its still flowing artesian well out back. On either side of the property, wealthy landowners took pride in their deer-hunting clubs with nicely graveled roads and high fences, so this area sat as a quiet, independent region far from the maddening city.

Tom envisioned the homestead long before they arrived. There the old beech tree he used as a tree stand, here the oak limb where he strung up the buck the very first time he stepped onto the property with Mike. This abandoned relic of a home had many connections to Tom's past, even to his own father, though those memories seemed too distant to touch any longer. Countless trips resonated from when he and Mike had come to camp, to run lines on the river, to shoot squirrels or hunt deer or turkey, and Tom sensed the affinity with his own little shack back on the Catchahoula where there too he didn't own the land but benefited from the anchor of an old promise. It felt odd to return to this larger river without Mike, though Tom had permission to go any time. Today, the place spread before him as fascinating as a new museum, and he wanted to show proper respect.

"We'll turn left up there at that gatepost. Darn thing's about to fall down. See that iron wheel at the bottom? It marks the turn. That thing's been there long as I can remember. Mike told me it was from an old plow his grandfather used when he was a boy."

Beginning to get excited, Lee said, "Oh, I remember this! Yeah, there's an old windmill right up here, isn't there?"

"Yep, they used to grind up corn back a long time ago. Part of the mill is still standing. Kinda like me, not so much grinding anymore but gumming," Tom said as he looked straight ahead.

Abruptly, the truck stopped. "Here we go. Mike and I always used that bluff over there as our backstop. I brought some targets we can put up." Soon the paper bull's-eyes and a few tin cans were set up, and the sound of shotguns and Lee's .22 rifle peppered the solitude of the place. They took turns laughing at each other and proposing ridiculous challenges, but in the end, they had simple fun testing the pattern of the shotguns and seeing who had the better eye with the rifle. Lee was impressed his grandpa could still shoot so accurately and even showed how from thirty paces he could light up a kitchen match with a rifle shot, something Lee never managed to do even after a dozen tries.

Finally, tired of games, they took a walk down to the lake. The black water and heavy trees blocking the sides gave it a mysterious feel, but soon Tom found the opening he and Mike used to slide their skiff in to fish for white perch around the cypress trees. There, he and Lee sat down to enjoy the crisp afternoon.

Deciding to ease into the conversation, Tom said, "Looks kinda like the Devil's Throat, don't it? You know, with just this cut running out to the middle." Lee smiled, and Tom saw the boy remembered that day fondly, the day he got to play the hero part the way Tom always had done before.

Not taking up the conversation, Lee stuck to what was on his mind. "So, what's this thing you wanted to talk about? You know, with Don Newland."

"Well, so much for small talk, I guess. Gotta get right down to business." Tom felt uncomfortable with being rushed and without realizing it let irritation fill his head rather than what he'd wanted to speak about with Lee.

The pushback caught Lee off guard. "No, not really, I just thought ..." Tom knew he was being too prickly.

"I'm sorry, son. Just being ornery. Don't mind me. Look, I don't know everything myself. It's all so old in my head I can't really remember what was real and what I might have made up or dreamed along the way. Things aren't as clear with me now." Tom's meandering start surprised him, and a wisp of worry formed as now he couldn't quite remember where to go next or even what he had intended to discuss. He hated stalling like this but hoped the words would magically come to him if he could only hold open the moment long enough. And a distracting thought further puzzled Tom as he considered that's all life is really, just holding open the moment long enough for something real to occur.

Lee stepped in to help. "I want you to know I'm sorry. I know I pushed you too hard about all this Newland stuff. It's old news, and I guess it doesn't matter anyway. Saralynn's letter got me to thinking about this stuff, but it ain't my business anyway, so maybe we should just let it drop. I'm okay with that." Now Tom remembered the letter from yesterday and his mom's diatribe thirty years ago. He also remembered Mike's Thanksgiving revelation about Don, and a swirl of injustice began to turn in his stomach.

"Look, this is hard for me;" Tom said. "I don't like all this personal talk, but the long and the short of it is that Mike told me something a few weeks ago that I never knew. Said Don made a pass at Oui many years ago. He was drunk, and I was out of town on business, so she threw him out. Then he tried it again. That time Oui slapped his face; he got mad and threatened that he'd get back at me, and it would be all her fault. The whole thing sounds crazy after all these years of not knowing. Guess I've been a damned fool."

Unlike before, this time Lee didn't get angry. "Grandpa, you weren't a fool; you didn't do anything wrong. He was your friend, and you trusted him; that's all you did."

Tom took in the words but still felt edgy. "I guess so, but it makes me crazy that Oui and Mike never told me. It's like they made fun of me." As Tom became clear, he realized his frustration was with both Don for the original slight and with Oui and Mike for creating this embarrassment he had in his gut. Anger rose. Though Tom sensed renewed strength, he knew these volatile feelings contained an unhealthy core, something he couldn't quite control.

"Grandpa, they were only trying to protect you—I mean Granny Oui and Mike. They didn't want you to do something crazy, I'm sure."

As quickly as his temper had risen, it subsided, and Tom let the idea sink into his mind. And quite unexpectedly, words came to him.

"When I six, one Sunday my parents took my older brother and me down to the Pearl River to swim. Louis was a little rowdy, so Mom was trying to keep a handle on him, and without realizing it, I kept inching forward into deeper water. I remember like yesterday. I took one more small step, wanting the water to touch my chin, and then down I went. I didn't know what happened, but I was gone. Some big root at the bottom of the river wrapped around my foot." Tom stopped.

"So then what?" Lee turned to face Tom directly.

"Well, I didn't panic. I didn't do anything. Didn't try to swim or jerk myself loose or anything. I just stood there half-floating like I was in a daze. But I knew something then—the river wanted me. It pulled at me like I was supposed to go with it. And I didn't know how to resist." Tom stopped as if he'd used all the words he had. After a few seconds, he looked up speaking softly.

"Son. That's the way I feel these days. Like that river pull is back at me."

Lee became concerned. "Grandpa, what happened that day?"

Tom leaned back against the big tree they sat beside. "I was floating. Like there was no ground or anything. And then I was back at the surface sucking for air. My mom had yanked me up by the hair on my head. She saved my life, and I never did a thing."

A thousand thoughts passed over Lee as worry became ecstasy, but his response was decisive. "Saralynn. I knew it. She was always watching." And Lee laughed out loud. "You know what, Grandpa? She might not be here right now to fight that current at your feet, but dang it, I am. And I ain't gonna let Don Newland or anybody else pull you under. I'm with you, and you need to know that." Then Lee jumped to his feet.

Those words steadied Tom, though still not his old self, and he stood frozen in thought. Suddenly, swept back to a day sixty-five years earlier when he and Mike had climbed down into a dry well to explore, Tom felt the cool, dank air. The dangling rope up the well side hung now in his mind as the only escape, their lifeline out of the empty darkness of the hot summer afternoon, and again Tom remembered how that desperate thought had so worried him that day.

"I could see that rope. Like it meant life or death," Tom said aloud. Then he went quiet as the image of Mike's boyhood face cleared in his mind, and there he felt the connection to life again, the tenuous union to the current moment so erratic lately. And like the zoom of a good camera sharpening the moment, Tom was back at the lake edge with Lee where he felt safe.

Watching his grandpa's face bound between placid and agitated, Lee finally saw those clear blue eyes blink. "What rope you talking about, Grandpa? Are you okay? Here, have a little root beer; the sugar will pep you up."

A wave of strength began a stronger trickle. "Yeah, good idea. Didn't sleep too good last night. Zoned out a little there," said Tom.

Uncomfortable with how feeble he must have looked, Tom wanted to hide his confusion. "I've figured out something, Lee. I'm ready to go see Newland. Want to know why he came to see Glenna, and I want to punch him in the face."

Lee bounced up and down as if he were being dribbled. "That's the stuff, Grandpa. Let's go kick his worthless ass."

Watching Lee jump around made Tom happy, and though he knew his mouth was out in front of his mind, at least he had found the path again. But Lee's response sounded like he wanted to be part of going to see Newland; Tom hadn't considered that. It needed more thought.

So gradually they meandered back to the truck after checking out all the deer prints in the mud and watching the mallard ducks down toward the far end of the lake.

At the old homestead, heavy shadows hung under the huge oaks. All the walls sagged inward trying to hold each other up, and only the old chimney had any strength left in it, as even the brick foundation supports at each corner of the house crumbled under the dead weight. The images seemed too familiar, like something he knew in his soul rather than in his memory, and seeing the rotten porch swing near the front steps, Tom remembered sitting there with Oui back when the house was still functional, though ancient even in those days. The image reminded him of his own existence, his fleeting strength, the unreliable efficacy of the truth Mike's secret had taught him. Everywhere were signs of what no longer existed, what had passed into the current of time. Tom felt himself disappearing.

Walking back to the truck, Lee took the initiative. "So let's go see him."

The bluntness tricked Tom. "What'd you say?"

"You know, Don Newland, let's go find him. You said he was trying to get hold of you, right? So let's go see him." Tom couldn't quite digest the words quickly enough, so he stared back at Lee as if looking for a reason to object. Then he remembered, that's exactly what he had wanted to ask Lee—yes that was it, to ask Lee to go with him to see Don.

"So will you go with me?" Tom said.

Lee seemed perplexed at his grandpa's response, but no matter, they had a plan, so with that, they hopped into the truck and headed home with heads full of Yazoo City and revenge.

During the slow ride, Tom studied Lee, his happy mood, and those moments where surely he was plotting the mission ahead. This would be an adventure for the boy, a quest to right a long overdue affront. Tom wondered if Lee had visions of a fistfight, of calling Newland names and cursing him out in front of his wife and kids, then realized the boy's youthful enthusiasm didn't reflect his own thirty-year-old grudge.

So, Tom too began to swell with anticipation as to how he would approach Don, what he would say. He couldn't quite distinguish between a verbal assault and physical violence, as all he envisioned was anger. But then the pitiful scene of old men fighting played movie-like in Tom's head, and rather than revenge, it simply looked puerile, grandfathers acting like children, weakened fools no longer competent to wage war or defend the honor of women. The thought shamed Tom.

All these years of doubt about Don now reduced themselves to muted anger, until Tom remembered the pistol under his truck seat. Even Lee didn't know the gun was there, that same .38 special, the trusted ally against cotton-mouthed moccasins. The glistening barrel and the white bone handle lent comfort almost like a cabin lantern on a stormy night, and as the befuddled intent so overwhelming only minutes earlier began to clear, Tom knew the time for resolving old unknowns had arrived.

IV.

"I just love Wanda," Vic told Glenna. "She talks to me like she's known me forever and really knows what it's like to be a girl." Victoria's excitement gushed as she and Glenna chopped vegetables for the pork roast they were cooking. Glenna listened quietly, not wanting to break her daughter's stream of consciousness.

"This perfume she gave me is divine. I love it. I really do. Suzie told me it's very expensive and that it's the same one her mother uses, and you know how picky she is and what nice clothes she wears. And Wanda knew all about boys and exactly what I should do—"

"Oh, really. And what did she tell you about boys? I'm curious," Glenna said.

"Nothing really, only how girls need to keep control—you know, always leave boys guessing and don't let them have what they want too easy."

Victoria's words skipped along with cliché after platitude because she did not want to reveal any of the exact wording of her conversation with Wanda; she wasn't quite sure why, but it needed to remain private. Without realizing, she found herself compartmentalizing her relationship with Wanda as separate from her mom, separate even from her mother's friendship with Wanda.

Vic continued, "Can we have Wanda over again sometime? I'd really like to. Maybe we could do girls' night or something and just talk. Wouldn't that be fun?"

"Sure, honey, that would be a lot of fun," said Glenna. "We'll have Wanda over real soon, I promise." Vic noticed the slight frown on her mother's face, almost as if she'd had an unpleasant realization, but what possibly could be wrong? Vic was happy, and her new friendship with Wanda offered another woman's life perspective and how best to take full advantage. As Glenna offered her daughter a weak smile, Vic was certain her mom understood and that everything would be fine.

Chapter 9

I.

The ride home from the old Eli place passed uneventfully. Neither Tom nor Lee had much to talk about now that the mission had been decided, so each wanted to ponder the coming odyssey. They discussed briefly their plan to leave around nine o'clock and then once at Don's house to decide if they were too tired to drive back or spend the night in a motel. Lee would print the driving instructions, so now all they could do was anticipate.

A quick call to Glenna—Lee calculated she might react better to the idea of visiting Yazoo City if she had time to think things over before responding. Likewise, Tom thought about the coming day and couldn't quite decide how he felt about Lee coming along on the visit. The idea seemed innocent enough, someone both to spark his confidence as well as help pass the time on a several-hour drive, but the more Tom stewed on the matter, the riskier it all seemed. He simply wasn't sure how the encounter might unfold.

Why Don had come to see Glenna still hung as a mystery and could pose problems. So could Lee's explosive anger. The shift from Tom's initial reaction of outrage had become more lurching confusion, but he recognized things could become volatile when he confronted Newland.

Tom oscillated, unable to decide between going alone and accepting Lee's company. The comfort of having the boy there seemed natural, but that old ire was returning, that crazed consumption he'd felt after Mike's long-held confession.

Over and over the image of his pistol flashed as he sorted how the gun fit into the plan. Time blurred as the day's events and visions of the past pressed upon a new demand to plan and be prepared. Clearly the future was about to change, and Tom worried for his grandson.

Lost in thought, twice he almost clipped a mailbox, then a child's bicycle left by a driveway entrance, each jerk of the truck startling Lee to open his drowsy eyes. But both times, finding nothing of concern, he drifted back into the monotonous ride while Tom held his breath.

The fledgling concern of danger rooted into the fertile rancor of lost time, and Tom accepted that he might actually kill Newland. Not his plan or even his desire, but the idea took on a separate identity, something he no longer controlled but rather a reactionary possibility spawned by justice. The words spoken tomorrow would determine the path ahead, and Tom comforted himself with the thought that he was powerless to choose.

All the heavy thinking became exhausting. He knew he could not kill another person, and yet some virulent force seized partial control of his will. Then Tom knew. Lee had to go with him, the boy intent upon revenge, his ally strong enough to help sort the truth, perhaps stopping a mistake; Lee must come. And that idea of youth became a crutch to ward off demons of his past.

As the truck pulled into the driveway, Tom shook Lee gently to awaken him with a soft reassuring voice. "Don't worry, Lee. Everything is going to be okay. I'm sure of it now."

II.

Glenna offered surprisingly little objection to the Yazoo City visit. "All right, you can go," said Glenna. "Knowing you and Dad will both be there makes me feel better, and who knows, maybe it will be an adventure." Truthfully, she was happy to see the two of them together anywhere other than on the river. For Glenna, this event represented a social return for her dad, a chance to reconnect with an old acquaintance even if there had been some dubious emotions all those decades ago. She'd never heard her dad or mom speak much about Don, so bitterness from the past surely must have dissipated by now. Besides, having Lee along meant a voice of reason would be advising her dad. So with the decision in place, Glenna thought how wonderful it would be to have Wanda over for that girls' night Vic wanted; what perfect timing this all worked out to be.

After dinner, Lee and Tom reviewed the itinerary and the printed directions. Glenna made up a sack lunch for them full of ham sandwiches, moon pies, and potato chips. She had an early-morning meeting at the library to discuss the upcoming job fair, so she knew the next day would be squeezed but wanted to send the men off with something to make their trip easier. Could that long-lost friend help bring her father back into the normal world, the place where his family waited for him and he wouldn't have to be so alone? Surely things would work out for the best.

The morning slipped by unnoticed as a gray sky left Lee and Tom slumbering later than normal, trying to catch the sleep they had lost in the night's uneasiness. Finally, Glenna tapped at their doors, rousing them as she left the house, the smell of coffee and bacon lilting up the stairs.

As she pulled out of the driveway, a sudden chill fell over Glenna, and she wished she'd actually seen her father and son to tell them good-bye. Long drives always bothered her. Today that private dread cast itself upon the journey of the two men she loved the most. She knew she was only being silly, but nonetheless she spoke softly to herself, "Drive slowly, Dad."

III.

The early chatter of the trip soon transitioned into individual solitude comforted by the drone of wheels tracking the highway groove. The holiday traffic was light, so they made good time stopping once to hit a truck stop men's room and grab some hot coffee, then once again to buy doughnuts. Oddly, neither spoke at all about where they were going or why, a mental dullness filling their sleep-deprived minds. Their lives patterned one another now, both cruising at the same mental pace, waiting with the same anxious restraint and yet completely divergent on how they expected the day to end.

For Lee, confrontation stood as the primary goal, while for Tom equilibrium replaced the erratic bounce from anger to self-criticism, and he saw his mission as completing an overdue process now requiring execution. These many years had buried much of Tom's past clarity, and Don loomed as an unfamiliar person they were going to visit. A cycle ran now as loop in his mind—the door opening, words being exchanged, then nothingness. Though he had no certainty of the approaching moment, darting images of his pistol still danced as sparks of suggestion.

Soon the small towns and endless empty stretches gave way to long country roads off the main highway. Without incident, the truck eventually pulled up to an old country home with a sign out front, "Three Oaks." On either side of the house lay open fields that had been planted in corn, with the nearest neighbor well over a mile away. The old Victorian house nestled in a collection of oak and pecan trees that in summer protected it from the hot sun, and yet it looked sun-beaten and weary, the brick footings under the front porch crumbling and beginning to fail.

Tom smiled as if on an ordinary visit to some kindly uncle, but the grin belied the anxiety. Ahead of the dreaded moment, a callous hardness had formed, walling out the dreaded image of what waited inside the old house, and Tom prepared for the man he'd hated for three decades.

"You ready, Grandpa?"

"Yep." So with seemingly casual resolve, the sons of Saralynn unloaded from the truck. Tom slyly grabbed the pistol from under his seat and without notice slipped it into the right side of the Chesapeake coat he'd worn for twenty years, one with large, leather-flapped pockets ample for both hands and objects. He looked at Lee with cool detachment.

"Listen, you hang back a little once we get to the door," Tom said. "Let me do the talking. I don't really know what's going to happen here, so you stay back." Lee nodded.

The ground crunched under their boots, colder here than back in Hattiesburg and more frozen. The shutters on the house had peeling paint, and a railing on the porch hung loose; the place looked of winter and neglect with no reason for anyone to bother caring until spring. His own little porch came to mind and how he'd fixed the loose post but forgot to secure the railing around the side.

The step up onto the decking sounded strident in the chilly air, almost like a hammer hitting wood as their boot heels simultaneously clanked though the platform proved mushy. An old double swing hung off to the left side of the covered area, guarding the porch end from the four-foot drop-off to the ground, the old chains brittle with rust. Paint on the screen door seemed new, but Tom noticed one corner was loose, his mind imagining swarms of summer mosquitoes sneaking through into the dark interior of this stately but failing home.

As Tom rapped knuckles on the white doorframe, he gave a quick cough to clear his throat, stepped back a healthy pace, and winked at Lee, who stood off to the side. In a moment, the wooden door with two glass panes cracked open, and an elderly lady peeked around the edge without opening it more than six inches.

"Yes, may I help you?" Her voice creaked in a quiet monotone tinged with just enough concern that Tom knew she was frightened. This far out in the country, not many people dropped in, he imagined, especially two strangers.

"Excuse me, madam. My name is Tom Bradburn, and this is my grandson, Lee. I hope we're in the right place. I'm looking for a Donald Newland; he's an old friend of mine, of sorts." Tom started off confidently but then found himself talking more than he wanted, explaining details that he didn't really want to convey, so he went silent, letting the sounds he'd already made carry the moment, the word "friend" now lodged in his mind.

"Well, this is Mr. Newland's place. He's resting now, but I'll get him for you. Won't you come in out of the cold, please? I've got some hot coffee on the stove if you'd like to warm up a little?"

"No thank you, madam. That won't be necessary; we won't be here that long." Tom wasn't quite sure why he said these words; he really wanted something hot to drink, but he didn't want to establish any kind of familiarity with Don's home. Bracing for an altercation, a long-awaited moment to vent his anger and call Newland a traitor to his face, Tom felt strong. The cold steel of the pistol hung heavy in the jacket pocket, slightly unbalancing his thoughts, but he knew that in two seconds he could pull the gun out, and everyone's life would change forever.

Soon, they waited in the foyer as the door to a room in the back opened, and a pallid, elderly-looking man began slowly ambulating down the hallway with deliberate patience and a wooden cane in his right hand. Tom looked twice to see if this was the person he once knew, but couldn't recognize the man. Memories of their sophomore year as college roommates echoed as he remembered his lanky friend always playing pranks, forever the radical reactionary objecting to school policy this and foreign policy that as he defined his own world of libertarian ideals. That person surely couldn't be this wizened old man struggling with the twenty paces down the hallway.

It seemed to take all afternoon, but finally the specter approached. "Thank you, Miss Smart, I'll be fine for now. Just leave us alone if you will."

"Certainly, Mr. Newland. I'll get your medicine ready; you let me know when you want me to bring it in. Good day, gentlemen." And with that, she took her leave at the very instant Tom and Lee realized she was Don Newland's nurse. They both stood stunned in the presence of this decrepit figure, the object of so much angst, the mythical marauder conjured for years as such a devious threat. Tom touched the pistol in his pocket, and he felt foolish, as if he'd planned to bully a helpless invalid, and the anger he'd born for three decades fuzzed into an irrelevant memory without the electricity of resentment. It was almost as if Newland had stolen Tom's revenge just as he'd stolen his self-respect decades earlier.

"So how can I help you young fellers? Miss Smart said you know me from somewhere."

Entrapped in the visual discontinuity between expectation and what he saw standing before him, Tom floundered, completely forgetting that he too had to speak. All the words and opening lines, the sarcastic comments and intentionally churlish jabs he'd planned seemed absent now, and he couldn't remember a single syllable from the countless practices he'd drilled into his head. He stood mute, staring blankly.

"Yes, Mr. Newland, this is my grandfather, Tom Bradburn. I believe you know him from Overland Container. My name is Lee."

"Well I'll be a baker's bun. You are Tom, aren't you. My, my, my. You look terrific, strong as an ox, just like always. Lordy mercy. Oh, I'm sorry. Where are my manners? You boys let's step into the parlor here and have a seat. My old legs ain't what they used to be."

Tom still hadn't spoken though his composure slowly began to return; he was glad to have a minute to pass through the glass French doors into a room with a space heater disguised as logs in a fireplace. Don moved so slowly it gave Tom time to think what he wanted to say.

"We're sorry to bother you in your home, but my daughter, Glenna, said you'd stopped by her house in Hattiesburg a couple of Thanksgivings ago. I don't get off the river much, so I just found this out." Tom was proud he'd gotten that string of information out so concisely, so he leaned back, absorbing the heat from the fireplace, now noticing all the pictures of grandchildren lining the mantel.

Don's voice was frail. "Well, yes, I did drop by after I tried to get hold of you but couldn't find any way to get word to you. I used to know your friend's name down there, Mickey or something like that, but I couldn't for the life of me remember his last name."

"You mean Mike Hamlin?" Tom spoke flatly.

"Oh yes, that's it. I remember now. He called me once a long time ago, but I didn't really get his name in my head." Don looked at the floor as if remembering, and a forlorn look suggested he too carried corrosive memories. Tom imagined Mike calling Don to warn him never to speak to Oui again, and a smile leaked through. He wished his old friend had come along, but then the clock on the mantel banged its quarter-hour notice, and Tom looked again at the ghost before him.

All business, Tom spoke. "Look, we don't want to take your time here. Glenna said you wanted to talk to me, so here I am." The invective Tom carried in his head began to return as the initial sympathy at seeing this frail figure now gave way to the engrained image of Don thirty years ago.

Newland sat up straighter. "Look, I can see you are still angry after all these years. I'm sorry about that; I never meant things to turn out this way." A violent rip occurred in Tom's placid demeanor as he sat forward in his chair.

"Cut the crap, awright," Tom said. "You're not sorry about shit, and we both know it. You're a liar and a Judas, and I wanted to come here and tell you that to your face—that's all." Again, Tom blurted out more than he wanted faster than he'd intended, and though the venting felt satisfying, he knew he'd raced right by everything Don had to say. Calmer now, he hoped he hadn't tainted the possibility of finding out Don's version of the truth.

"I'm sorry," Tom said. "I didn't mean to be so blunt. I've been mad for a long time here, hauling around this feeling of how my fishing buddy turned out to be the biggest two-face I ever met. It's hard to sit here and pretend like we still know each other."

Don remained calm. "It's okay. I really do understand. I've been hauling stuff I didn't know what to do with either. Things I'm not too proud of, stuff I think you didn't really understand the right way. It's taken a big toll on my life. Hell, Tom, look at me. I'm barely alive."

Tom took dark pleasure from Don's words. "Awright. I'll shut up. You say anything you want, and I'll listen. When you're done, then I'm gonna talk."

Shaking his head, Newland seemed pleased. "Fair enough. But first, you sure you boys don't want something to drink? I could use a little coffee myself. And we got some of that Swiss Miss hot chocolate for you there, young feller, if you want it." So the moment quieted down, Nurse Smart served coffee and hot chocolate with a plate of ginger snap cookies she'd baked, and the diversion allowed the initial fervor of pent-up sentiment to settle into a more composed discussion.

After his nurse left the room, Don leaned back in his obviously familiar chair by the heater. A saturnine weight hung about him, pressing down on his attempts to rally his strength as memory, and Tom witnessed the pain in Don's demeanor, the void left by hope having abandoned this shell of his former friend sitting ghostlike before a muddled past.

Don spoke quietly. "First, let me say thank you for coming; I know it wasn't easy. When I visited Glenna, it took me days to work up the courage, and just the mental strain left me sick for a week. You see, I went to tell her I was having a lung removed right after Thanksgiving.

157

Cancer. Wasn't sure what would happen, so I wanted to try and find you to make amends before the Lord called me home."

Tom seemed touched. "I'm sorry. Didn't know. Are you okay?"

Sorta. I did fine with the surgery, but about six months ago I got some kind of blood infection, and now my red cell count is really high, and the doctor can't quite figure out what's going on. He wants to take out my spleen now—not real sure why."

"I see." Tom felt suddenly uncomfortable, as if he were in the presence of death. He looked at Don and saw the corpse that he soon would be, and the apparition disturbed him in a way he couldn't explain. Here was the person he'd imagined shooting with the gun in his pocket, and yet now he felt sorry he was dying. That too-familiar bewilderment returned. Tom wasn't sure how to cope with life anymore; things he thought he knew and understood reversed themselves, leaving him adrift. Here Don appeared to be dying, and yet Tom couldn't judge if that was good or bad. Did he feel satisfaction or pity? Suddenly he wished he wasn't sitting in this stuffy room listening to this doomed, guilt-ridden dirge, and Tom wanted to be back on the river in front of his own warm stove.

Don pressed on. "Let me get back to something. When everything fell apart back at Container, you left town so quick we never got to talk really, and I never got to explain things to you. I know people told you I got you fired, but it isn't so. I never did that."

Tom again sat forward. "Look, cut the bullshit. We don't need to be making up stories or rewriting history 'cause frankly we're too damned old for that. I don't want to hear some version of a lie from you; I want to hear the truth, that's all, nothing else. I'll leave here and won't bother you ever again, but you're going to tell me what really happened."

Newland seemed annoyed. "That's what I'm doing. I've had a long time to sort this, and there's nothing I can do to persuade you otherwise, so I'm going to lay things out just the way they happened, that's all."

"Good. Get on with it." Tom had begun to sweat from the heat and anger.

Don took a long breath. "A few weeks before Container let you go, management came to me and said that you weren't fitting in with the new president's plans for the future. Remember Eldon Budds? When he became president of Container and shook up all the management, he had his own group of cronies he wanted around him. Eldon came to me himself and said you had embarrassed him once in front of the CEO, pointed out some pecuniary discrepancy or something, I don't even recall, but he never forgot it. He told me he was going to let you go and that he wanted me to take your job."

"That's crap, Don, and you know it. I was away at Eldon's management retreat when Bill Henderson set all this in motion and ambushed me after I got back. I know you were behind that, scheming on me behind my back and trying to steal Oui from me too." Hatred radiated from Tom's eyes, his face ember red as he grabbed the balls of the chair arms, practically breaking them loose from their joints. Leaning forward almost to the point of standing up in a rage, Tom then caught Lee's eye as he held his right palm down, parallel to the floor, cautioning his grandfather to simmer down. Tom got the message, shaking his head, exasperated again by his temper but now back in control.

"Sorry, I forgot. I'm listening. Go ahead," Tom said petulantly.

Don had handled the outburst with self-control, never raising his own voice or allowing Tom's agitation to influence his calm demeanor. "Listen, these guys were playing games with you because you didn't fit in. They knew you were too smart and that you had lots of allies in the company. They wanted to run the show all by themselves, so dumping you had to be part of their plan. You don't believe this, I know, but I begged these guys not to fire you. I told them I didn't want the job and that I could work with you to help you better fit into their plans if they would give you and me the chance. They even lied to me, saying that's what they intended to do, and then they went and ambushed us both. On the day you got canned, I was as stunned as you."

"I notice you didn't turn down my job when they gave it to you, did you?"

"Well, actually I did. Said I didn't want it, that I'd stay right where I was." Don was adamant.

Almost sparking anger again, Tom caught himself. "So why'd you take it after all?"

"Because I had no choice. They were restructuring and said if I didn't take the promotion, then all the people who worked for me would be in jeopardy because a new guy would want his own team. I know some of that might have been bluff, but there was truth in that threat too."

As the dubious past became clearer, Tom again considered he'd misunderstood the whole situation. And the disturbing thought came to him that perhaps he'd misjudged Don.

But old bias is hard to erase, and Tom struggled still. "But everybody said you were the one who started the whole thing, that you went to Eldon and told him a bunch of lies about me."

"I know they did. But it wasn't true." Don paused, looking directly at Tom, and then sheepishly stared at the ground as he began speaking. "There was something else though. Something that was my fault, and I have a lot of guilt about it."

Tom cut off the confession. "It's about Oui, isn't it?"

"You know about Oui?" Don said and then his eyes dropped to the floor.

Wanting to get the whole story, Tom proceeded slowly. "According to what I just heard, I didn't know anything back then, so why don't you tell me this self-serving story too?" Again, Tom caught his ire rising, but a cool stare from Lee kept the tension under control.

"Okay," Tom said. "Give me all the bad news you got." His exasperation now felt consuming. More difficult to listen now, Tom's mind raced to paint mental pictures.

Newland tried to be sympathetic. "I know this is hard; it's hard for both of us. Look, I lost the best friend I ever had those last few days before you left, and I never even got to settle up with you, to tell my side of things."

"I don't give a shit about your side of things, you hear? I want the truth. For Christ's sake, get on with it." Jaw clenched tight, Tom nearly oscillated in his chair as he struggled to maintain equilibrium before what Tom now saw as a plea for forgiveness.

"Hey, guys." Don diverted attention. "That coffee ran right through me, so I got to hit the head right quick. You two relax a minute, and I'll be right back. There's another bathroom there on the left if you need it; my medicine is in the back."

Don's exit was painfully slow. The instant his bedroom door closed, both Tom and Lee sprang to their feet.

"Did you hear that sack of crap?" Tom said, nearly screaming. "He expects me to believe he didn't have anything to do with what happened to me, that he was my defender. Bullshit. I ain't buying that pack of lies." Pacing like an anxious watchdog, Tom struggled to focus. Lee saw the confused anger.

"Let's step outside a second," Lee said quickly. "It's stuffy in here."

The shift proved timely, and after a couple of minutes in the chilly air, Tom's flushed countenance returned to its normal craggy off-white appearance. Lee said nothing, allowing Tom to search the past hour for the things he wanted to analyze. Gradually the pacing slowed, and as Tom leaned against the porch column looking out across the distant grain silos, he wondered if he was being manipulated again.

"I think he's telling the truth." Lee's soft words were met by a hard stare. Head hanging low, shoulders slumped, Tom knew Lee had not only heard Don's story but wasn't angry, as he had listened without such deep prejudice. Old images of his friend flickered, the straightforward thinker, the unemotional problem solver, and with a quick glance back at Lee, Tom realized that today his grandson was the one not overreacting.

"You really think he ain't lying?" Tom tried to pull back his strained emotion. "Sure sounded self-serving to me."

"Yeah, I know," said Lee, "but, Grandpa, he's dying. I don't think he's trying to make up a passel of lies. He's trying to find peace; he needs forgiveness."

Tom misunderstood. "Don't start on all the Christian stuff; I don't want to hear it, not now." The surge of irritation moved Tom off center, and his tentative pathos faded.

"It's not about that," Lee quickly inserted. "It's got nothing to do with church. I'm talking about this poor beaten-down guy making peace with himself before he dies. He can't do that unless he tells you the truth. I think he's trying to forgive himself. It doesn't matter if you believe him; he just needs to say it."

The door opened with a squeak, and Nurse Smart poked her head outside.

"Gentlemen, forgive me for interrupting, but Mr. Newland is very tired right now. Would you mind terribly if he rested a while? Perhaps you could come back later."

"Of course, yes," Tom said before he realized. "I'm so sorry; we didn't mean to put him out." Then having lost his sense of direction, Tom paused to catch the thread. "Would it be possible for us to come back in the morning?"

"Yes, that would be lovely. Mr. Newland has breakfast at eight. If you'd like to come back then, I'd be happy to fix some grits and eggs for you gentlemen as well."

"Thank you, madam," Tom said, feeling the situation again under control. "I saw a hotel back toward town, the Long Valley Inn. Is that an acceptable spot?"

"Why yes, it's quite nice, but you're welcome to stay here if you like; there are extra rooms, and it would be no bother at all."

"No, no we couldn't do that." The idea of sleeping under the same roof as Don Newland nearly made Tom nauseous. "We will see you at eight in the morning."

IV.

The girls squealed as Wanda pulled out her negligee and showed them the lovely black teddy her husband had given her before he died. Of course, she didn't intend to wear it for the sleepover with Glenna and the two girls, but she wanted to scandalize them a bit with its delicate fabric that left little to the imagination. With Glenna leaving the room to get some water, Wanda wanted to get the girls excited for the night together playing Monopoly, eating popcorn, and talking about nothing but girl stuff.

The invitation to Glenna's came as a ray of daylight for Wanda after the tedious holidays. Now she only wanted to clear her memory of the lingering loss special occasions always brought. Though doing well all by herself, Wanda remembered clearly the days being adored by her late husband, those cushy times she rarely worried about utilitarian matters. Since the loss, she had learned to be forthright in her business affairs, and that strength served her well even as she enjoyed cultivating the eccentric persona so at odds with the sedate habits of many traditional south Mississippi women.

Glenna called the festivities to order. "Do you girls want to watch a movie first or play Monopoly? I found *Fried Green Tomatoes* in the movie drawer."

Lucy was quick to answer, "Oh let's play a game. I want us to be able to talk and laugh, so let's save the movie till last." Everyone thought that a sensible plan, and soon the smell of popcorn filled the room while Glenna slid the teddy deftly back into Wanda's bag.

The friendly company soothed the lonely wounds Wanda kept hidden. "Glenna, love, thank you so much for inviting me; it's so much fun to have the girls here without men trying to show us how much they know about everything." To titillate the sisters was part of her therapy tonight, but in her heart, she still hoped that Tom might be back later that evening. His Christmas conversations had touched upon a longing for a strong man she could flirt with and still feel completely safe around.

"It was all Victoria's idea," Glenna responded. "She wanted to have a girls' night, so when Dad and Lee decided to visit a friend in Yazoo City, I figured we had our chance. I must warn you though; Lucy is merciless at this game."

"So are you there, girlie?" Wanda said, smiling. "We'll see about that. I'm showing no pity tonight." Wanda felt the thrill of her bluff as in truth she had only played Monopoly twice before, but to forget that big empty house of hers was already a win this evening.

"Mrs. Spencer?" Lucy asked.

"Please, Lucy. You girls call me Aunt Wanda. That's what my nieces call me—and Monopoly queen, of course. Wanda loved the bravado of repartee that seemed to be her comfort zone in social situations, preferring a more challenging modern style not exactly like many of the women she'd grown up knowing. It never occurred to her that she couldn't control any situation, and that confidence mesmerized the girls.

Lucy continued, "Okay, Aunt Wanda, I want to know something. I plan to be a lawyer when I grow up. Have you ever had a job like that?"

"Now, Lucy," Glenna said, ever on guard, "that's a bit offensive to Wanda, I mean, Aunt Wanda, so let's be a little more civil, okay? Wanda's professional life is really none of our concern." Glenna sat back as if she had set the rules for the evening.

"No, no, Glenna," Wanda said, feeling the thrill of personal engagement. "It's perfectly all right. In fact, I like Lucy's approach, self-assured and focused on what she wants. My kind of girl. This night, ladies, nothing is off base with me, so ask away." Wanda knew she might have opened herself a little too much, but the words left her mouth before any filter applied. She didn't really care; she wanted to be challenged, maybe even outdone. A fragility had crept into Wanda's thoughts lately, carrying a yearning for real human contact with both women and men.

Lucy became impatient, so her interrogation resumed. "So, Aunt Wanda, what was the most favorite job you ever had?"

"Well, Luce," Wanda leaned back as if travelling in thought, "I've done everything from being a secretary to a bee keeper along the way, including some bartending and waitressing." She whispered the two less laudatory jobs, and both Victoria and Lucy squealed with excitement. Glenna grinned and looked toward the kitchen. "But the best job I ever had was when Ernie and I used to play in a band out in Las Vegas; those were the greatest days of my life."

Now, Vic leaned forward. "You played in a band in Las Vegas? Holy cow!"

"Yep, when Ernie and I first dated before we got married in Reno." Her mind drifted slightly. "Anyway, we used to play offbeat places in Vegas and Reno—not the big names you'd recognize but tired, little spots that had regulars who travelled through, people who liked a strong drink and maybe a wild romance for a night. Ernie played bass, and I played rhythm guitar. We had two or three other guys who came in and out of the band. You know, a couple of drummers and a lead guitar fellow named Eldredge Brocolade. That El could sure play. Unfortunately, he could also drink whiskey."

Quick to jump in as Wanda took a breath, Glenna looked impatient. "Well, that's a nice story, but maybe we should get back to the game. Look, everybody seems to have their money ready to go." No one moved. Wanda knew she'd drifted a little far from the shores of rectitude, but she also saw the girls' enthralled look. A decision to push on or acquiesce presented itself, but Wanda remembered she was a guest.

"Yes, of course. I'm sorry. Sometimes my mouth can't find the brakes. Here, give me that thimble, and let's roll these bones."

Before long, the game was in full swing, and popcorn passed around like the offering plate at a Baptist revival. Arguments erupted between the two girls, but Wanda loved seeing their competitive nature. Glenna observed quietly while Wanda recalled days of young motherhood before her own daughter discovered that virulent captiousness that changed them both.

The game finally ended in what was called a draw between the two girls, most of the anger having subsided. Victoria had been quiet most of the evening but now wanted to engage Wanda in more earnest discussion.

"I think it's amazing that you were in a band in Las Vegas," Vic began cautiously. "Did you get paid for playing? I mean, in those days Las Vegas must have been pretty small, huh?" Glenna cast a serious look but said nothing.

"Yeah, the place was nothing like it is today," Wanda began, "but we did get paid. Ernie handled all the money, so I didn't have to worry about that, but we made enough to eat and travel around like gypsies. To be honest, we only did it because we loved playing music. I got to sing and play the guitar. We had so much fun that life seemed like one big vacation."

"So you were the lead singer?" Vic asked.

"No. We all sang really. Ernie had a great voice. Our band changed all the time, so it was hard to lock in any one singer or style, so we floated with the day and did what we could."

Even Glenna seemed fascinated at such an unconventional life. "Were you married then? I mean, was this before Jocelyne?" Glenna asked.

"Lord yes, long before she was born. Ernie and I played together for four years before we got married—you know, parties and all. We'd go see his uncle, Ben Statler, in Reno, and that's how we got started in the clubs. Ben had a friend or two in the business."

"I think it's so interesting that you didn't really worry about anything then," Vic continued. "You know, having kids and such. Or did you?"

Wanda sat back again, looking toward the kitchen to catch her thoughts.

"I don't think a woman ever stops thinking about family and kids. That's how we're different from men. They think about sex and money. Women have to realize that it's our job to get family and kids wedged into the relationship with men or they will fiddle around until a woman can't have kids."

"That seems a little harsh, don't you think?" Victoria responded.

"No, I don't," Wanda said calmly. "Listen, a woman has two choices in life, to use her energy to look for a man that can provide for her or to use her brain to provide for herself and hope she can find a good man along the way. When I was young, that second option didn't really exist, and all we could do was target the right fellow and hope he wasn't as stupid as he acted."

Now Glenna felt compelled to step in. "Now, don't you think you are being overly dramatic? I mean, you make it sound like some kind of hunting expedition."

"It is a hunting of sorts," Wanda continued, "and when you and I were young, we were just as calculating as girls today, only we didn't have as many options. Our goal was to be taken care of, and the smart ones knew that what she carried between her legs was the real weapon she couldn't waste on the wrong prey."

Victoria and Lucy squirmed with excitement. Wanda didn't seem to mind Glenna's frown.

Vic was bursting to speak. "In our Social Directions class at school, we had a two-day discussion of women in the twenty-first century; each of us had to write an essay and present it to the class. Lots of girls talked about marriage or church—but not me."

Glenna spoke eagerly. "So what did you talk about? You didn't say you weren't going to have children, did you? It would break your dad's heart." Glenna blushed, looking as if she'd said out loud what she thought she'd only spoken to herself.

Vic hardened. "Well, let's forget Dad's broken heart because I'm not going to mess with his Chevelle." Jaws dropped all round the table. As Wanda studied the dynamic, she wondered how Glenna really felt about her marriage to such an itinerate husband as Harold. Then Wanda intervened.

"Now, whoa, let's not be rude to your mom. After all, your father is away earning a living so we can sit in this nice, cozy house eating popcorn while he's out on the road God knows where." Though Wanda tried to defend Glenna, in her heart she didn't even believe her own words.

Vic remained undaunted. "But that's my point. Men have manipulated women into believing that because they provide money for the family that it's only their agenda and values that are important. Look, I appreciate that my dad provides for us, but where is the love? Where is the nurturing for my mother who slaves to keep this house running and, might I add, to stay out of his way when he comes home like some warrior back from the crusades, glorious and unapproachable? That's crap; my mom is the hero here, and I don't see anybody in our society standing up for her."

Now Lucy was inspired. "Yeah. Men suck. They think they're more important because they have all the money, the power too." Glenna looked like she wanted to speak but kept quiet.

Sensing her friend's shock, Wanda addressed Lucy. "Love, men don't suck. They aren't evil." Wanda allowed the statement to take root as emotions cooled. "Men are creatures of habit developed over centuries by doting women who taught them to feel overly important."

Vic jumped to her feet. "I agree. That's what I talked about in my class speech, how many cultures treat women like kept animals and not like equals. This isn't the Dark Ages anymore. We aren't hunting wooly mammoths; we're using computers and social networks to communicate. That's women's stuff."

"Exactly," Wanda said. "But sex is still at the heart of everything; it's where our power begins not ends."

"You're right," Vic agreed, "but it's still all about power."

"Yes, indeed," Glenna finally said, "but those cultural norms are changing, and there really are some terrific men in our society today, though some not too terrific as well." She looked down as if studying her shoe suddenly.

Wanda knew she'd set disruption in motion, but that was her nature. Clearly Vic had slipped into her classroom presentation persona, and Wanda was impressed with how comfortable the girl seemed effusing that voice of informed opinion.

Lucy now joined, speaking directly to her mom. "No, it isn't easy, but we don't need a big plan or organization; we only need to change the way we live in our homes."

"Yes," Wanda said. "But what about the power of money? In some countries, women can't drive or vote, and even here, brutal necessity traps women who don't have means or education."

Lucy continued, "We don't need money; we can make men do what we want; we can control them." Wanda thought Lucy quite precious in her oversimplification, but she also saw the strength that ran through this young girl.

With Glenna's energy clearly dissipating, Wanda began steering the conversation back toward fun, but she wanted to make sure Lucy understood the gravity of things a little better.

"Yes, Luce, but we don't want to become overbearing like men with skirts on, do we? We don't want to take on those values of reducing relations to the power struggle of money where one side wins and another side loses."

"Exactly," Lucy's voice was now almost loud. "We have to use our power of family as the secret weapon, you know, delay their gratification to get our own power. It's like chess. Protect our backline and use pieces to weaken opposing strength." Everyone looked at Lucy in astonishment.

Distracted, Wanda finally regained her thought. "Yes, I suppose that is true, but you really must remember that the goal is not to dominate men but to bond with them. Money is problematic since women only earn seventy-one cents on a dollar to what men do for the same work. We have to recognize that and let it motivate us toward change." Then Wanda sensed Glenna zoning out and staring at the kitchen door, obviously searching for a reason to leave the table.

"Okay, girls," said Wanda, "you've worn me out, so let's have some *Fried Green Tomatoes*." With that, everyone clapped and passed the popcorn bowl yet again. But Wanda saw in the collapsed look on Glenna's face that she'd begun to realize her girls were becoming a very different type of woman from the one she'd grown up as. Now Wanda wanted to know, did Glenna also glimpse the kind of woman she too might become one day?

V.

The afternoon in town proved anxious for Tom, though he and Lee found a local snooker hall and spent a couple of hours shooting racks. He struggled to grasp that after all these years practically everything he'd known about Newland's betrayal had in fact been erroneous. This upside-down reality left Tom struggling as the rate of change these past few weeks far outpaced his capacity for adjustment.

The uninspired billiard play gave way to a dinner of fried chicken, black-eyed peas, and hot biscuits, but even that didn't seem to break Tom's puzzlement. He remained vacant no matter how Lee tried to jolt him into thinking about the delicious food or the crazy woman in the corner with a hat that looked like a bird's nest. Nothing seemed to penetrate that veil of distraction behind which Tom seemed to have disappeared.

By eight o'clock, they were in their room preparing for sleep. A communal television down the hall provided Lee with a few minutes of distraction, but Tom went to bed immediately after dinner, saying nothing except that they needed to leave by seven forty-five the next morning.

A night of intermittent sleep lingered, Tom fitful in his twisting unease looking for a comfortable spot his mind could rest. He kept seeing Don's feeble form as a costume of sorts, a Halloween show where at one moment he was the sophomore college roommate and then at another a devil in specious form. Faces distorted, a horrible, craggy stare becoming a smooth boyish smile and then an angry sneer. Tom tumbled through the night hiding from the images, avoiding the parade of transformation that tortured his dreams.

By daybreak, he lay exhausted, wanting only to dress and leave for home. But he could not face Lee's anger, so he considered faking illness. That idea passed quickly as well. The only comfort was a dull blue neon light from the drugstore down the street that sent stripes of dark and light through the prisonlike blinds; the color reminded him of morning fog back on the Catchahoula.

Wondering what Newland's night had been like, Tom hoped he too had tumbled in dread, and then the pistol flashed into his head. Maybe today should be the end for them both; maybe no more thought was necessary. Showering but barely noticing the water peppering his face, Tom lost himself in the sounds of a thunderclap, he thought, or perhaps something else. Then a sound interrupted the storm in his head.

"Time to go," Lee said.

Platitudes about frost and the color of the sunlight reflecting from the puddles in the road barely penetrated his stoic face, though Tom once managed a weak smile. Then gradually as the sun peeked and hid, he began to feel the boy's energy reaching for him. Soon a driveway, an opening door, and as if transported through time by some wizard, Tom sat before a plate of steaming grits with two fried eggs mixed in, dark splotches of black pepper hinting at the zing he needed to feel.

"Mr. Newland will be right here, gentlemen. The doctor is with him now. He seems to have had a difficult night, and it looks like he will have to go to the hospital for tests today. But please, he wants to see you first." Tom smiled faintly at the news, experiencing the first alacrity of the morning.

Soon a creak of the hardwood floor revealed a dark creature slowly ambling toward the kitchen, this time using a walker instead of a cane. In the silhouette of light from the bedroom, Don appeared corpselike. Nurse Smart quickly swept to assist as Newland entered the light of the kitchen.

"I see you boys are having some of the best grits south of Memphis. I tell you, Miss Smart can make some fine cheese grits too, but Doc says I got to lay off them for a while."

"Yes, sir," Lee responded, "these are mighty fine, and this coffee is stiff, like that stuff you get in New Orleans."

"My neighbor works in New Orleans sometimes," Don said. "He always brings me coffee from the Café Du Mont. Still reminds me of my honeymoon. You know at my age coffee's about as good as arousal gets." Lee turned red, but Tom missed the comment entirely, though the mood in the room seemed much improved over yesterday. Soon, dishes cleared, the men sat at the kitchen table nursing a little apple cobbler.

Don led off slowly. "I'm sorry about disappearing yesterday. I got a little faint and needed to lie down a spell. Happens when I get too tired."

"It's okay," Tom answered casually. "Shouldn't have barged in on you like that anyway." Remembering carrying the pistol into the house and wanting to catch Don off guard, today that hostility seemed like a picture Tom could no longer touch.

"Look," Don rallied his energy. "You boys don't want to stick around here all day, so let's get to it. I need to get my say in while I got a little strength to spare."

"Fine," Tom said, feeling almost sympathetic, "but if you're not up to it …" Tom hoped to avoid the whole discussion, the thing he'd wanted for years now, and yet Don raised his hand to silence the false protestations.

"No, that won't be necessary." Don paused to sip his coffee and take another bite of the cobbler, then stared directly at Tom.

"When I got word the brass planned to fire you, I went directly to Oui. Understand, I was under strict orders not to say anything to you, but they didn't say anything about Oui, so I took that loophole as a sign."

Remembering what Mike had told him at Thanksgiving, Tom had a powerful urge to smack Newland with his fist but forced himself to remain calm.

"I know what you did," Tom said bitterly.

Unfazed, Don continued. "Just relax, okay. So, I told Oui about management's plan, and for a couple of weeks, we talked about it on the phone every day—you know, what could we do, should we tell you? That sort of thing. Tom, this is the part I feel really guilty about because all during that period, I really did care about you and how to help save your job. But something happened to me then. I don't understand it all, but the more I talked about you and listened to Oui, the more I started thinking about her, you know, how I felt sorry for her with Glenna so young and you fixin' to get fired."

"Bullshit. You didn't feel sorry for anybody; you only lusted for my wife. And you son of a bitch, you're telling me you were talking to her for two damned weeks. I'm gonna bust your ass!" And Tom was on his feet, leaning over Don with fist balled, ready to slug the frail old man who drew his body back slightly but obviously with little physical ability either to fight or run. Tom hesitated when he felt Lee's hand on his drawn wrist, strangely grateful that he'd also left the pistol in the truck.

"Sit down," Don ordered. "Please, sit down and let me finish." Don too began to lose his patience. "If you'll contain yourself, I'll tell you what happened, but if you're going to keep jumping in my face, then you can clear out of here, and that will be that. Tom glared sullenly but took a seat.

Newland resumed. "During this period when Oui and I were talking, I think I fell in love with her. She seemed so vulnerable; told me how she didn't know how you would react to getting fired, that this job meant everything. But that wasn't the thing that got to me, Tom."

"Then what was it?" Tom barked.

"Oui told me about the guy back in Picayune, you know the one she almost didn't accept your marriage proposal for?" Tom's breathing stopped, and he felt the blood in his face drain away. "She told me how you went to PRC your freshman year and how you were so in love, and then that other guy talked to her about not going off to State with you and staying in Picayune instead."

Tom had little idea what Don was talking about. He remembered a spat the second semester he was at PRC but recollected it was about something he said about Oui's brother, not about another guy. Now he couldn't decide whether to confess his ignorance and hear the truth or feign familiarity with the story and save face. The dilemma disrupted

Tom's thinking so dramatically he was unable to speak as a loop of erratic images replayed in his brain.

Newland didn't notice Tom's distress. "Oui said that other guy didn't want to go to college, so she wouldn't have to leave her family."

Words continued to fall from Don's mouth, but to Tom they sounded like a phonograph record on very slow speed as a viral thought emerged that this other man might have been Mike. Had yet another best friend deceived him? Shaking his head without speaking, Tom could not process that possibility.

"When she talked about this other fellow," Newland continued obliviously, "I knew then I could be that same guy too. She was scared for the future, knew you'd go crazy when you got fired. You hear me, Tom? She wanted to be loyal, but she was scared you'd crack. That was what set me off; I knew I could make life easy for Oui. She'd never have to worry with me 'cause I wasn't so hotheaded like you."

With glazed eyes, Tom imagined Don and Oui criticizing his temper and judging his difficulty with people, his tendency to withdraw. Streaming images burned through his eyelids as secret phone calls day and night and traitorous whispers filled Tom's imagination. Then he erupted.

Fist again raised, Tom lunged to hit Don as hard as he could, but again Lee stopped his grandpa's arm, pulling Tom backward. No one spoke. The moment dripped with hatred. Finally, Tom turned to Don.

"You took advantage of Oui, didn't you? She was scared, and you slipped that knife right into my back, you two-faced bastard." The words flowed thick as cold blood.

Don tried to stand but couldn't. "No, it wasn't like that. I did everything I could to build you up in Oui's mind, to save your job. I did, Tom. It's not what you think."

"So I guess all this stuff I heard about your coming over to Oui's when I was at the retreat was just talk, huh? You were in church I suppose?"

"No, I was wrong there. I had been out for a few beers and on my way home stopped by your house. I guess I was drunker than I realized. But she threw me out, Tom, honest."

"Well, did you leave?"

"Yeah, I did, but the next night I went back sober. Tried to tell Oui I loved her and that I couldn't save your job but I could save her. Things got all crazy, and I tried to kiss her. She slapped me hard, yelling for me to leave; it was a mess. I was afraid a neighbor would hear or Glenna would come in, so I left. But I lost my temper when she called me a traitor. I went nuts and started saying she deserved what she got. Stupid stuff. I don't know what came over me. It's the biggest mistake I ever made."

Tom ripped his arm free from Lee. "I've heard enough of this shit. I'm leaving. If you weren't such a puddle of scum, I'd whip your ass, but right now it looks like God has already done that for me. In my book, Don, you're already dead." And with that, Tom slammed the screen door hard, then stood on the porch where he could still overhear his grandson.

With deep voice and icy-cold eyes, Lee spoke slowly. "Mister. You deserve the special hell you're already in. My grandpa trusted you as a friend, and that was a mistake. Listen to me now. Stay away from my family. This time I stopped my grandpa from hurting you, but me, I'll use your sorry ass to wax my car if I ever hear your voice again."

As the door slammed, the top hinge broke, and Tom flipped Lee a quick grin. Both had lost their tempers but had at least sampled the vengeance they came to find. The road lengthened as the day warmed, and each sank into silence, but then about fifteen miles from Newland's house, Tom hit the brakes. He looked at Lee. "We're going back."

"What for?" Lee asked.

"I'm going to hit that liar as hard as I can. I ain't going to let him bend the truth and make Oui sound disloyal like he did. This is my last chance, and I'm taking it."

The determination on Tom's face made arguing pointless. Lee began to dread what might happen next, as whatever governor restraining his grandpa from revenge all these years had now been removed. He was proud to see his grandpa call out Newland's lies, but suddenly, imagining Tom in jail, Lee began to hesitate and hoped the drive would cool Tom down.

A half hour later, after near total silence, the truck stormed into the driveway. This time the doctor's Buick and Nurse Smart's Toyota were both gone.

"Looks like everyone's gone to the hospital already." Lee's words drooled with a tinge of relief.

"Let's see." Tom pounded on the front door. No response. Then he walked to the back door hammering again. No answer.

"Damn it." And he kicked the back-porch step. But walking back to the truck, Tom noticed the crumbling bricks of the front foundation pillar that held up the porch and the front of the house. His grimace became a grin. Off to the truck he scampered, happy to have a task.

At first Lee simply watched, but then Tom opened his toolbox and pulled out two rather long steel chains. "What the?" the boy said, mystified.

"Just get over here and help me." Tom was all seriousness. Within minutes, he had repositioned the truck almost up to the front steps but facing down the driveway and had looped both chains around the crumbling right house footing. In this wet low country, no one had large basements, and Tom knew exactly how unsteady such old foundation footings became with age.

Once secured to the truck hitch, Tom adjusted the chains so each carried the same amount of tension. Next, he dropped the truck into four-wheel drive. As Lee stood sentry, the scene unfolded like a wild video game.

With one mad accelerating pull, the truck heaved against the pillar and at first simply stopped in place with tires spinning, sending up a cloud of dust. Tom repositioned the chains nearer the top of the pillar at what he thought would be a better tipping point. On the second pull, a loud crack shot through the truck cab as the crumbly bricks leaned forward. With a huge crash, the right side of the house and porch fell forward, smothering the broken pillar while leaving a deep gouge in the ground where the corner of the main house dug into the front yard and the front porch snapped off like the lead of a pencil.

Both Tom and Lee looked up and down the road for cars, but this remote homestead stood alone. As Tom moved toward the house, he thought the whole structure looked like a cat leaned down on one knee with its front paw nestled underneath, big haunches still high in the rear. A mischievous smile crossed his face, and then he got busy.

Quickly the chains were removed and the toolbox locked. As Tom started the truck, in the rearview mirror he surveyed the ruins one last time, the arched back of the house, the groveling front porch, windows blankly peering into nothingness while the inside curtains fanned in the stiffening breeze seeping through the broken glass of the windows. A drizzling rain now fell with passion.

Hitting the accelerator, he turned to his grinning grandson: "Must've been an earthquake or something."

Rain had already begun obliterating the tire tracks, and preoccupied with the thought, Tom mistakenly turned right out of the driveway instead of left as he seemed more intent on gathering words than driving. Seconds later, without even glancing sideways, Tom calmly pronounced his summary of the event: "It's a terrible thing to have your home wrecked, terrible thing for sure."

A half mile up ahead, a huge highway sign grew larger, a thirty-foot-high man in a flannel shirt holding a massive, translucent container half-filled with blue liquid. Underneath, a caption read, "Overland Container: We Fill Your Life." Tom studied the sign from a quarter of a mile away. The oaf holding the giant plastic jug reminded him of his days working at the plant and the way he'd been treated in the end. So scrunching his face about a hundred yards from the sign, Tom put the truck into neutral to coast by. His glare never left the sign as if some secret conversation was taking place without speaking. Then, without a word, he grabbed his pistol from under the seat and, shooting left-handed, put two bullets dead center into the lower quarter of the container. The blue liquid inside began leaking out instantly as two streams of alien urination, Tom thought, and a devilish smile enveloped Tom's whole face.

Unexpectedly, he mumbled, "Fill that, jackass."

VI.

The morning after girls' night came early. Glenna knew a long day of cooking lay ahead, but nothing could have made her happier. By six thirty, she was already chopping onions and celery and orchestrating a dozen kitchen tasks, all with precise synchronization.

No one else had arisen when she put the coffeepot on at seven fifteen, and Glenna was glad to have quiet time to get her work done. As she stepped into the dining room to retrieve a silver ladle from her mother's antique sideboard, she happened to glance through the open curtain facing out to the street and noticed an old tan pickup with no hubcaps drive slowly by the house. No real concern, but the truck barely moved as if looking for something. But at such an early hour it was probably only some handyman.

Glenna returned to the kitchen tasks, forgetting the strange vehicle. A few minutes later, a slight tapping sound came from the back door that led into the kitchen. Again she thought it odd at that hour, but perhaps Sue needed to borrow some coffee or eggs, as they often did from each other.

"Sue, is that you?" Glenna asked with familiar intonation. They had coffee together a couple of days a week to share the news about their kids and the neighborhood. But Sue did not respond. Wiping her hands on the black-checkered dishrag, nothing in mind except the pie crust she wanted to make next, Glenna turned the knob to the back door while suddenly remembering she'd forgotten to turn down the eggs cooking on the stove. As she spoke, she glanced back at the stove for just a flash to make sure everything was okay.

"Good morning there, Miss Early Bird ..." and with startling suddenness she realized a complete stranger stood at the storm door, a rather tall man likely in his fifties, wearing shabby clothes and muddy shoes. Glenna's cheery disposition evaporated.

The man spoke. "Excuse me there, madam, my name is, a, Wilbur Simmons. Is this here the Mitchell residence?" Glenna said nothing. "I don't mean to disturb you none, but I met your husband over in Memphis a few months back, and he was telling me about this Chevelle he was restoring. I was wondering if I could see the car; you know, I might want to buy it."

Glenna knew immediately something was amiss; that car was her husband's pride, and he would never sell. She screwed shut her mouth tightly without moving another step toward the door.

"I'm sorry, Mr. Simmons, but my husband will have to deal with that. I'll have him contact you when it's convenient to come back. Right now we have a house full of holiday guests about to come down to breakfast." Making sure her voice remained icy, Glenna wanted to know how this man knew her address, but she didn't want to engage him any further. A creepy chill crawled over the hairs on the back of her neck while images of Wanda and the girls upstairs flashed through her head. She prayed no one would come downstairs.

"Well, Mrs. Mitchell," the stranger said, his voice now more insistent, "that's not going to work for me. I'm passing through on my way to, ah, to ah, Florida; I live in Florida. I need to see the car now."

Her stomach turned, and from the corner of her eye, Glenna spotted a butcher knife on the counter. She nonchalantly drifted in that direction.

"Mr. Simmons, I'm sure you will appreciate that I have a large gathering of people to attend to, so if you would, I'll have to ask you to leave now. I'll be sure to tell Harold you stopped by." Her tone satisfied Glenna; she'd been decisive yet courteous, now expecting the stranger to leave quietly. Instead he pulled hard at the storm door that fortunately was locked and then hit the Plexiglas panel hard with his right fist, cracking it right in the center.

The sound echoed through the kitchen like a shot, and Glenna froze in fear. Suddenly the man's face glared red and swollen, lips sneering angrily. "Open this damned door or I'll rip it off the wall, you bitch."

Glenna slammed the wooden door, locking it in the same motion, then sprinted toward the knife as the stranger rattled the storm door.

"Go away! I'm calling the police!" her frantic voice yelled.

Upstairs, Victoria had already arisen and put on sweatpants to go out for a run before breakfast. She heard her mother's voice and then a crash of some kind, so she ran down to see what had happened. At the head of the stairs, she heard her mom yelling.

"The police are on their way!"

Then a man's voice rumbled as Vic looked out an upstairs window to see the stranger at the door. She shot down the main staircase to the front door where Glenna caught a glimpse of her daughter going outside, but Vic was gone before Glenna could react. In seconds, the girl circled around the oleander bushes that lined the back side of the house; no one ever walked around there. She saw the stranger at the back door, a pistol bulging from his right pocket.

Through the kitchen window, Glenna saw Vic approaching the stranger from behind, and she had the quick idea to keep the man distracted.

"Okay, Mr. Simmons, I'll get the key. I have it right here." Glenna saw the man smile and also watched Vic pick up a piece of rebar leaning against the gate that she'd driven into the ground for twining her nasturtiums in the summer.

"Okay, I'm opening the door now. Here's the key." The man stared ahead intently as the wooden door opened. Vic raised the rebar like a baseball bat and then without a sound swung as hard as she could, catching the stranger right behind the kneecap on his left leg. He buckled like an imploding building suddenly having lost structural integrity. As he hit the ground, his head bounced off the concrete patio pavers, and he groaned in pain. In an instant, Vic grabbed the pitchfork her brother used to pick up fall leaves, and immediately the tines indented the stranger's throat.

"Listen, buster," Vic said, standing over him, "if you move, you'll lose a gallon of blood in thirty seconds, and the heaviest thing you'll ever lift will be your eyelids. So shut up and don't move." Wanda had joined Glenna at the window; they both gasped. In seconds, they jerked the back door open wide.

"Are you okay, Vic? Oh my God," Glenna said.

"I've called the police," Wanda said. Vic nodded without emotion.

Wanda smiled at Victoria, who had the man whimpering in pain with a broken leg and a pitchfork ready to disable him for life.

As the sirens pulled into the driveway, everyone felt a wave of relief, and Victoria finally released a slight half grin. Wanda took two steps down to the patio, giving the girl a thumbs-up.

"Vic, darling, I forgot to tell you something last night. Women have to teach men many other things besides just how to love, but, dearie, it seems you already know that, don't you?"

Victoria smiled proudly and then spoke to Wanda. "See, I guess it's a woman's world after all."

Two policemen came racing around the side of the house, guns drawn, badges flashing, yelling, "Everybody freeze, police! Don't worry, we've got this under control."

Raising her eyebrows, Wanda growled, "Men."

Chapter 10

I.

After finally getting all the police activity taken care of and the girls settled down, Glenna sat alone in her room. The morning had so disturbed her, she couldn't quite find the rhythm of the day again, and the mountain of work she needed to do for the meal felt like unwanted pressure. She decided to call Harold.

"Is everything okay?" Harold said. He was in Little Rock and stunned to hear from Glenna, as she never called.

"Actually, no." Glenna almost broke down crying but held herself back. "A man with a gun tried to break down the back door today. Said something about buying the Chevelle and wouldn't go away." She could hardly remember the details now. "His name was Wilbur Simmons."

"I don't know a Wilbur Simmons, Glenn. What did he look like?" After Glenna gave the details she could remember, Harold knew.

"I think I know who this is," Harold said apologetically. "He's a guy I met in Memphis. Some pickpocket stole my wallet, and this guy happened to find it on the side of the road, or so he said. No money or credit cards of course. He called me asking for a reward, so I met him and gave him fifty bucks. I think he's some kind of drug dealer for truckers, as he tried to sell me amphetamines and got mad when I wouldn't buy anything."

"So is that how he got our address?" Glenna was too upset to be angry.

"I reckon. From my license." She heard the sincerity in Harold's voice.

"But he knew about the Chevelle, too." Glenna had reservations.

"Yeah, I had a couple of pictures of Lee and the car in my wallet. Clyde and I talked about how I wanted to give the car to Lee one day."

"Did you tell him you wanted to sell it?" The pointed question tightened the tension on the line.

"Of course not. I would never sell that car. Not for any reason." She was convinced the situation wasn't malicious on Harold's part, but her emotions roiled.

"I can't live this way any longer, Harold. I'm too lonely. You come through just to change clothes, and I have to take care of the kids all by myself. You don't even care what's going on with any of us." She started weeping.

"That's not true, Glenn. I care. I care a lot. But I don't feel like anyone cares about me. I'm just a doer that does the money getting." Deep in his voice was a dark, lonely place that Glenna recognized as the same place in her. She sat without speaking. Harold continued.

"I've got something I want to discuss with you, Glenna. I'll be back day after tomorrow. Let's you and me go to the Sea Lodge for dinner. Got a hankering for one of them big lobsters." Glenna erupted with a bawling she hadn't experienced since her mom died.

"You're not going to divorce me, are you?" she asked near hysteria. "I couldn't take that right now, Harold." Then, the minutes on his cell phone ran out, and the line went mute.

II.

To burn up some of the morning's anxiety, Glenna threw herself into preparing the big meal for her dad's return. The girls helped, and Wanda too, but Glenna withdrew into her own quiet world of preparation.

"Will somebody please get that doorbell? My hands are covered with flour." Glenna knew she needed to try being less grumpy.

"I got it, Glenna," Wanda said casually as she headed for the front door. The girls' night had been a big success, lasting until after midnight watching movies and talking. Though the stranger's disruption to the day had thrown off Glenna's timeline, everyone was anxious for Tom and Lee's return.

Wanda primped her hair in the hallway mirror before opening the door, always ready to be on stage with any cue to be sociable. Pulling open the front door, she found herself a bit nonplussed. Wanda expected Tom to be at the door, locked after the morning's disturbing episode, so when she saw a shorter man wearing a John Deer cap, she wasn't quite sure what to say. She then recognized Mike from the pictures Glenna had shown her. Odd but he reminded her of Ernie with that cute smile and air of humility.

"Well hello there, handsome. Is my tractor ready or are you here to volunteer for the charity escort auction? I'm the head judge." Wanda couldn't help slipping into a coquettish humor, and seeing Mike's ears turn red and jaw open like a broken nutcracker further inspired her.

"Seriously, mister, I'm lining up men in the kitchen to test their worthiness, so let's not waste time. Get yourself in here for proper evaluation." With matter-of-fact tone, she grabbed poor Mike by the hand and hauled him inside; he couldn't even grunt let alone speak coherently but allowed himself to be yanked inside by this strong redhead.

"Who is it, Wanda?" said Glenna. "Is it Mike? He called and said he was coming to talk to Dad."

"Well there, young fellow, so your name is Mike, is it? Mike Hamlin, I presume." The defenseless creature stood as bewildered as a deer in the middle of the interstate, and Wanda aimed straight for his manhood. "All the girls tell me you're quite the buck and that a poor little doe like me won't stand a chance against that charm of yours." And with that, Wanda stepped so close to Mike she could hear his heart beating. She bent near him, swishing her hair by his face, allowing him to smell her perfume, then cut her green eyes directly toward him.

"Well show me your stuff, big boy." Mike was so shaken he dropped the bag in his hand, spilling out a mess of turnip greens he'd picked from his garden right before leaving Picayune. Wanda looked down at the bright color spread on the wooden floor then winked at Mike, "Oh, I see, green, yes, very green indeed." She then turned and left Mike standing in the hallway with turnip greens spread at his feet and all the blood in his body now drained to his toes. Glenna appeared from the kitchen at last.

"Oh, Mike, how are you? Dad isn't back yet, but he should be here shortly. Did you meet my friend Wanda?" To an outsider, Glenna appeared perfectly normal.

Wanda leaned against a column separating the living room and kitchen, her ankles crossed and long, lean body spread against the pole but said nothing, only cutting a seductive Lauren Bacall look toward Mike.

Struggling to remember Glenna's question, he finally answered. "Well, yeah, yes, we, ah, I did, I think … How do you do there, Miss Wanda?"

"Listen to that. The little dear called me Miss Wanda. Do you call all the girls by their first name, sonny, or am I special? People tell me I have very special talents."

"Now, Wanda, stop that." Glenna immediately saw what was happening. "Leave Mike alone. He's a good friend of our family, so don't make him uncomfortable."

"Well, excuse me there, Mikey, but since you stood us up for Christmas dinner, I thought I'd give you a little taste of my medicine. But enough; your bodyguard has given me warning, tractor man." Finally, Wanda dropped the act, allowing Mike to relax his shoulders that had hunched up to his ears.

"Come on with me to the kitchen, Mike," said Glenna. "I have stuff on the stove."

With that, Wanda wheeled and walked into the kitchen with complete superiority, leaving Mike to gather up his greens and his disheveled manhood.

Entering the kitchen, Mike mumbled, "I picked you some greens, Glenna. They sure are good since we had some cold weather on 'em." The more settled images of the kitchen helped calm Mike—Glenna at the sink, the girls at the kitchen table, and smells of chicken broth steaming up the windows.

"Why thank you, sir. I'll cook them to go along with the dumplings tonight. And make us a big pone of corn bread too." Wanda observed

Glenna's chipper mood so suddenly transformed and realized how skilled her friend had become at compartmentalizing life, a talent useful for alleviating immediate pain but perhaps not the healthiest habit Glenna could cultivate. Then she moved to exploit the cornbread comment.

"Oh my," Wanda said. "A cornpone, huh? So you're a cornpone kind of guy?" Speaking slowly with exaggerated drawl, she considered devastating Mike in front of the girls but knew Glenna would object, so she let mocking do the job. Already Wanda had poor Mike sized up as a simple country boy, and one caught off guard at that.

"Well, Miss Wanda, is it? I'm not only a cornpone kind of guy but a corncob fellow as well." The feeble double entendre launched a whirl of "woos" and "woes" around the room, but no one loved the retort better than Wanda, as a spirited repartee from a manly man was something she'd come to miss in her life. Her sultry look and half grin consumed Mike, though she said nothing, allowing her silence to speak instead.

Glenna barely noticed. "Listen there. How about taking this pot off the stove for me and setting it here in the sink? That chicken is a little heavy for me."

Mike moved the pot with his usual amiable ease, noticing Victoria and Lucy whispering to one another with excited little giggles. He turned to Glenna again with a question.

"So, when I called, you said something happened this morning. What's the story?" His pleasant tone revealed Mike did not know any of the details, so Glenna scanned the room, searching for a way to proceed.

"You know, I'm kinda busy here. Vic, why don't you tell Mike about our visitor." And a fifteen-minute recitation followed.

"So finally, the police arrived and took the heathen away," Vic said after the long speech. "He's in jail now, and his truck was towed to the police station. I know one thing; if my dad had been here, that creep would be in the hospital." The comment halted Glenna, who turned with a loving look at her daughter, which Wanda noted as well.

"Or Tom," Mike added. "Good thing the old bear was off chasing beehives. His big smile showed he was proud of his comment.

Hands wiped, Glenna stepped toward Mike. "About that. When Dad and Lee come home, let's try and downplay the drama a little, okay?

You know how he blows up sometimes, and after a long trip, I don't think getting him too agitated is a good idea." Mike scrunched his face like he didn't totally follow the logic, but ever the soldier, he nodded in agreement. Wanda studied the interaction, noticing Glenna's tendency toward secrecy and Mike's toward agreement. Even Vic's comment about her dad was revealing, as perhaps this family wasn't quite as fragmented as she'd believed. Now Wanda wanted to see Tom's reaction, as she always enjoyed a round of fireworks, especially ones she didn't have to light.

III.

The drive home from Yazoo City passed uneventfully. A few times Lee tried to recount the two days and what had happened, but his grandfather only grunted and pretended to be mono-focused on driving. Face scrunched obviously with deep thinking, Tom barely flinched even as Lee referenced things he saw along the road, a stand selling "The Best Pralines North of Gulfport" or "New Orleans Antiques." But Tom would have none of the palaver.

Piecing together what they had learned at Newland's was tricky as Lee sorted the surprisingly sketchy details. The whole sequence now appeared convoluted, and Lee wasn't sure what had been truthful or what had been missed because of Tom's temper.

That comment Don made about the "other guy" kept ringing as Lee remembered the letter where Saralynn referenced a similar episode, but none of the dates or people seemed clear. He began to understand the bewildering complexity of relationships between men and women, how they seemed so straightforward in the movies but in real life didn't follow any simple line of logic. He wondered how his own parents had wandered into their estranged world of pretense where his dad behaved more as a visitor than a member of the family. What had happened to them along the way? Was there treachery in their past also, or had closeness simply died of neglect?

"Listen, Lee," Tom finally said. "We'll be home in a minute, so let's keep all this Newland stuff between us. I don't want to answer a bunch of questions, so you just say we saw Don, but he was too sick to talk much. Glenna worries too much anyway, so let's let this all slide away." The plaintive tone in Tom's voice had a depth Lee wasn't sure he understood. His grandfather appeared worried about the day's events, preoccupied as if details needed lots of thinking and considering before they could be exposed to the scrutiny of outsiders, especially his daughter.

"Okay, no problem," Lee said. "You can count on me, but I sure would love to tell Mom how we crippled Newland's house." Lee smiled and wanted to say more but knew the timing was wrong. But then just as mysteriously, Tom broke into a laugh that Lee matched as they vented the stultifying tension of the drive home.

"Yeah, son, we dropped that baby like an eight-point buck, didn't we?" The bubble around Tom depressurized briefly, leaving a faint smile, his spirit lifting slightly, Lee thought, and the boy felt that friendship feeling again with his grandpa, that shared closeness new memory uses as bonding.

With a slight smile, Tom half-joked, "I think your mom would be the last person to appreciate our little outlaw prank, but a little revenge was called for in this case, and it could have been a helluva lot worse." The pistol popped into Lee's head, then the fistfight he'd hoped to see. And as alternative realities popped in and out, he decided a dead house was better than a dead person.

Then Tom spoke quietly. "Thank you for going with me, son. Having you there helped me stay clear on things. I know what I did was wrong. Broke the law. But sometimes what is wrong has a way of being right." His voice trailed off as Tom finished, and a hint of sadness touched Lee. The moment overripe, Lee simply reached over to give Tom a quick little fist punch on the arm, silent love shared in the language of men.

IV.

As they pulled in front of the house, Lee got excited. "Looks like a party. There's Mike's truck, and Wanda's Cadillac too. This outta be fun."

"Yeah." Tom smiled, secretly hoping the celebration would distract people from asking too many questions. So, focused on avoiding the social spotlight, Tom figured to make a big entrance as camouflage for slipping into the background when the talkers took over.

"You go in first," Tom insisted. "I'll trail behind. Remember now, our secret, okay?"

Thinking the kitchen would be a safer place, Tom drove to the back of the house. His scheme, of course, was dead wrong. The two men noticed the broken panel on the storm door, but that door often got stuck, so Lee figured somebody had pulled on it too hard. The second Lee opened the wooden back door, however, a wave of chatter and heat poured from inside, the smell of chicken and dumplings blanketing the men with the balm of home.

"Well, Lordy mercy, we got another couple of handsome men slipping in the back door," and Wanda grabbed Lee to give him a kiss on the cheek and a big hug. Then Tom crept in. "Hey there, handsome, good to see you again," said Wanda, more amiably than the virago Tom remembered at Christmas, her soft smile calming the edgy moment. The compliment surprised Tom, as he actually enjoyed being called handsome.

Within seconds, the room burst into conversation, with Lee's sisters talking about girls' night, Glenna asking Tom if he was hungry, and Mike and Wanda deciding who would be in the Super Bowl.

Mike caught Tom edging toward the den. "So, how was your trip? Did you get to see Newland?"

The question seemed innocent enough, but Mike's unexpected presence left Tom wary. Without dwelling too much on substance, he dispatched with the inquiry. "Yeah, we saw him for a minute. He's real sick—dying, I think—and he had to go to bed."

Across the room, Lucy couldn't wait to talk to Lee and pulled him aside. "Did you hear about the terrorist? Broke the door there. He had a gun and I think maybe a bomb too." Scrunching his face, Lee thought the story might be a joke.

"Oh yeah? Where is he now? I don't see any strangers." Lee smiled.

"He's in prison. The police took him." Her definitive answer sounded more legitimate.

The noise was driving Glenna crazy. "Okay, guys. I can't hear myself think in here. Everyone go to the den and let me finish dinner. We'll be eating in about an hour." With that, the crowd drifted away, leaving Lee to investigate Lucy's claim.

Helping Glenna make a salad, Lee spoke quietly. "So what happened to the storm door?"

Eyes flashing, Glenna knew Lee was onto the secret. She cocked her head. "Lucy, right?"

They both laughed. "Yeah, she said a terrorist with a bomb was here." Again they had a good chuckle.

"Not exactly a terrorist but a scary stranger anyway. Some loser that found your dad's wallet and knew our address. Found pictures of the Chevelle too." That seemed enough information for the moment.

"So Dad knows?" Lee asked.

"Yes. He's on his way home." Glenna really didn't know what else to say. "Look, go send Grandpa in here so I can tell him myself. I don't want him flipping out on us."

A moment later, Tom appeared with a concerned look. "Lee says you got some news for me."

Trying to look as busy as possible, Glenna wasted no time. "Look, Dad, some guy broke the door. He'd found Harold's lost wallet and knew where we lived. Saw pictures of the car and pretended he was here to buy it." She felt embarrassed. "Vic broke his leg, and the cops hauled him away." Tom only laughed.

"What? Broke his leg?" he said.

"While the guy was yanking on the door," Glenna said, "she snuck up behind him and wacked him with a piece of rebar. He dropped like a dishrag. Don't be upset, Dad; everything's okay. Harold is on his way home." Tom sat down.

"That girl definitely has some Saralynn in her." They both smiled. "But I apologize, hon. I should have been here instead of off babysitting that dead man in Yazoo City." Tom's mind drifted to the broken house.

"So did you have a chance to visit with that guy?" Glenna asked.

"Yeah, he had some stories from the old days. Nothing important. Just a bunch of tales."

Her dad and Glenna chatted a few moments, but Tom showed almost no emotion. Even he was surprised he didn't react with more volatility. Then, as if they'd discussed the day's pedestrian duties, Tom returned to the den as a dull film began covering the memory of the past two days.

The girls chattered away and then scooted out of the den, so Tom stared at the concert playing on the television. A few moments later, the experience produced an unexpected effect. On stage, a man sang to what appeared to be hundreds of thousands of people, mesmerizing them with his power as in unison they all rhythmically moved to familiar sequences exactly mimicking the performer. For an instant, Tom felt pulled into the power of that scene, feeling the synchronicity of tens of thousands of people.

Lost in the exuberance, Oui's beautiful blue eyes sparkled in his mind as she called to him through this lovely scene before him. Staring dreamily, he remembered how Oui used to sing in the kitchen as birds played outside at the feeder.

The familiar image gave rise to other sensations, and Tom recalled those many afternoons on her mother's porch swing with Oui all those decades before, and for an instant, Tom was sure he understood the eternity of time, that place his own chinaberry swing had hinted at that afternoon.

The odd euphoria swept him upward as he leaned forward in his chair, emotionally reaching into the crowd to feel what they felt, and Tom merged into the love between performer and audience. For a moment, he peered high above the treetops of his cluttered thought out toward the horizon of his life, and the air stroked him as lightly as a June morning.

"Hey there, big fellow." Wanda spoke abruptly. "Rock and roll fan are you? Amazing, isn't it? I watched it a few nights ago."

The words penetrated Tom's trance, but he didn't remove his forward stare until the song ended. Then he spoke. "This guy is something. Got that audience right in his hand, like some religious thing, musical sex maybe."

Even Tom was surprised as those words sprang. His eyes locked on Wanda, but neither spoke. And for one of the only times since Oui's death, Tom stood comfortably in the presence of another woman with no urgency to flee.

"The other night, I bumbled into this concert," Wanda said. "You know, a little lonesome, and then there was this presence in front of me with bedroom eyes, some desperation in them that the audience understood."

"I've never been to a concert," Tom responded quickly. "Don't think I'd like it. Too many people." The high awareness waned now as habitual thought resumed control, but something special had flashed from Wanda, a moment that pulled Tom back to a region he'd forgotten existed.

She spoke softly. "Can you imagine yourself being in that crowd?" Then she paused turning directly to Tom. "Life doesn't have to be routine all the time; sometimes it can be absolute joy." Wanda's sincerity, her hushed frankness froze the air.

"Maybe I can see that," Tom said. "See myself there trying to feel that, but it's hard, like maybe I don't know how to do it right."

She stepped even closer. "Feeling the moment, that's the secret, not trying to feel it. Music lifts your soul to where it can see over the confusion of things without needing a single word." And without warning, the intimacy delicate as a resting hummingbird fluttered away on the intrusive sound of normalcy.

"Supper's ready." Came the call from the kitchen.

Heavy gaze falling to the floor with Wanda touching his hand lightly, Tom lifted a slight glance then disappeared into the slavery of habit. Turning, he left without a word as Wanda mustered a frantic, "Music is where you can find Oui again, Tom." The dying sounds left only loneliness as companion for Tom, who would not allow Wanda's lure to touch him any longer. Listening to the cheering crowd adoring the man under the lights, Tom heard the clunk of his own boots and thought they sounded almost military. And once again, human connection, intimacy almost, stalled beneath the indifferent march of lost choice.

V.

Dinner proved to be a festival. Tom smiled and mumbled small talk, the two girls chattered about girls' night, Mike and Lee envisioned the Chevelle and how in two weeks his dad was going to let Lee drive it for the first time, while Glenna and Wanda reminisced about how wonderful family time could be without conflict. The size of the group made one big conversation impossible, so all around, discussions lurched and plodded through quieter moments. The threat from earlier in the day had completely evaporated in the warm, friendly atmosphere of denial.

The sounds at the table and thoughts of the concert tumbled in Tom's mind, how that singer had brought a single guidance to the crowd noise, organizing the singing, yelling, and dancing into an effortless synchronicity. He understood now why his family must be united in a physical place and not just aware that each other exists in remote corners of the river or suburban boxes, and he almost craved the permanency of one channel in time with its communal flow. The buoyancy felt almost unrecognizable with its welling of hope, a fullness difficult to find when on the Catchahoula alone.

Glimmers of wife and mother flitted, and he missed their voices, their indefatigable energy around the table, but tonight Tom chose to be convivial as the raucous conversation rose. Looking across the family, he imagined Ouida smiling, Saralynn listening, and there he was joined into the wholeness of things just as he had been while watching the television concert. Separation and connection merged as the stuff of life tonight, and the quiet drift of time passed as a slowly building sunset marking not the end of a day but rather its blended essence.

"Hey there, big fellow," Glenna said to Tom, "want some more cornbread? You know, Dad, you look so peaceful tonight. I'm glad you got to talk to your friend. It's good to see things differently, don't you think?" Glenna plopped some more chicken and dumpling down in Tom's bowl, placing beside it a big slice of cornbread with a fresh cayenne pepper. Smiling, she bent over and kissed her dad's forehead. With her sweet breath touching his brow, she whispered, "I'm so glad you're here with us; we've missed you."

Everyone saw the delicate exchange. Mike and Wanda smiled at each other, and she gave a quick wink, but miraculously Tom permitted himself the moment of attention. He smiled at his daughter, noticing how much she looked like Oui this evening, how beautiful, and he understood then that Oui was indeed there with him as life force living in his daughter's cells, in all these grandchildren, just as Saralynn was there too. For a lingering moment, Tom's childhood home, the homestead he'd shared with Ouida, his cabin on the river all emerged as part of the same mosaic woven together by the flowing tide of family. The project he wanted to get back to on the river nibbled again at his thoughts, and the cohesion around the table made its distant relevance even more urgent.

So, relaxed into the permanence of the moment and without thinking, Tom raised his tea glass to make a toast. Mike saw the gesture and tapped a spoon. "Here, here, folks. Tom wants to say a few words, so quiet down. Go ahead, Tom."

"Well, okay. Listen, it's been quite a day, and I'm so full of thoughts I can't quite sort yet, but let me say a bit of what's on my mind." He paused to take in the eager faces. "Some folks say there's nothing but selfishness in the world. Some say there's nothing but hate. I say look around this table tonight, and you'll see those folks are wrong; there's all the love and hope we need right in front of us. Here's to family and friends wherever they might be tonight."

With that, Tom raised his glass to a chorus of accolades and "Here! Here!" He sat down thinking he hadn't really said things right because he wanted to mention Oui and Saralynn's presence, but surely everyone understood, and Glenna's adoring smile spoke all the words Tom needed.

Chapter 11

I.

The day ended perfectly, jubilant people simply grateful to see one another before beginning the assault on another new year. A happy simpatico spread around the room as balance against the weighty considerations year-end brings, while slowly each person sorted potential hope, scorekeeping the previous months and predicting things to come. Encroaching maturity brings solace against the private torture of life as youth becomes confused adolescence, adulthood shrinks from the parasitic fear of inadequacy, and old age gathers the remorse of imperfection. But this night, this meal, Providence had found its way into the hearts of a clan bound by ties of blood and friendship in a home open to its mystery.

A bountiful sentiment arose leaving Tom with an overall impression of safety, he thought, a cocoon of protection for the whole family. Inside, he simply felt serene, undiluted contentment since the mesmerizing experience watching the concert. Here, walking around the block after dinner, catching the early evening chill against his face, the slowly mounting wind brought in the north air, and he ambled alone with thoughts of this strange day's losses and gains.

Glenna and her daughters quickly cleaned up the kitchen with practiced ease while sharing words of mechanical regimen. They too knew the charm of the evening, the stretch of the ranging discussions, the healthy presence of Tom and Mike, even the catalytic influence of their newly adopted aunt. Each, replete in her own way, adroitly moved to reorder the kitchen, the hum of satisfaction overshadowing not only any serious personal thoughts but also distancing recollections from the morning's shock.

Glenna, Vic, and Wanda each compartmentalized the day's early threat, the ugly intrusion of evil into their Elysian holiday, and no one wanted to remember the distant images. Wanda and Mike had drifted to the den, finding a couple of family photo albums. Complete histories of children lined page after page as each smiled through fat baby dimples to Easter dresses and school day dread. Mike remembered many of those moments with Oui and Tom.

He recalled Glenna's cute little face when she and Oui came home after the Yazoo City imbroglio, remembering how the child had carried herself with such confidence, speaking with perfect diction like a little lady. There the distracted look on Oui's face held his thoughts, the cozening to trick little Glenna into believing all was well. Those days reverberated as far-away thunder while he wondered what had happened with Don Newland on Tom's trip, and he plotted how to drag the story from his stubborn old friend.

Drifting too into reflection of her own marriage and motherhood, Wanda remembered the odd combination of success and its reluctant partner, failure. She wondered had Jocelyne softened a bit now that they were not near each other to irritate the wound between them with daily aggravation, and then pondered, if Ernie were here, would she feel so lonely when she thought of her daughter?

Calming herself, she enjoyed Mike's steady presence sitting next to her, thinking how he must be rooted to a life so different from hers. Then the stranger from earlier, the suddenness, the vulnerability each of them had experienced, the memory that danger is never far from comfort. Having Mike's gentle strength alongside as they slowly stepped through decades of Tom's friendship seemed to restore some of that eroding foundation she had forgotten how to share, and the sweet smell of his Old Spice aftershave reminded her of another lifetime.

A sly glance at Mike caught him absorbed in pictures, remembering his past even as she relived the tender moment shared earlier with Tom, the instant when he almost unshackled himself from grief. Tom seemed lost to Wanda. Even as she relived the evening's connection and his stately eloquence, she knew some essential piece of his foundation was missing. Something he needed to anchor progress to a different kind of healing had disappeared, and not only could Tom not find his lost will, but to Wanda he no longer knew how to search.

II.

Strangely, Lee carried a glum cloud away from the evening's festivities, a response largely different from everyone else's. The light table banter about anything other than the Chevelle had left him bored, so he wandered outside to be alone in the garage. The day's images of conflict and betrayal perplexed him, and he felt unequipped to understand. There was his grandfather raging like an old lion at Newland again, but the thing he had wanted so badly, resolution, loomed hollow in the chill evening of remorse.

What now began to worry Lee was his deep concern that perhaps Don Newland had not been lying. An unsettling notion grew that perhaps he and his grandfather had ignored the truth and destroyed a man's home for the wrong reason, and the once seductive violence that had ensnared his imagination now left nauseous stirrings as Lee remembered his own caustic last words to Newland.

"Hey there, what ya doing?" Tom's words broke Lee's trance.

"Oh, looking at my car. You know, wondering what it will be like to drive it."

"I see. It'll be a great moment for you. But you know something? It still won't match what your mind is conjuring right now. Life almost never can. Thoughts and words are just pictures, not the real things, and what looks so clear beforehand comes through different in reality."

"Yeah, Grandpa, I know. I was just thinking about Don Newland ..."

Tom stepped away. "Stop right there. It's over. No sense rehashing all that. Sometimes you have to make a stand, even if it's wrong. We did that. Now it's done. Life ain't all good or all bad; it's only one thing leading to another."

With that, Tom squeezed Lee's shoulder in that familiar way and drifted back up to the house. Watching his grandpa's slumped form, Lee then strolled around the Chevelle, its sleek lines crisp in the raw fluorescent light. It sat as a new car thoroughly renovated from the dilapidated hull it had been when his dad towed it home. Now it gleamed with new vitality, proud to be reborn, to be given a chance to live its seasoned life in a spirited new form. Lee thought of when the car had been brand-new, what it must have been like strutting about town with powerful rumble and shiny paint glowering disdainfully at its pedestrian rivals. Ruthless, arrogant it must have been in that heyday, much like his granddad probably was with his important job in the plant, his cadre of friends all looking up to him. All except Don, or had he too really tried to be a friend who just got trapped in the complexity of living?

Unlike cars, life seemed irreversible. Images of the old man they'd seen earlier in the day and even his grandpa's weariness felt more like museum artifacts that couldn't be altered in any way, and Lee mulled the injustice that cars could be reborn but not bodies. The harsh fluorescent light sprawled over the evening like an otherworldly presence hiding the truth of things. Then Lee pondered Saralynn's unwavering belief in Jesus, how she never doubted He would renew her life after she died. It wasn't the dying part that seemed so hard to comprehend; it was the trap of old age that didn't seem fair.

Hollowness inside, and Lee didn't believe in his grandmother's vision of death and everlasting life; the material world seemed more permanent, something that could be restored in the ways a living life couldn't. Lee knew that Tom's old image of friendship had succumbed to change, never had a chance against the quickening pace of age with its greedy need to hold on to judgment. For the first time in his young life, Lee felt old, wearied by life's flow and worried about someone other than himself. The glaring garage light made the room feel like a basement without a staircase.

The world had shifted. Lee's unwavering certainty now gave way to doubt, a creeping suspicion that he'd heard the truth from Don but had refused to listen. Disquiet, a demur sensation of fault now absorbing the details of the day, the superficial actions that had surged like instinct in the moment but that now revealed bravado to be simple bad judgment.

This beautiful car more than twice as old as Lee gleamed unaffected in this new light, its wounds relieved by a second birth. Lee slipped into the driver's seat to feel its untainted hope, its spirit patient with anticipation, and he knew things were building secret energies all around him, quiet caldrons ready to erupt, to speed, and the car comforted Lee, helped distance his worries. This machine felt like a true friend, as if both were in motion, grounded, tempered by mistakes but strong and, at least for the present, invincible.

A sound pulled him back to the moment as Glenna's voice pecked at the car window. "Lee, honey, come on in. I've made some hot chocolate and popcorn, and we're going to watch a movie, so turn off the light, please." Lee stroked the beautiful tucked and rolled front seat, smelled the new leather, and almost as if a spaceman on a foreign planet, he landed his thoughts among the burned gases of dread and hope permeating the eerie gray light.

III.

At the same instant the garage light flipped off, Tom stepped onto the front door step then turned to face the street. He stared into the darkness almost as if he heard someone calling him from the clouds hanging low between the streetlights washed in a dull grayness, an opaque, one-dimensional wall. He wondered if Don was asleep—surely so, probably for hours now, but where? Tom experienced an odd sympathy of regret. The surety that Don had been a scheming thief of a friend drifted away, estranged from hot belief, leaving no replacement of the familiar comfort long-held resentment had provided. "I can't believe it's true. It can't be."

The darkness tugged at the new hole in his understanding as Tom shoved his hands deep into his coat pockets, hoping to turn off the mistake clamoring inside his mind. Things loomed wrong in this light of new regret, the warmth of the family evening fading now before the rising wind rolling down the from the dark northern sky.

IV.

The day had passed as frozen time for Don Newland, each instant lecturing him with strident detail on his failure, clocks ticking by the second, shadows thick as refrigerated honey moving across the hospital floor while his heart thudded what felt to be the last moments of the world.

Images from the two days replayed endlessly—Tom's fractious mood, the boy's scorn, and all those hollow words. A howling awareness of failed friendship stormed over the long night, stretching across the horizon of his thought as a windswept ocean too broad to cross. Estranged from his dream of hope, robbed of redemption, the hopelessness of life mirrored the as yet undiscovered foundation of Don's home waiting crippled in silence.

For years Don had kept himself alive by clinging to the idea that one day he could rectify his mistake by helping Tom know the truth. It was all misunderstanding, he knew, but the rift of disloyalty lives as chronic loss, and Don's last true wish was to make things whole with his old friend.

A corrupted hope hung heavy about the room as thoughts of simply giving up pounded at the windows, demanding entrance. Dreams had forestalled death for years, but now the peeling paint on the bedroom moldings, the sputtering furnace, the stale air of an old and dying house reached across the miles to this sheltered room working nimble fingers of humiliation in search of entrance into a soul robbed of love.

Yet in this moment of drifting descent, a shiny thought glimmered, a brief glimpse of hope held faint but steady. What if he could penetrate the loyalty, the commitment Lee had for Tom? What if he could help Lee understand the truth as a way to reach Tom? Don had briefly seen that empathy in the boy's quietness. And then sleep came upon Don, the sleep of a lifetime, a coma from which perhaps he would never awaken, and alone Don slipped into the unknown land of final earthly rest, neither alive now nor dead, much as his hope had been for thirty years.

As Don's eyes wavered shut, he saw a ray of light from the late-day sun strike the stainless steel arm of the chair by the window, and the flash fired an image of him back at college when he was twenty years old, and still alive, still Tom's friend, standing before the river of misunderstanding they both would soon follow. And Don felt the river's cold tug grasping at his feet, a yearning pull terrifying but irresistible.

V.

At eleven o'clock, the movie ended with people sprawled all over the den, mostly asleep. Only Glenna remained fully awake as images from the morning conjured sharp pokes of fear. As she was about to wake the sleepy group for bed, a car stopped out front and then went dark.

"Dad, Dad, wake up." She shook Tom's arm. "Someone's out front." Tom jumped to his feet as simultaneously the door opened. Everyone awake now, Glenna gave a minor scream and covered her head like a bomb had exploded. Then Harold walked in.

Glenna howled. "Oh my God, thank heaven." She flew to him as if he'd come home from a long-lasting war, and they embraced with passion.

"Dad, Dad!" Vic yelled, and both she and Lucy attacked Harold with joy. Standing back not quite sure what he should do, Lee simply watched.

Tears streaming while words bubbled, Glenna rambled, "What, what are you doing here? You're in Little Rock. I can't believe it."

"Glenn, my damned phone died, so I said screw it and headed straight here. Pushed off my load in Tupelo and rented a car so I could get here quick. There was a big wreck in Jackson or I'd have been here two hours ago." For perhaps the first moment since his kids began their teenage years, Harold felt genuinely happy to be home. More importantly, he was welcomed with the loving arms that he'd forgotten he'd ever known. And within minutes, tales of pitchforks and rebar filled the room as screeches of laughter erupted. Sue even called asking about the strange car out front, wondering if everything was okay. That too brought an avalanche of laughter.

At last, everyone settled down, so Glenna and Vic told their story in detail. No one interrupted, though they all squirmed thinking of what might have happened. When they finished, Harold stood up and walked over to Glenna, planting the biggest kiss anyone there had ever seen him do. Then he hugged Vic and turned to the group.

"I ain't no scholar. Guess you all know that. But I want to say something. I'm sorry to my family; I wasn't here when you needed me. I'm sorry for the years I've been gone. But I always loved you, and I love you even more right now." Harold found a tear in his eye and didn't quite know what to do as his voice quivered. Lee did; he went to his father, put his arms around him, and hugged him till they both turned lollipop red.

Finally, Lee stepped back, allowing his dad to finish. "One more thing. I know this in my heart. If I'd been here, or Lee or Tom or Mike, there'd be one less piece of human shit in this world tonight." And the room exploded.

Then Tom and Mike as well gave Harold a hug, and so did that gorgeous redhead Harold remembered was now part of the family. She looked him dead in the eye, then uttered, "Now would be a good time for a handkerchief to wipe the tears from your wife's cheek."

VI.

After Wanda left and everyone went to bed, Glenna and Harold finally had a moment to talk.

Looking at her husband, her heart filled with both anger and sympathy, and then she sobbed.

"I don't know what to say. All day I buried this morning, trying not to think about it, but we could have died here, Harold. All of us. I keep thinking he could have killed us all like in the Capote novel."

Harold began slowly. "I know, hon. I do. But I don't think Clyde would have hurt anyone ..."

The fuse lit. "What in the hell are you saying? This wasn't important? Not dangerous? Just some long-lost friend dropping by with a gun in his pocket? This is exactly what I can't take anymore. You skim the surface of how we live here, but you aren't part of it; you don't experience this family like a father, let alone a husband." Glenna whizzed around the kitchen, slapping the dishtowel against the countertops.

"No, no, that's not what I'm saying." Harold scrambled. "Look, I know it was dangerous, sure I know, but ..." And words failed to form. Glenna saw her husband's collapse, and a moment of empathy came over her. Then he spoke. "Glenn, that guy was a petty criminal, but my friend Wayne from Tulsa told me today that Clyde had begun dealing more dangerous drugs and was on the run from the law. Headed to New Orleans we think. I'm sure it was just an impulse to steal money when he drove through Hattiesburg and remembered he had my address."

Not really knowing what to think, Glenna felt certain Harold really didn't have anything to do with that lowlife, but her heart was full of something she'd needed to say for a long time.

"I need to tell you something," she began. "I've been thinking for a long time that maybe I've wasted my life." Harold tried to interrupt, but Glenna put her finger to her lips indicating silence. "The kids have become my whole world, and I've found happiness through them. I love that, Harold, but it isn't enough; they are growing up, and I need something else. I want to be loved—loved by you." And words too failed Glenna as her anger melded into sadness. He rose from his chair and wrapped his arms around Glenna.

"Hon. There ain't nothing in this world more important to me than you. Nothing. Not even the kids. I love them, but I know I've been a poor father, and they love you more. I accepted that a long time ago. But, Glenn, if you'll let me, I promise you I'll show you the man I really am." And they whimpered in each other's arms.

Two hours more of deeply personal confessions and comforting followed, producing an emotional catharsis both had needed but didn't know how to find. Then Glenna went to Harold and sat in his lap, stroking his face gently.

"You know, I've got some of that ice cream and whipped cream you like so much. If you want, you can have a little dip." And though Glenna still felt oceans of frustration, she found herself relaxed with the thought that Harold would be her husband until she died.

"All right!" Harold said. "And tomorrow night, I'm gonna buy you the biggest lobster they got in this town." Harold smiled bigger than a sunrise, and Glenna knew he was truly happy to be home.

VII.

The next morning, his mom was ironing her favorite blue blouse as Lee entered the kitchen. He knew she was still upset the cleaners had ruined her nice lavender one, and though he hadn't seen her use the iron in months, there Glenna stood carefully creasing the collar. She looked so content, he thought, completely adept in her world of domestic management. Lee had often wondered what his mom could have done had she gone to college and pursued a career; she tended to be so even tempered, organized, that he was sure she could have run most any business.

"How was practice?" Glenna asked Lee, freshly showered after the grueling workout.

"Oh fine. I made twelve points in the scrimmage. Coach says he wants me to try out for the varsity. With four seniors graduating, he thinks I've got a good shot next year." As always, Lee was modest. In fact, the coach had told him he was all but assured a starter slot if he continued to work hard and progress and if he attended basketball camp in the summer. Lee hadn't told his mom yet about the camp or the four hundred dollars it would cost; he wanted to wait for the right moment to spring that news.

"Listen, hon," Glenna said, "with all the company we had around yesterday, I never got to hear much about Dad's trip to Yazoo City. You know Grandpa doesn't give away many details. How did things go?"

"It was good. We got to see Mr. Newland and talk to him twice. The first day, he got tired and had to go to bed, but the second day he was better." Fixing a banana sandwich with mayo on white bread, Lee considered parallel universes and how people navigate the moments of their lives in silent worlds. His distraction evaporated when his mom cleared her throat to catch his attention.

"Did Dad find out why Mr. Newland had come here—I mean the real reason? I don't know, but Mr. Newland seemed like he needed to reach out or something; it's hard to describe."

"Yeah, Mom, I think you're right. He talked about how he tried to help Grandpa back in Yazoo City, like he went to bat for him, but it didn't help. Something about the big bosses had already decided to fire Grandpa." Lee replayed the two meetings searching for details, but he wasn't quite sure what all his mom knew. No need to worry her with Newland being a traitor or hitting on Granny Oui. He especially couldn't divulge the secret about Newland's house. So, Lee opted for diversion, and though a twinge of guilt gave a quick shudder, he decided not to allow it a voice.

"There was something else," Lee said. "I remember reading one of Granny Saralynn's letters where she talked about some trouble Grandpa and Granny Oui had a long time ago. Some guy tried to steal her or something like that, but anyway, Mr. Newland said something about a guy in Picayune who tried to talk Granny Oui out of going off to college and getting married. Grandpa flipped out, so we didn't get the whole story."

"Oh, is that so? Did he say who that guy was?" Glenna feigned deep concentration on her ironing without having to look up, but Lee knew she was more than mildly interested.

"Nope. Just said someone who lived close to her in Picayune. I got the feeling she knew this other guy pretty well." Lee paused to let his words sink in, and then continued, "I kinda remember Granny Oui's old homestead from when I was a kid. Maybe it was somebody from her neighborhood, or school I guess."

A stern demeanor came as response. "That's ancient history, son, and it's personal stuff I'm sure your grandpa would not want us to be discussing behind his back." With that, Glenna found her own silence.

Lee and his mom shared a sideways look, but neither spoke. He was sure his mother knew more, but he too felt uncomfortable with such personal talk, especially since he knew what Newland had tried to do. Without realizing the full depth of things, Lee caught a glimpse of how Tom and Oui were real people, individuals with lives and complications. Perhaps for the first time he began to understand that their roles as grandparents had so dominated his understanding that his awareness of them as separate people, as a man and woman who once were not even married, now began to take on meaning outside of their family roles.

That letter Saralynn wrote explained how Oui was a woman and not an object to own, that she had choices, and Tom's job was to have her choose him, not merely the other way around. As he looked at his mom in this sobered light, the hue of adulthood now finding its way into his thinking, Lee wondered why his mom had chosen his dad as her husband, what he had done to deserve her conviction. But that thought seemed far too heavy to lift, and he contented himself with the good feeling that his dad had come home early and Glenna was grateful. He decided to save that discussion for another time, fearing the intruder episode had left emotions already frayed. Lee tasted the ginger snap cookie he pulled from the jar, remembering the cookies Nurse Smart had given him, and he wondered what would happen to her now that the house had fallen down.

VIII.

Within hours, the entire town knew about the home assault and the phone wouldn't stop ringing. Neighbors, teachers, school friends, and even the local television station all wanted to know the scoop, so Victoria and Glenna talked to people at length, never getting tired of telling the same versions. Killing time until noon, Tom finally decided he needed the refreshment of some river air to clear his head, his secret about Newland's house still rumbling around his head with no place to exit.

The drive back to Picayune helped provide the tonic he wanted to relieve the discomfiting cloud cluttering his mind all morning. The air in town hadn't felt right with its scathing northern air sharpness, an unfamiliar intruder Tom kept pondering. Though he had slept comfortably, dreams made for a morning greeting with a stiff neck. Fleeting images of people flickered, but no words could touch the place they now hid, so Tom instead talked internally, hoping to coax the mysterious beings out of hiding.

The prolonged good-byes and insincere promises to call exhausted Tom, and now he merely followed Mike's truck without having to think about anything practical. Soon the "Welcome to Picayune" sign startled Tom while Mike flagrantly signaled he was turning into Wal-Mart just as the two men had agreed. But Tom only waved and tooted his horn twice as he drove straight on with deliberation. He didn't want the noise of the store, the bright lights, all the decisions he would have to make, preferring the peaceful cabin porch instead. Knowing he didn't have fresh milk or bread didn't seem to matter as lately he'd eaten and discussed more than he could digest. The three nights away from home had drained Tom, separated him from the calm riverside ease he preferred to the overstimulation of people and food.

Listening to the Chevy purr so comfortably reminded him how fixing his truck had changed things, excommunicated him in a way from his old life of simplicity where denial of things needed was the daily routine and not the exception. These days, necessity and want became choices ceaselessly invading his privacy. The tradeoff of mobility felt like contamination now, as if he'd been polluted with too much of everything, cities, people, driving, and even guilt. The long-awaited revenge he'd sought had gone so wrong with losing his temper and then wrecking Don's house. Now it all seemed dirty in retrospect, and Tom needed the clean air of the woods to filter the pollution of complexity.

His little boat bobbed in his mind, the traps he'd set down by the blocked stream where beavers had made such a mess. He thought of the salt lick he'd put out for the deer and the field corn he'd spread for turkeys as he'd already begun to think about spring. But when Tom's mind travelled to the tree swing hanging from the chinaberry tree, a renewed blaze of inspiration bolted, and he remembered the project he'd planned. With wry smile, he gave the old Chevy a little more accelerator, and before long the bouncing and banging down the road led to his cabin so forlorn-looking without any smoke coming from the chimney. Here now time wound itself back to the cabin door and the entrance to his old life. This time the door was still closed.

With a few hours left before dark, Tom moved with dispatch to gather up some bait for the lines and head down to the river. There were still two nice-sized catfish in the holding pen, so he knew he had dinner, but tomorrow he wanted to check traps, so today he needed to catch a couple of fish for the coming days. He also thought of the smokehouse and how it was time to smoke up a new round of meat, perhaps another duck. Life returned to normal almost instantly as the familiar patterns unfurled like rose petals in May, but inside a disquiet lurked, impish images of Don Newland decades earlier, ominous sensations of that decrepit body now awaiting the season of death, and then the thorn of Sheriff Barker crept into mind.

After two hours of checking and moving limb lines, baiting and untangling hooks, Tom returned to the familiar cypress tree to tie off the skiff. From the low angle of the river he saw the top of the chinaberry with its abnormally bent limb seemingly calling to him, so he took his sharpest skinning knife from the scabbard on his belt and walked deliberately to the misshapen old tree, it too pondering the release of death. With two swift slices, the rope holding the swing seat severed, and the board fell to the ground. Such a nice piece of ash wood, sturdy and heavy, exactly the kind he needed.

The two ropes hung from the high limb like vines in the swamp, serpent-like with slow wiggles in the breeze. How useless they hung in the afternoon air with no function any longer, not even a boy to come along and swing Tarzan-like on them the way he and Mike had done in the swamps a million times as boys. How might he use them to hang up a deer or a turkey? But he needn't bother with the details until the time was right, until some utilitarian purpose arose. So, for now, the ropes awaited new duty.

After removing leftover strands from the knots, Tom studied the beautiful piece of wood, though sitting out in the rain had slightly darkened the light grain. He decided to take it inside for cleaning before he used it again; he needed that white, almost sandy look once more, like when Mike had given it to him.

Washed and dried the board sanded out nicely lifting the rich grain. What a thick, heavy mass the seat really was, so much larger than it looked hanging from the tree. Tom began envisioning exactly what he wanted, how the turns and dips would go. And the beach—he saw the lineage of his life and the homes he had loved turn slowly down the grain toward the great finish he had planned. Then, sitting the board by the potbellied stove, Tom fixed a nice meal of catfish and potatoes as he listened to the river gurgle its soft music in the late daylight.

IX.

A strong sun and pleasant weather brought the morning, and with a pot of hot coffee and boiled eggs, Tom planned the day. Still pondering the swing seat as he carved off a hunk of old cheese he'd forgotten at the back of the cupboard, he wanted to sketch out some detail until he heard what sounded like several vehicles coming down the road. He always recognized the rattle of Mike's old Ford, but this was different.

A few minutes later, two sheriff vehicles wheeled into the yard evidently trying to enter with as much bravado as possible. The noise irritated Tom. Sheriff Barker and the two deputies, Chris Wolf and Leon Portman, got out of the car. Tom wondered why they needed two vehicles.

"Well hey there, Chuck. What you doin' way out here? You boys get lost?"

"That's Sheriff Barker to you, Bradburn. And to answer your question, we're not lost at all; seems like you didn't get the message from our first little chat, so I thought I'd give you a personal reminder. That's the kind of guy I am. I like things personal."

"Well, I hope you brought your own coffee 'cause all I got is some bark tea, but I'll be happy to whip up a batch if you like. Keeps you regular, you know, and from the tight look on you boys' faces, it seems you might have a corncob or something shoved up there that could use a little dislodging. How 'bout some shitty tea there, Sheriff?"

"We don't want any of your swamp spit tea; we're here to tell you for the last time to move out of this house. Like I done told you, the state of Mississippi owns this and seven thousand more acres around here, and they intend to make it a state reserve."

"Listen, Chuckie, I explained this once already, so maybe turn up your hearing aid a little this time, or maybe these kiddie cops of yours can write it down for you. Ouida's cousin, Sam Seldon, told me forty years ago I could build this cabin on his property and could stay here for as long as I wanted, and that's exactly what I'm doing; I even got a note he wrote in his own hand and signed."

"You do realize," said the sheriff, "Sam died two years ago, and his niece sold all this land to the state. Now I know you understand all this. You ain't nothing but a squatter here; you got no claim."

"Now, Chuckie, I don't give a crap about all that 'cause the guy who owned it when I built this place said I could stay here as long as I wanted. So, that's the way it is."

Barker lost his temper. "You're as dumb as you are stubborn. Here's the official papers I'm serving. You got thirty days to clear off this land or you'll be arrested for trespassing, and you can bet I'll come do the handcuffing myself." The sheriff's sneer struck Tom as genuine hatred, but he didn't care, as he'd known Barker all his life to be a bully and a bore, a man that liked to be respected but didn't have any qualities to respect other than the badge his rich old man had bought for him twelve years ago in a crooked election.

Barker's first visit to announce the adoption of the "Catchahoula Land Preservation Act" had been clear enough, but Tom hoped it would get hung up in legal wrangling and wouldn't take effect for a while longer. Frankly, he couldn't imagine the government getting anything this big done in a whole lifetime, let alone a few months, but he'd underestimated how long the process had been unfolding and how supportive the landowners were who accepted the above-market offers. Clearly the big money in Mississippi politics had greased the system sufficiently.

As the sheriff and his deputies headed back for their cars, Barker turned toward Tom one more time. "Sure would be a shame if a game warden caught anybody shooting a turkey or a deer out of season. I hear sometimes they even put repeat offenders in jail. You might want to spread that word around to any other savages down here you might call a friend, or even a wife."

Tom jerked his head up and marched straight for Barker. The insult got to Tom, whose mind filled with the horrible suffering his long-dead Oui went through before her death. Had the deputies not stepped in to restrain Tom from getting his apology, surely a night in jail would have followed the heavy piece of hickory in his hand and the rage in his heart. As it was, he already wondered where he would be sleeping a month from now.

"You piece of dog shit, when you come to throw me off this land, you better bring more help than these Boy Scouts here because you're damned well gonna need 'em." Tom's icy words delivered the warning that everyone knew left no room for compromise.

The sheriff, comfortable with two deputies holding Tom, relished the moment. As he turned to get back in the police cruiser, he taunted Tom one last time. "Don't forget about that game warden. Surprises can be unpleasant; you should remember that."

X.

Two days after returning to Picayune, Mike's truck pulled up. Parking to the left of the cabin to avoid some project Tom had scattered about, he immediately noticed the two empty ropes hanging from the chinaberry, parallel lines in the dull, foggy light. A chill ran up his spine, and though he couldn't quite imagine what had happened, clearly something had changed.

"Dang, I can't get rid of you, can I?" Tom said. "You're bad as a stray dog looking for some scraps." Tom's crotchety greeting seemed perfectly normal.

"Well, you ain't very appreciative for a guy getting groceries delivered to him; some folks might even be grateful." With that, Mike opened the passenger door and took out two brown paper bags of things he'd picked up in town. "I knew if I wanted a decent cup of coffee and a doughnut, I'd have to bring it myself, so that's what I did."

"Okay then, don't complain to me because sounds like you did it more for yourself than for me." Funny how those words cut through things, called out part of the reason Mike always came to visit Tom—to help out, sure, but also to draw from Tom's venerable strength a dose of that independence their friendship had shared for a lifetime.

"You're right. You caught me," Mike said. "I got up at six to go buy groceries so I could drive down this rabbit trail of a road for an hour to have a cup of coffee with a grousing old piss like you. Yep, I do like to irritate myself in the mornings." Mike's tone showed he was a little tired himself from the trip to Glenna's. He too was ready for a little rest and catching up on matters neglected, but first he had to settle a couple of things about the past, to find out where Tom stood on the Newland visit.

"Awright, awright, get on in here, and I'll make you some coffee. I finished my own pot, but I know how you hate coffee without hazelnut latte yoga flavoring." Tom finally lightened up a little cracking a smile, but Mike knew something was bothering his friend, a new smoldering in Tom's well-guarded ways.

"So I see you took down the swing. Why's that? You didn't burn it for firewood, did you?" Again, Mike made a joke but really asked a serious question, but entering the cabin, he saw the board leaned against the wall. Tom never bothered answering.

"I kinda figured you'd be sleeping in today, not out visiting this early. You're lucky I'm here as I was gonna go check traps but decided to catch up a few chores first. I'm hoping I got myself a nice pig out there wanting to come home with me."

"Yeah, I thought about that, but since you didn't stop at Wal-Mart, I figured you needed a few things, being gone so long and all. Just being neighborly, you know; you ought to try it yourself sometime." Another zinger rang across the room as the two old warriors rooted their way around trying to find the old rhythm that seemed so disrupted these days with trips and people and old problems lurking at the edge of life.

"No thanks," Tom said. "My experience is that people can take care of themselves and don't need me barging in on them. If somebody needs me, they know how to find me." The words sounded so normal, trite almost, but Mike couldn't help noticing how absurd normal was for Tom.

"Oh, yeah, they know where to find you all right. They just need a four-wheel drive with a wench, a full tank of gas, and an Indian guide to get out here to this lump on a log. You ain't exactly in town, you know."

Not paying any attention to Mike's derision, Tom turned to making fresh coffee, ham and eggs, and even a nice hunk of rye bread Mike had picked up special. Full and comfortable, they soon moved to the porch to watch the sun build among the trees and to listen to the birds in the chilly morning light where Mike enjoyed his double-glazed, jelly-filled doughnut for dessert.

"I'm only cleaning the white ash board; it got a little moldy in all that rain."

Mike didn't bother to comment, as he knew whatever he said would only irritate Tom.

"So we didn't get to talk much at Glenna's. I'd come up to Hattiesburg not knowing about your trip to Yazoo City—you know, in case you wanted me to go along after all." Mike knew this wasn't exactly true, as Glenna had explained that Tom had already left for Newland's, but the fib seemed a good ploy to pull his old friend into the discussion.

"Yeah, Lee and I had a good trip up there together. It was fun being on the road with the boy. But I tell you, teenagers are something these days, all talking about faces with books and snap caps on their phones. I didn't know what all he was talking about half the time. I just listened close so I didn't have to talk."

As if they had begun to play a board game with strategy, Mike saw Lee as a way to loosen up his old friend. "Yeah, Lee's a good kid. Not many teenagers would go on a trip like that to listen to two old codgers talk about the old days. You know swapping stories that must be boring to anybody under seventy." Hoping any nudge would prompt Tom to sharing a little information, Mike then focused on his doughnut.

"Don sure looked bad. He's had cancer and now some kind of blood thing. I don't think he's long for this world. Seemed friendly though."

"Did you find out why he went to Glenna's last year?" Feigning disinterest, Mike now trimmed his fingernails with his pocketknife.

"Yeah. He was getting ready for lung surgery. I think he was trying to set things right in case he didn't make it. Said he'd tried to find me, and you too, but couldn't."

"Me? Why'd he want me?" Mike asked.

"He knew we were friends, remember, but he thought your name was Mickey and couldn't get it straight enough to track you down. He recalled you though."

"So did he talk about that time when I threatened him for messing with Oui?" Mike treaded delicately.

"Not so much. He mentioned it, but it didn't seem to carry much memory for him." Tom paused, then stood looking down the path toward the river.

"Don said I had it all wrong about what happened. Said the brass was about to fire me when he tried to step in, but they wouldn't hear of it. Threatened to fire all his people too if he didn't get in line."

Mike seemed irritated. "That's a bunch of hooey. Too simple if you ask me, like a Perry Mason story. I guess he said he didn't make a pass at Oui either, huh?" Mike in rare fashion had begun to lose patience quicker than Tom and now sorely wished he'd been there for the confrontation. A steady seepage of guilt began filling Mike, and he knew he'd let his old friend down just when he needed help most.

After a few seconds, Tom answered. "No, he talked about all that. Said he and Oui had been talking about my getting canned even before I knew; said they were trying to figure out what to do and how to tell me. Then things got too familiar between them, and he got drunk and said some stupid stuff. Admitted he was wrong to tempt Oui but insisted he had nothing to do with getting me fired."

"I can't believe you didn't punch that Judas. Hell, you grouch me out for bringing you coffee, and this guy got you fired and tried to steal your wife, and you listen to his bullshit like it's the nightly news." This time Mike's ire rose in extraordinary fashion as some fissure in his soul released an unexpected spasm of emotion.

Remaining calm, Tom displayed little reaction. "I didn't say I didn't get mad. I got real hot and stormed out of his house before I got to ask all the questions I wanted. I wish I hadn't done that."

"What kind of things did you want to know?" Mike said. "Like how he made moves on Oui? If he said anything bad about her, he's a damned liar." Mike's face now bright red.

Slowly Tom's gaze lifted from the floor, and Mike observed his loyal friend, lifelong fishing and hunting buddy, craggy now with wrinkles on his aging face, rough knuckles and calloused hands tired perhaps but strong. Could this be the same man he'd known all his life as a rock of stubbornness? Tom had a distant look, one that seemed to weigh disappointment too heavily and anger too lightly. The fire had cooled in Tom's spirit for some reason, yet still Mike could not understand why.

Pondering the recent changes in Tom's life and hoping for clues, Mike suddenly noticed a milky glaze come over his old friend's face.

"Tom, you okay? Hey, settle back and rest." Staring blankly ahead, appearing not to see anything, Tom's complexion turned white, and then he faded into a sleeplike state.

"Wake up. Wake up, Tom." Mike felt panicked.

Groggy, Tom blinked but seemed still in a stupor. "Oh, hey, hey there … sorry, must have been daydreaming. Drifted a second, didn't I? That big trip I guess, still a little tired."

The episode scared Mike. Then he helped Tom lie down on the couch and got him a glass of water. He knew something had happened; perhaps a diabetic thing, he thought, as Tom lately had not looked as strong and seemed to get confused. All the travel and maybe even all this Newland talk might have pushed Tom too hard, and again a wave of guilt rose. The one thing he knew was that Tom was going to the doctor for a checkup.

For the first time, Mike witnessed Tom's mortality. Here lay a man who wanted no help, disdained being treated as if he needed a friendly hand, let alone a handout, and obviously preferred the solitude of woods and rivers to the officious concern of people. Here was the old loner now circling back on his own life where retreat had begun. And Mike stared into the offing of things as if he were looking at his own vulnerability.

After a few minutes, Tom looked up, shaking his head from side to side. "Hey there, fellow, you still here? That dang coffee got me. Lately, if I have too much, I get a little lightheaded. Listen, you don't need to stick around here. I'm gonna rest. Then I'll be back to it. Got to get that pig out of my live trap. Why don't you head on back to town and let me take a little nap?"

"That's a good idea," Mike said. "You drift on off, and I'll get out of your hair. Here's another blanket, and I'll throw a log in the stove too." With that, Tom closed his eyes, falling into silence. The day felt slow with the blanket weighing heavily on his chest, and Tom succumbed to its weight.

Resting in the chair by the door, Mike picked up the copy of *Walden* that Tom had obviously read a dozen times as half the pages were earmarked and the spine fell open easily. He thought of how intently Tom must have studied that book out here all alone, and as he listened to his friend's breathing, Tom's wonderful life paraded past. Mike had no intention of going anywhere until he saw his friend standing.

Outside, the river gurgled over the new logs that had washed down, fresh voices in the openness of the Catchahoula, and Mike sat quietly in the warm cabin wondering about the changes ahead, what forces were at work within his old friend's solitary life. Listening to the river, he recognized how Tom felt sitting out here in the cabin all alone, how the world outside these trees didn't seem to exist. And as that sensation of one place and then another passed through, Mike thought of sitting on the couch with Wanda and how safe he'd felt with her.

Chapter 12

I.

His rest on the couch led Tom deep into the feverish moment leeching at his strength. At first fitful, he pushed on through the restless early drowse as he travelled down into locked regions fully retreated from the outside world. Lingering in this twilight dream state, he sensed being awake, and there he rested, observant of his consciousness. Eyes closed, soon a slow oscillation from side to side began as if reading, and Tom waited, peacefully aware of himself as both the watcher and the person being watched.

In this stasis, he began to hear familiar sounds, perhaps voices, almost a language but not and yet emanating from inside his body. The sounds gradually grew louder, and then Tom realized he was listening to his own heartbeat and other bodily functions all in unison, rhythmically processing. The muffled pounding and flowing grew louder, bringing with it sensations of everything growing larger, expanding as if his awareness were a balloon inflating, and the sounds magnified the entirety of Tom's life.

After what seemed an endless clog of time, brightness began to appear, first a small point far away but then accreting itself with intensity into Tom's consciousness as it melted away bodily sensation. This phenomenon was not a ray of light perceived through his eyes but a radiance from inside his retreated thoughts, a beacon now blending with the hidden chorus of external sounds he suddenly recognized had been there all along. The bright sensation grew, and Tom lost all awareness of concern, of observation; he found himself relaxed by the flooding submersion of his physical life into an ethereal soup of unfamiliar perception.

Almost without notice came a nondescript voice neither male nor female, sensuous, almost haunting. "Can you feel it, Tom?" But Tom could not speak; he didn't even recognize his body any longer, disconnected, removed yet still contained. "You don't need to speak, Tom; we can hear you." And Tom yielded to deeper relaxation. He felt the distance between each molecule in his body releasing the tensions of binding themselves to one another, and with the ease of morning dew rising, he welcomed the unfurling of his life as something familiar yet unknown.

Where am I? he thought.

"You are everywhere, Tom. You are every single thing that ever was or ever will be."

Am I dead? Am I dying? The thoughts seemed so easy, and though Tom could perceive them as separate from the thinking he usually indulged, the sounds appeared differently, separate and voiceless but unified, as if the words he thought were redundant to carry intention.

"No, Tom, you are absolutely alive."

But where?

"With us—with all of us. We are all here with you. We've been waiting."

A spark piqued every atom Tom knew as him, body and mind, each speaking a singular voice in unison, and instantly he accepted the shimmering light, its faint movement that at once seemed a human form then just as quickly that of a mountain, or clouds, or a herd of buffalo, radically evanescent yet concrete.

"Tom, when you talk to yourself, who do you think is the listener? Who is the speaker? You see don't you, there is no separation, no plant or animal, no you or them, ever; only thinking creates separateness."

Strangely, Tom already understood, the words striking him as a memory of something already learned, maybe even before he'd been born. Yet still he struggled. *Am I in the future?*

"No, there is no future, no past; there is only now, and you are always in it. You will understand soon."

Then, as quickly as that crevice to the dream world had opened, it closed with Tom receding from the strange moment and with complete certainty he heard his mother's voice, and Oui's too, as a faded image appeared, a lake—or was it an ocean with a little island—a place he could see the two women talking on a shoreline but which seemed so far away. Almost without notice, Tom realized he could hear every person he'd ever known and remember all their faces at one time, and then he understood that the time had not yet arrived to yield to the distant vision pulling at his spirit, nor was there any more need to worry.

Precisely in this moment, a cold washcloth draped across his forehead, dispelling the feverish dream. Eyes peeked open; the only image he could make out was sunlight trickling through the window behind the silhouette of Mike bending toward him, and Tom thought how much like the old chinaberry tree his good friend looked and how comforting that image appeared.

II.

Pushing the lobster carcass away, Harold smiled. "Now that was about the biggest crawfish I ever ate." Glenna laughed and then leaned over for a little kiss. The server was a cute college student enjoying seeing this old couple so happy.

"So, you guys did pretty well on the lobsters. I hope you saved room for a little tiramisu; it's the best in town." Harold looked at Glenna, who shook her head no, but she really wanted to try it, as she wasn't sure what it was really but had heard Wanda mention that it was delicious.

With the air of a billionaire, Harold addressed the waiter. "Bring us one of that tiramessum stuff you mentioned and a cheesecake like that feller over there has. This is a special night for my lovely bride, and nothing is too good for her." Both Glenna and Tina, their server, turned red.

"Are you crazy, Harold? Those things probably cost ten dollars each." She protested but truthfully was proud of her husband. .

Continuing as if he had an agenda, he said, "You let me worry about paying the bills tonight. You get plenty of turns at doing that." Glenna smiled and felt flush. "But seriously, Glenn, I've got a couple of things to talk to you about, so let's have ourselves a nice coffee and relax a minute here. This place stays open till ten."

Two coffees served, Harold became serious. "I know I've disappointed all of you. Acted a selfish fool, I guess you could say. But I've got something to share now, Glenn." Her big smile became a strained grin as Harold pressed ahead. "I can't make this decision alone, so you got to be the brains here." He seemed almost confused. "But I've been offered a job here in Hattiesburg. An old friend, Stephen Reid, owns a car auction place and a body shop; well, he wants me to come do custom remodeling for him. You know, like I did on the Chevelle." He paused with a look of doubt covering his face; Glenna moved closer.

"Is there a salary? What kind of money can you make?" she asked cautiously.

"Yeah, a thousand dollars a week to start, plus 20 percent of the profit on every job, parts and labor. Steve says he's already got a dozen cars lined up, and he'll hire me a couple of helpers too. Oh yeah, insurance included." The discussion quickly became financial, and Glenna determined the money would probably work out about the same, but Harold would not be travelling.

She looked him straight in the eye. "Look, this is your call, not mine. You got to go to work there every day, so you need to do something you like. But for me, having you in Hattiesburg all the time, that's a dream." So with cheesecake and tiramisu along with a Sambuca as nightcap, Harold and Glenna lounged with their peers in the Sea Lodge restaurant, celebrating the single most expensive meal they'd ever tasted.

While waiting for the bill, Glenna remembered something. "Oh yeah, you said you had two things to talk to me about." She paused anxiously. "Now don't you go spoiling my Cinderella evening here, Mr. Prince." A lovely blush came to her cheek. Harold was ready.

"Okay, so I guess I'll wait till later. But I really wanted to give you this. And with those words, Harold laid on the table the most captivating pendant Glenna had ever seen, a handmade sterling silver item that looked like a picture frame an inch tall and three-quarters wide. An intricate palm tree in the foreground connected the sides of the structure, but what made it fascinating was the stone embedded in the background, the color of the ocean or sky. The piece looked as if the observer peered through a window at a palm tree with a lovely white, speckled blue horizon behind it."

"It's Larimar. From the Dominican Republic. Only place in the world it's found. Bought it in Santa Fe from a guy who made it himself, used to live down there in some place called Cabarete." Tears the size of sweet peas rolled down Glenna's cheek, and she erupted with a shower of kisses. But Harold's nicely pressed initialed handkerchief flew to the chivalrous task, and all decorum was restored.

III.

"You still here? Dang, I ain't no child," Tom said. "But that nap did me good. Just some kind of bug. Heck, you could be a fine wife, or a nurse, for some lucky girl."

The quip gave Mike confidence that maybe Tom had made the same express rebound that had taken him away so suddenly, but he knew something wasn't right.

"I don't mind staying," Mike said. "I don't feel like driving that old pothole road this late anyway. Be my luck I'd get stuck and have to walk back here in the dark."

"Your choice, but I gotta ask you something," Tom said.

"Well, I ain't marrying you if that's what you're asking," Mike joked. "I'll tell you that right quick." They both got a good chuckle, but quickly Tom turned the moment to seriousness.

"Before I got stupid and went off on Don," Tom began, "he said something about Oui that didn't sit right with me. Said Oui told him she almost didn't go up to State for college, even almost didn't marry me. According to Newland, some guy she lived close to tried to talk her into dumping me while I was at PRC. Any idea what he was talking about?"

The words poured down as a pelting rain, soaking every part of Mike. He heard the concern in Tom's voice, felt the ooze of long-hidden fear rising, and understood how vulnerable his old friend was at this moment. Everything depended on Tom's capricious temper. Weakened perhaps by the day's strange fit, Tom didn't appear as irascible as usual, so Mike proceeded carefully with something he had long dreaded.

Changing the proximity by walking over to the potbelly stove, Mike searched for advantage.

"I don't know how much good can come from talking about things sixty years ago," Mike said. "You know, memories change, and things ain't always the way they're remembered. But I'm gonna try to tell you this as truthful as I can." Still no words from Tom.

"When you went off to PRC, it confused everyone. Your folks were disappointed you didn't use your scholarship to State, and the rest of us just figured you were plum crazy. People said you were afraid to leave home 'cause you were a momma's boy. But the person who took it the hardest was Oui."

"What in the hell are you talking about, Mike? I went to PRC so I could be with Oui that year; I wanted to be around for her senior year, you old fool. Damned, what kind of spin doctoring are you up to here?"

"Now let's get something straight," Mike said. "You asked me to tell you about this, and I told you I'm going to give you the God's honest truth. But if you're gonna jump up and yell at me every time I say something you don't like, then we're done." Unexpectedly Mike also lost his temper and started for the door.

"Wait up, you old cuss. Damn, you're a pain in my butt. Look, I got a little riled, that's all. Settle down and finish your story. I ain't feeling good enough to argue anyway. Git on with it, you old piss." Tom slumped into the couch.

"Anyway," Mike said, "Oui was overwhelmed when you turned down that scholarship, felt like it was her fault and she was holding you back. Heck, Tom, you were the hometown hero—smart, football star, prettiest girl in the school for your girlfriend, big-time scholarship, and we all felt it was part of us getting all those breaks when we watched you." Mike paused to let the idea take root.

"When you threw that touchdown pass that put us in the state tournament, Picayune High School was your kingdom, buddy; we all lived in your world, wanted to be you. Some of us tried to become you.

Our friend Tom made us all feel better about ourselves, like we too could have it all since we'd grown up just like you. Heck, everybody thought that if you could escape, then we all might."

"Escape what? What are you talking about? I didn't want to escape anything. I loved this place. I wanted to spend my life here."

"That's just it. You were a hero here, and we worshipped you. When you passed up that State scholarship, we knew that if you couldn't get out, none of us could. Disappointment felt like a life sentence to us. Oui was heartsick that she had ruined your life. Did you know that? Did you know she agonized every day about seeing you on weekends 'cause she thought she was burying you in this swampy little town? Made her sick to her stomach, Tom; she cried all the time."

"You're wrong." Tom's voice was getting louder. "Oui and I were in love, and every time I saw her, it was like magic for us both, like shooting stars and homecoming parades. There's no way she felt wrong about what we had."

"She didn't feel wrong about what you had; she felt wrong about what you would give up for her, how much you would sacrifice to be with her, and she hated having that power. She wanted you to go to State and win championships and become famous, Tom, simply so she could stand next to you. Oui's life was so tied up in you that you didn't realize how she needed to live through you. You were her hopes and dreams, just like for the rest of us. When she saw you almost throw everything away for her, she smothered herself in guilt knowing she'd get the blame if you failed."

"That's plumb crazy. Not taking that scholarship was my choice, not hers; she never even asked me to stay here." And Mike saw Tom's realization, how he'd made their relationship about exalting her when all she wanted was for him to take over the world and let her come for the ride. The brilliant Tom furrowed his brow, and Mike knew that at last Tom understood he had discounted her objections without noticing the pain she was experiencing.

With Tom deep in thought, Mike continued. "All our senior year, Oui and I talked about nothing but you, how it was a mistake to go to PRC, how her mom was furious at her for making you do that, how you were ruining your future. It went on endlessly, every day after school, at lunch, on Saturday's down at Roy's before you came home. I listened to her. I told her how I didn't think you were ruining your life but had just made a mistake, that's all, a little setback that could be fixed when she graduated, and you two could leave together."

"That was the plan," Tom said. "You know that. I knew it was stupid to stay here, but I couldn't live without her. I didn't want to be anything if I couldn't have Oui by my side. Don't you see that?"

"Of course I do. I saw it then, and I told Oui that, but it was harder for her than you realized. She put all this pressure on herself to do good in school because you were so smart, and to be in student council because you had been president, and to try and play basketball because you'd lettered in every sport Picayune had. She wore herself out trying to be your equal, so people wouldn't laugh, so she wouldn't feel like a second-class person next to a celebrity."

Tom looked up at Mike with a ruthless stare freshly fed with tangled emotion, a glare that now began to feed on truth.

"Did you do something then to steal Oui from me?" Tom said. "Tell me now, and if you lie, I swear I'll feed you to the bobcats."

IV.

After the fundraiser over at the Red Oaks Country Club, most of the ladies broke into small groups to have coffee after lunch, but Wanda and Glenna decided to leave. Wanda needed to drop off some papers at the bank before it closed, and since the two women had ridden together, Wanda asked if they could have a little afternoon coffee at her house instead.

The papers delivered and wild car ride to Wanda's home finally successful, Glenna tried to compose herself from the speeding, the red light running, and the mindless lane changes that Wanda assumed to be the way everyone drove. Feeling a bit disheveled as they pulled into the driveway, Glenna had seldom felt so happy to escape from a ten-minute roller-coaster ride as this harrowing trip back to her friend's house had proven to be.

"Next time, I think I'll drive," said Glenna. "I haven't made my last life insurance payment yet." The redhead only smiled.

"Honey, that was nothing. You should have seen me when I drove my Corvette." Nothing seemed to trouble Wanda. Her confidence flowed from a place of self-assuredness that didn't need input from anyone, as she was her own fuel cell with unlimited capacity.

Soon they settled on the veranda off the kitchen, a nice covered area all marble with gorgeous tile facing the pool. Large stone columns created an effect of a Greek colonnade where a variety of large planters overflowing with flowers in the summer would cultivate a civilized, almost hotel type feel, but here in late winter, it seemed hungry for life. Glenna loved how beautiful the space felt with the flowing white curtains and stately columns but sensed that it was too large and impersonal to be a home.

The afternoon warmed, so they sat at a lovely wrought-iron table with large marble top and soft padded cushions on the chair seats. Wanda's maid, Estelle, soon brought coffee and homemade chocolate-chip cookies, and then the two ladies relaxed in the welcome afternoon sun that felt so good after the recent cold.

"I cannot wait for spring; I so love when all the flowers bloom and my planters come back to life. They're like children, you know, and I enjoy seeing them flourish in the summer." Both women sensed simultaneously the oddity of the statement, how peculiar Wanda's life really was with her daughter estranged and unwilling even to talk to her mother. Glenna's friend sat here today supremely confident yet alone in a gigantic house with no one in it but a maid and with planters burgeoning only in the past. Glenna couldn't help feeling a bit sorry for her friend even as she gazed at the clear opulence in which she lived such a lonely life.

"Have you ever thought about getting married again?" Glenna asked. "I mean, having someone around all the time?" Glenna almost ventured too far and mentioned that since her daughter was now gone from home, but she caught herself and let the follow-on comment pass unspoken.

"Yeah, sometimes," Wanda said. "But I like my independence to go where I want when I want, and I don't really mind not having a man around. They can be such a bother, you know." Wanda winked at Glenna when she made the quip, leaving her more traditional friend slightly disquieted. A chronic discomfort crept back into Glenna's thoughts, one she'd learned to deny all these years but which always managed to slip into her inner thoughts at the most inopportune moments to remind her of what she'd not pursued in life. But with deft familiarity, she put away the image like an ironing board once the laundry is finished.

Apparently still thinking about Glenna's question, Wanda spoke again. "Seriously, I think about what it would be like to have a man around, but I'm not sure there is another one out there like my Ernie. He was so devoted to me and didn't have that tediousness most men seem to have inherited genetically from too many generations of indulgence by doting mothers and socially acquiescent wives. If I could ever meet the right man, one who could get his ego out of the way, I think I would like that companionship again. But he better not tell me what to do."

"Yeah, I've wondered myself what things would be like with a different man." Glenna spoke habitually before she'd considered her words.

"Well," said Wanda, "how thoroughly modern of you. I didn't realize you had such progressive thoughts. Imagine, getting rid of a man who is never around and is emotionally unavailable even when he is. Darling, I'm afraid you either have to upgrade your choice or become a car that needs to be restored, and then you might get some attention." Wanda howled at her quip, but Glenna felt pangs of guilt as she hadn't updated Wanda on how well she and Harold were doing or on his new job offer.

"I've always been afraid Harold was too set in his ways for rehabilitation," Glenna said methodically, "but I must say he's been really coming around." Glenna didn't want Wanda to feel even more lonesome, so she remained low-key with her comment.

"Oh really," said Wanda. "What's Harold been up to? Did he give you a new set of whitewalls or an oil change perhaps?"

Without a word, Glenna pulled the pendent from underneath her blouse. "He gave me this. Took me to the Sea Lodge too." Wanda sat back with a huge grin.

"My, my, my, looks like someone did get an oil change after all."
They both howled.

After a second cup of coffee, Glenna adopted a plaintive look and
began to speak softly. "What do you think of Mike? You know, Mike
Hamlin?"

Wanda drew her head back with wrinkled face as if she'd smell
something fetid. "Mike Hamlin?" She pretended to be a little surprised,
but of course she'd had designs in her head from back as Christmas when
the sense of family had become so revived for everyone at the Mitchell
house.

"Mike is my dad's oldest friend," Glenna said, "and we all love him.
He's one of those avuncular guys that really cares about the kids when
he's around, and he's always been the best to me, nothing but thoughtful
and kind."

Wanda followed along. "He really seems to be close to your dad—you
know, brother-like in a way."

"Oh yes, absolutely. I'll tell you the truth. Mike is the only reason I
have any peace about Dad living out in that dreary old cabin. Dad stays
out there all by himself and won't come to town unless a new century
rolls around, but Mike keeps an eye on him. Shoot, he's my mail system
to Dad." Glenna's voice reflected genuine appreciation for the sacrifices
she'd always seen Mike make for Tom, the unprompted generosity to keep
an eye on Tom and to take him food and supplies though never asked
to do so. Then Glenna spotted her chance to redirect the questioning.

Meaning to drop a joke, Glenna tried to be clever. "Why you're not
interested in my dad's friend, are you? I'm a bit suspicious here."

"Don't be silly," Wanda said flatly. "That calloused old shoe is
too gruff for me. He doesn't even have a college education, does he? I
don't know what we'd even talk about." Wanda's words sounded false
to Glenna, as if they were designed to be superficial, to be discovered
as insincere. What had begun as a playful question unexpectedly had
revealed a hidden clue. Glenna saw immediately her friend's interest and
knew how delicate such things could be, how they could be snuffed out
with the turn of a brow or the slash of an unkind word, and a guileless

longing seeped to the surface of Wanda's usually composed dominance. But no words frightened the vulnerable emotion back into hiding.

Cautiously, Glenna decided to discuss the man she knew. "Mike Hamlin is probably the most honest, sincere man I know. He may not be as sophisticated as some, but he has something most men don't, something I've always seen in him—he knows how to love. You see, Mike isn't a man of words, but he is one of deeds. Watch the way he will always help out, how he genuinely talks to the kids and listens to what they say, how he wants to know how everyone else is doing and how he can help. Mike is a tough old coot on the outside but is a sweet, sensitive gentleman on the inside."

"Yeah, I can see that. I watched the way he was with Tom, how he always has his radar up for anything that your dad might do to complicate things. It was weird, but he always looks out for Tom like a big brother or something. I'm not sure."

Glenna laughed affectionately, looking up at Wanda. "My dad is pretty much a straight-on brute, hard, unyielding, blunt. He says things he doesn't mean sometimes, and he loses his temper over minor details, and that tends to cause problems for him. I think it's one of the reasons he likes to be alone; he doesn't have to worry so much about saying the wrong thing or offending people when he doesn't mean to. It's easier to be alone for him. Mike understands that and helps Dad almost like a translator, a social go-between in a way."

"You know, that's so odd because your dad is really smart. I can see that in the way he thinks. He's not a man of a lot of words, but there is intelligence there. Your dad graduated from college, right?"

"Yeah, he did; he had a double major in history and industrial engineering. He even used to have a big corporate job up in Yazoo City before he and my mom came back to Picayune."

"Really? He doesn't strike me as the corporate kind of guy; I can't see your dad brownnosing people too well."

"No, he isn't too good at that, for sure, but he used to be a lot more amiable, more social. When my mom died five years ago, he took it really hard and has never quite been the same. At Thanksgiving was the first time I'd seen him in three years; he almost never leaves the river. If it hadn't been for Mike, Dad would have probably just disappeared into that nasty old swamp."

"Wow. I get the feeling there's a real story there, Glenna. Maybe a story I'd like to hear someday."

"There is, for sure, but I don't think I know it as well as Mike does. That's a guy who knows more than he says, and though he doesn't have the education a lot of people do, he's more aware of how people think than most of us. I always have the feeling Mike understands things more deeply than he lets on; he gets things intuitively without having to mince through lots of words. Strange really, but he almost understands things—people, I mean—more like a woman than a man. Is that crazy? Does that make sense at all?"

"Yeah, that makes a lot of sense to me," said Wanda. With that, the day's conversation ended, as Glenna had to get home before the kids got back from school.

As she drove through the quiet back roads home, Glenna wondered about her new friend. Was there a place she too hid her fears and hopes alongside the singed emotions of half-attempted failures, the broken trophy closet of her mind? Glenna simply knew a woman existed there who could become a true friend if only she could find that soft core Wanda hid so carefully beneath her self-assuredness. The loneliness in Glenna's life had begun to lift now, and with new hope she was learning to see the world as the place she too could become her own deeper self, and she wondered if Wanda sensed the loneliness of her life, the sprawling, unpopulated places in her womanly spirit that now had begun to feel the early callings of spring. And as she turned onto the street leading home, an interesting insight occurred—Mike still knew how to love, but Wanda had stopped trying.

V.

The accusation about trying to steal Oui away all those years ago caught Mike unaware, but before reacting, he remained collected enough to let the words echo through his thoughts. Tom often blurted terse summaries of complex matters, syllabic walls intended to halt discussion, but this festering idea Newland had planted was one Mike knew needed to be excised. Both men felt the starchy tension as each maneuvered carefully between thoughtful question and impulsive response.

Mike formed his defense. "That's just a bunch of bull hockey, and you know it. I didn't try to steal Oui from you back then or any other time. You know, sometimes I think you're plain old nuts."

"Oh no, buddy, you're not pulling that trick on me; there's something rotten in the state of the Catchahoula, and I can smell it. Let me have it, Mike. Tell me the damned truth."

"Okay, you old possum, I'll tell you. But it's a lot less dramatic than you think, so just sit there and do something you've never tried before: stay calm." Mike felt he'd gotten his friend about as disarmed as he could, so with a little pacing and chin stroking, his story began to unfold.

"Back when Oui and me were seniors, it was a tough year. You being at PRC caused so much commotion that Oui was always upset. You didn't see most of it, but every day I got to hear the crying and depression. She was like a movie of every extreme emotion, and every day she'd lay a new load of blubbering on me. It was brutal."

Pausing to look at the stove but really only observing Tom's reaction, Mike saw his old friend staring at his shoes, hands crossed in his lap.

"One particular night," Mike continued, "she came over and told my mom she needed help with her science homework, so we went into the den to study. In about a minute, she went off like an alarm clock and started jabbering about the fight you two had, about how she couldn't take it anymore and she wanted to run away from home. It was a nightmare; she was hysterical." Tom looked up as if to say I'm listening but not reacting, so Mike continued.

"After she finally got all that vented, we started talking, and she said some crazy things. You were too much for her—too smart, too popular, and that kinda stuff. She needed someone who wouldn't make her feel so, what was it she said ... oh yeah, Lilliputian—you know, real small. It was like the more she thought about being with you, the smaller she got in her own mind."

"How can that be?" Tom finally spoke. "I loved her more than anything in the world. How could I not know she felt that way? Am I that stupid?"

"Not exactly stupid but self-centered. You are so damned sure that everything you think is right that you forget that other people might have the same opinion of their own thoughts. You act like your way is the only way. What's worse is when you get exactly what you want, half the time it turns out to be precisely the wrong thing. Oui was afraid. She knew you'd get her just like you wanted, but she wasn't sure it was the right choice for you or her, at least not that senior year."

"You know," Tom began, "I remember her being antsy a lot that year, but I thought it was because I wasn't around all the time like I had been before. Because we only got to see each other on weekends, it was harder to be close, I think."

With Tom revealing a slight hint of vulnerability, Mike took advantage. "Now I need you to relax for me here, okay, but that night something else happened." Mike paused with a mounting sense of dread as if he were about to enter a courtroom. "Oui kissed me, Tom. She grabbed me, holding me while she was crying, and then before I knew what happened, she took her hands and pulled my face to her and kissed me."

"So there it is, huh. Blame Oui because you're a lying, thieving rat."

"Just shut the hell up," Mike said. "I told you you're getting the truth, but lock that complaint horn of yours because you don't know what you're talking about. I didn't do nothing but try to comfort her. After she did that, we both withdrew from each other instinctively, scared almost, and she looked at me and said, and this is the God's honest truth: 'I need someone like you. Tom is too big a personality for me, and I get lost in his shadow.' That's the truth."

Looking scornfully and appearing weak again, Tom spoke as if he'd given up. "What did you do?"

"I told her she was wrong; said she'd get tired of someone like me, simple, not flashy, and that she just hadn't discovered her own power yet. Tom, I told her that she'd be making the worst mistake in her life if she left you."

"Did you mean it?" Tom asked.

"Yeah, sort of. Truth is I did believe you two were the perfect couple, but I think I loved Oui too. I loved her the first time I ever laid eyes on her, and the same way you made her feel small, she made me feel that same way too. I knew I could never hold Oui in the long run, I just knew it, and that's what I told her."

"And?"

"Well, for a couple of weeks, it was touchy. When we talked, it was stiff, artificial like. Then she came over one night, and we went through the same thing all over again, but she said she wanted me to tell you she was dumping you. Tom, she was all jittery and nervous, almost crazy kinda, like she didn't know what was real. I could tell she was vulnerable, and she kept grabbing me to comfort her, but it was more like a friend than anything, and I knew it. I saw then that your friendship was on the line, and though I dreamed sometimes of Oui and me, I knew the idea was crazy. I wasn't tired of living just yet either, but really I knew she was too much for me even if you hadn't been in the picture. She finally settled down and left that night, and we both understood then we'd always be friends but nothing else."

"Is this all on the level?" Tom asked.

"Yeah, it is. Nothing ever happened between us except in my dreams."

With that anticlimactic ending, the two men both went silent, listening to the crackle of the oak log in the stove. Tom found himself drawn to thoughts of days long since receded into the past. How blind he'd been, how bullheaded and unable to sense Oui's true needs even as he saw her distress that year. There too the quiet moments, tender times when he sensed her fear though he never quite understood. Images sorted, the supremely confident man defiant of opinion, single-minded and often misguided, leaned back against the couch pillow in silence.

That young man he used to be stood now in his thoughts as domineering and insensitive, hardly recognizable as the person he'd envisioned back then. So shallow. How hard Oui and Mike must have thought him, and the rising truth left Tom diminished this night, surrounded by creeping old age and the leaden burden of lost time remembered. Weakness had activated in Tom's body, and the downstream pull of life tugged harder in its call from a distant gulf he could almost see. Heavily into the blankets and pillows, searching for solace not to be found this night, Tom discovered that his warm little cabin with his best friend there to help could bring relief from the rising darkness in his soul but not from the changes he could not control.

Mike too slipped into a deep, mournful silence. On his face, only a vacant look after he'd poured the lifeblood of his secret guilt into the moment. Whirlpools in a turning river of the past ate at the firm footing of this lifelong friendship, eroding the constancy of loyalty, and Tom listened to the distant chorus of the Catchahoula, hoping to hear Ouida's faint voice steadying him against the capricious currents ahead.

Their three lives had become a sloshing sea of confusion, even without Newland. And yet Tom's old nemesis had dredged the truth from the past using his cultish tools of betrayal and confession. Hunkered on the couch, mired in the collapsed aura of faded youth, Tom struggled to imagine the path ahead now that the dark cloak of guilt had been removed and the ancient myopia exposed.

"I'm going to sleep now," Mike said. "But I want you to know something." Tom didn't move or respond. "You and Oui have been like family for me my whole life. I got pleasure watching you two grow up together, sorting out things, having a family, and I couldn't have asked for more than to be close to you two like my own kin." Mike paused; Tom remained silent.

"When Oui made me promise not to tell you all that stuff about Newland, she told me if I did, she'd never speak to me again or let me in her house. That was about the scariest thing I ever heard, and I couldn't let that happen."

No kind response from Tom, no bond that said past and future were healing in the new light of frankness, only a barely audible grunt, "Uunnh." And so the evening ended with Tom drifting further away from life and Mike paddling hard to catch him with outstretched hand. Clouds of fear were forming, and Mike knew he must brace for increasingly uncertain moments ahead. Outside, the cold night air sunk heavy across the river with muffled songs struggling in the dark even as deep roots feeding on the river began to give rise to early spring already sipping on the chill.

Chapter 13

I.

The days after Mike left found Tom with fresh energy to tidy up around the cabin. He cleaned out the garden and got ready for the early broccoli and cabbage plantings, he repaired furniture and a broken porch step, and he started his new project with the white ash board, sanding and polishing the wood until the clean fibers stood up and awakened the wood's color. Then with a piece of smokehouse char, he carefully traced out the scene he wanted to construct. Working from the right-hand side back to the left, he puzzled why he had done it that way. Was it the passage of time flowing right to left, or was it the river current behind the cabin that set that image in his mind? Did things go backward or forward? The more he thought, the more unclear he became, so he worked instead, leaving the words behind in a place he could visit later when he could be troubled with their awkwardness.

Soon a serpentine image sprawled itself across the board, end to end, spilling into the holes cut for the swing ropes. Tom wanted to incorporate both those chasms into his scene, as they seemed to mean something to him, symbols perhaps of origins and cycles.

Soon he found his woodworking tools and began routing out a gorge between the two parallel lines that snaked their way from side to side, including sharp twists along the way with unpredictable changes of direction. Carefully scooping out the hard wood, he gouged out the long trench, leaving behind curled rolls of ash wood carefully abscised by the sharp tools. Each of these white folds was saved, as Tom enjoyed how they were the same but different, some larger and broad, some small and delicate, each evincing its own shade of wood color and twist of the grain. The wood being so hard, this process took longer than envisioned, but hour by hour, he worked lifting spiraling fragments from the channel he so thoughtfully prepared.

When the two holes in the board finally connected with the meandering trench, Tom took several of the saved shavings and began to see how they could be fitted together to form a structure, how they could be joined to a triangle-shaped scale of a pinecone. Each shapely segment from the cones had been collected in his search for the most geometrically pleasing forms. Soon intertwined pieces mounted one scale atop each of the five miniature creations he'd assembled, tiny little houses an inch wide. Gluing pieces together with the sap of pine resin, Tom soon sat back to admire his labor, three days of intermittent effort now coalescing in a form that had rattled around his brain as undefined wish.

Soon he knew exactly what he wanted to do. Mixing used coffee grounds with a bit of mud and pine resin laid in the routed-out trench, Tom watched a chocolate-colored river flow from one end of the board to the other. Into that stretch, he carefully placed tiny shredded pieces of wood shavings, gradually taking on the look of river logs and piles of debris trapped in the twists of a current. The coffee grounds gave a lovely, deep texture, Tom thought, the same hue the oak tannins gave the Catchahoula, and he felt a strong familiarity with this simple little microcosm of his life.

As Tom surveyed his replica of the river, he studied carefully the seven bends he'd intentionally scripted into the design. The biggest and most radical turns were at the second and fourth bends, then again at the seventh switchback. At these critical junctures, Tom placed the five little houses with pinecone steeples he'd so carefully assembled, each having been soaked in a tea of berry juice and coffee to give a darker appearance but one lighter than the river hue, and he thought the colorful tints of the houses beautiful and familiar. Affixing them to the board with sticky resin to hold the houses firm, Tom lived again among the memories of these sanctuaries from his past.

Across from the houses on the opposing shoreline, Tom sprinkled a mixture of salt and sand onto the resin, creating what he thought to be respectable sandbars, and all round the rest of the board he tinted the white ash with a green stain from grasses and leaves he'd stored last summer, things he used as herbs in his cooking. The only thing that remained to be done was to fill in the two large holes from where the ropes used to tie off, and for this Tom placed an individual hunk of soft wood he'd collected from the river, something supple enough to be worked into an exact fit, plugging the holes yet remaining below level with the rest of the board, a floor Tom thought, a bottom to the two lakes, one to be the headwater for the river, the other the mouth where the current ends.

To fill the lakes, Tom took the remainder of the routed wood and broke it into smaller pieces, soaking them overnight in a brew of dried huckleberries; he wanted the bluish-purple color to absorb into the wood fibers. And the next day after drying them, he placed the pieces carefully into the shallow lakes, sprinkling over them dried huckleberry bits as highlights. The lakes took on a deep appearance from the dark color, and the texture created by the wood and berries gave the impression of wildness, a choppy water illusion if a person allowed his imagination to run free. And as Tom sat pondering his work, he pictured himself floating on that lake in his little boat, searching, searching for something he couldn't quite describe.

After a few days of fine-tuning, affixing, coloring, and admiring, the diorama of Tom's life lay finished on the table. With two hooks at the top and little fanfare, in minutes his creation hung from the back of the smokehouse, nestled perfectly into the larger blackened section of the mural, a second portrait of time captured. He thought the dark scruff from the charcoal backdrop offered the perfect matting for his new artistry, a rich contrast to the white ash and heightening the symbolism of a bright little island of life in the middle of a surrounding ocean.

Several times a day, he loved to walk by and admire its uniqueness, how vibrant his little sculptures made the entire panorama, and Tom felt gratified at having left the heart of his mural undamaged though trapped by the charcoal harshness now become its edges. He saw the two worlds as a story he was sure had now been told without having to speak.

Each morning, he studied the scene, looking at the first house and bend, thinking of his childhood and the deep longing he had to see his mom again, how wonderful it had been to play in his family home and to laze around on the rope swing out back or dig in his first garden when he was just a boy, with his mom reading poetry from the porch. He looked at the second bend and the house, thinking of his teenage years in Picayune, growing up with Mike, meeting Oui and falling in love, being the hometown football champion, halcyon days of joy. Then the third house and the triumphs and rejections of Yazoo City, of his realization that he wasn't invincible, that friendship could be a specious thing, and Tom felt a powerful urge to race downstream away from those memories, to escape back into the reliable arms of these woods he loved so deeply. The simple little fourth house, the place he and Oui had raised Glenna in Picayune, seemed nondescript, like Old Mother Hubbard's humble place that belied the love inside, and Tom appreciated the quaint, simple existence of those best years of his life.

Looking at the final house situated on the seventh river bend, he thought of his own life in the cabin, so alone after all these decades but happy with the woods and his beloved river. He wondered what Oui would think if she were here. Could she stand this isolation? Would she insist on being closer to Glenna? And a thought emerged as if raindrops from a blue sky, sudden, overpowering. Deep churnings that had begun some time ago as mere inklings, those sequestered rumblings of ineffable angst now began to seize a new form, a foothold upon which to hoist itself into the world of things done and choices made. A surge flowed through Tom, a swiftly moving pull from thoughts hidden but now unleashed to compel him onward. But again Tom hesitated.

The new creation struck a familiarity with the birdhouses his mother had made, those physical flashes of beauty from her soul, and Saralynn seemed so close in the moment, so alive. Remembering the time he almost drowned before his mother yanked him by the hair, Tom sensed the hungry river. And again the clawing water swallowed his shackled foot, begging him to come along. A cold dread lay against his heart as he remembered that mother long since absent, her promise to be with him always now stranded behind the wall of time like his secret universes hanging behind the shed.

Slumping to his log bench, staring at the creations, the delicate touch of the present and the vastness of life merged in a swell of completeness, as if he'd already been everywhere, seen everything. The cabin again lured Tom to its sanctuary of stillness hunkered against encroaching darkness, and slowly the disconcerting impressions of towns and places began disappearing like dew in a soft breeze, leaving the quietness of his river world to its permanence. And Tom began to accept his mother's end, and his own, as life rested on the gentle fragrance of passage.

Don Newland too drifted into the blur of lost thoughts, and not even those images seemed worrisome; in fact, he barely recalled the trip to Yazoo City. Even Sheriff Barker's threats retreated into the ignored place behind awareness as Tom studied his creations, allowing mellifluous river songs to wash away the unpleasant past. Contented by his quiet world again, he paused to imagine each of his broccoli plants adding new florets as they too performed their dutiful work. And Tom calmly leaned against the shed post to adore the cool day, and into the arms of an imaginary river goddess Tom slipped, welcoming to his riverbank her idea of perfect change—the return of spring.

II.

In mid-February as Lee's sixteenth birthday approached, he got more and more anxious about getting his full driver's license. His dad had promised he could drive the Chevelle on his birthday, and Lee wasn't about to forget such a momentous occasion. All week before the big day on Saturday, Lee slipped out to the garage to sit behind the steering wheel and feel the seduction of this perfectly restored muscle car now become a shared dream with his dad. The smell of the interior, the shiny chrome shifter, the immaculately clean dashboard and perfectly transparent windows created a magical world for his imagination.

On the Saturday he was supposed to take the car out for the first time, Lee was up at six and sitting with Glenna at the motor vehicle agency when it opened. His dad, true to his commitment, waited for their return.

At last Lee strolled into the garage. Donned in a red polo shirt and khaki-colored Dockers his attire was of a fraternity kid home from college, a rich boy spoiled by the easy pressure of wealthy life, and he enjoyed being the poseur showing his father how mature he had become. New license peeking from his hip pocket, Lee had never felt quite this grown-up. A manly confidence filled his casual swagger, and he was certain he'd captured exactly the right impression to sway his father.

With a huge smile, Lee stepped into the fluorescent glare giving his dad a quick wink. "Well, look a here. Mr. Rockefeller, I presume," Harold said.

With the focus of a jeweler, Lee strolled slowly around the car, wiping away with his handkerchief any specs of dust from the pin striping set so subtly against the seductive yellow color. He enjoyed pretending close attention to the detail, but the car stood as clean as an operating room. Even in the strong shop light, Lee saw his dad's amusement as perhaps he too recalled special moments from his long-passed teenage years.

"She's beautiful, just beautiful," Lee remarked. "You did something really special here, and I'm proud of you, Dad."

"Thanks, son. I appreciate all your help too. She looks like a brand-new dream and is worth every skinned knuckle." The room filled with unspoken emotion.

"So, are we going to fire her up today?" Lee asked with a bit of reticence. In the past, Harold had a way of disregarding the feelings of his kids, not realizing how demeaning his capricious decisions felt to them. Lee had known many moments of unrequited affection with his dad, times they had planned to go hunting but his dad forgot, times when Lee had a baseball game but his dad was busy shooting pool down at the Stony Road Tavern. Taking his new job the past few weeks had revealed a whole new Harold, but deeply ingrained patterns left Lee wary.

"Well, son, I don't really know. What day is this, anyway?" Harold smiled and gave away his trick, but Lee went along with the ruse.

"Saturday, the twenty-third. You know, time to christen the Chevelle." Lee grinned at his quip even as his head filled with the noise of old promises.

"Oh, yeah. Seems like there's something else going on today. What is that? Maybe it's the Braves playing?" Harold paused as he lost the thread of his joke. "Oh, I remember, it's the day you get to drive the Boss." Solidly delivered, his dad stood up straight, reached out his right hand to shake Lee's, and then handed him the keys. "Happy birthday, son."

Lee erupted, losing his cool and jumping up and down while at the same time grabbing the keys and hugging his dad's neck. "Thanks, Dad. You're the best." With the deep embrace, Lee sensed his dad's happiness, and as Harold unexpectedly gasped, Lee knew his dad had almost begun to cry. They held their closeness. Finally, Harold broke, immediately opening the driver's side door.

"Crank her up, son. Drive me around the block a time or two just to make sure you're comfortable with everything. Then you can take her out by yourself. This car has more power than anything you've ever ridden in, let alone driven, so you gotta respect her or she'll hurt you. She's the Boss, and don't ever forget that." Lee sat down as if in a spaceship about to leave for another world.

With the engine firing, the sound gurgled with a low rumble as menacing as a cornered tiger, and raw power echoed in the grumbling noise even with the headers closed. Lee slowly pushed the clutch down, slipping the Hurst shifter into reverse, and instantly the car died. His dad smiled.

"The clutch is a little tight, so you'll have to get used to it; try to find that smooth place between a steady release and just enough gas to make her go without complaining."

Soon Lee had them on the road and stopping at signs, making left and right turns, even backing up and parallel parking in the church lot until his dad felt comfortable. Harold smiled and grabbed his son's neck affectionately. "Okay, bud, take me home. But remember, this car is a beast, and she will eat you the first second you don't respect her. Treat her like danger, then she'll love you forever."

Within five minutes, his dad was deposited in the driveway, and Lee made his way out to Highway 59 to feel the new suspension and the raw response to the horses in the engine running free. Cruising at about fifty, Lee back shifted to third gear, suddenly stomping the accelerator; the Holly four-barrel carburetor snapped opened, sucking in air and fuel like the edge of a waterfall. The roaring sound reminded Lee of the hot air balloon ride he'd taken while on vacation years ago, and instantly deaf, he sizzled with excitement. Shifting into fourth gear, the throttling roar calmed into a laser-like sprint forward, the sheer, sleek bullet performance of this magnificent beast now set free on the prairies of the interstate highway and allowed to stretch her muscles with attack speed.

The sound of the engine numbed Lee to anything but the hunger of acceleration, and all his faculties focused on keeping the car steady as it merged the white lines into a blur of blistering speed. Never had Lee felt so powerful, so alive. Never had his young life known the supreme dominance of anything the way this car made him feel as it controlled the road with not a whisper of concern, it racing with ease and Lee riding high as its master.

As the speedometer crossed one hundred, Lee became frightened as things shot by so quickly he couldn't keep up. Hills in the road flattened out as they came upon him in a compressed blur, the car lightly touching the highway, more like it was surfing the road than gripping it. Then slowly he began letting off pressure to the accelerator allowing the car to plane out in a high-pitched rattle, almost the sound of Nascar, a whining scream of tight, angry power.

Returning to sixty-five, Lee felt like he was walking. The scenery moving by so slowly, the road elongated, adding distance almost faster than the car seemed to move. Lee's heartrate began to slow down again, his breathing deeper. This animal beneath him seemed to own the moment, to have all the answers for overcoming any resistance in its way, and Lee stoically absorbed that magnificent feeling of authority.

Soon off the highway and headed back to the neighborhood, Lee thought of his grandfather and wished he'd been there to see him drive this supreme machine, to see what a man he'd become and how nothing scared him, nothing could stop him from devouring the life that he wanted to live just the way he wanted to live it. In the dashboard mirror, handsome in his red shirt, perched in his cockpit with his left hand casually laid across the steering wheel at his wrist, Lee admired the insouciant, invincible man smiling at him. "Yep, Grandpa would love this for sure." The words slipped effortlessly from his lips, and Lee thought of his dad, his mom, his sisters, and how everyone would know what a man he was now, a man of sixteen and dauntless courage fed by the power of the Boss.

III.

Over a month had passed since the home invasion scare, but the town still buzzed with tales of bravery. Interested more in forgetting the incident than leveraging its notoriety, Vic tried not to discuss that day, but Hattiesburg wasn't quite ready to allow the event to die quietly.

"Come downstairs, honey," Glenna called out. "I've got something to tell you."

Excitement continued swelling as Wanda's phone call replayed in Glenna's head.

"Yeah, what's up?" Vic said cheerily. "I'm working on the essay the principal asked me to write."

"I know, darling, and I don't mean to disturb you, but this is important. Wanda is on her way over, and she's got some news for us that I'll wait and let her describe it. She didn't tell me much but sounded thrilled. So, while we're waiting, what's this essay thing you're working on?"

"You remember my research report we talked about on girls' night? Well, my teacher was so impressed with my class presentation that after the intruder story got so much attention, she and Principal Reeder asked me to write an essay for the school newspaper. Cool huh?"

"Yes, honey, that's impressive. So what are you writing about?"

"I met with them, and we discussed a few ideas. I told them I wanted to focus more on what women can do *not* to become victims in life— careers, that sort of thing. I'm still trying to sharpen my thinking on what to say, but I'm focusing on how women often end up really poor in old age because of their early life choices."

"I like it; that sounds great because it's so practical. Maybe you could even contrast that with women in oppressive societies that don't have many choices ..." The doorbell rang. There stood Wanda in a green pantsuit with a gorgeous red silk scarf.

"Wow, you look like a movie star. Where you been?" Glenna asked.

"Oh, had a little luncheon with an old friend, that's all."

"She must be rich, or is it a he? I'm betting on the 'he' option." Glenna smiled and grabbed Wanda's arm to give her a hug. These past few weeks, they'd become best friends, and even Wanda and Harold now enjoyed each other's company more since he and Glenna had begun marriage counseling.

But Wanda had a little secret she had not shared, a bouquet of flowers sent two days earlier on from some anonymous stranger. The shock of the surprise left Wanda with a warm glow she wanted to share. But first, business was pressing.

"So where's my girl?" Wanda asked. "Oh there you are. I love that shirt you're wearing. Abercrombie, right?" Wanda, carrying a bag of pastries, swished into the room, hugging Victoria with movie-star affectation. Victoria glanced down at her blouse bought on sale at Target.

"Listen, girls, let's put on a pot of coffee and dig into these goodies. My friend bought these this morning at the best bakery in New Orleans. She—I say that for your benefit, Glenna—had a meeting there yesterday and drove up to see me this morning. She's the most divine, elegant woman, a sorority sister of mine from Ole Miss, you know." Wanda was talking so fast while unpacking the pastries, taking off her light jacket, and spreading out some papers on the table that both Vic and Glenna could only stare in passive amazement at the multitasking storm in the kitchen.

"For heaven's sake, slow down a minute," Glenna said. "I can't make heads or tails out of what you are saying. Just relax and let me get this coffee going. Now let's start at the beginning. Who is your friend?" As always, Glenna clarified, and Wanda charged ahead.

"Well, here name is Sarah Marion. She's from Massachusetts. She's the former director of admissions at Smith College and one of the most accomplished women I know; she's written six books, has a PhD—oh she's simply amazing."

"Here's your coffee," Glenna said. "Now breathe deeply and let's take this slowly enough we mortals can understand, okay?"

"Yes, well, anyway. Sarah contacted me because she's the national chairperson of a foundation that focuses on women's issues— everything from violence in the home to educational opportunities for underprivileged kids. Right now she's organizing a national campaign to promote awareness through a series of women's competitive events— golf tournaments, tennis, bridge, a whole range of things that can help raise money. Sarah wants me to organize something in this area for next year's campaign."

"Cool," said Vic. "What kind of things are you going to do?"

"Well, love, I'm not sure. That's why I want to talk to you. See, I had this big idea, so I called my neighbor who is the station manager out at WRQG Channel 8 and asked him if they'd be willing to help us out with some publicity if we got something together. Rob Janson is the best, and of course he said yes, so I want to float a proposition by you."

"Wait. Before we float off," Glenna said, "I have to tell you this is the finest piece of fluffy, confection-covered whatever I've ever tasted." Glenna's words again slowed Wanda to a word-per-millisecond speed understandable by humans, and once again Wanda labored to recalibrate.

"Okay, what do you think about this. Vic, you're in every newspaper in Mississippi right now because of that idiot you clobbered. Rob even told me they are trying to get you to do a television interview, but you're too scared."

"Yeah, it's not scared really. I'm just, well, terrified," Vic said.

Wanda laughed and patted Vic's hand. "It's okay, honey. Everybody's afraid to be on television. Heck, I don't even like it, and I'm not exactly the potted plant type." Vic and Glenna each shared a quick smile at the delicious audacity Wanda carried so effortlessly.

"Anyway, girls," Wanda said as she turned to Vic, "Rob and I were thinking that if I got some things going, that maybe you could help me as my youth cochairperson and focus on teenage women issues and events. Then we could dovetail with a television interview about that butt kicking you gave the cretin—you know, to help bring some visibility to our women's awareness events. Brilliant, right?"

Both Vic and Glenna looked so stunned their faces froze as each tried to process Wanda's pronouncement. Finally, Glenna spoke.

"Oh, my God. Are you kidding me? That's unbelievable." Glenna turned to Vic. "Honey, did you hear that? Wanda wants you to serve as her youth cochairperson. And go on television."

Victoria's mouth gaped open. "But I wouldn't know how to organize anything like that. The principal asked me to write an editorial on women's issues for our school paper, and I've been working on that for a whole week without finishing."

"Well, there you go. See, you're having good ideas already. I love it, women's editorials in high school newspapers all across the state. We could sponsor an essay contest and give a scholarship to the winner. That's fantastic, Victoria. I love it!"

"Well, yeah, I like that too," Vic said, "but if I was a cochair, I couldn't participate in the essay contest, could I?" Immediately Glenna recognized Vic was intimidated and looking for a way to avoid committing.

Wanda barely paused. "Listen, let me explain something to you. What we're talking about is going to take a year and a half to pull off, all the way through next summer. We've got planning to do before we get to the execution stage."

Though at first prepared to urge her daughter to participate, now the time line disturbed Glenna, and she stepped in quickly. "That sounds like a lot of work, and I don't think Vic will have enough time. She graduates in three months, you know, and she has a five-thousand-dollar scholarship to Mississippi State for the fall." Glenna was sure that would keep the conversation focused.

With dramatic slowness, Wanda stood, poured herself another cup of coffee, and then leaned against the breakfast bar with outstretched arms guarding the entire space. With cocked head and a deadly stare softened only by the smile on her lips, she peered at Glenna and Vic, who looked like two puppies waiting for treats.

"My heavens, girls, you two really are from the same gene pool, aren't you? Now if we could only get you to join the rest of us in the twenty-first century."

Vic and Glenna thought that sounded like an insult but weren't sure yet, and at the pace Wanda was speaking, they might not be able to decide until tomorrow, so they each sat back and stared blankly.

"Let me break this down for you. Victoria, if you help me with my plan, you will have pulled off one of the most amazing women's rights feats any teenager in Mississippi has ever accomplished. Do you think a prestigious college like Smith might be interested in that? Do you think my sorority sister who was director of admissions at that school for sixteen years might be able to put in a good word for one of her cochairs? You know, a cochair teenager helping change southern society for the benefit of all women?

"Look, over half the girls that go to Smith get financial assistance. When someone with your brains and initiative, especially being from such modest means—please forgive me, Glenna—applies with these credentials, then I think you might just have an edge on getting accepted to that school, don't you? You offer geographic diversity too, which schools love. Heck, I bet your application essay could tie together how you crippled that savage and how that sparked your interest in women's rights. You'd be a shoo-in."

"Do you really think so?" Vic asked diffidently. "That they'd want me?"

"I guarantee it, sweetie. Look, I'll make you a deal. To help me, I know I'm asking you to pass on going to State this fall, but for some reason if this project doesn't work out and Smith doesn't accept you with a full free ride, then I myself will pay for your entire college education to whatever school you choose. You just have to work with me this next year. I'm looking for a commitment."

Glenna's jaw dropped like the crystal ball on New Year's Eve. "Holy cow, Wanda, you can't do that; we can't let you do that. That's not right. It's too much money, and we'd never feel good about it."

Looking at her friend's serious concern, Wanda then spoke kindly. "Glenna, darling, you're so sweet, but you don't have a clue about me yet, do you, sweetie?" Wanda paused to let everyone catch up. "I've already cut the deal with Sarah Marion. I just have to deliver my cochair and get this party started!"

All three women screamed with joy, kissing and hugging each other, enjoying something human, something feminine beyond friendship and deeper than good will. This moment represented a healing, a reconstituting of the soul for Glenna, and for Wanda, and both allowed their deepest feminine spirit to continue thawing. The future unfurled as if time had jumped its boundaries, leaving an anodyne of friendship and family to nurture that bonding essence their individual lives had begun to share.

After a few moments, Vic looked at Wanda, a sudden moment of trepidation in her voice. "Aunt Wanda, what if I can't do it? What if people won't do what I need?"

Wanda didn't hesitate. "From this moment on, Victoria, I want you to talk about only what you want, what you expect, what you need—and never, ever tell me what you cannot get. Do you hear me?"

The girl smiled and understood, or at least thought she did. Glenna reflected to herself what great advice Wanda offered and how she planned to start thinking the same way too.

Glenna squeezed Wanda and her daughter with the grateful pressure of a life rejoicing in the nourishment it needed but had struggled to find. Proud of her daughter, Glenna for one of the few times in memory could find no words, and so she smiled at the two women, now friends on a common mission to change their world, and hers.

"And now, girls, I have a mystery to share," Wanda said. "It's about a bouquet of flowers I received."

IV.

Almost a month passed since Tom made his new creation and hung it on the smokehouse wall, and now he felt the full force of spring returning to the river. The early chartreuse of new leaves filled the winter-thinned woods, and life could not be resisted as it surged back to his tiny corner of the world. The garden filled with a chorus of onions, cabbages, broccoli, and asparagus. Fish fed eagerly in the warming river and strengthening sun while the air shook off the doldrums of cold. Everywhere jonquils and daffodils, spanish bluebells, and creeping periwinkle slipped from the underbrush, blooming, nature's own little secrets smiling at the spring air.

Mike visited the cabin a couple of times, and the two men discussed new plans for a trip up to Hattiesburg to see Glenna and the kids and especially Lee. Though not saying so out loud, Mike hoped to have a chance to see Wanda again, his boyish interests piqued as well by the new season. But the two old friends couldn't calculate the right time or make a solid plan, and soon the days and weeks turned warm without notice, leaving the friends to their own rhythm of the fresh season where weighty discussion seemed out of place.

Slipping into a new routine, Mike volunteered at the high school, helping teenagers learn to work on cars after their automotive teacher, Mr. Kraft, broke his leg. The time with the teenagers surprised Mike, as he looked forward each day to talking with them and hearing about their lives. Tom even let the students work on his old truck, changing out the water pump and radiator and replacing a tire rod that bent after he accidentally slid into one of the river road craters.

One Saturday in late March, Mike stopped out at the cabin, hoping to pick up a couple of nice catfish or white perch to cook up for supper. There he found Tom sitting on the steps.

"What's the matter, little boy? Lose your lunch money?" Mike's quip went over Tom's head by thirty thousand feet, as the most he could do was look up without even a smile and not a clue that Mike was making a school joke. No words found their way out, so Mike tried again.

"Hey. Lookie here. I brought you a brand-new trotline I picked up at Wal-Mart for half price. Got this nifty little thing to roll it up on and everything. Good hooks too. I was hoping I could trade you for a couple of yearlings for supper tonight." No answer.

Mike took a seat. "Is anything wrong there, fellow? Something happen?"

"I told you before. Don't you remember? You know, about Barker. That letter yesterday he left on my truck. The extension is almost gone."

Not sure what Tom was jabbering about, Mike tried to get some specifics. "What in the world are you talking about? Who's Barker? You don't mean Charlie Barker, do you?"

"You know, like I told you before, you know." Tom began to get agitated.

"Now listen," Mike said, "I don't know what you're talking about, but we're going to figure this out right now. Let's start again. Tell me what Sheriff Barker said to you."

Tom started to walk away as if his friend hadn't said a word. When he reached the chinaberry tree, he turned and looked again at Mike, then mumbled, "You know, I told you before. It's like I told you." And Tom walked to the river, got in his little skiff, and pushed off, leaving Mike standing bewildered on the bank.

As fast as he could drive the Ford down river road, Mike headed for the sheriff's office and barged in with a huff.

"Where's Sheriff Barker?" he asked the policewoman at the receiving desk.

"He's in conference and not available."

"When will he be available?"

"I suspect in about forty-five minutes. I can tell him you came by if you'll give me your name."

"That won't be necessary. I'll wait. Please, Officer, this is an urgent matter, and I need to speak to the sheriff personally. My name is Mike Hamlin, and I'm an old friend of Charlie's, so thank you for your help, ma'am."

So anxious he popped up every two minutes, picking up a newspaper, magazine, and some old coupons to the Pizza Palace in Slidell, Mike tried to kill time. After an hour, the door to the sheriff's office opened, and a beautiful woman of about thirty wearing a tight skirt and dangling turquoise earrings tinkling under her auburn hair walked out after shaking the sheriff's hand. Oddly familiar in the handshake, Mike thought.

"You can go in now, Mr. Hamlin."

"Thank you, Officer. I appreciate your help."

Sheriff Barker leaned back in his swivel chair, looking for all the world like a stereotype redneck Sheriff in a B movie, fat gut hanging over his invisible belt, white socks pulled up to his calves. On his face, a sneer intended to look menacing, but to Mike, he only looked like the ignorant brute he'd always known Barker to be.

"Well look what we got here. If it ain't Mike Hamlin. I ain't seen you since we impounded your truck for leaving it overnight down at the Wal-Mart. Tell me, did you ever git it back?"

"Yes, I did. But your boys down at the impound seemed to have walked away with my front winch. You know anything about that?"

"Well, I heard that it was missin' when my boys hauled that piece of crap out of the parking lot; musta' happened before they got there. You know, we try and keep things respectable around here; don't like junkers abandoned in the parking areas of our nicer stores, you understand. But I'm glad you got the old bucket of bolts back; that would be a real shame to lose such a valuable antique." The unctuous look on Barker's face, supercilious, crude, brought back the old hatred Tom and Mike had for the Barker clan for decades now. They were a ruthless, cutthroat group, as venal as the worst politicians and as mean as water moccasins.

"So what can I do you for, Mikey? You having some trouble?"

"No, Charlie, I'm fine. I'm actually here trying to find out what's up with you and Tom Bradburn. I understand you sent him a letter, and he seemed pretty upset to me today, but I couldn't really get all the facts straight. Thought you might clarify things for me."

"Well, Mikey, it's like this. Tom is trespassing on that property where he lives, and I got a court order that says he's got to get his grumpy ass off that land by May 15 or I'm gonna put him in jail. See, it's real simple like; maybe even the two of you got enough brains to figure this one."

"Why does Tom have to leave? He was given permission to build that cabin and to live there; he's not breaking any laws."

"Well, see, an old fool like you is out of date, just as I figured the case would be. The owner of that property, Seldon Tompkins, died two years ago and left the land to his estate. Now, his niece has sold the land to the state of Mississippi, part of the new Catchahoula Land Preservation project, you know. Ain't that grand? Hey, maybe Tom can apply to be the ranger out there? There's a good idea for you."

Genuinely concerned, Mike leaned over, putting his hands down on Charlie's desk. "There has to be some mistake. That preservation act stops miles away from Tom's cabin.

"You'd think, wouldn't you? But see, that rise Tom squats on is the highest point within ten miles, and when Dotty Feo approached the state about affixing her inheritance to the land act, they decided it would be a good place for a fire tower. You know, to look out over all them woods for any troublemakers." Barker smiled like he'd made a clever joke. "Ain't it good to know we're doing all we can to support the safety of the fine citizens of Mississippi?"

"So doesn't there have to be some kind of notification to Tom well before eviction?" Mike asked.

"Well, call me a pickled potato; you ain't as dumb as you look, Hamlin. But you see, there was. Numerous letters was sent to Tom's last recorded address in town. I'm sure he musta read 'em. No matter though. Tom's moving May 15 if I have to drag his worthless ass off that land myself."

The hatred in Barker's eyes glared, and Mike knew this was real trouble. Surely they could file lawsuits and drag out the eviction, but Tom had no money, and neither did Mike. Not knowing what to do, the only person Mike knew he could talk to with the brains and knowhow to deal with a situation like this was Wanda, so he headed to the truck.

V.

Wanda's cell phone took the message, but Mike couldn't wait, so he headed north to Hattiesburg. He'd copied her address from a card he saw on Glenna's table last Christmas, but for Valentine's Day, he'd gotten caught up in thoughts of approaching spring and a few days afterward had sent Wanda an anonymous bouquet of flowers, signing the card only as "A distant admirer." Though his gesture was sent well after the holiday, Mike still thought he'd been clever. But what a fool he felt like now. Torn between whether she even remember his name and thinking him a stalker, Mike's mind raced wildly. But no matter how nervous, he didn't have a choice; he had to find help. Calling Glenna wasn't an option either, as he didn't have his facts sorted yet, and worrying her before he knew the details didn't sound prudent. The answer was Wanda.

As he pulled up to the outskirts of Hattiesburg an hour later, Mike's cell phone rang; she was returning the call.

"Hello there, Mike. Nice to hear from you. How are you?" Her voice sounded like pure sensuality, sultry, husky, all woman, and at first the words in his head flew away leaving him mute. Then after what seemed an eon, Mike regained composure.

"Oh, hi there, Wanda. Don't mean to be a bother, but, a, yeah, a, I need to talk to you about something, about Tom."

"Mike, is everything okay?" Wanda's voice immediately became serious. "Tell me what's happening. Do you need help?"

"Well, yeah, I do, sorta. Look, I'm almost to Hattiesburg. Would it be too much trouble if I came by so I could talk to you in person? I'm having a hard time driving this truck and thinking and talking all at the same time. You know, I'm more of a single tasker."

Wanda softened. "Yes, of course. Come on by. Let me give you my address."

"Oh, I got it all memorized," Mike said.

"Oh? Well, good, I'll see you in a few minutes." Then she paused a few seconds. "I'll put some flowers in a vase, and we can have coffee and talk." As she hung up, Mike's mouth dropped open and eyes glazed over. An 18-wheeler almost crawled up his bumper because he'd slowed to twenty-five miles an hour on the interstate, the blare of the horn jolting Mike back to reality. It was all he could do to glide into the rest area outside of town so he could catch his breath and reconstruct his personality.

"Damn. She knows."

VI.

Mike wasn't the kind of guy to be afraid of too much, but Wanda terrified him more than anything he'd ever encountered. After years of giving up on the idea of ever finding another woman to care for, he now looked at Wanda as if she were a Kennedy or a Vanderbilt—unattainable, educated, wealthy, a sophisticated goddess as far above him as the sky is from the center of the earth. He enjoyed the idea of thinking about her, of remembering the conversations they'd had, of even recollecting how she toyed with him with such skill so as to humor herself but not hurt him insultingly. To Mike, Wanda was the adult version of what Ouida had been for him as an innocent adolescent, the unattainable princess.

Thinking through the situation, he felt uncomfortable that his boyish secret admirer stunt now complicated a situation that required full attention and precision of response. He feared Wanda might hold herself in reserve because she wouldn't want to lead Mike on, and he wrapped himself around the thorny paradox of asking for help without getting too personal. Ideas of intimacy intruded with suffocating bewilderment, an infatuation he wanted to keep secret. Or did he want her to know? The labyrinth loomed before him, a Herculean challenge at precisely the moment his strength evaporated.

"I'm doomed." And he rang the doorbell.

The sound echoed through the house, cavernous behind the gigantic wooden door. He expected a maid to answer, so he remained calm, though now he couldn't remember a single thing he wanted to say. The door opened with a heavy swoosh, and Mike looked up, prepared to be direct. There Wanda stood.

She wore tight blue jeans and a bulky aquamarine sweatshirt with no jewelry, and Mike hardly recognized her. A simple charm emanated, a beauty that she loved to glorify with expensive clothes and jewelry, but there she stood as ordinary looking as any housewife on the street but elegant as a sculpture on a pedestal.

"Hello there, Mike. Good to see you again." She thrust out her hand in a formal greeting, and Mike was glad the teasing banter she so loved to torture him with had been put aside. "Do come in. Would you like some coffee, or iced tea perhaps?"

"Oh, well, no, no thank you. I'm fine, thanks." Mike thought he heard a waterfall and then realized it was his blood sloshing through the arteries in his neck.

"Here," said Wanda. "Let's have a seat on the sofa and chat a moment before we get down to business. Tell me, how have you been? Still teaching at the school, Glenna tells me."

"Yes, yes I'm helping, teaching a little." His mind still seemed to be outside the house, but then Mike began to calm down. "Trying to show them kids how to do things the right way. Even got two girls in class. You know teenagers today want to jump into things quick like and sometimes don't think things through too good." Mike suddenly felt dumb dribbling on about chatter Wanda couldn't care less about, but he didn't know enough about art or politics or even business to start up an educated conversation, so he slumped a bit, weakened by the aura of Wanda and wishing he'd planned his topics better.

"You know," Wanda said, "I think it's terrific you donate your time to those kids. Your experience, your gentle ways are things many of them benefit from, I'm sure. I bet some of those teenagers don't have a kind parent or grandparent, don't even have anyone who will take the time to show them important things about life, things like patience and an open mind." She reached over and touched Mike's hand with her own, and he noticed the beautiful pearl color of her nail polish and the intoxicating smell of her perfume.

"I assure you that you touch those young people's lives in important ways they are too shy to tell you. But it's okay. I'm telling you for them."

Realizing he had forgotten to breathe, Mike gasped a quick gulp of air and squirmed as the compliment seemed to have plugged his trachea. Wanda never moved, never took her eyes away from his. When he saw the plaintive look on her face, the sincerity in her soul, he knew she understood who he was, the innocent creature he kept hidden behind the ruddy leather of his appearance. Something was happening between them, but he couldn't allow himself to think it was real, that he was worthy of such a moment, and as he prepared his emotional retreat into his own simple view of himself, Wanda squeezed his hand again.

"I loved the flowers you sent. But you do know, Valentine's Day is not on the 19th?" His heart stopped, and he felt a tear draw in his eyes.

Then she broke the spell. "We'll talk about that later, Mike, but right now you have to tell me what's happening with Tom."

For the next hour, he poured out everything he knew about Tom's circumstance, about the May deadline, about Sheriff Barker's grudge from Ouida's ancient rebuff of Barker's older brother, and about the inheritance land sale. Wanda listened intently, taking notes, asking questions, pondering angles of attack. Mike saw the rich mind of this spirited woman, the years of business experience, the education and poise as she continued to grow into the persona Mike knew could advocate for Tom. Before another hour passed, Wanda had complete control.

"Listen," she said, "this situation is critical, but we have a little time before the eviction can be executed. This can be fought as a breach of contract and improper notification. We may not win, but we can hog-tie this swine until a better plan can be developed.

"I'm going to call my brother-in-law down in Pearl River County; he's a judge there. I'll get the scoop plus find out who the best lawyer in town is to handle this for Tom. These people may think they're taking out the trash down there, but let me tell you something. I know who controls the trash industry in Pearl River County, and trash can be a delicate thing."

"Thank you so much," Mike said. "But I have to tell you something. Tom won't fight this. He doesn't have any money, just a small pension and some social security. You know him; he's a stubborn old mule and won't accept charity. I'm telling you he won't. His temper too, he'll more likely do something crazy."

"I know. Let's just see how this goes. My brother-in-law will know how to handle it. There are ways, don't worry. So, Mike, listen to me. Tom is not going to be thrown off of that property, not as long as I'm breathing. I promise you that."

"There's something else," Mike said. "Can we keep this between us for now? I don't think Glenna needs all this stress. Maybe we could figure out a plan before we drop this storm in her backyard."

"I don't know about that." Wanda frowned. "I got a bad feeling about keeping Glenna in the dark, but for a day or two, let's see what happens. I'll work the legal angle; you go to Tom and find that permission Seldon Tompkins signed. Can you do that?"

"You betcha'."

The day began to slow to normal rhythm, and Mike felt oddly comfortable. Wanda gave him confidence in navigating this sophisticated world so unfamiliar to him, the world of lawyers and businessmen, of decisions determining other people's futures. The fragmentation he'd known since his wife died had slowly begun to aggregate itself through Wanda's new influence. Now the idealism of earlier times began restoring, enriching the emotional dormancy that for years had lain idle beneath the glacier of practicality upon which Mike lived.

Something important had entered his life, a force bigger than fixing cars or killing time on the river. Here was a woman who knew how to assemble lives, to construct relationships through the resolution of difficulties, and he could feel himself lured by her strength. He studied carefully that trickling idea, the loving way she had as a woman, that instinct to connect subtly beneath the bravado she used to disarm people. And he relaxed into the idea of her as ally even as the quiet closeness with Wanda left him spinning in circles of delight.

"It's almost dark, so I know you can't get back to Tom on the river today. How about you join me for a glass of wine on the porch. I've got a nice new planter filled with colorful pansies we can admire, and then you can talk about the note you forgot to write me."

VII.

Rising early, Tom was in New Orleans by nine for his follow-up doctor appointment, and the results were much what he'd anticipated. Stopping by the library on the way home, he completed the writing project he'd worked so hard on, then took care of his mailing errands, including the special package he made sure would be delivered promptly, as well as the important letter to Glenna. Afterward, he didn't feel like working any longer, so he took his time this special day visiting some of the old sites in town, places he hadn't seen since Oui died.

The bright sun felt so inviting that Tom decided to reminisce a little, so off to the old church and the duck pond he ventured and even to the giant old beech tree they used to climb as kids going up a spiral staircase of limbs, but today Tom was firmly grounded and in no mood to climb trees.

On his way back to the river, he passed Sheriff Barker's squad car over at the Po'boy Pirogue restaurant. He thought about going in and flattening Barker with his hickory club but at the last minute decided it wasn't worth a night in jail. Tom had a better plan, and it was already in irreversible motion as of today. So on down the road home he bounced and slipped as his dreamy thoughts wafted over the trees and fields like rising mist searching out a new day.

Pulling into the yard, he saw fresh tire tracks and knew Mike had visited this morning. Hadn't been gone too long either. A little note stuck to the cabin door fluttered in the breeze, announcing Mike would be back tomorrow afternoon after his dentist appointment. "Don't leave until I talk to you tomorrow and find Seldon's agreement giving you permission to stay at the cabin; we have a plan." Tom smiled. Mike was always the one to help, the person he could count on to be by his side no matter what the situation. He was sorry he'd missed Mike today especially and thought hard to remember the plan Mike mentioned but couldn't.

This year Tom didn't seem able to rise to the occasion of spring the way he always had. He loved nothing more than gathering little seedlings from the riverbank and then bringing them back to the cabin or planting the hundreds of seeds he meticulously gathered each fall. From his garden and all up and down the river, Tom selected each type of seed, storing them in a dry, cold place in the eve of the smokehouse so they'd be ready to sprout in the lengthening daylight of spring. These days, thinking about tasks often served the same purpose as physically doing them, and Tom spent more and more hours drifting through the woods listening for sounds he thought he heard in his head but couldn't quite identify. Often now, random images floated by, and distant voices from the past scrambled themselves into an indiscernible chatter that never seemed to turn off inside his mind, a static that drained energy from his practical thoughts, leaving simple tasks half-finished or forgotten. The separateness of things muddled together these days as wobbling vibrations and then just as quickly back to separate disconnected islands, each of which spoke to Tom accusingly as if he were still separate and detached from the flow of his own life where he'd failed to grasp some essential responsibility of living.

The contrast baffled him as he stumbled and talked to himself, asking who he was speaking to and then remembering the dream where he'd heard the answer. Drifting toward that echoing voice each day now, Tom thought he heard clues in the wind, in the river song, and he patiently looked, waited. These days increasingly overwhelmed Tom as he slipped further from his normal reality into a deepening befuddlement where the clear outlines of his world blurred into hazy ideas of things rather than the concreteness of the existence he'd always known. Tom drifted now in a current he increasingly could not compensate for as the volume of unfamiliarity deepened estranging him from the shores of his own consciousness. That pulling sensation felt so familiar, so real, and yet he couldn't quite recall where that deep memory had started. Perhaps it was just an idea instead. He let that drawing feeling tug at his legs now as he walked the curving bank, stepping through the river's invisible fingers.

Rest helped restore his strength temporarily after such a long day of travel and thought, and the following morning, with the sun feeling good against the still chilly but not so brisk wind, Tom walked over to the nearby horse stable. His neighbor had brought the animals back for the spring to enjoy the new grass he'd seeded, and though no one was around, old Bucky waited, nibbling away at the young shoots. He couldn't help but smile at his old friend, slightly thinner from the winter but fit enough and still spry as ever, though the years too now left a gray tinge to his boot-brown coat. After treating the horse to fresh carrots and kindly pats on the neck to remind him of their acquaintance, Tom mounted up, deciding to take Bucky out for a little exercise, to clear both their minds from the clutter of spring.

Down the road they went and out across the field of grass so beautiful in the morning sunlight, over to the old pond to see if any ducks still hung about after winter, then back toward the cabin the old duo loped along, enjoying the wind in the warmer morning light, Bucky happy to be out for a run and Tom lost in his foggy bewilderment, now relieved briefly by the distraction of the ride and the power of the creature underneath him.

As the wind blurred Tom's vision, galloping hooves drowned out all other sound as Bucky eased off onto a side trail. Tom felt himself light in the moment, weightless in a dreamlike instant of complete rapture, lost in the freedom of immediacy. The sound and feeling conjured in his mind a distant image, the ancient artesian well at his childhood home still flowing endlessly and watering his boyhood garden. Beneath him, the horse's strength rippled under the lightly held reins, blending with the earth's oozing life vibrating around him. Tom now young again in the moment, racing through the sunlight chasing dragonflies, it felt almost as if he were flying, soaring above his own being. Sounds from far away hummed in his crowded mind, memories flashing into the present as if time had reversed, and Tom seemed to evaporate into the chill of the wind as one more invisible light beam rippling through the sky.

There too in his mind sat Saralynn on their old back porch reading from a book, speaking with slow deliberation as if declaring the truth of the world to young Tom covered in garden dirt, filled with pride. These distant sounds now marched forward into new memory, Saralynn's voice melodic with Walt Whitman's free verse even as the image of the artesian well in their yard spilled its cold liquid onto his newly planted garden those many decades ago. Clear as a church hymn, his mother's voice spoke the lovely words, and Tom couldn't help joining her recitation with his own voice as in his mind he whistled down the trodden lane of the past. Bucky and the blue sky seemed to listen with delight as the poem spilled from Tom's lips:

I have heard what the talkers were talking, the talk of the
Beginning and the end,
But I do not talk of the beginning or the end.
There was never any more inception than there is now,
Nor any more youth or age than there is now,
And will never be any more perfection than there is now,
Nor any more heaven or hell than there is now.
Urge and urge and urge,
Always the procreant urge of the world.

As the final words fell from Tom's lips, a cloud darkened the sun, and Bucky broke pace back into a canter as Tom seemed to relax from his hunched sprint. The halo of euphoria evaporated now as he realized he had ridden much farther than intended and he wouldn't be able to hear his mother's call for supper, so the pair slowed to a trot, then an easy walk to allow his old friend a rest on the trail.

Stopping by a small creek, Bucky drank from the cool stream, and Tom thought of the poem he'd remembered, the day his mother first shared those words and how proud she'd been of his first garden, how the spirit of nature lived in that youthful labor in the soil and how Saralynn had recognized the artist in Tom as no one else ever had, the sensitive essence she'd always seen in her son. It all seemed so close now, the memory, her words and the gentle touch she gave him as she handed him the first volume of poetry he'd ever owned, *Song of Myself,* and now the memory of how they'd learned these lines together, day after day prompting each other while hauling buckets of water from the well to the garden or chopping at the hungry grass, all the while mumbling their memorization of Whitman's rhythmical verse. Tom felt timeless, invincible, as if the storybook of life would never end, and he wanted to go home to Ouida and his mom and have that Christmas turkey he'd shot just for them and a big pot of those fresh beans he'd grown—yes, those beans that were so crisp and ready.

The minutes muddied, and without notice, a half hour later Tom found himself back at the cabin. Dismounting with deliberation, he fed Bucky a bowl of oats along with some fresh water and then wondered how he got home so quickly. He also began tying away at the thing he had pictured in his head for some time now. Soon the rope assumed the familiar shape he wanted, and with not an instant of reflection, Tom was back on the horse. Bucky fretted, unsure what to do.

All around the birds twitted, and songs floated down the river on the breeze. Every single creature sounded fully informed of the seasonal change and of new responsibilities to adjust to the routine of lengthening days and warming temperatures. Each understood the singularity of the moment and how things intertwine in spillage from the past to the future, always connected, always studying the pull toward the reprisal of life's spring ballet.

This oneness engulfed Tom, comforting his body and mind. He thought again of the strange dream he'd had of the spirits speaking to him, and their presence lingered as the muffled river sounds chanted underneath the hum of the wind. He couldn't quite grasp the dazzling light or sound sensations all blended as chorus now, inviting him somewhere it seemed. And the odd idea flashed that he'd love to swing on Mike's swing just one more time to see if he could get high enough to see over the treetops down to the other side. Torn between acquiescence to pause and a submission to the mysterious urge to push forward, Tom found himself halved by his own existence, sliced again into portions of halting action, caught in the dilemma of duty and abandon.

Perched in this detached rift, Tom sensed an unknown presence comforting him, assuaging the incompleteness that seemed so large suddenly. Inchoate images of lost decades tumbled randomly through his head, as did the leaves blowing overhead in the morning wind, all mirroring for Tom his inability to touch reality anymore, to escape the exile of his mind. And his misfiring brain sputtered with directionless violence, pausing one last time before the threshold of oblivion.

With a long, confused gaze about the yard, the dulling lens of his mind faltered under the crouching chinaberry as Bucky fidgeted, uneasy with his task. Lingering smells from the smokehouse trailed on the breeze, reminding Tom of his damaged mural while the prate of the whispering river seduced him to follow her home. At peace, the paradoxes of life resolved as unimportant, he surveyed once more his garden, that tiny world, and Tom's heart smiled wide as the gulf of childhood.

Contented as he could be in this earthly life, Tom gave a sudden swift heel to Bucky's haunches, and the horse bolted as if a canon firing into the daylight, and with a giant bow in the old limb above, Tom hung instantly dead, dangling from his friend's swing rope beneath the weary chinaberry. The last firings of electricity in Tom's brain brought forward Oui's face the day they got married, luscious as fresh cream, resplendent in her white veil and mother's jewels struggling hopelessly to match the crisp cerulean blue of her loving eyes.

And the world returned to distraction, Bucky slowing finally to munch on a nice patch of freshly sprouted wheat Tom had spread for the rabbits, and a mockingbird sprung to life with a riotous chorus of arrived spring.

Chapter 14

I.

Mike awakened with the oddest sense, disconsolate for some reason even though the weather peeked into his bedroom with bright rays of sunlight and a cool, windy feel to the air. He thought he might be getting sick, as pollen often clogged his head in spring, but his eyes weren't red, and he had no sniffles. Things seemed out of joint this day. He burned his toast, accidentally knocked the coffeepot off the counter and broke it, with a huge mess left as reward, and then the phone rang. Another dentist appointment reminder, the fourth since Christmas, and though this should be the last one, Mike fibbed, saying he had a cold and couldn't make it. The day simply was not right for responsibility.

After a few disheartened efforts to clean the house, he decided on a break from the routine, so he had the idea to buy some smoked salmon and bagels and let Tom tell him how crazy he was for wasting his money on something so silly as overpriced bread and stinky foreign fish. He smiled as he thought of his cantankerous friend always ready to opine about things pecuniary with his continuous plea for simplicity, but the repartee had become entertainment long ago, and Mike needed a little cheering up today. The strategy concocted with Wanda and the permission document for the cabin all seemed distant reminders of the practicality Mike struggled to invite into his discomforting morning.

In Wal-Mart, he splurged and bought a bag of hazelnut coffee because he knew how flavored coffee most irritated his friend, but Mike liked the nutty taste and considered Tom's repining similar to the negativity of the news, something to hear but nothing to listen to seriously. Two other stops to pay bills and pick up a rebuilt starter, and Mike finally headed off to the river expecting to catch Tom after lunch.

All down the old rutted Catchahoula road, Mike thought of the upcoming trip to Hattiesburg and how today they would actually pick a date to go up for a visit, maybe Easter since it was imminent. Mike was sure Wanda would look splendid in a new Easter outfit, and he always liked a bite of chocolate, which surely would be close at hand with little Lucy around. So a plan formed as he wondered would Wanda hate an onion bagel? But at least he knew Tom would; he hated all bagels, so that would suffice.

The humble little cabin looked sleepy, no smoke from the chimney and only silence around, but maybe Tom was off still checking traps and hadn't made lunch yet since he was expecting Mike in the afternoon. Surely the scene was a stroke of good luck though the clanking of the truck made the only sounds of life about the yard. Tom would be preoccupied and probably irritated at being interrupted by friends with big-city coffee and smelly, store-bought fish, but feeling a little low today, Mike needed some familiar banter with his old friend to reset his dreary mood. Besides, now he could tell Tom about Wanda's brother-in-law and the breach of contract idea that could prove useful.

Pulling up on the right side of the yard, Mike noticed immediately the Chevy parked there as well, but clearly the place was deserted, front door closed tight, no coffee cups or water glasses sitting on the porch. He blew the truck horn three times in succession, hoping Tom would be close enough to hear the sound, but even after repeating it two more times, no response came, so Mike decided to kill a little time looking around, expecting Tom to come walking out of the woods at any moment.

Rounding the right side of the house, something felt wrong, cold, a strangeness hovering over the yard even in the warming light. The panoply of trees along the border of the woods all shimmered in the chilly wind, sending a rustling noise that matched their vibration. Mike froze, looking around carefully, the hair on the back of his neck now standing up with a shiver down his spine.

"Tom, Tom, you 'round here?" Strangely afraid, he inched forward as if hunting. Only the new leaves on the trees danced their odd ritual, and then his eye caught a different shape moving down by the river, something behind the brush line sprouting of pale green. Instantly Mike knew it was Tom, but he couldn't help remembering the movie he'd seen once of an alien spaceship landing in remote Kansas where the old farmer and his wife were turned into the walking dead, so he cracked a slight grin and kept walking.

"So there you are, you old goat. Why didn't you answer when I blew?" And just as the question fell from his lips, Mike tripped on a hoe left lying in the grass and had to catch himself before he fell in the mud.

Down by the river, Bucky finished his nice fresh drink and, now ready to play again, began walking back up the hill through the bushes. It was Bucky that Mike had mistaken for Tom.

Distracted by his misstep and wiping the dirt from his hands, Mike jumped to his feet, still talking loudly as if Tom could hear him down at the river.

"Damn, Tom, don't you ever pick up anything?" He looked up, but the shape he'd seen moving had disappeared. Again, the chill tickled Mike's neck, electrifying the hairs to attention. Stopping short, through the three young catalpa trees he saw the top of the chinaberry crouching its top branches lower than normal, unnaturally haggard-looking, Mike noted, as the tree looked frail, probably missing its handsome swing, he thought.

"Tom, where the heck are you?"

Hearing the call, Bucky pushed through the bushes, giving a little jump from the shadows into the sunlight. Mike sighed with relief.

"Hey there, boy. Where's the old man?" Comfortable again, Mike strolled toward the horse as a gust of wind sliced a small opening between the young catalpas. A glimpse only, but a flash of the draping horror, then only green. The air in his lungs froze. Time stopped, allowing Mike to catch up to the recalculating image he struggled to believe. Then, after what seemed an eternity, he was running as fast as he could.

Tearing through the young catalpas, he saw Bucky nudging the slumped form hanging from the chinaberry, its dull weight gently answering the horse's insistent push with a jerky meandering swing in and out of the shadows, a broken pendulum twisting in the wind.

His own scream startled Mike. "No, Tom, no!" as he grabbed the limp shell, lifting it as high as he could. The noose hung out of reach, so Mike eased the weight back onto the rope, then broke for the cabin. "The ladder. Where's the ladder? No, the truck." With a skip in time, the Ford plowed through the yard until gently allowing the body to sidle up to the hood, then onto the windshield until finally it lay completely across Mike's view, the shoulders blocking the sunlight. With another jump in time, Mike stood on the hood with his skinning knife, slicing the rope.

Sawing the thick twining with this favorite knife he always wore affixed to his belt, the gift Tom had given him two decades earlier, the blade seemed to tell the story of how it had always known this duty would come. But Mike frantically sawed until the heaviness collapsed into his lap, a burdensome blanket smothering him.

Off the truck hood onto the ground they both slid, only a lifeless plastic feel left in Tom's cool body, as Mike knew gravity had finished her work. The crushing weight of an accumulated lifetime crumpled in his arms, and as he slouched to the dirt, he was buried by this lifeless thing he no longer knew, and with a bolt of understanding, Mike realized his friendship with Tom was no more.

An urgent fear emerged. Had some evil done this to Tom? Was there a murderer hiding and watching? Eyes twitching, head jerking in sectional views of the yard, Mike studied the surreal moment, looking for what he could not imagine and experiencing what he could not comprehend. Then, as if wounded by the acceptance of truth, Mike saw the world without Tom's living presence, no strong close friend, no paragon of loyalty and straight talk, no vulnerable old pal battling encroaching old age. Too numb to realize his actions, Mike stretched Tom's semirigid form out on the ground, praying it might help, and then laid his ear to Tom's silent chest. Endlessly rocking in the peering sunlight, the old friend groaned with hollow despair as Bucky insistently nudged his new friend to pick up the ride Tom had failed to finish.

Above, the shivering young leaves froze, and the march of spring paused before its fallen soldier. Beneath Mike, the cold ground thirsted for the warm beads of sweat forming on his brow even as truth floated across the nothingness of his soul. And ever so gently, Mike now heard the rattle of young leaves discussing the grinding turn of time as out by tree line, soft gurgles of the river murmured a language of release, a fresh voice awakened into its current, and a vast emptiness reached within Mike for the thing it too might release. Disbelief and unripe grief, those opportunistic bystanders of untimely death, sprang to the song of the mockingbird preaching of the new spring twirling among the river eddies and dancing the music of never-ending change. To the silence of grief, Mike rocked his old friend in disbelief.

II.

Glenna took the news very hard, so badly in fact that she broke down completely and had to be hospitalized for what the doctor described as "severe exhaustion." From the moment Mike and Wanda came to see her, Glenna knew something was wrong. Mike had the look of death on him, a pusillanimous weakness that hardly allowed him to speak, dribbling instead only incoherent mumbles and apologies.

Wanda spoke softly to Glenna. "Love, listen to me now. I have some bad news. It's about your dad. Something has happened, Glenna, and God has taken Tom home to rest."

Caught in a wandering babble, Mike yielded to an ineptness he had rarely known in life until Wanda preempted his incoherent gibberish, telling Glenna the story with the frankness for which she was known. She couched her friend in the soft, supple arms of female pathos, heartfelt, strong at a time when strength is so fleeting then let Glenna cry as she rocked her childlike, gentle strokes of her hair hearkening a mother's tenderness. Wails of anger and remorse, fits of despair interleaved like movements of orchestral music unfolding a dirge of unfettered agony. Mike too wept a sobbing he'd never known as both he and Glenna clung to Wanda's strong arms as she tried to help them find the bottom to their free fall of shock.

Harold kissed Glenna as he held his own wound, then left for Picayune to take care of the burial arrangements. The coroner had pronounced the death a suicide, and Harold asked that there be no autopsy, only a quick burial. Lee and the girls had withdrawn into utter isolation with their mother, but there was no consolation for Glenna, no solace for her journey into the depths of innermost pain. Crawling deeply into her grief, closed off from all external influence, she secluded inside a solipsistic shell impenetrable from the outside. For now, Glenna was gone.

Victoria never left her mother's side, holding her, sitting with her, stroking her face gently even as her own heart heaved the pain of loss, the regret of young life now forced to find its own root of courage. Sedated, Glenna languished, barely regaining consciousness, then again drifting away into that untouchable place away from the pain of life. Not once did her children leave her side as now Lee and even little Lucy sat with her around the clock, hoping against hope their mom would open her eyes and see what she had not lost.

On the second night in the hospital, Vic stood looking out the window at the sun settling over an aerated lake next door. The breeze blew gently as she watched a willow tree dance in the pleasant air with its long, thin branches trailing in the moving water. She recalled her mother's timid speech when she turned thirteen, that day she entered the difficult teenage years. Glenna had told a story of her grandmother Saralynn as a young girl one Saturday asking to go fishing with her dad and a neighbor, but when they got to the river, the men put out in the small boat while Saralynn was left alone to watch the horse and wagon. The story went that adventures followed. A large dead oak limb fell twenty feet from the girl, terrifying her and the horse. Then, while she investigated the river's shoreline, she almost stepped on a water moccasin sunning in the May air. But the part Vic remembered most clearly now was how Saralynn sat so patiently at the river's edge watching the leaves of the willow tree thrill in the passing current, float and fall on the undulating wind. Glenna had described it as dancing with the current teasing the tree to come deeper into the river. And these years later, Glenna's words lingered as a poetic image of grace among the intricate complexities of life Vic had now begun to glimpse.

Now she realized her mother had told her the story not as mere entertainment but as a veiled attempt to summon the girl's fortitude and at caution about the temptations of sexuality, probably exactly the same as Oui had done for Glenna. But today Vic cared less about temptation than about strength, and she prayed her mother could find her own depth of will to resist the darkness the same way Saralynn had done that lonely day she discovered her youthful courage. Vic saw clearly now the willow's thin limbs orchestrating its life in the wind, and the idea that this tree was her mother became so powerful that Vic began to walk about the room with animation. Her mother's deep well of strength had always flowed artesian-like for the family as Glenna with her steadfast way nurtured each of them to happiness and wellness, and Vic so wanted to tell her mom the story of the willow tree, to remind her mother what a monument of guidance she'd always been.

Returning to her mother's side, she kissed Glenna's forehead, whispering, "It's okay, Mom. I'm here with you. I'm right here."

III.

"Hey, Sheriff, did you hear they're gonna plant Tom Bradburn in the ground tomorrow? Betcha' nobody even shows up for the funeral." Deputy Adams had known Tom but was several years his junior, the same as Barker. The Sheriff's older brother, Ted, had tried to court Oui in high school before she rebuffed him. Then he joined the marines where he was killed in a training accident. Barker's hatred of Oui and Tom had not abated over the years. The deputy knew enough to subscribe to the sheriff's bias, as a promotion was under consideration, and timing wasn't good to irritate the county's top law officer.

"Well, the guy was a complete loser," Sheriff Barker said, "so I don't know why anybody would waste their time. He always struck me as touched in the head, just like that crazy mother of his. But at least now we don't have to go evict his sorry ass."

"Hey, by the way, happy birthday, Sheriff! What's this one—about ninety, I'd say?" and Roy Adams got a big laugh at his cleverness.

"Nope, sixty-four and as virile as the day I left for the Marine Corps," the sheriff bragged.

"Look, I forgot," the deputy said, "but this box was delivered urgent for you. Don't say who it's from, but it smells like perfume or something. Probably some babe wishing you a happy, happy birthday. There's a little card taped on top."

Barker snatched the card and read the brief note: "Been thinking about you. Hope you'll think of me."

Sheriff Barker became genuinely interested now as the idea of a secret admirer tickled his giant ego, reminding him how women drooled at his power. He wondered what kind of temptation might be inside.

"Look at this, Roy. Bet there's something yummy in here, so let's open her up. You throw on a fresh pot, and I'll get the scissors. Can't disappoint one of my fans now, can I."

The sheriff cut through the considerable packing tape that seemed to encrust every corner of the box, but it was a slow day, and he didn't have much to do anyway. The thought of a sexy young thing drooling over him flattered the sheriff, and he couldn't wait for the surprise he was sure he deserved.

The box sat on the sheriff's desk, and as the last corner was sliced open, he pulled back the wax paper covering the contents.

His sweet tooth aching with anticipation, Barker leaned over to see if he could catch a whiff of chocolate cake or candy, and without warning, a white blur flashed from the box. Stunned, gulping for breath, Barker froze in the longest second of his life just as an angry cottonmouth moccasin sunk both fangs deeply into the sheriff's left face cheek. He stood immediately staggering with the three-foot-long snake holding on by its fangs. Barker spun around in a circle screaming like a demon in some perverted voodoo ritual, afraid to touch the creature. Finally, two deputies ran into his office to see what the commotion was about, both halting at the door as Charlie pirouetted.

The snake dropped to the floor, and as it tried to escape, Deputy Adams impulsively pulled his pistol and fired. The bullet wounded the snake but then bounced off the filing cabinet, rebounding right into the right butt cheek of the sheriff. Such a howling ululation of curses has never been heard since in Pearl River County as Barker fell forward to his desk where he saw the snake writhing in a screw-like spin as its head was half-gone.

Finally, with the help of a plastic garbage can, the snake was contained. Barker lay apoplectic across his desk as underlings scrambled.

Three minutes later, an ambulance screamed into the parking lot, scurrying Barker away to the hospital, but as the EMTs loaded him on the stretcher, the secretary, Nancy, found a separate card that had fallen from the inside lid of the snake box. Walking alongside the gurney removing the sheriff, Nancy, while doing her best not to faint with excitement, read Barker the brief message:

Happy birthday, Chuckie.
Something personal for you, special from me.

Tom Bradburn

IV.

Avoiding public scrutiny, the family kept the burial plans quiet, but on Friday in Picayune, Tom would find his place next to Oui in a lovely spot outside of town under the sprawling arms of an ancient live oak. Few people attended. Tom had long since ignored almost everyone except his family and Mike, and the scourge of suicide tainted the small goodwill he had managed not to erase through years of social neglect.

The children's vigil continued unbroken until Harold and Lee made the trip south to lay Tom to rest. Amazingly, Nurse Smart sent flowers on behalf of Don Newland, indicating his health would not permit him to attend. Tom would have jumped out of his coffin if Don had shown up, and Lee remained silent as to how Nurse Smart had heard the news. Slumping under the load, Mike, Harold, and four pool hall friends served as pallbearers, a morose crew of reluctant helpers all trudging through heavy thoughts. Glenna remained fully sedated and didn't even know what day it was, her daughters at her bedside.

With an easy grace, Wanda's thoughtful eulogy recounted successes in Tom's life, his marriage, college education, child, but when speaking about his character, her sincerity seemed deepest:

"Tom Bradburn lived the life of a man untainted by situational morality. To him, loyalty was never calculated for effect but reached out as a personal gravity influencing those around him. Tom was a man of integrity and true character in a world of fleeting genuineness. In the brief time I knew Tom, I came to see him as a poet who struggled to find the right words but also as a sensitive man and unwavering paternal force. Gentle and strong, his days were loving and long. We will miss the large shade his presence provided us all from the overbearing heat of our lives."

In her moment of conclusion, even Wanda felt fractured as she tried to ignore the nagging reality that Tom had abandoned his family, so selfishly some thought, and she felt a weakness within, a horrible ingestion of some sickly venom she needed to expel. The moment drew interminably long before a thought touched her heart, something kind. Then, as if given a gift, she recognized that her words had referred to Tom's life rather than so much his death. Was the reprieve her mind's trick to deny the harsh truth? Wanda did not want to know. The paradox suited the complexity of the man she thought unassailable, loyal even to a dead wife he carried in his every thought. Her eyes lifted to see the stares boring into her, and though she felt the full hypocrite, she turned and blew a kiss to Tom's coffin.

The words lilted easily for Wanda but left a seeping trepidation in her own quiet struggle against loneliness, the sticky pull of desperation ever drawing at her soul. Faces spoke to her around the room, wordless agreement of entrapment and smothering guilt, but Wanda drew comfort from her shared understanding with Tom that the reality of life is that it is fervently temporary.

The cold, steel chair warmed as she thought of permanence, noticing not being able to remember the past few minutes of her eulogy. The sensation absorbed Wanda as if she had been away on a journey, an internal quest, and that somehow Tom had counseled her through, releasing her to feel her own conflict of truth. Time disjointed now, the moment felt irrelevant, not somber. An odd smile drew across Wanda's face, incongruous yet genuine, undetected under her draping veil. Then, silently, firmly, invisible hands stroked that cold place deep within the ache she could not soothe alone. And she knew that touch lay upon Glenna too in this very moment and that both hearts now might be warmed again.

The Reverend Garland next introduced Lee, who had asked to say a few words. Gangly, his long legs seemed to walk with abnormal slowness to the podium, his pivot to face the crowd awkward and cloaked in red-cheeked whiteness.

"My grandpa was the strongest man I ever met." Then tears took his breath, and he had to pause, a vibrating spasm welling in his stomach.

"Grandpa knew what most of us don't; he knew nothing matters but the quiet stuff. He didn't care about material things, but he knew how people stay linked to one another."

Then Lee broke down and had to take his seat, everyone's eyes now burning at the brevity with which he'd spoken, the Tom-like quality of his words, the aloof demeanor of the family legacy struggling to harness words inadequate for understanding.

As the crush of grief subsided, Lee felt embarrassed and wanted to hide behind a door in his mind that no one could enter. Then, a distant sound, the voice of Mike Hamlin from the front of the room, released Lee back to the moment. There his grandpa's proud old friend standing in front of the casket, his soul leaking vitality without regret.

Cheap twenty-year-old suit, clip-on brown tie, and a white shirt that looked like he'd bought it the day he left the army, Mike grasped the small podium as if his only support. But grueling as it was, he stood before the small group, looked at the family, made note of his hope that Glenna would be okay, and then delivered what were probably the most soul-searching words he'd ever spoken. Mike with sincerity brought fresh oxygen to the room with an anecdote about how he and Tom used to get in so much trouble in school that one time their teacher encouraged them to join the foreign legion. But after a little chuckle from people remembering the cantankerous Tom, Mike paused as he stared at the top of the doorway in the rear of the room, seeming almost to listen for a distant voice.

"I've known exactly two people in my life that knew the secret of things," Mike said, pausing to grip the podium a little tighter. "They understood from the first time they met that heaven is a place we can find on this earth if we know where to look. It's the place we don't have to die to go to, but to find it, we must learn how to love. There it is. Tom and Oui knew that place. They were angels sent to my life so I could learn how it will be when Jesus takes me home."

No one expected such delicacy from Mike, or spirituality. With tears dropping, Mike looked at the few people seated in the stillness, then turned to the flower-covered casket: "See you down the river, Tom. You and Oui wait for me, okay?"

V.

The ceremony ended in a whimper, disbelief filling the vacuum of emotional exhaustion. Awkwardly, the small crowd wandered off, uncomfortable with staying to talk, disturbed by leaving. Wanda and Mike stared at the casket, sharing their emptiness even as Lee began to hear birds chirping and feel the sun warming his shoulders. Under the giant oak, a seeming permanence gaped from the hole in the ground, and then a light hand touched Lee's shoulder. His dad too found no words and only squeezed his son's neck firmly, without a sound, then turned for the car to go be with his wife. Lee watched his dad's shuffle as he walked away, thinking how erratic life is when the things we think can never happen suddenly fall across our path.

In his suit pocket were the handwritten instructions Mike had found in Tom's cabin giving Lee the responsibility to decide the distribution of his belongings, all except his boat and motor, which were to go to Mike along with everything at the smokehouse. His books were also to be Victoria's. Sketchy words at the bottom of the note seemed only to add more confusion:

"You'll understand soon. Please forgive me now. Tom"

The evening ended in perfunctory detail, brave attempts to act normal, and the following morning, Mike, Lee, and Wanda visited the cabin. While bouncing down the broken road nearly getting stuck twice,

Lee remembered last fall when he'd come to visit, how his grandpa seemed so alive and vital and open to sharing secrets about the family. How could that have changed so suddenly? Lee wondered if his pressure regarding Newland had caused some break in his grandfather, had he pushed too hard about things he didn't truly understand. Before him lay a chasm Lee instinctively knew he must avoid, a pit from which he might not be able to climb, so he pushed his thoughts away from the brink by thinking of the task ahead, the sorting of his grandfather's belongings.

The little homestead waited peacefully. Lee tried not to look at the chinaberry tree or the garden or the smokehouse or the fruit trees or even the river, as each image contained sharp barbs. Instead he stomped around in sulky anger, sorting things as if preparing for a garage sale. Brooding confusion tinted a perfunctory handling of objects he could no longer see as relevant—mere junk, he thought. And the three of them slipped into a work ritual that avoided thought.

The meagerness of Tom's world lay sprawled in the back of the two pickups, strange mounds of the stuff no one wanted: rudimentary furniture, animal hides, worn-out tools, while to the side of the cabin a lovely garden flourished, claiming nothing had changed. Mike and Lee tried not to look at each other, to think the same thoughts, as the gulf of loneliness continued to swell with waves of guilt.

The afternoon waned in segregated business, but before leaving for town, the three gathered on the porch, finally feeling the pleasant spring breeze wafting the smell of honeysuckle up from the river. The men idled in private images of Tom speaking quietly, cooking breakfast, or dragging them into the Devil's Throat. It simply wasn't possible to be on this porch and hear this river without Tom there with them. The breeze so sweet with the spring smell, the river so happy about the journey, they sensed momentary peace with Tom outside the gravity of time.

Wanda broke the silence. "Listen, guys, before we leave, I want to say something to you both that needs to be spoken here on this porch with Tom's spirit all around us." And both Lee and Mike felt tears well in their eyes and a gasp suck air from their lungs.

"Tom didn't let many people into his world. He didn't need to. His world was about this cabin, about nature and his family, and I sense that completeness in this beautiful spot. He loved this place, and really no one but you two knew him in his world, how he behaved here, what he looked like as he sat on this porch or walked in these woods. You see, you have something in your mind's eye right now that is priceless, something only you can see." And Wanda let that thought suspend.

"Look," she continued, "as the years go by, we will all wonder, and we'll be tempted to blame things on someone, maybe even ourselves, but you need to know that is wrong. Tom wouldn't want that. His decision was personal, and that needs to be respected." She felt a little choked, so she stepped off the porch gazing down to the river, then finally spoke again.

"Tom spent the past five years missing Ouida, dredging up every detail of his life with her, and I'm not sure in the end if that worked for him. All those stories of Tom you're carrying around in your head are the same for you, and they can be turned into good memories or into ugliness. You have to make a choice." Then Wanda went silent. Mike and Lee only stared at the ground.

The men remained silent, so Wanda tried again. "Did you see those copies of *Beowulf* and *The Odyssey* in the cabin? Those stories are still in this old world because tribes of people kept them alive as oral history they shared around campfires long before books were invented. Heroes lived on that way and kings, and the storytellers were poets who memorized thousands of lines so they could entertain weary warriors after a day of battle. Those poems were history those bards instilled into the hearts of great fighters. Tom was a man of history; he knew. He had a heart that could sense the pain of life and also the beauty, and I think that he was beginning to learn that expressing his understanding allowed him to cope." Again she paused, this time watching Lee squirm, so she addressed him.

"That school project where you found out so much about Saralynn; that's exactly what I'm talking about. She was kind of a heroic figure for your family, and Tom was her bard keeping her life alive within the family."

Lee only stared back at Wanda as if he'd heard a call from another dimension in time.

"I know you think I'm crazy," Wanda said, "but you two could do that for Tom. You can keep him alive for all of us with your stories." Then Wanda drifted toward the garden.

With Wanda out of range, Lee spoke. "How could he do this, Mike? To Mom?" And he kicked the post Tom had repaired, the nail coming loose, producing a prophetic sag in the roofline.

"I don't know," Mike said. "Can't figure it myself. Your grandpa was the toughest old goat I know, and I can't imagine he gave up like that. Just can't see it." Both stared again at the floor, afraid to look up.

Wanda drifted back within speaking range. "Listen, fellows, this isn't about you or your grief; this was about Tom.

"Now, Lee, don't get upset, but your grandpa was being forced to leave this cabin. The land has been sold, and the sheriff is a jackass with an old grudge. Mike and I just found out. I could have stopped it, but I didn't have enough time. But the point is Tom had his reasons. He just decided he was done."

He had been sitting quietly, but Lee now stood. "Bullshit. Grandpa didn't quit. He was a man, not a weakling. He couldn't give up—no way. He would have fought that jackass sheriff. It don't make sense, I'm telling you. What about the rest of us? Did he give up on us too? Did he think we weren't worth fighting for either?" The question allowed Lee to escape his real thought, the memory of how his grandfather had almost given up on the idea of revenge against Newland before getting bullied into the trip to Yazoo City. Now the barbarians of guilt banged at the gate of Lee's quiet sanctuary as well, and he knew there was a hidden lie inside him he could not release. Mike came to the rescue.

"Son, I knew your grandpa for seven decades, and one thing I can tell you for sure is he didn't give up on things. He was showing us something. That's what he always did. He let his actions speak and let the words catch up later. I don't quite understand it yet, maybe never will, but he was showing us something important. I know that."

"Yeah," Lee said sneering, "showing us he didn't love us anymore."

Now Mike stood. "Don't you go saying things like that; it ain't true. Your grandpa loved you more than anything, and you know that. This here mess is about things we don't understand, maybe about this eviction stuff or just a powerful need to get back to Oui. I don't know, but whatever it added up to in Tom's mind, this was how he saw it ending."

With a guilt miasma settling over the cabin, the three decided to leave while the light was still strong. With each lap around the same dismay, each had found a deepening uneasiness that some essential honesty was missing, and as that unguarded threat slipped insidiously into the privacy of self-talk, all three scampered to avoid thoughts they did not want.

As the sun drifted behind the tree line, the three made their way to the trucks loaded with ignominy. Lee drove Tom's truck back to Hattiesburg, silently pondering the fishing and hunting trips in the old Chevy and the trip up to Newland's house. The idea of stories circled in his head as he considered what Wanda had said, and he felt slightly shifted but not quite sure how.

As the truck whined its familiar complaint to the highway, the idea of memories so poisonous they can kill a person stomped through Lee's thoughts. Could they turn into cancer? Surely violence. And Lee became confused whether his grandpa's suicide had been about anger or acceptance. And so he drove into the darkness of words he wished he'd said and ones he wished he hadn't.

It became comforting to realize his grandpa could live through stories the same way Saralynn did, though the thought weighed with too much permanence for the moment. And yet another impression slipped into mind: these stories could be a family duty intentionally left to him.

As he made the last turn onto his street, the load in back shifted when a basketball suddenly rolled into the street from two boys playing in a driveway, and Lee jammed the brakes. A few things in the back fell over, but nothing seemed to break; however, from underneath the driver's seat next to Lee's right foot, his grandfather's pistol slid out from its hiding place. That same gun Tom asked Lee to play sheriff with as they made their way out of the Devil's Throat and which punched two holes in the Overland Container sign, that gun Lee loved to hold.

Parking in the driveway, Lee sighed and then picked up the pistol. Still loaded. Looking about with a strange sense of guilt as if he'd done something wrong, he quickly wrapped it again in the blue bandana it had slipped from and then pushed it back under the seat. With a flash of disconnected images, Lee oddly thought of Don Newland and how this gun could easily have changed the world for everyone, and he felt overwhelmed by the idea that tiny moments can destroy lives or save them. The idea loomed so large that it dipped over into a new thought, a thought that maybe Wanda was onto something when she talked about saving the stories of Tom's life. And without fanfare and wanting no one else to know, Lee decided to begin keeping a journal of his grandpa's life and their time together, an historical record of hunting trips and anecdotes. He also decided to make note of details such as the gun slipping from underneath the seat and jot down ideas of how those little moments might have gone differently and how they might become a different kind of story, one not true but certainly just as real. Maybe one day these tidbits and adventures could come in handy as perhaps for the first time Lee had the adult thought that one day he would have his own children looking for their own understanding of their great-grandfather, and even of Saralynn. A good made-up story might be as entertaining as a lived truth.

VI.

After Lee left for Hattiesburg, Mike took Wanda back to her car, which was parked at the funeral home. She wanted to make it back home before it got too late.

"That's crazy," Mike said. "It's dark already, and you don't want to drive back to Hattiesburg now. Listen, let's go down to Viola's grill and have a nice baked flounder and chat a while. My sister is at a revival, and I don't really want to be by myself right now. You can stay in the guestroom and head back in the morning."

The little-boy look on Mike's face touched a gentle cord with Wanda, and soon they enjoyed a nice bottle of white wine, an excellent fish, and a tiramisu that Mike believed was sent from heaven.

"I need to ask you something," Wanda said. "Did you come up with that eulogy all by yourself or did some female have a hand in it? Your girlfriend, perhaps?" She snickered.

"No, that Pulitzer Prize pontificating was strictly me." Wanda sat back, a bit astonished on many levels.

"It was beautiful, Mike." Wanda reached across the white tablecloth, placing her hand on top of Mike's rugged paw which fidgeted a tiny bit uncomfortable among all the glassware on the table.

"What was she like, Mike? I mean Oui." He sat back, slightly nonplussed, but Wanda saw his mind turning.

"She was the loveliest woman I ever met. Uh, present company excluded of course." They both laughed quietly. "But seriously, Oui was a person that lit up the whole world, I think, and when she died, God put out most of the candles he had in heaven because he didn't need them anymore."

"Now you see, that's what I'm talking about," said Wanda. "That kind of talk isn't really blue-collar Picayune language, and I'm a little curious where it comes from." Mike acted as if he were insulted.

"What? You think I'm just puttin' on airs to match you being educated and worldly?" He looked a bit shamed as he stared down at the table.

"No. To the contrary, I think that elegance is exactly who you are," Wanda stated firmly. "In fact, you've been pretending to be this roughneck more comfortable with carburetors than conversation, and I think I've found you out, mister. In fact, I found out both you and Tom." She stopped abruptly, but Mike stroked her hand, unfazed.

"You're partially right anyway," Mike said. "Tom, he had an elegant way about him and saw the little details of life having big meaning." Mike sat back as Wanda studied the plaintive look.

"Yeah, that could be." She glanced at her watch. "I had a chat at Glenna's with Tom, and he seemed mesmerized by a concert on television; couldn't get over how moving it was for him. Was he really that sensitive a man?"

"Tom was as hard as a brick, but peculiar. Had these poetry books around and even used to go to museums and such in New Orleans with Oui where he would show her paintings, and he'd talk about how scenes would symbolize different things, and colors too. Oui used to tell me all about it after they'd go."

"So you never went?" Wanda asked.

"Only one time. Went to a tractor museum in Natchez, and I really enjoyed it."

"Sounds poetic." They chuckled again.

"But seriously, that's what I mean by Oui being an angel. She didn't really care for all that stuff, but she knew Tom had a secret place in his soul he kept hidden from everybody else, except maybe his mom. Once Oui figured that out, she'd go to museums and ask Tom to read her poetry and such; made it look like that's what she wanted, so he'd do it for her, but really it only gave him an excuse to treat a part of himself that got neglected for most of his life. See, I think Tom was an artist at heart. He felt things different, like the wind and the colors of leaves as the seasons changed. I'd note things, but he'd be inside of that change listening when all I knew how to do was talk."

"You're too hard on yourself there, Mike; sounds like you're pretty inside of things yourself. I watched how you treated Tom, looked out for him, and guided him without his even knowing it. You're an old softie yourself there, Mr. John Deere." Mike smiled. "But tell me something, Mike. How did Saralynn know about Tom's soft center?"

A puzzled look bounced back to Wanda, but she knew Mike had something to say. "Well," Mike stumbled to find a beginning, "you've gathered how straight-on rough Tom's mom could be, but she was even more peculiar than Tom. She painted birdhouses and things all the time, even wrote poems. Heck, I remember once when we was about twelve or so, I walked down to his house through the woods one day, and as I got close, I heard voices, so I kind of slipped up on the backyard to see what was happening. Tom was hoeing his garden like a pilgrim, and on the back steps set Saralynn readin' out loud from a book of poetry. She went on and on just like it all made sense, and Tom listened. Every once in a while, he'd look up and ask her to repeat a word or a line; it was like he was memorizing it as she spoke. Dangest thing I ever saw."

"I knew he was a poet!" Wanda exclaimed.

"What's that?" Mike asked.

"Did you ever see Tom write any poetry or stories or anything?" Wanda now had radar set firmly on finding some buried treasure, but Mike stalled her theory.

"No, not Tom. He wasn't much for words. Never wrote much of anything that I could tell. But I reckon he listened pretty good to Saralynn; she knew how to spread words around like fine dried horse manure on top of a freshly turned garden."

VII.

The day after the funeral, Harold finally checked the mailbox for the first time in days, and there he found a letter to Glenna with Tom's name at the top. With Glenna still largely incapacitated, he made the decision to read it.

> Dear Glenna and Family (both blood and bond),
>
> A few weeks ago, I was checking lines down on the river, and I suddenly realized I didn't know where I was or which way to go to find the cabin. The experience scared me, and I knew something serious was wrong, something that wasn't likely to go away. Two days later, Sheriff Barker came again threatening trouble, warning me to evacuate the property or I would be arrested and put in jail for trespassing. Imagine, put in jail for living in my own home. These two events so shook me that it became difficult to sort out what normal was anymore or what my place was in this old world.
>
> Now leaving any home is a hard thing because that place grows to be a part of us, much like how our lives connect to family and friends without any planning involved. A real home is a sanctuary, not just a structure; it's a skin that contains our lives and hosts activities that sustain us and is where we find meaning. Leaving any home is a form of shedding an old life for a new one, and though some people easily wrap themselves with newness, for folks like me, it isn't so simple.
>
> At first, I didn't know what to do. I considered fighting, going to war with words and lawyers, even with guns and violence, but I knew resistance could only bring pain to those I love most in this life. I also knew such action was a form of denial, just like hiding in a hospital would be, all full of needles and drugs while my body disappeared. You see, I went to the doctor in New

Orleans a couple of times, and I have an inoperable brain tumor; I knew I was going to wither away. The doctor's report is here in this package. When I thought of my medical options and all this sheriff business, I decided that rather than clinging to the emaciating seconds of a long and happy life, I would leave this world as a strong man, still owning my freedom.

Now listen, I know I'm running off at the mouth here, but I don't want you to be angry with me. Frankly, when my mom died, I felt resentment and a powerful anger because I felt like she gave up. I know you must think the same thing, but, hon, I only wanted to live on my own terms.

Look, I apologize to all of you for the pain I've brought. But please know that exiting this world with dignity rather than desperation stood as a conscious preference; I simply couldn't allow you to see me wither away sickly and weak. I especially couldn't give that jackass Barker the pleasure of throwing me out of my cabin. Besides, let's be honest, you know what a lousy roommate I would have made anyway, so don't try to deny it.

All right, let's call it time to hand over the reins of the family to someone else. I figure you and Harold can take things from here because in the end, we'll all find each other in the same holding place downriver. I'll see you there.

Dad

VIII.

The news of Tom's revenge on Charlie Barker spread like a spring flood, and soon everyone in town was laughing at the arrogant sheriff's humiliation. Down at the local bar, the girls had coined a new dance called the Barker where they would all spin in circles until they fell down on the dance floor. For some reason, everyone just loved spinning around like they were five years old again.

Barker's birthday surprise spawned a wave of not only dances but jokes and conversation that spread instantly over Pearl River County. It seems Tom's present to Barker had launched a new generation of creativity in town, and soon the water tower had graffiti on it proclaiming that "Snake Man Cometh" and "An Eye for an Eye," as sadly the sheriff lost vision in his left eye due to the snake bite. Unexpectedly, everyone in town suddenly loved Tom Bradburn like he was a high school hero all over again, though frankly most of them had never even heard his name. Graffiti popped up on barns, abandoned buildings, and most every unattended flat surface available.

Mike too was inspired by the events, though the city authorities tried to keep the snake episode quiet the first few days. He wished he'd known earlier what Tom had done because it would have made a great story for his eulogy, but Mike only snickered, enjoying Tom's creative revenge. Then he had an idea of his own, something he too wanted to contribute to this season of exuberance spreading across Picayune, but not something aimed at Barker.

Knowing he still had to pick up Tom's boat and a few other things, Mike had an idea he thought Tom would appreciate no matter what the state of Mississippi had in mind. So down the Catchahoula road he bumped and slid one last time.

After pulling into the yard, he went to work methodically taking his wheelbarrow over to Tom's worm bed and with dispatch shoveling the virtual army of squirming, crawling creatures into two large buckets. They did not like being removed from their comfortable home. Into the fenced garden he took load after load and filled three large holes he'd dug about ten feet apart, a nice proximity that made a perfect triangle. Then from the back of his truck, Mike hauled over three dogwoods he'd bought at Wal-Mart that morning, two six-foot white ones and one five-foot pink one, all balled and ready to plant. On top of the worm mounds now set down in the holes, each tree was planted comfortably in the middle of Tom's garden, a new living sculpture of life lending some formality to the now abandoned vegetable patch.

When finished, Mike closed the gate to keep out any creatures that might want to nibble at the new plants and then admired how beautiful the three trees looked sitting among the broccoli and brussels sprouts, neighbors of sorts in the newly launched season, the last living things Tom planted this spring, the things Mike had decided to let go to seed without being picked. He figured his old friend would appreciate the seeding idea.

Next, Mike got his chainsaw from the truck and walked straight to the chinaberry tree. One rope still hung dumbly, the other had been removed. With barely a thought, the chinaberry fell to the ground, and Mike felt the thrill of vengeance seeing the deformed old crone humiliated in the sunlight. He thought to cut the limbs off and roll the trunk down to the river, but it seemed too much trouble. Then remembering Tom had saws and tools behind the smoke shed that he and Lee had forgotten to load up, Mike headed over to have a look.

Coming around the back of the smokehouse, he first noticed the big black smudge on the rear wall, then the white ash board hanging prominently alongside the charcoal-framed mural. Here the two pieces of Tom's art waited as stoic vestiges of a life no longer nimbly weaving itself around the silent poetry of his thoughts, and Mike imagined he was in a private museum.

His first gaze stopped on the swing seat, a river beginning and ending with lakes of some sort, seven bends with houses and sandbars all detailed immaculately with the care Tom gave to things he admired. And Mike knew instinctively the scene to be a snapshot of Tom's life.

Then, to the right of the diorama, he noticed the remnants of the mural, realizing it had been partially destroyed, its simple edges now framed with crude charcoal smudge that covered what used to be additional sections of the mural's landscape. But in the center, there it was, his old red Ford, and sure enough an image of Mike himself leaned up against it along with what looked to be Lee. Even Tom's long-dead dog, Shep, was off to the side. Tears formed, and Mike had to look away to the pear orchard to keep from breaking down. A sense of respect welled as he studied the two works, and he had the dim memory of that little museum in New Orleans Tom had made him go to almost fifty years ago, and that past dimness melded with the shed's showy portrait of a world greatly emptied now by the absence of an old friend. Mike felt again the heaviness of Tom's ending, the slumping body draped across his arms, and now the atmosphere under this simple little haven filled with a thickness of regret.

Soon, the caw of a nosey crow broke the trance. The board down from the wall revealed how the river had been routed out, the wood shavings and pinecone scales fitted into little houses, even the enhanced sand so sparkly in the sunlight. Tom's touch filled every crevice, and Mike looked twice down by the river for the voice he kept hearing grumbling about too much company.

"Well, I'll be damned. You old goat." Holding the board in his lap, Mike thought of when he'd given the swing to Tom, how objections had been his thanks and what a frivolous idea it was. Tom had now returned the gift, made it utilitarian and artistic all in one swoop, so typical of the sensitive brute sworn to the secrecy of a withdrawn life, and through the rustling pear trees the sunlight danced in the sky.

Days as boys together returned, camping on the riverbank thrilling at the brilliant night sky. Mike knew these thoughts must stand in for his friend now just as Wanda said. An idea occurred to give the board to Lee. Would that help the boy? But he didn't think it would, and Mike was sure Tom had left the little gesture for him. Then a simple thought occurred as he looked at the river flowing into the huckleberry lake, an idea of generosity that seemed to make so much sense at this particular moment. So Mike stood and walked straight to the river.

The little skiff hadn't been used for over a week now, and the rains had dislodged it from its protected little spot by the cypress tree, so now it pulled downstream hard against the rope. The boat seemed eager to get back into action, bored with sitting around waiting for some human to sidle up for the duty of running lines.

"So you left this thing for me, did you?" Mike smiled as if speaking to Tom as he looked at the anxious little boat, and he had the flash of a sensation that Tom was listening, studying the discordant moment. The boat tugged at the rope, lapping a little tune to the current, like an animal anxious to move, to go do something, and with deliberate speed, Mike untied the knot, placed his boot on the front of the boat, then pushed the captain-less little friend out into the river flow all by itself.

The skiff seemed confused at first to be set free alone on the river with the motor still cocked up out of the water and the tie-off rope trailing in the dark brown river, with no Tom there to guide its course and set the routine. The skiff seemed to smile at him, Mike thought, emancipated from its toil, alone on the river without a job to do, and he gave a little salute as the river took the offering with acceptance. Mike watched Tom's familiar working partner dip behind the willow trees being tickled by the current, then pause at the base of a large cypress wading in the shallows before catching an upstart breeze that ushered it deeper into the river's movement to follow its own winding passage to the gulf.

Sparkles of light glinted from the river as the boat played hide and seek with the trees along the bank and then Mike gave a quick, "Adios, amigo," then turned back up the hill to the cabin. There the fallen chinaberry rested in the newly allowed sunlight, and Mike admired how much brighter the path to the river seemed now, how much easier it was to see things out of the shadows. The tops of the new dogwoods peeked over the brush, each with a good view of the river through the new clearing, and instinctively the perspective seemed natural. Tom's love of this place hovered all around in the gently whispering leaves and dappled sunlight, the flowers and trees, the wind gliding down the river, these things Tom had known each day as his private world. Strong on the riverbank, the honeysuckle told Mike that Tom was happy the skiff was set free and that the old chinaberry had bequeathed her rule of the place to the new dogwoods, and for a moment Mike almost felt he was chatting again with his wise old friend.

The pink and white dogwood blossoms soaked up the river breeze, reminding him of the two trees Saralynn had him plant at the little rental house decades ago. The tradition now continuing, he was sure Tom and Saralynn were watching and very much approved of the new additions. But with that thought, Mike had yet another fresh inspiration, so off to the truck he walked with a quick step and a churning mind.

He found his little notebook and pen in the glove compartment and then scribbled out what he'd mulled over while down by the river, quickly stuffing the handwritten words into an old tobacco tin that had rattled around the glove box for a decade. Then off to the garden. Mike couldn't help wondering if this little can had been waiting all these years for this special role it must play, but wisely the can had known to be patient. Wedging the little red box into the largest fork of the bigger white dogwood, he stepped back to admire his work, and Mike noticed what a good sprucing up he'd given Tom's place, a homey touch, he thought, where things got removed and things left for good. Surely Tom was pleased.

Moments later, saws and a few odds and ends loaded into the truck, Mike strung a last long gaze across the yard and cabin before remembering one final task. With the knife on his belt, he quickly cut the remaining rope from the felled chinaberry, and as he coiled it, he gave the tree one last comment. "You won't be needing this one, so I'm taking back my rope." Then, without emotion, Mike found himself bouncing down the river road, bogged down in thought about the four-foot section of smokehouse wall he had riding with him in the back. His work had been good, like he'd honored that soft center of himself that Tom had understood but never discussed—but maybe only painted on a smokehouse wall. Yes, today the two old friends shared something new down by the river, not just coffee and fun jabbing at one another but a protected repose of expression each had carried silently for a lifetime. Glancing at the diorama sitting on the seat next to him, Tom's last creative gift, Mike thought again of his own simple words left for Tom in their new dogwood home, and again he allowed the words to dribble from his own mouth, though suddenly his voice sounded like a stranger's, some unfamiliar person Mike didn't recognize as himself. The discordant thought struck him as significant, something he needed to ponder later, and with a smile he realized that's exactly what Tom would have thought as well. Then, the words fell out almost without sound:

"For Tom and Oui"

Flowers on the hill
Blooming still,
Following your way
Like I always will.

Mike

He liked the sound of those little words, how they reached out across time to an image of when they were kids running through the woods, and Mike felt contented with the changes he'd put in place down at the cabin, the new order of things. He'd left his best friends with a little touch of his own creativity, and the gift felt strangely right alongside Tom's art carving resting on the seat like a familiar pet. But Mike had the image of the mutilated mural tattooed to the back of his eyeballs where it wouldn't leave his thoughts—his old Ford truck, the garden, Lee, those simple images formed by a river spirit were the very last things Tom held to at the end, final vestiges of a life now flowed past the last bend before the big, wide opening downstream. Again the ash wood comforted Mike as he could see the final pooling place Tom searched for and where surely Oui was waiting. And though sadness rode with him on the passenger side of the truck, Mike was sure Tom counted on him to understand the end and to help Lee do the same. Surely that's why the two creations had waited in secret behind the shed where they could tell their story after the shock of truth had passed.

A big *wham* jolted Mike as the pickup fell into a deep mud hole. Rattled a little, for some reason he thought of smoked salmon and onion bagels and realized his old friend through these final creative gifts had gotten the last word. It was okay. A wry smile carried him on down to the main road, but this time a fresh sensation swelled, a new bend in the river of his oldest friendship, and as Mike pulled out onto the black asphalt, he lost himself completely in the thought of what Wanda would think of his little "Flowers on the hill" poem. That strange idea so pleased him that he decided to stop by Wal-Mart and pick up a volume of Walt Whitman as a little gift for Wanda; maybe she could show him a nice poem or two he could study on for a while and maybe memorize.

Chapter 15

Two weeks after the funeral and mired in ennui, Lee trudged through a daily routine no longer affording pleasure, no basketball or fishing, not even casual thinking about Saralynn. Though the letter his grandpa left Glenna offered solace and at least a realistic understanding of events, Lee still could not accept his grandpa's abandonment. These days, he rarely spoke with that boyish energy, and nightly dinner conversations left him bored, until one Saturday when he really wanted to be left alone.

After emptying out the cabin, Lee had simply dumped Tom's possessions into a vacant spot inside the garage—no sorting, no attempt to catalogue or preserve things, but this Saturday they finally had to be organized. Before him lay a mountain of rejection he frankly didn't want to touch, but the idea of being completely alone at least brought some comfort.

Everything looked different as Lee picked up boxes of clothes, tools, kitchenware, and what looked like junk in the light of Hattiesburg, but handling individual items without anyone around to make comments brought unexpected energy, and the more structure he created through the sorting, the less impossible the whole task appeared. Out went the old rug, the creaky homemade cabinet, the mismatched dishes and ancient flatware. Time brought a jaded new perspective of what fondness felt like; and though Lee didn't want to consider that thought, he did allow the flow of motion to carry him through the keep-and-pitch process until he came to a green metallic box with the word "Documents" handwritten in black marker across the top.

From such a numbed vantage, the box provided little interest as likely its contents would be useless, but finally he considered an old marriage certificate or diploma might still be around, so with confirmed disinterest, he opened the lid. Sure enough, most of the contents were ancient bank account statements, checkbooks from the 1980s, and receipts mostly too faded to read. But there was one notable article at the bottom of the box—a brown manila envelope, nothing written on the outside.

Mechanically, Lee removed the rather new-looking item to find handwritten on the underside: "Lee." A chill doused his lackluster mood, and his first thought was that some new Newland information might be inside, or maybe more Saralynn letters. But the package was not heavy, so he remained calm.

Peeking inside as if another rattlesnake might be in queue, he found nothing but a bunch of papers, mostly gibberish as it seemed to have been a note or letter that got rewritten over and over to the point it no longer made any sense. But halfway through the pile, he found a cover page entitled, "The End of Saralynn." Lee was terrified to look at the next page but flipped the cover over to find a note:

Lee,

I don't know how long it has been between my leaving you all and you finding this box, but I hope it has been enough time for your disappointment to fade. Surely I've let you down, and I know you must think poorly of me, almost like I did when my mom left me. But life keeps flowing, son.

Listen, you're a good boy, and I can't have you wasting time on being angry; I did enough of that for the both of us, and all it brought me was sadness. I need you to stay strong because your mom will need that; she'll need all the family. There is a soft spot in your heart that I've seen, and though life will nudge you to follow the hard part of your spirit, it's important you listen to that gentle center of your nature. To help you a little, I want to give you a gift.

This is the only poem I ever wrote. Surely my skill tells that plain enough. But in the days before my mom died, she muttered all the time. Her eyes would flash like she was watching a movie, and then she'd mumble out loud like she was talking to somebody. Even heard my name a few times. I tried to write it all down, and the notes are scattered in this envelope here, but mostly it was crazy stuff.

You know, that genealogy report of yours got me to thinking about those moments with Mom, and the more stories of her life I dredged up for you, the more my brain kept sorting through all those disconnected ramblings of hers back in the hospital. I even tried writing a story about all that, but it needed too many words, and they almost drowned me. I ended up cheating and writing this little poem instead, which is more like Mom anyway.

I tried to catch a few flashes of her life and match them up with some of that incoherent gibberish she mumbled in the hospital. Might not make a lick of sense to you, but I had to try and leave you something from my heart, and hers.

So, take this offering as a kind of compass heading to the past, and use it to go find your future. I'm where I need to be now with my Oui and Mom, so you go find your own life, then learn to love it.

Grandpa
p.s. By the way, read this poem out loud. That's what mom always did for me and it kinda' brings the words more to life. TB

"The End of Saralynn"

I.

"The Girl"

A dark night, that night
On the Pearl River,
Fog dripping its obscurity
Over the silver-covered trees
In a night of swaddling fear.
Heaving,
Mom all alone,
Us all alone,
And that cold wind blowing
Groans of exhausted pain.
Into this world I came that night, already strong.

"Momma, you gotta push—hard, Momma.
You gotta breathe—deep.
I'm here. We don't need him.
I'm coming now, Momma. I'm coming to help.
Breathe for me, Momma; I'm here."

But I remember that day he tricked me, too.
Left me on that riverbank
All alone
By that big oak root
That felt so much like home.
Him and that friend, liars,
Slipped off in the boat, alone,
Left me with the horse and wagon,
Left me to fish with no pole,
To watch that big limb fall
Then roll on the ground to die.
Left me to run
From that big blue hole
Jumping out of the sky,
That showed me not to fear,
Taught me not to listen, to him,
Or trust any other lying man.
Can't suffer a liar, even family;
Can't trust a man with no soul.
But that willow tree dancing
That day,
The breeze touching her leaves, that way,
Courting in a chocolate river sway
With spring flowing through the sky,
With me all alive
When I stepped on that snake, almost,
When I ran from myself, almost,
When that willow trilled in the breeze,
With me trusting in belief,
Beside my friend who kissed the wind
With her leaves all happy and free.

"I hope that snake is gone, Tom.
But I wasn't scared, not too scared.
This oak root here feels so safe
I'm gonna hold on.
But that willow, she just dances

All naughty with that breeze
And the current touching her knees
And me sittin' here with me,
Just waitin' and listenin'
'Cause I'll hear him first;
I'll do the tricking this time,
Like he fooled me last time,
But I ain't gonna forget;
And he better not forget."

Old Man Dearman hoarded apricots,
Grumpy old troll;
Shot at us every year with salt and rice.
And his dog was quick as a hawk,
But I was smart.
I divert, you see,
Like that Sun Tzu fella' Teacher had me read;
I divide the center to the sides
Then slide when the time falls true,
And those kids knew when the moment was right,
While Katie climbed that fence
And my soldiers
Fought for the moment of youth
With our troves filled of sour fruit
And the golden gains of war.
But we knew when to run and hide,
How to divide then unite
Round a clubhouse hour
That was nothing but ours
And stuffed with the power of youth,
'Cause we had time, you see,
And time you can't steal, I believe.

"These plums are tart, Tom.
Feel that sharp pain
Like mumps behind your ears?
Did you see Dearman's dog?
Tricked to the wrong sound
Like it was a bone.
Katie and me laughed so hard
Climbing them limbs,
That old fool mean as can be.
But listen, Tom; I hear Katie. Quiet.

Dearman's on the prowl. Quiet.
We got to be silent tonight.
We don't need fun, or town;
We got all we need.
Momma sewed clothes from flour sacks
And toys from boxes and trees,
Old kitchen spoons and worn-out dungarees,
All the provisions we need.
But we got to be silent tonight
And wait for Daddy; he's drinking.
But Katie don't mind,
And I don't mind,
'Cause I'm strong,
For Momma, you see.

And he was wrong
To hit my momma,
But years made me tough, so I watched;
Tears made me tough, so I watched
Till that day
Daddy hurt Momma, again.
Till I put that knife next to his skin,
And his kidney felt the heat
That I'd kill 'em in his sleep,
And vengeance wouldn't hold, not again.
So I stole to keep Momma from Momma,
To keep her from her desperate heart
Bruised by the scream of power
Till that hour I stole my own future,
To save Momma,
To prove
He couldn't scare me, or Momma.

Oh, I remember that little brown bottle,
Mercury, it said, quicksilver,
The day I helped Teacher inventory,
Deceit, really,
A shiny bond of broken trust.
Silver circles dividing,
Rolling into one, then dividing.
So I knew about one, at first.
So I knew there was lots of ones,
So I saw people divide, then hide

Behind trust.
Broken, healed,
Broken, then broken.
The way of things,
The way things want to be, it seems.
With Jesus, then alone,
And the one dividing,
And the whole staying whole
Where we began
As woman and man
Before the big mystery
Of rolling shiny things,
Dividing into me.

"I was stupid to steal.
Don't blame Katie, Tom, I'm the thief.
I'm the one who tricked,
You know, deceit.
What did it hurt?
Nothing broken, really.
Teacher never knew.
What does it hurt a heart
When it can't imagine the truth?"

II.
"The Woman"

Early mother picked too soon
From a vine of handmade dresses
And restaurant dishes
Flowering with carefree men
Flirting through the season of youth,
Whispering with time's urge
Not to worry with wishes.
It was that day, dabbling in the stream
Swollen from the rain,
It was that day the river took my Tom,
Reached hungry for a leg
While I wasn't watching,
While he slipped from me
Without knowing, without knowing.
The hiding sycamore had arms,

And the rolling current wicked charms
To take him that day from me,
But the Watcher was watching, always,
Watching hunger stalking
The ungiven gift
Tricked by the liquid brown
Craving to steal again.
But a mother knows
Not to be alone,
And a son now knows
What the river wants
On its twisty journey home.
And the Watcher watches
The winding and dividing,
Watches the wholeness
Of never being alone.

"You're safe, Tom. Oh, you're so cold!
Breathe, son, breathe.
Hold on to me.
Feel this blanket, this warm sunshine
Strong like you?
I'm right here, son, right here with you."

All that grassy grass he bagged,
All those wheelbarrows of heavy slag
And dried manure.
And how many buckets of water
Soaked that happy dirt?
A boy filling home
With a bounty of beans and
All those greens and onions,
And squash, such a sight
That first night of the feast,
Like rich folks sitting with kings,
Treasuring onions and beans
Together.
Poor boy shoveled
To the center of the earth, it seems,
To where the roots of life begin, I believe,
To the heart of you, and maybe of me,
To the seed of dreams we dream.

"Listen, Tom, can you hear me?
I want us to work on that line,
That one urging and urging,
The one Walt loved, you know,
And that angry mother ocean too,
Growling so, and
Calling souls to seek their seek.
I tell you, son, it's like your garden talking
In that way you understand the dirt
And what might come
And what must go
And what can be learned
And then foregone.
You got that soulful touch, for growing,
And that hopeful way of knowing
How nature speaks and when she changes her mind."

"Now dang it, Harlan, tell that boy you proud
Or I'll show you how things go.
Tell him you want more beans
And those white perch he caught just now.
Tell him how proud
You are, out loud.
Don't you cross me, Harlan.
Don't you cross me now."

I felt so lost that day,
Life always cheating
With the grind of lying people
And greedy old time
Pulling at me when
I couldn't see my boy
Or get to that traitor in time,
Or I'd have snatched his hair
And he'd know where justice lives.
He'd know just fine.
But that day Ouida talked to me,
Asked me how to help.
Oh that day indeed, but
I forgot to listen, to her,
Forget to show I cared, about her,
Marched right over, her

Concern
When she needed a friend right then.
And these years been lonely since,
These years here alone,
These years I couldn't make a friend
With my sweet Katie gone.
And so helpless I've been
With my Tom in the cheatin' land,
Helpless, except a phone, and alone.
And all these women past,
And all who should be friends,
And all those could be friends,
And those not my friends,
They stare from memory's home,
Stare at me alone so long.
And why is Ouida frowning?
And why did I not learn
To listen, then,
To a yearning heart
Needing just a friend.

"Now, Oui, you know my boy.
He has a sensitive center.
He'll be okay; you just love him.
He'll need you beside him though,
God love him.
But I see a hurt on your brow,
Like I injured you just now, without trying,
Like you're pulling away, and sad,
Like those other women did,
But you got to love my boy.
That's all you got to know;
It's all I ever needed,
And he needs us now, you know."

My, my, my there's a lovely Miss Hattie.
See that hairdo? I did that.
See these pretty women? Did that too
For this silver dance tonight.
And Tom's cookin' chickens
While the preacher thanks us all,
But I gotta sneak out of here
Before he calls my name;

Never can stand that light on me
With all that prideful stain.

"And they all got their hair done
And danced under the moon
Till ten that night when the lights went dim.
And the ladies closed like flowers.
And, oh what a day, Tom,
And what those hours found.
Reminds me time may not be a wall
But a garden for planting around."

"But where are you, Harlan?
You didn't even try to show
Some respect to these ladies
For all the life they've known.
You never do, Harlan;
You never shelter people;
You got no center to you,
Only thoughts forlorn.
But Tom was here and working.
He danced and cooked and read.
Tom was right here with me,
So people wouldn't see instead
How you never show,
Never even try to know
What lives need while being."

This hospital, so ugly white,
Why can't they use a color?
The sight makes me sick,
And these needles always prick me
With pokes and pushes through
And quiets and rude you must do's
Till I wonder what I'm doing here
With all this pain run through me.
But look there, my boy, he's crying.
Such a soft soul inside.
This cancer
May pull him under, too,
'Cause I forgot to tell him
How I'll be with him in the wind,
How I'll never leave him

Till we're all home again.
He's a man that feels too much,
Gets confused, lost at times.
Gotta learn to love himself,
To find some peace inside;
But I forgot to tell him that,
Forgot to make him know
That love links to the golden home
Where the river wants to go.
But Oui will show him now,
Never leave his side, I'm sure;
She'll help him find his truth,
The Lord will show her how.

"Don't cry, son.
Can't you see Jesus needs me?
I'm goin' by his side.
But I'll be the wind, you see,
Singing in the mist
And chatting up that breeze,
So you listen for me, Tom,
'Cause every nature's sound
Is where I'm gonna be.
But now I got to jump,
Jump that wall of time
Beyond the edge of me.
So do me one last favor, Tom,
And tell me one last time
That line we learned back on the porch,
The one Walt wrote
For me,
The one about souls and leaves and things,
And all eternity:

> *'Onward and outward ... and nothing collapses,*
> *And to die is different from what any one supposed, and*
> *Luckier.'"*

Chapter 16

I.

The next few weeks brought unexpected optimism for the family as each person worked to reconcile that Tom's death had been inevitable, though no one wanted to examine the truth too closely. Lee shared Tom's poem, but the girls didn't seem to follow it too well, so he tried telling his grandpa's stories, making up details where needed. Each night he pulled some tidbit from the past, and one night as he lay staring at the ceiling thinking, he thought again of those old bards Wanda had brought up and what a responsibility they had carried. The idea so stimulated Lee that he got out of bed and started jotting down some of his own family tales, trying to sort out what he knew as fact from what he'd added as embellishment; maybe one day those details could be important.

Oddly, Tom's poem brought solace to Glenna. Gradually recovering her strength, each day she read the poem and the letter her dad left her as she drifted through her own years with her mom and dad, and Saralynn. The grief counseling helped greatly, and soon she began to leave the house and volunteer again, especially with helping Vic and Wanda on their new projects. She even pitched in at Harold's shop and got all the paperwork in order so well that his boss offered her a job working three days a week, which she gladly accepted.

Almost imperceptibly, a new center for the family began to form, though no one addressed the shift, but the malaise of grief had begun to lift, and new light filtered through the dim haze of remorse. Dinnertime conversations returned to normal pace with discussion now not about sadness but often about stories of Tom's life, or Saralynn's, and even about their own stories of Mitchell childhoods. Soon Glenna had revealed regions of her life her children had never known, like how she won the Latin award in high school for having the highest grade point average in the class. Even Harold talked about his aloof mother and how as a result he'd been closer to his dad, who had died young. With time, tangled emotions began to unravel as everyone allowed themselves the chance "to know the past but find the future," one of those newly invented lines Lee made up in a tale attributed to his grandpa.

A few Saturdays later, Mike called saying he needed to come by and drop off something he'd found at the cabin. He wouldn't say what it was, but Glenna thought it might be a good chance to have a Sunday lunch and invite Wanda over too, so the next day she cooked a roast beef with mashed potatoes and green beans.

Though Glenna had talked to Mike a couple of times on the phone, she hadn't seen him since the day he and Wanda told her about Tom. She was a bit afraid that old memory would intrude again, but as soon as that green hat stood at the door with a big bag of fresh corn in hand, Glenna knew all was well.

The dinner went fine, and surprisingly, Wanda and Mike shared that they had enjoyed more contact than Glenna realized; lately she'd missed quite a few details it seemed. Wanda and Mike had tales of museums in New Orleans they had visited, a terrific sculpture park, and even the Audubon Butterfly Garden. The girls listened carefully but did not submit their guests to thorough interrogation. Finally, Mike spoke.

"Well, folks, I can't tell you how pleasant this has been. And, Harold, it is such a treat to have you around again, as I finally have someone to talk to that loves cars as much as I do." Mike was proud of his tribute.

"Thank you there, sir," Harold said. "My boy and I do pretty good with 'em. Pleasure to have you here with us, Mike."

"Anyway," Mike quickly moved to change the conversation. "I found something at the cabin I thought ya'll might like, so I got it out in the truck." Everyone strolled outside, happy to stretch their legs after the heavy meal. Mike pulled back a tarp covering something fairly large, which left Lee gasping, almost forgetting to breathe.

Offering docent guidance, Mike spoke softly. "Apparently, this mural was something Tom had worked on for a while. You can see he mixed up his own colors from plant dyes and such, and I think these little pears from his orchard were done with egg yolk from what I can tell. This whole thing was on the back of Tom's smokehouse under the shed; nobody ever went back there. When I visited the cabin last, I took my chain saw and cut out the mural. Trimmed off some of the black smudge but left three inches as matting for the wood frame I built. Don't look quite so rudimentary this way." He winked at Wanda. "I figure the Mitchell clan can have the mural, and I'll keep this here diorama that was hanging right beside it. I think I know every piece of the history Tom put into this little life drama he created." Everyone nodded heads in agreement.

Funny how some things just touch a heart, but Glenna wrapped her arms around Mike, hugging him as if for the last time in life. Then Lee spoke up.

"I want to put the mural on the big wall by the patio where Vic KO'd the cretin. That way it gets to stay outside but protected like Grandpa wanted. When we're barbecuing, it'll be like Grandpa is here with us." As the new story formed for the family, each person took away a moment the years ahead would likely bring pause to in considering the black smudged border and what had happened to those other images, but today the sense was only gratitude.

Later as the house grew quiet and Harold's familiar snore increased its rattle, Glenna lay in bed thinking how her dad's trust in his friendship with Mike had reached back into her life through his painting, and that notion brought a healthy calming to the disquiet she could never seem to lose. And with the thought, Glenna closed her eyes to her husband's snoring and the comfort that all three of her children slept peacefully under her roof.

II.

Saturday basketball practice ended with full-court sprints leaving Lee winded but energized. After a cool down and a long shower, he was ready to drive the hour west to Columbia to help with Wanda and Vic's charity event, and he looked forward to sitting in the Chevelle and letting the engine do all the work. Harold decided it was good advertising for his business to let Lee strut around town in his prize specimen, so Lee was perfectly happy to show off his dad's fine work.

Within seconds of leaving school, the steady throttle of the Boss hummed, and Lee's tired muscles allowed thoughts to drift away into that place between the present and times long since passed, or not yet arrived. A throaty purr from the engine seemed to carry him into that intoxicated state where the mind frees itself and the body pauses to allow the mental world to fill itself with the currency of the moment. This surging optimism lifted Lee to where the simple truths of his life became visible, and on that mild euphoria, he cruised.

The months since his grandpa's death passed quietly as the family adjusted, but for days now Lee had thought of that line from Tom's letter to Glenna: "To my family both blood and bond." These simple words tumbled endlessly, wearing away the obscurity of familiarity, now leaving glimpses of an idea Lee was beginning to conceive.

As the rural country stretches zipped by, images swooped in and out of Tom sitting by the river telling stories. And there again this feeling of closeness from the mural Mike gave to the family. Stitching together scenes from the past, Lee knew now his family story was compelling him to action. Tom, as connector of the family's past, to Saralynn, stood so clearly and yet in such contrast to the aloof antisocial man people misjudged him to be before his death. And the more the interplay of past and present tumbled in Lee's thoughts, the greater the sense of duty he understood.

There too came the humble flashes of Mike remembering Tom in that brotherly way, gentle as breezes chatting in trees, connected by a past so rich that words stranded themselves in pools of irrelevance. The slow seepage of reflection continuing, Lee realized yet another insight that even marriage must begin as friendship and that the blood lineage of children must also begin as the deep bond of friendship. And the filling eddies of thought blended family with the bond of friendship in a way that Lee knew was indistinguishable.

The taut purr of the Boss led on through rolling reflections, waves of sound elongating in images fluid as a Dali painting, and he imagined his own children as yet unborn, unconceived, those souls that might already exist outside of time merely awaiting their moments of presence. Were his children there with Tom and Oui, and Saralynn? The car's sweet vibration, the fusing images of roads and trees sweeping into a blurring wind of sight, all these universes now swept over Lee as a swirl of rolling light.

Blrrrrrr! Blrrrrrrr!

But a pickup truck blew his horn rudely at someone who cut him off, and the Boss instinctively slowed amid complaint for the disturbance of her loping stretch, and as the philosophical moment fractured, Lee realized the entire family was binding itself behind the great impact of loss.

The euphoria subsiding and shifting from his philosophical mood, he thought of his duties ahead as host at the senior citizens Silver Fox Ball, the second time he'd performed this function. He looked forward to seeing the ladies dressed in their finest clothes with hair freshly coiffed, they too revisiting their past, reviving their own hopes of love and life. These women were so grateful for a young man's attention that it touched Lee's heart and reminded him what a lonely life Saralynn had led without real friendship or a loving marriage to fulfill her. But even with truth marking the trail of his thoughtful journey, Lee sensed the coalescence occurring all round him, lives adapting to new paths, bonds joining from life broken tragedy, and he sensed the contraction rebinding the family.

The mural sparked in his memory regularly, the dark smudged borders that destroyed part of the truth his grandpa wrestled, the blurred connected order that in the end Tom found difficult to sustain. Yet, there again, he and Mike stood by the old truck floating on some sliver of memory that would never pass away. Nor would the anxious little boat waiting among the flowering trees. *Forever and never must be the same*, Lee thought, and he shifted the car into top gear for a sprint.

Up on the highway now, again into idealistic regions Lee flew as the country roads yielded to swatches of green pine distorting in the sunlight, and he realized he knew almost nothing of the truth of his grandpa's life, only the fragments left by undocumented time. At the idea, he thought of retreat, maybe the project of gathering the past was too big, but he wanted to be the investigator, the hero saving truth from slipping beneath the waters of immediacy.

Back to the cabin visit a year ago, how simple things seemed then with easy picture book answers and childlike awareness. His grandfather both revealed and symbolized the difficulty in truly knowing anyone. It wasn't through objects left behind that we know a passed life; no, we know a life through the stories, through the cool, lonely oak root by a flowing river or a happy willow tree flirting in the sunlight or the pulling, hungry river grasping a child's foot. And Lee pondered, how would he share his grandpa with his own children? With their children?

Alone and quiet, he imagined Saralynn as a young girl playing with the speck of mercury, watching it divide and then reassemble so perfectly, leaving a spark in her mind of matters larger than mere physical life, of possessions, and Lee began to understand that his grandpa's retreat to the river had been a fracturing, and his return to the family a cohesion only to be fractured yet again.

Pieces fit now through the storied lens his grandfather left. The family was healing, Victoria flourishing under Wanda's guiding hand, and Glenna too discovering the importance of her capabilities. The hole in their lives had become a new vessel into which their heartache could be poured to create an elixir of service to others, an emotional balm they each shared as freely as sweet tea.

Thinking of his mom and Vic, their courage, the parallel path they journeyed, and especially their close bond this past year, more pieces aligned, but perhaps most of all Lee knew how happy his grandpa would be next month when Mike and Wanda would be married. Everywhere it seemed new eddies of life gathered themselves along the bank of family and friends, little drops of earth swirling about, bumping into one another and then blending into the conjunction of life that merges people and creates the future.

He thought of Mike's humility when apologetically he asked Lee to be best man. As starkly announced as an orchid blooming in a leafless tree, Mike had blurted out in his inimitable way, "Dang it, if Tom Bradburn can't be here to do it, then I want the same blood he came from; I want you to be my best man, Lee." And chuckling to himself, Lee understood again the unfading friendship that still connected the two men as if Tom were only down at the river checking his lines and grumbling how he didn't want to get all dressed up anyway.

And here it was late summer again, and life spread out in front of Lee as clearly as a winding river. The world so huge, so complex. Maybe that's why Tom had retreated to the river, to study why life sometimes works against human intention. Shaking his head in confusion, it was all too big to consider right this moment, and he'd better let the thought drift along for a while longer.

The western horizon began lighting up with soft pastel colors as the road slipped by without notice, and Lee considered the one thing he'd dreaded doing had completely changed his life. If not for the genealogy class he so resisted, Saralynn would be a stranger still, and his grandpa would have died without finding the reconnection to the family they all so earnestly needed.

The worn-out copy of *Walden* sitting next to his grandpa's chair hinted at Lee's thought, how the solitude of that book represented for Tom one extreme of desire while family represented the opposite. The tension of those pulls seemed balanced, and in that moment of perfect stasis, Lee decided he wanted to study literature in college, along with forestry, considering the essence of nature and of people might be exactly the same thing, surely an insight his grandpa had understood all along but simply forgot to tell anyone.

The sun winked through the canopy of pine trees, ready to rest for the day as Lee realized his world was expanding and resting all at the same time. He glanced at himself in the rearview mirror, sensing traces of his grandfather's hair and cheekbones in his own visage, a genetic echo from further up the river of family, and the connection spread across his young spirit like a warm cabin blanket on a chilly night. Spontaneously, loving words slipped from his lips. "Okay, Grandpa, let's get going; we got work to do."

With that salute, the sun continued making up the colorful horizon as Lee pulled off the interstate, downshifting into third gear, triggering the tight, angry roar of the Boss. He couldn't wait to see Mike and his dad, to help cook up burgers for the girls, and then go to the dance and be adored. He especially looked forward to seeing Sally, his new girlfriend from Columbia, so he could bask in those blue eyes of hers that made him feel so much like a man.

Ahead, a yellowish-pink-and-blue sunset began changing into her evening wear, and a subtle new thought popped into Lee's mind. For Mike and Wanda's wedding, he would build them a birdhouse and paint it exactly these dazzling colors ahead, a blended sunrise and sunset, something surely Tom and Saralynn would have done themselves, something they could do now through Lee's own hands as their tool.

Satisfied, arm draped at the wrist over the steering wheel, Lee felt his heart steadily rise into his eyes blurring with alertness, an acceptance of soaring life embracing him as a young man, as carrier of the family story and historian of the lives that had so profoundly opened his own. With the Boss humming her chorus of strength, a cascade of invisible hands stroked softly Lee's soul as the endless sky blushed with pastels of humble pride.

The End.

> On our earth, before writing was invented, before the printing press was invented, poetry flourished. That is why we know that poetry is like bread; it should be shared by all, by scholars and by peasants, by all our vast, incredible, extraordinary family of humanity.
> —Pablo Neruda

About the Author

Arthur Byrd is a retired computer technology executive and CEO who splits his time between the beaches of the Dominican Republic and the forests of northern New Jersey. Raised in Petal, Mississippi, he has a master's degree in English from USM and taught high school and college in both Mississippi and Oklahoma where he enjoyed years of fishing, hunting, exploring nature, and the study of literature. He and his wife have three grown children.

CPSIA information can be obtained
at www.ICGtesting.com
Printed in the USA
BVOW08*0825020217
475150BV00003B/6/P

9 781532 008252